Going Out
the IN Road

Also by RA Cook
Calvin Splinter & His Splendid Splinter Ideas
GIGANTA, An Epic Tale
Lola's Muse, Limited Edition

Going Out the IN Road

An unexpected odyssey to the past and beyond

RA Cook

HMAPUB

Publisher of Books, Stories & Cards

Going Out the IN Road
Copyright ©2023 by RA Cook
All Rights Reserved

Disclaimer
The author and publisher shall have neither liability nor responsibility
to any person or entity with respect to any perceived loss or damage caused,
directly or indirectly by the information contained in this book.

Cover and interior design by Rebecca Cook
Illustrations and cover photo by Rebecca Cook
Author photo by Libby Cook

Text set in Adobe Garamond Pro

Library of Congress Cataloging-in-Publication Data
Rebecca Cook
Going Out the IN Road
by RA Cook
1. Fiction 2. Magical Realism

ISBN: 979-8-9883778-0-1
Library of Congress Control Number:
2023907994

Printed in the United States of America
HMA Publishing
109 Pelican Way, Friday Harbor, WA 98250
www.hmapublishing.com

First Edition

DEDICATION

To my daughter, Shawn;

my sister, Libby;

and to the lost, may they be found.

Table of Contents

Finding the IN Road

1958

The dream as I remember it.

The air is still, the room dark. Above, a rustling sound wakes me from a night's sleep fraught with dreams. Drowsy, I twist my body toward the window and pull the shades open to peer out. It is then that the dream penetrates my thoughts again, haunting me, enticing me to fall back to sleep. Outside, dawn approaches. I hear the faint chirping of birds as I slip back onto the pillows. "Oh, it's just a dream, just a dream," I whisper, and push further under the comforter. I surrender to the dream. And it lingers.

I drift, reliving every scene, every nuance. An odd sensation rumbles through me from a deep, cellular level. I can't explain it even now. At hyperspeed, a vibration circuits through my body. I feel light as if I've traveled weightlessly through space for eons. In my mind's eye, a kaleidoscope of surreal, vivid colors swirl, filling my head. All my visual senses explode like fireworks, and I wonder if this is kundalini energy running through me. I've read about the awakening of one's serpent power and know such a transformation comes either through meditation practice or spontaneous.

As I am mulling this over, my thoughts prick my senses, signaling me to be more aware of my outer surroundings. I have an acute sense that I am not where I am supposed to be. All of this happens in a split second, mind you, but by now I am awake. My eyes dart down the bed and navigate around the tiny room. Most of the surrounding backdrop seems normal. The cats are sleeping at the end of the bed; Karina, my dog, snuggles against me. But after closer inspection, I realize that nothing else in the room—not one thing—looks familiar. My eyes open wider. Karina raises her head when I say, "Where are we?"

The last thing I remember is lying in bed in my studio. I am not in my studio, and for a moment I wonder if someone has kidnapped me, though I have no memory of a struggle nor am I restrained. I do not feel any fear, only mild confusion. The thought comes to me that I've been transported to this place in a dream. *Is that possible?*

Bewildered, trying to sort out my whereabouts, I stare at the tired, outdated wood paneling. The grain of the veneer looks as if it has been through a time warp. I have a vague hunch I've gone through a mysterious, multidimensional portal—a time warp. I shiver and again wonder where I am.

The air, moist and chilly, forces me to dig deeper under the comforter to keep fear at bay. Karina yawns and squeaks a little, reassuring me in her canine way that we are okay. Gatito, my gray and white fluffy cat, comes toward me purring. Standing on top of me, he looks into my eyes, exuding confidence, and bless the boy, he licks my cheek. I reach out of the covers and stroke his large, fluffy head. "Where are we, Gatito?" I say.

Just then Moon leaps off the bed and meows, urging me to get up and fix breakfast. I toss back the covers. "All right, I'm coming," I say, and swing my legs down. Without a thought, I throw on a tatty navy blue sweater hanging near the bed and investigate the area.

Despite Moon's insistent meowing, I take a little time to survey the small living space and discover the interior to be an old but well-kept Airstream. There is an aura of backwoods charm throughout. Several well-used Pendleton jackets hang by the door. Next to them is a small closet lined with pressed blouses and a few pairs of woolen slacks. I take a moment to look through the clothing and finger a starched shirtsleeve, testing it to make sure the fabric is real because I am now toying with the possibility of being in a dream continuum.

I'm drawn to a small vase of fresh-cut flowers sitting alongside several pairs of half eyeglasses. Above the bouquet, an old fifties-style brass lamp dangles over the miniscule dinette table. On top of the table rests a manual Royal typewriter, the keys worn, scuffed from years of use. A well-used dictionary and thesaurus plus a few highbrow magazines skirt the typewriter—*The New Yorker* for one.

All of this paraphernalia belongs to someone else—a woman with educated tastes. By the contents of the trailer, I suspect the resident is female. I am no judge, but whoever *she* is, recently stepped out. The thought tightens my stomach a notch. I feel uncomfortable. *What will I say when she finds me here?* The thought of her walking in the door makes me shiver again.

I notice my feet are ice cold, so I slip on a pair of her discarded slippers and scan the room for a heat source. I spy a little potbelly stove standing in the corner, ready for action. Tucked near the stove is an empty kindling box. I will have to go outside to retrieve wood, if there is any. I assume there is. *Later,* I think, and search through the cupboards and cabinets for food.

"Hey, you guys are in luck," I say, opening an overhead cupboard. "There's pet food in here, canned *and* dry. It's not your brand, though." I chuckle because at this point I know laughter is my only safeguard—a nullifier if you will—because what I feel in my gut borders on hysteria.

Karina saves me from further turmoil by scratching on the metal door. The noise brings me back to the moment, pressing me into action. "Okay, girl, just a second. Let me finish feeding the cats." I spoon food into bowls. Gatito and Moon rush over and tackle the food as if they haven't eaten in days.

When I open the door, I see huge terra-cotta pots stuffed with flowering plants standing like centurions across the deck. At least five or more pots line the edge of the wooden porch, sheltered by the little trailer. The sky, a dismal overcast gray, is drizzling rain on the deck and lush foliage. Walking out into the cool, moist air, I sigh with relief. *So far, so good,* I think. I don't know how, but I know we're alone. I still do not know where we are or how we arrived in the middle of a dense, green forest.

Undeterred by our bizarre circumstance, Karina jumps off the porch and scurries down a narrow pathway into the woods, barking, chasing something. I don't know what. Panicking, I follow. I yell, "Wait, Karina! Stay close!" But she takes off racing like a greyhound. I know I can't catch up with her, so I stop. Breathless and a little shaky, I turn around, hoping she'll come back soon. I don't know what else to do.

Trudging back up the trail, I notice an outside camp kitchen to the left of the porch. On a small table sits a miniature gas stove top, a coffee pot, a few pans, and two cups. I want something warm to drink, so I walk over, fill the pot with water, and light the stove. Remembering a tin of coffee in one cupboard, I head inside to help myself.

As I turn to enter the trailer, Gatito and Moon peek out the door. Both cats stop short. Their tails fly straight up. "I *know*," I say and giggle at the startled pair, glad for the comic relief.

Gatito, who always loves adventure, hops off the deck and sniffs the forest's edge as I suspected he would. I wish I had an ounce of his courage, but I am more like Moon, who slithers underneath the porch.

By the time my coffee brews, Karina has scampered back. "Find anything, girl?" I ask. Karina wags her tail around and around as she always does. I swear she smiled. Cradling a cup of hot coffee, I take her jaunty cue and walk down the path, pretending I own the place. The rain has stopped, and the breeze carries the scent of ionized air. With Karina by my side, knowing she will warn me if there is trouble, I feel much better, less confused. "This is not so bad, is it?" I say to her.

Still, I am perplexed about our situation, and unable to reconcile a thing. I don't know what to do or where to go. If I have been transported to God knows where, how will I return home? *Or can I return?* My wanton foe, apprehension, creeps in.

Before my fears can solidify, I push them away and concentrate on keeping a steady pace down the trail. Maybe this is *just a dream,* and I am fumbling my way through. I've read of such things. Maybe I will wake up in my studio, laugh at this silliness, and settle down to work. But I am hard-pressed to cling to such a tenuous idea because, deep down, I know this is real, and I'm in a strange environment, barely treading water.

As I walk along, I try to reposition my dilemma, reframe the dream, but the images are vague, the details gone. Giving in, I let my mind wander, hoping for a reprieve. The dirt path becomes wider and soon is wide enough for a compact car. When we come to a juncture in the road, I notice a marked crossing. Several old, weather-beaten signs are tacked to a huge Douglas fir. One sign has a large arrow pointing back toward our camp. In faded Gothic lettering, the word *IN* is written in capital letters.

"Hot damn, Karina! We're on the IN Road going out," I say. No sooner are the words out of my mouth than in the distance, I hear the roar of an engine. My heart teeters. *Should I hide or stand my ground?* Unsure, I deliberate whether to dash into the bushes or not, but before I can decide, a 1940s pickup truck rumbles down the road. Smoke billows out the back, the tailgate rattling. We've been sighted. It's too late to do anything except stand by the roadside.

Screeching to a halt in front of us, the driver leans out the window. "Say, girlie, how ya doin'? Haven't seen you for a while. Where ya been?"

"Do I know you?"

"Sure ya do! Did you forget me already, Georgia?" The driver, a scruffy-looking man, chuckles. His laughter disarms me.

"Already? Ah, well—" I stall, deciding to smile back at him to avoid confrontation.

"Yeah, Georgia, 'course you do. Nobody forgets the mailman, do they? It's me, John, the mailman. I deliver mail around these parts every week. Remember?"

"Oh, yes, of course. John the mailman. Sorry, I guess I forgot." Hesitant to say more, I give him a long look. He is a hefty man somewhere in his late forties, I guess. His chubby face and jolly demeanor help sway my sense of caution. He looks harmless, but his appearance is too crusty around the edges for my taste. I decide to continue our conversation. "Say, John, I know this sounds kind of stupid, but...where am I?"

"Where are you? Well, Georgia girlie, you're right here with me! We're talking just like we always do on mail day."

"Oh." Still mystified, I counter, "How often *is* mail day?"

"Well, now I don't rightly know. Guess you'd have to say when there's mail, if you know what I mean. Seems like every week there's mail, though. All depends on the weather and if the boats are runnin'."

"Boats? You mean boats deliver mail here?"

"This is Orcas *Island*, Georgia. For gosh sakes, have you lost your marbles?" John pauses, stares at me, and then laughs. "Aw, Georgia," he says, shaking his head. "There you go again, joking with me. Well, it's your lucky day cuz it's mail day." John winks and hands me a small bundle of mail. "Here ya go! See ya next time."

I am dumbfounded. Clasping the handful of mail, I don't respond. John revs the truck's engine, tips his hat, and shifts into gear. The truck, dodging potholes, waddles like a duck down the road and spurts out black exhaust as before. Right before he rounds the corner, John sticks his arm out of the window and waves.

"Well, I'll be." I sigh and wave. "Orcas Island. At least we're not alone, Karina. He seems to know me—or thinks he does. Who the hell's Georgia girlie anyway?" I now think since John the mailman informed me we are on Orcas Island, this *must be* a waking dream. My mind is swirling again. I can't get a handle on it.

I glance down at the mail and sift through the pile: a few letters, a postcard, and a local newspaper. Everything is addressed to Georgia Swan, IN Road, Orcas, Washington. "Huh. There's Georgia girlie—and Orcas Island! We *are* on an island."

Still, I am mystified because I've been to Orcas Island while visiting my sister, and the island looks nothing like this. The Orcas I know is a bustling green island with a reputation for summer fun. Streams of tourists on vacation pack the ferries every year. They invade the small island in the summer, bringing with them bicycles and SUVs burgeoning with kids, dogs, and camping gear.

The Orcas locals don't appreciate the massive influx of tourism and are often rude or discourteous, claiming they are overrun with outsiders, which they are. I was an outsider then. Now, by some odd twist of fate, I am here sequestered somewhere on Orcas Island talking to the mailman as if I'm a local. *What the hell?*

Perplexed, I sort the mail again, looking for postmarks or any other clues. Hidden in the newspaper's fold, I find a thick letter addressed to Georgia L. Swan. The stamped postmark shows the year 1958—fifty years ago. "1958!" I swallow hard. *"Good God!"*

Karina barks and licks my hand. Her tail is wagging. Her actions tell me we're okay despite what I think. "Let's go back to the trailer, girl," I say. "I don't know what we will do, but I'll figure out how to get back to 2008. I promise I will." Little did I know then how convoluted it would be.

In hindsight, not knowing turned out to be a good thing. I didn't know what the future held then, so when I hear an inner voice say, "Do you want to go back? Life might be better here."

I shake my head. "Yes. No. I mean, yes," I blurt out. That I'd consider staying fifty years in the past surprises me. The year 2008 *was* a rough year for me. I shake my head again. "No. I can't... I can't stay here. It's not possible."

As I start back to the trailer, I can't help but wonder when I will wake up from this dream. As the thought leaves me, I hear a swishing noise behind me and swing around to see tree branches extend and then intertwine with the underbrush on the pathway. Gobsmacked, I stare as the vegetation snakes across the trail, winding together, twisting long, leafy tendrils into taut ropes. Several form an eerie, wild-looking, crisscross-like barrier that looks reminiscent of a medieval gate. It isn't long before the opening to the road disappears. Within minutes, I can no longer see the road or the *IN* Road sign.

"Spooky," I whisper. I shiver and hurry along, clasping the pendant hanging around my neck. I glance down at the plastic disk. The talisman always gives me a boost of courage. On one side is the Medicine Buddha. His dark blue body sits amid a throne of fire and lotus blossoms. When I flip the amulet over, I see a picture of His Holiness, the Dalai Lama. He is smiling at me.

Someone gave me the pendant at a Tibetan conference in California. Early one morning, my sister and I trekked down the interstate through heavy freeway traffic and sat all day in the hot, dry sun to hear His Holiness speak words of wisdom. Being in his presence healed me, and I remember feeling grateful to have been there.

I am as grateful now to hold the pendant with his portrait on it. I rub the plastic disk. "Please stay with us, your Holiness. Keep us safe," I whisper.

Karina nudges my leg again, reassuring me. There is nothing left except to go back to the trailer. I pet Karina's head. "Okay, let's get something to eat, girl."

When we arrive at camp, I put out a bowl of food for Karina, which she gobbles up. My stomach is in knots. I am too nervous to eat so I skulk around the trailer. Georgia Swan. *Who is this woman?* I am also curious why John has mistaken me for her and, more importantly, why I am here.

To this day, I don't know how, but I know Georgia isn't coming back. This realization gives me the added freedom to rifle through her belongings. I sift through papers, books, and magazines. Every item is dated with the year 1958.

In a heap of periodicals behind the easy chair, I find an article about Georgia Swan in a *Newsweek,* an old popular weekly news magazine. A black and white photograph of Georgia Swan is embedded in a lengthy article about her newest work, a book of short stories. According to the reporter, each story is illustrated with her stylized pencil drawings. The short story collection, published in February 1958, commemorates her fiftieth year. The article ends with a brief paragraph about Georgia's mysterious disappearance six months after publication.

I study her picture and then walk over to the mirror. I have to admit there is a remarkable likeness between Georgia and myself. It occurs to me that if we were both living in the year 2008, she would be 100 years old and I would be fifty—my exact age to date.

Going over the *Newsweek* article, I reread the part about Georgia's accomplishments. According to the news story, she was an award-winning writer and illustrator. "Well, we have several things in common," I say. "We're both artists and writers." I am aware Georgia reached a pinnacle of success, which I have not. This heady thought makes me feel inadequate and a little dizzy, so I collapse into the easy chair. *What in the world am I doing?*

When I close my eyes to wait for the wave of despair to dissipate, a gossamer-like vision comes into my mind's eye. My sight clears and like a camera on a movie set, a scene tracks in on Georgia sitting at the dinette table in the camp trailer. Coastal breezes float through the windows, billowing white lace curtains and ruffling papers on the table. I can almost feel the balmy air. I see Georgia typing on the Royal typewriter, oblivious to her surroundings.

The image pans out to include a big tabby cat sitting underneath the table. The cat's long tail, loosely wound around Georgia's ankles, flicks back and forth like a nervous metronome. With a furrowed brow, Georgia continues typing and then stops. She rips the typed sheet of paper out of the typewriter and stands up. Pacing back and forth, she lights a cigarette. Exhaling a cloud of blue smoke, Georgia turns and looks straight into my eyes.

Taken aback I say, "Oh!" and the vision snaps shut.

At that moment, things click for me. I understand why John the mailman has me confused with Georgia. In an instant, I know the resemblance is more than casual—more than coincidence. It is not lost on me either that I was born a few months after Georgia disappeared in 1958. Now I am her age and can't help wondering about the depth of the connection.

Just then, Karina, who is outside nosing around, barks an alarm. I walk out to see movement in the trees and underbrush near the trailer. The cats scatter. Karina continues to bark. I can't imagine what was going on, but when the commotion stops, out pops a small boy with curly, blonde hair and a cherub-like face. The child reminds me of my grandson.

"Hello. Are you lost?"

"No. I'm looking for Kitty. Have you seen her?" the boy says.

"I don't think so. What does your kitty look like?"

"It's really Nana's kitty. I just pet it," he says, pointing a finger at me.

"Oh. What does Nana's kitty look like?"

"It's brown and black and has a striped tail like that one." The child motions to Moon, who is skittering across the yard, desperate for a place to hide.

"Well, that's my kitty, not Nana's kitty. Maybe if we call your kitty, she'll come."

The boy gives me a knowing frown. "I don't think so."

"Why not?"

"'Cause Nana took Kitty when she left. I saw her do it, but Momma doesn't believe me."

I walk over to the boy. "I believe you. Where did Nana go?"

"I don't know. She wouldn't tell me." The little boy's eyes fill with tears. "I really miss her, and Kitty too."

"I'm sorry. Can I help?" I pull a tissue from my pocket and wipe the tears from his chubby little face.

"No, not unless you can find Nana." I see the child's little lips quiver, and it looks as though he might burst out crying.

"When did Nana leave? Do you remember?"

"No. It was a long time ago, I think. That's what they told me." The boy scuffs the ground. "They won't tell me everything. They think I don't know Nana's not coming back." Tears stream down his face.

"Oh, I'm so sorry." I reach out, and we hug for a few minutes. Then he stares at me.

"You look like Nana. I thought I heard her. I ran and hid in the bushes from Momma. She says I'm not allowed here anymore. She says it's not safe."

"Ah. Does Nana have another name? Do you know?"

"Yeah, I know." The little cherub child twists his fingers and looks down at his feet. By his gesture, I think he is hiding something. "John, the mailman, calls Nana *Georgia girlie*," the boy says. "He brings the mail, but he doesn't live on the IN Road. Only Nana, Momma, and I live here—and now you." The young boy's face turns red, so I decide not to prod him for more information.

"Would you like a cookie? Nana left you some in the trailer."

"Yes!" The little boy's eyes gleam, and he adds, "Please."

In the trailer, I hand him a cookie from a tin cookie box and check to see if there is any milk in the small refrigerator outside. There is. The boy takes the glass of milk in both hands and drinks it down. He gobbles up the last of the cookie. "Can I have some more?"

"Sure." I hand him more cookies. "More milk too?"

"Yes, please!"

The treats have changed the boy's mood. He is happier now and I sense we are becoming friends, so I question him again. "What's your name?"

"Billy. I'm five. Momma says I'm too big for my britches sometimes."

"Oh, Billy, you seem okay. What does Nana say about that?"

"She says I'm okay too. Are you a friend of Nana's?"

"I guess so. She seems to have invited me here." My voice trails off. I'm not sure what to say. His grandmother,

Georgia/Nana, is still a mystery to me. All I know is what I've read in the *Newsweek*.

"Nana *always* tells me stories," Billy says, and reaches for another cookie. "She likes to draw too. Do you draw?"

"Yes, I'm an artist and a writer like Nana. I think Nana wanted me to visit for a while. That's why I'm here." I hesitate and then ask, "Billy, do you know how to get out?" I don't go into detail, for I assume the child knows what I'm talking about—and he does.

"Yep. Nana says it's easy if you know how. She says the hard part is getting back in. I know how to do that too." The little boy looks at me with his head cocked, as if he is wondering about my ability to comprehend his meaning.

"I'm not sure how to get out without help. Would you help me, Billy?"

"Yeah, I can. Kitty knows the way too. Follow her!" Excited, he jumps up and runs outside, calling, "Here kitty, kitty, kitty. Here kitty, kitty!" Each time he yells for the cat, his voice goes up a notch in singsong fashion. I smile at his enthusiasm and search for the cat too.

"There she is!" he cries. "Hurry, she's getting away!" The little boy scrambles into the bushes. "Come on!" he hollers.

I run after him, but his compact frame is more agile than my fifty-year-old body. It's hard to keep up. Gasping, I stop to catch my breath. I hear him calling for Kitty in the distance.

Gathering momentum to continue, I move on and arrive at a clearing in a few minutes. The fresh, dewy meadow ahead is scattered with daisies and other wildflowers. Robust apple trees are stationed throughout a well-kept orchard. Billy is standing near one of the older apple trees. He waves and I trot over to him.

"She went there," he says, and puffs out his little chest. "I told you it is easy."

"What do you mean?" I catch my breath.

"Go there," he instructs and points his child-sized fingers to a wide, indented space between two apple trees. "Nana does it *there*. I saw her." Looking very much like a little toy soldier standing erect and ready, he puts his hands on his small hips and commands, "Try it!"

I stand for a few moments, unable to move. I try to decide whether I should follow the little urchin's command or not. Then I see a soft, almost imperceptible light shimmer between the two apple trees. The movement reminds me of heat waves in the desert. I stick my hand into the shimmering light. "What will happen when I'm on the other side?" Surprised to see my hand wavering, I quickly withdraw it.

"I don't know." The little boy shrugs. "Nana never lets me go. She says I have to stay here with Momma and go to school. I never get to do *anything* fun."

"Oh, Billy, I'm sure Nana knows best about this," I say with a calm deliverance. But in reality, I feel torn, in turmoil. *Should I take the chance?* I glance at the boy. He seems to know more than he says. I scan the area, searching for Karina, but she is nowhere in sight. "Well, I guess I could try it," I say. "If I make a mistake, Billy, what do I do?"

"Just follow Kitty. That's what Nana does." Then Billy turns around. "I hear Momma. I gotta go. Bye!" Before I say anything, he takes off like a rocket and runs into the forest.

"Wait, Billy! Come back!" I yell. But it is too late. He's gone, and I am left staring at the shimmering, vibrating air between the apple trees. "Do I really want to go back?" *Maybe, but then again, maybe not.*

The year 2008 had been problematic for me and everyone I knew. The economy plummeted, putting scores of jobless people on unemployment benefits. There were long bread lines; thousands of people lost their homes, and some were living on the streets. A war erupted in the Middle East. France was against U.S. policies—England and Ireland too.

The financial system was a calamity, and I was a casualty when the magazine I worked for went defunct. I lost my job. I scoured the want ads, made every attempt to apply to any job I qualified for, but there were thousands of applicants and too few jobs. Forced to live on credit, I watched my credit card debt pile up. I knew I wouldn't be able to withstand much more. Life was grim.

But despite my worries, I spent the last of my meager budget on a steak dinner and a bottle of wine last night. After a satisfying meal and brief conversation with my daughter and five-year-old grandson, I went to bed.

To quiet my mind, I ran through some visualization techniques. Nothing unusual, stuff I'd done a hundred times before. My meditation consisted of imagining my bed as a life raft. Like Noah's Ark, I'd pile everything I needed on top, including my pets. Then, I encircled the raft with light, and drifted down a white gold glistening river.

I'd used this meditation before, but this time, something unusual happened! I woke up on the IN Road, fifty years in the past. Now, I am contemplating staying here. *How can I be so fickle?* What about my family and friends?

Holding my breath, I clasp my pendant and bow my head. "What should I do, Your Holiness? Help me." I keep still until deep within the cortex of my brain, I hear a faint reply. "Go back."

Without thinking, I trust the command and take a deep breath. The air between the two apple trees is still wavering. I stand between the trees and wait for something to happen. A subtle buzzing sensation surrounds my torso, and I feel buoyant, as if I'm weightless. The instant I close my eyes, I hear a slight *vroom* noise, and when I open my eyes, I am home, standing in the bathroom. The shower is on and I am soaking wet.

I grab a bath towel, wrap it around my body, and dart into the bedroom. I see Karina, Gatito, and Moon resting on the bed. Karina lifts her head and wags her tail. Everything looks just as I'd left it the night before. Everything is the same, except me.

The memory of the IN Road is vivid—scenes flash before me, every detail emblazoned in my mind.

Deep within, I wonder if I'll ever return to 1958, never believing for a moment that it would happen.

Part One

Visiting Lisel

2001-2006

Margot sat waiting for her flight and watched passersby hurry along the crowded corridor. As her gaze shifted up and down the long, shiny hallway, she imagined each of the harried travelers' dramas, their life stories as they rushed past while in the back of her mind, she tried to pinpoint the first time she'd heard of Orcas Island. It must have been the summer before her senior year in high school when Michelle, her best friend, returned from Orcas after a two-week sailing adventure.

Margot chuckled to herself, remembering how Michelle cooed about the trip. "Oh, I had *so* much fun. What a blast!" Her friend swooned. "We went sailing almost every day, and

I met these *really* cool guys from Orcas." Michelle twirled. "See my tan."

To show off, Michelle spun her svelte, tanned body.

Margot bit her lip. "Wow," she said. Margot wasn't jealous of her friend then, not really. She didn't care about Michelle's tan, sailing, or Orcas. She wished she'd been the one who'd met those cool guys.

As a teenager, living on an island had not occurred to Margot; it would be years before Orcas Island showed up on her radar. Margot hadn't thought about the island at all until thirty years later, when in the middle of a long, cold winter, she flew there for a respite. By that time her sister, Lisel, lived on Orcas.

In the late 1980s, Lisel crewed on a sailboat. On one cruise, they anchored in Deer Harbor on Orcas Island for a few days to collect supplies and a fresh round of passengers. At the time, the San Juan Islands and island-style living impressed her so much that Lisel later returned to Orcas intending to stay.

"Why there?" Margot said. "What's so special about those islands?"

"Why not, Margot? I love it here. I can't think of any other place I'd rather be. Why don't you visit and see yourself?"

"Hmm, maybe later. Can't now. I've got to make some money." Margot dismissed her sister's comments.

Sparked by the need for income after a long span of unemployment, Margot hired on with an oil service company for the Alaskan pipeline. She somehow snagged a good-paying field office job despite having no construction experience. Hoping for a big bankroll, she grabbed the opportunity.

Margot had not anticipated life to be difficult in the remote Alaskan construction camp. Almost immediately, she found the work tedious and camp life suffocating. Six months into the job, she hated everything: the workload, the cold, and short, dark days. She felt like a prisoner and couldn't wait to leave.

"You have a common malaise, Margot," a seasoned co-worker said one day in the cafeteria. "It's called cabin fever."

"Grrr-eat," she said, and piled more mashed potatoes onto her plate. Staring at the mound of food she was about to consume, Margot whispered, "I have to get out of here. I'm too old for this." Margot bit her lip and ladled another spoonful of rich gravy over the potatoes.

Later that evening, Margot wallowed in depression. She wanted to go somewhere, anywhere warm, away from the frigid, dark, and boring days. She checked her savings account. By her estimation, she had accumulated enough money to at least contemplate the dynamics of leaving. Margot sighed and collapsed across the bed. It was then she remembered Lisel's invitation. Staring at the ceiling, Margot heard her sister's voice. "Margot, why not come here?"

"Wait—what?"

At first, subtle, faded images floated into her mind's eye. Within a few seconds, the fuzzy edges sharpened, and the vision cleared. She saw herself lounging on a sunny deck surrounded by cascades of potted flowers. A large tabby cat lazed next to her. As the daydream panned out, she spied a small orchard in the background. Beyond that, a wide expanse of sparkling water that spoke island came into view. She wanted to go *there*. That set the tone, and with her resolve in place, the dreamy scene faded. With her jaw set, she lay on the bed and flirted with the idea of island life. Maybe, she thought, she'd head to Orcas Island where Lisel lived and check it out.

The next morning when she peered through the frosty window, her intention embedded itself with firm resolve. Shock waves reverberated through her as she stared at two feet of fresh snow blanketing the ground around the camp. "Shit! It's *spring*! It's not supposed to be snowing!"

After she spat out the words, something inside her snapped. "My God, I have to get the hell out of here fast." Margot grabbed the phone and dialed a travel agent. "Hello? I want to make reservations to…to Seattle, Washington. Yes, that's right. Well, the sooner the better."

The instant she made the reservation, her ennui dissolved. That night Margot threw her suitcase on the bed and packed for Orcas Island.

Though a small plane service from Seattle to the San Juan Islands was available year-round, Margot decided to take her time and drive up the I-5 Corridor. According to Lisel, spring in the Pacific Northwest was lush, and after the frigid, gloomy days in Alaska, she had a deep desire to see green— bright, cheery, spring green. So she planned to rent a car and drive through the colorful tulip and daffodil fields of Skagit Valley, then take Highway 20 over the bridge to Fidalgo Island and coast down to the quaint town of Anacortes where she would drive onto the San Juan Island Ferry to Orcas Island.

Lisel cautioned Margot to expect a sixty-minute ferry ride to Orcas on the waters of Puget Sound. Once off the ferry, there would be a thirty-minute drive halfway around the island to Lisel's place. None of this bothered Margot. In fact, meandering up the highway, unwinding as she cruised through a wash of green, breathing in balmy air sounded sublime to her.

Margot would eventually appreciate the remote aspect of island life, but on her first visit, getting to Orcas was not the leisurely trip she'd hoped for. Rush hour traffic with back-to-back cars for half the journey turned into a gut-wrenching experience. *What was she thinking?*

"Give yourself plenty of time to get to Anacortes," Lisel said. She estimated it would take her sister half a day to get to Orcas. "Remember, the ferry schedule is nonnegotiable. They won't wait for you." Lisel also recommended stocking up on a few items before crossing Puget Sound. Specialty items were almost nonexistent on the islands. "If you want your favorite shampoo and conditioner, better bring it with you." Lisel paused. "Think about packing some warm clothing like socks and fleece vests. Oh, yeah," she added, "don't forget rain gear!" *Rain? She didn't want rain.*

Reluctant to even fathom dreary weather, Margot took her sister's advice and made a few brief stops along the highway corridor. Time seemed to lag as she pushed her cart through Fred Meyer until she glanced at her watch. "Yikes," she said, "it's getting late." She shoved packages into the car and prayed she wouldn't miss the ferry, driving like a maniac on Highway 20. Lisel had warned her about speed traps in Anacortes. Margot held her breath as she careened through the small town's residential areas, pushing the speed limit, tailgating elderly drivers. It took all she had not to break the sound barrier.

That day the gods smiled upon her. The ferry docked late. Margot drove onto the ferry with ten minutes to spare. "Whew, made it." Margot sighed. Her heart was still pounding as she walked up the stairs to the main cabin.

Later, she would learn she'd passed the true test of a seasoned islander: pushing the speed limit, driving helter-skelter through Anacortes, swerving around slow drivers while attempting a frantic, last-minute shot down to the ferry terminal, just making the ferry.

Hidden within the Pacific Northwest, a region notorious for its gray skies and wet weather are the San Juan Islands. Tucked within the Puget Sound waterway, the archipelago boasts a climate akin to a mini-banana belt. The locals swear by the temperate climate. But on her first trip, Orcas Island felt bone chilling—more so than the dry cold of Alaska. Thinking temperatures would be mild and warmish to mimic her vision, she did not bring enough clothing despite Lisel's advice.

Several days into her visit, Margot sat shivering in two layers of clothes, sipping hot tea. "Well, I admit to being foolhardy." She frowned. "I was expecting balmy weather. You can bet I will *definitely* bring copious amounts of fleece and wool socks next time."

"It's the damp." Lisel laughed at her sister. "I told you so." She grabbed her extra down vest. "Here, you can borrow my vest to wear when you head to Lopez tomorrow."

Puget Sound is renowned for its deep green water and seasonal tides. Minus tides are not unusual. Water is the standard way of passage from island to island and the mainland, and that always includes a boat ride. For most everyone, that means relying on the Washington State Ferry system.

While commuting back to Orcas from Lopez Island, Margot found, to her surprise, she was the only car on the interisland boat. That ferry route makes regular daily stops at each island

and is usually bustling with commuters all year, but on this night, Margot's car was the only vehicle on the ferry.

As the *Evergreen* pulled out of Lopez, heading to Orcas Island, Margot stood alone outside her car in the center of the shadowy, cavernous lower deck. When the ferry made its normal gradual turn, a gigantic rainbow materialized in the distance and arched across the Sound. Long shafts of light spread across the sky and plunged into the deep water. Under the center of the rainbow was the blackened silhouette of her car parked at the bow. Off the port side, the diminishing sun caught the waves just right, sprinkling the rippling water with shimmering light. "Oh, my God," Margot said as she caught her breath. "It's a sign!"

Her voice echoed down the empty hull of the ferry. Spooked, Margot looked around. Just at that moment, she saw something move out of the corner of her eye, a blurred image behind the staircase. When she pivoted to look closer, she saw nothing. Uneasy, thinking she was being watched, Margot locked her car and hurried up the flight of stairs to the mid deck.

That evening during twilight, the sisters stood outside on Lisel's deck and Margot retold the story, leaving out the part about feeling watched. "I wish I'd been there. Sounds wonderful," Lisel mused. Peering at the emerald green water below, she said, "I think the only thing that might have made it better would have been a pod of orca whales swimming by."

"Yes," Margot sighed. "That would have been a nice touch."

Margot had to admit, Lisel's island-style living was enchanting. She wondered what it would be like to live year round on the islands. "I'm liking it here, too, Lisel. How would you feel if I moved to Orcas?"

"Well, there are pitfalls," Lisel said. "Island living isn't for everyone, especially if you're trying to earn a decent living." Lisel squirmed a little in her chair. "We have local businesses that fill most of our needs, but making a living is scant here and steady income is not easy, not to mention there's not enough adequate housing. I've been lucky so far."

Lisel had succeeded in a blend of caretaking and gardening for her livelihood. But it had taken years to get the right clients and seasonal positions; some years were better than others. Car repair, major injury, or illness never factored into her financial situation unless it happened. She made a living by sheer determination and a desire for an independent, island-style life. Her credo was not uncommon. Locals almost always lived meager lives.

But it would take a few more visits before Margot discovered her sister was right. Island living wasn't for everyone and she wasn't sure it was for her either. It didn't take a detective to know who was living marginally. One look at the old, often rusty car or truck, frayed overalls, and crusty lifestyle, and Margot could tell who was a diehard local.

"Well, I guess you have a point, Lisel," she said one day. "If I want to live here, I'm going to need an income stream."

"It is a struggle some years." Lisel raised her right arm. "Remember when I broke my arm? That was a hell of a hard year. But, you know, Margot, I wouldn't live any other way."

"Yeah, I know. If I want to live here, I need to figure out how to make a living on the island," Margot said. "I have an excellent skill set so I *could* make it." She set her mind on the idea, but it wasn't until she met a woman named Wanda that fate cracked the door open.

One day at the local market, Wanda, a casual friend of Lisel's, invited Margot to her fiftieth birthday bash. Unbeknownst to the owner who was off-island for the winter, Wanda, who was caretaking the property, planned to host her party at the owner's house.

When Margot walked into the festivities, she found the house filled with locals drinking and partying. Not knowing anyone and taken aback by the raucous party, Margot wandered around until she found Wanda.

"Should we be here, Wanda? I mean, the owners, they're out of town," Margot said.

"Oh, don't worry. I'll clean up the mess. They'll never know. Come with me. I want to show you the house."

Wanda paraded around the well-appointed home, showing Margot all the cupboards filled with antique dishes, hand-blown glassware, and delicately embroidered linens. When they wandered along the gallery hall lined with island art, Margot stopped in front of a framed news article hanging on the wall. A stark black and white photo of a woman sitting by a typewriter caught her attention. "Who's that?" she asked.

"Oh, that's a famous writer. She used to live on Orcas. They say she disappeared, vanished decades ago. No one knows what happened to her."

Margot stared at the photo and read the caption. "Georgia Swan. Huh. She looks interesting."

"Yeah, she was a talented writer. I read one of her books."

"Ya know, I think I've seen this photo somewhere," Margot said. "But I don't remember."

"Maybe the library. They have her books." Wanda opened another closet. "Look at this. Nice, huh?" Wanda fingered the navy blue satin fabric and took the beautiful embroidered Asian jacket off the hanger. She put on the garment. "What do ya think?" she said as she twirled in front of Margot.

"Yeah, nice," Margot said. Aghast at Wanda's lack of propriety, she wanted to leave. "Uh, I gotta go, Wanda." Margot backed out the door. "Thanks for the evening." Her voice trailed down the hallway. She escaped out the kitchen side door, sidestepping the partyers. In the car, she scribbled Georgia Swan's name.

Fishing, farming, and a lime kiln industry drove the early San Juan Islands' economy. As the natural resources depleted, the economic base shifted to real estate and tourism. By the 1980s, the trend had ballooned to epic proportions. Though part-time residents and summer visitors were a rich source of income, there was a downside. Overwhelmed by the encroachment of summer people, locals had a tendency to be testy and rude toward visitors and wealthy part-time residents. Lisel had tons of stories about the scourge of summer tourists. She claimed Orcas was part of the heart chakra of the planet, and with seasoned authority, told Margot that often vacationers came to the islands to drop their emotional shit.

"They do, Margot. They're acting out—adults and children. I've seen it," Lisel asserted. "After a few days, they leave feeling light and airy because they've left their pent-up emotional shit here. It's getting so I dread summer and can't wait for fall!"

"Oh, Lisel, come on." Margot looked away. Secretly, she knew she'd done the same thing. "What should we have for dinner tonight?" she said.

It was festive at Lisel's hobbit house that night. Primed by wine and marijuana, the sisters reverted to their childhood days, poking fun at each other. After a few more glasses of wine, things shifted, and they hissed about memories of their shared family history.

"No, it wasn't like that, Lisel."

"Yes, it was. I remember distinctly, Dad wanted you to fly. You didn't want to, but I did! He always deferred to you. You were his favorite."

"No, I wasn't. You're misremembering."

"Aw, bullshit."

"And baloney to you too."

Back and forth it went until neither of the women could muster the energy to squabble anymore. Their mood changed again. Soon, the women told quirky stories, reminiscing about childhood escapades and adventures until they were laughing so hard their sides ached. It was a cathartic evening, bringing the sisters together.

When morning came, they gathered at the table, hung over and stunned by their excesses. Feeling miserable, they promised one another they'd go straight. But that evening as they lingered on the deck at sunset, Lisel rolled another joint. "Want some?"

Margot raised her eyebrows. "Sure. Why not?" she said, and reached for the marijuana. They passed the smoldering number back and forth, chatting about the day's activities. When the conversation lulled, Margot got up, opened a bottle, and poured the rich, red alcohol into tall wine glasses.

"I'll get some munchies." Lisel pulled out a bag of chips and dip. Before they knew it, the sisters launched into the next round of talk story and they kibitzed way into the night. This party cycle dissipated after three or four days, and so did Margot's melancholy. Later, she'd remember her first visit to Orcas as one of the best times she'd had in years.

Theater and music play important roles on the island, and local productions bring out the best amateur talent around. Most everyone on the island gets involved on some level from selling tickets, front theater participation, and/or audience support. The year the new Orcas Center opened, Margot helped the production crew build sets and design costumes for its first theater performance. One day, a five-year-old boy was playing outside the theater, kicking dirt. The child came over when Margot walked out. He looked into her eyes and said, "I bet you don't know I know your name is Margot."

"No, I didn't know," she said in total surprise. "How do you know my name?"

"We know each other—from before," the little boy said, gazing at her. "From a long time ago."

"Wow," said Margot. "What's your name?"

"Billy."

"Well, sorry, Billy. I…I guess I forgot."

"That's okay," the boy said, and ran off to kick more dirt clods.

"Bye." Margot waved and wondered where she'd met the kid.

Lisel drove up and rolled down her window. "How's it going?"

"Fine. What brings you here?"

"I was in town and so I stopped by to see what you'd like for dinner."

"Oh. Uh, I don't know. Pasta and a salad, I guess. Something light."

"Okay. I'll pick up wine too. We're out." Lisel chuckled.

"The strangest thing just happened, Lisel. See that little boy over there?" Margot pointed to the field where Billy had gone.

"What boy?"

"That one—" Margot said, turning toward the field. "Well, he *was* there just a minute ago. He's about five years old, said his name was Billy."

"Well, he's not there now. What about him?"

"Oh, nothing. I just thought…well, never mind. See you later."

For islanders, the San Juan County Fair on San Juan Island signals summer's end. Temperatures drop. There is a feeling of winding down the day after the fair. Locals let out a sigh of relief. Traffic diminishes and ferry lines thin after the Labor Day weekend. In fact, islanders count on it and often pray for deliverance from the hubbub of summer.

On one extended summer's visit, Margot found she had the same grim wish to see visitors leave after three frenzied summer months of living as a transient local. In private, she chided herself for counting the days until summer's end, but couldn't stop feeling glee once the season ended. Labor Day weekend meant the finale of tourist season for the year; it also signified the end of her income.

And so, after that long, endless summer, the luster of island living vanished, and Margot decided it was time to try mainland living again. "I think I'll go to California for a while," she told Lisel, and packed her car.

The night before she left Orcas Island, Margot had a vivid dream. In the dream, a woman, panicking, runs through a pasture. A stocky, darkly clothed man chases her. When the man closes in on the woman, he reaches for her arm. Just before he grabs her, the woman disappears into thin air.

"I had the strangest dream last night." Margot snapped the bungee cords on top of her car. "Yep, those are tight enough."

"What about?" Lisel said.

"Well, I'm not sure of the meaning, but it had to do with a woman. She was running, being chased, and disappeared."

Margot frowned. "I woke up feeling disturbed, like something was wrong."

"Huh, odd," Lisel said. "Are you sure you want to leave, Margot? Maybe it's a sign."

"A sign?" Margot laughed. "That's funny coming from you! I thought you didn't believe in signs."

"I don't…but you do. Maybe you should just stay here and not go to California."

"No. There's more opportunity for me there. I feel it. Besides, I'm all packed." Margot gave her sister a hug and slid into her car. "Well, see you later, gator. Thanks for everything."

Lisel shook her head but said nothing. Thinking her sister nuts to leave island life, she waved to Margot as she drove out of the driveway, her car chock-full.

Margot grinned and waved back. California sounded right to her, and she was more than ready. She knew she'd be back one day, but she didn't realize until later how soon it would be.

Part Two

Returning to the IN Road
1958/2008

For the second time in her life, Margot had the strange, uneasy sensation she was not where she was supposed to be. Finding herself sitting in Georgia's easy chair on Orcas Island again in the year 1958 wasn't startling to her, but it was nonetheless baffling. *How had this happened?* She must have dozed off while meditating.

Margot glanced around the small trailer's enclosure. In slow motion, she moved her head from side to side to check her perimeters. Off to the left, shuttered by Georgia's white lacy curtains, a faint morning light shone through a slit in an open window. A hint of ocean breeze crept in the window, fresh and damp.

Oddly, she remembered the lace curtains, the ones she'd seen in a vision of Georgia months ago. Yes, they were swaying just as she'd seen them.

She peered at the antiquated clock through the hazy light. The little hand was on numeral seven. It's morning, she thought, and picked up her thick, orange fleece off the floor. She zipped up and closed her eyes to reach in her mind for a reference point—something. What had she been meditating on when she blacked out? She couldn't remember now.

Combing through her memory to recall her meditation, Margot jolted upright when she heard a sharp noise outside. Her eyes popped open. She shot a glance at the door, which had opened a crack. "Georgia?"

Near the door were two sets of worn rubber boots: a black high top pair and a low cut green pair. Margot inspected the green boots. They were smeared with fresh mud. She touched the still moist goo with her finger. With some trepidation, she pushed the door open and listened. Nothing. Margot stepped onto the deck expecting to encounter Georgia.

To her surprise, no one was there, only large terra-cotta pots, gushing with bright summer flowers at the edge of the deck. Along with the pottery centurions were two wooden deck chairs and an adjoining table intermingled with a few more big flowering pots. On the table were several half-empty glasses and a full ashtray. It looked as if someone had just been there. "Georgia?" she called out, but there was no answer.

Low, dark gray clouds hung over the land, threatening precipitation. "Looks like rain," she mumbled. Almost on cue, she felt a few drops. Margot gasped when she saw her hands tremble. "I need some coffee," she said, and dashed inside.

At the kitchen counter, she filled the shiny percolator with water and ground coffee. Her hands shook as she lit the propane stove. *Why was she here—again?*

Struggling to make sense of her situation, she hummed a Buddhist mantra to help calm her nerves. "Om mani padme hum," she whispered over and over until the coffee finished perking. Then she heard another noise. This time it was a cat's meow. She pivoted toward the sound, and for a second, saw a large tabby cat's nose around the front door. "Kitty?" The cat meowed and then darted out the door.

"Kitty! Here kitty, kitty, kitty." Margot rushed out of the trailer, but the feline was gone. She scanned the terrain, guessing the cat must have darted into the forest. Off to the side of the trailer, Margot spotted an almost invisible game trail and followed it into the dank underbrush. By now, the drizzle had turned into a downpour. Her clothes stuck to her body. Drenched, Margot moved deeper into the forest along the narrow path, ignoring her discomfort. "Kitty! Here kitty, kitty," she called.

She wandered into the dense forest until the trail ended. Exasperated, finding no trace of the cat, Margot called out once more. By now the squall had passed, and there was a hint of blue sky. Within minutes, the sky opened, the sun came out, and the air felt much warmer.

Soaked to the bone, Margot shivered and decided to let Kitty—if it was Kitty—come back on her own. She traipsed back to the Airstream. Still, she wanted to find the cat. Kitty had to be a conduit, a connector—something. Margot didn't know what, but without the cat, she knew she wouldn't get home. She had to find her. *Dang. Where is that cat?*

In the Airstream, Margot toweled down and peeked in Georgia's closet for something suitable to wear. "Ah, yes," she said, when she saw a pair of soft flannel lined jeans and a loose-fitting sweater. She slipped into the dry clothing and stretched her arms up over her head, wondering what she would say when Georgia saw her wearing her clothes.

Stiff from the damp chill, she drew a clear, deep breath and pushed the thought away, then warmed up for yoga practice. She needed to do something normal, and yoga seemed right. Practicing a few asanas would center her enough to sort through the confusion. Meditation might help, too, she thought. *No! Wait. Wasn't that how she got here in the first place?*

For a moment, Margot felt frightened. She hesitated and dropped her arms. "Oh, don't be silly." She extended them again and bent over slowly. Exhaling, she touched her toes, paused for a few seconds, and then took another deep breath. She rolled up her spine and imagined each vertebra flexible, her body supple, just as she'd been taught. Over and over again, she repeated this simple technique. *Breathe. Don't think about anything else right now. Stretch and focus on your breath.*

Yoga had been with her off and on since her early twenties. Sometimes, she was a faithful student and followed a practice; other times, she ditched yoga as casually as she would toss a pair of worn shoes. Today, *she* felt like an old pair of shoes. Payback, Margot thought, and stifled a laugh as she bent over. She would think about the ramifications of that later.

As she breathed deeper, the frantic voices in her head subsided. She noticed subtle changes in her body and felt better. Yoga was one thing Margot held onto even while living through turmoil. If she missed a day or two, her mind would cloud over, and her body would yearn for more oxygen and prolonged stretching. Then she'd get back to her practice. She had to; yoga kept her sane.

Once *Savasana* was over, Margot slowly rolled her body up and went into the bathroom. She wanted to feel clean. Her face was grimy to the touch; her teeth felt encased in fur. *When was the last time she'd brushed them?* Rummaging through the tiny bathroom drawer, she found a toothbrush, an old-fashioned tin of powdered Pepsodent toothpaste, a washcloth, and a bar of hand soap. "Thank you, Georgia," she said and kissed the air.

Margot swept back her hair to examine her face in the mirror. She had not aged appropriately. She was not as old as she looked. "How did you leap back fifty years?" she asked her reflection. It all seemed crazy, and for a moment, Margot wondered if she was hallucinating. "No, you're not. Don't be stupid, Margot." She motioned to the mirror. "Come on, old girl! Let's snoop around."

As if by magic, an orb of light hovered over the dinette table and shone down on the Royal typewriter, beckoning her. Inserted in the typewriter carriage was a sheet of white paper. She had not noticed this earlier. When she scrolled the paper up, there were five words typed in the middle of the page.

Tell Billy I love him.

"Billy," Margot said. "*Dang,* I forgot about him." She glanced around for her laptop, then caught herself. "Oops." She laughed. "That's right, this is 1958. No personal computers yet."

She moved to the stack of papers and magazines by the easy chair and flipped through the top magazine. Nothing. Tossing it aside, she leafed through a few more periodicals until she found a brief article about a retrospective of Georgia's post modern work in *ARTnews.*

The abbreviated piece reviewed Georgia's past work and described her ongoing career. Her list included one novel, a book of short stories with original color illustrations, and a children's picture book about a lost boy. There was also mention of another book coming out in September 1958.

Margot sat down hard. From the outward evidence, it appeared Georgia was still alive and might walk through the front door at any moment, but where was she?

As mist formed across an expanse of cool water, a three-dimensional vision emerged in front of Margot. She stared into the translucent scene as it came into sharp focus. A single hanging lamp spotlighted Georgia as she typed. A cigarette burned in the ashtray beside her, along with some crumbled pages on the table. The detail was incredible, right down to the fine strands of Georgia's hair and her subtle expression as she hammered away at a page of text on her Royal typewriter.

Fascinated, Margot watched Georgia work as she pounded the old Royal's keys with rhythmic force. Margot heard the keys clack. Then suddenly, Georgia stopped. She pushed back her hair and studied the prose with a furrowed brow. A large tabby cat jumped up on the table and nosed Georgia's hand. She ran her hand over the feline's back and read the text. Then the cat meowed and jumped down.

Again, just as she had in Margot's former vision, Georgia turned and looked straight at Margot. Taking a deep drag of her cigarette, Georgia exhaled smoke toward Margot. When smoke evaporated, the apparition was gone.

No sooner had the vision disappeared than Margot heard a light knock on the door. It did not surprise her to see Billy standing there when she opened the door.

"Hello, Billy. I thought that was you."

"Where's Nana? Is she here? I want to find Kitty." Billy's voice was weak, and his eyes filled with big tears.

"Come in." Margot said. "I don't know where Nana is, but I think I saw Kitty wandering around a while ago. Would you like to have a cookie?"

Billy nodded.

"Good. Come, have a snack, and then I'll help you look for Kitty." Margot set out a small plate, grabbed the box of cookies and put a few on it. She took out a miniature glass from the cupboard and poured in some milk. It was obvious the boy was upset, so Margot said nothing and watched him gobble up several cookies. She wasn't sure what to say anyway. Better take this slowly, she thought.

"Can I have another cookie?" the boy said. Margot handed him the box. He took a handful of shortbread cookies and stuffed a few in his mouth. "Thank you," he said, his voice muffled. "You kinda look like Nana."

"Really?"

"Yeah, but I know you're not her."

"That's right, Billy. My name is Margot. I came to visit. Where is your momma?"

"At the store. When Momma goes to the store, I'm old enough to stay home now Momma said. I used to come and play with Nana, but—" The little boy choked back tears.

"How 'bout more milk?" Margot reached for the milk in the refrigerator. "Here you go." She sat down across from him and watched as he drank the milk right down. "You were thirsty!" Margot smiled at him. She kept her voice soft, wanting to question the child as gently as possible.

"Momma says Nana is her momma."

"Yes, that's how it works. How old are you now, Billy?"

"Five!" Billy held up his right hand and spread all five fingers wide apart. "But I'm almost six." Billy stuck out his other forefinger to add to the count. "One, two, three, four, five, six!"

"Would you like to hear a story?"

"Yeah," Billy said. "Nana tells me stories. She likes to draw too. I know where the crayons are."

"Well, let's read a little and then color." Margot looked through the bookshelf behind her and pulled out a storybook. She turned the front cover toward Billy. The book was an old Hans Christian Andersen story, one of her favorites. "Will this story be okay?"

"I like that one!"

"Me too. Now, let's see. Once upon a time…"

Halfway through the story, Margot and Billy heard a cat meow. They looked at each other in surprise. "There she is!" Billy's voice quivered with excitement. "That's Kitty!" Billy jumped from the chair and bolted out the door. "Kitty! Here Kitty, Kitty," he called.

Margot snapped the book shut and hurried after him. Just as she stepped off the deck, she saw Billy disappear around the bend and head toward the apple orchard. "Billy! Wait!" she shouted and jogged after him.

Panting, Margot stopped just short of the apple orchard and bent over to catch her breath. Her heart raced. With her hands on her knees, she took a few deep breaths and cocked her head toward Billy, who was knee-deep in wet grass. With both arms up, he stood between two of the trees and yelled to her. Margot straightened up, but she couldn't quite make out what he was saying. "Get going," she said to her wobbly legs, and with all her might rushed over to him. That was when she saw Kitty clinging to a top branch in one tree. The cat howled at them.

"She's up there!" Billy yelled. "Can you get her?"

Wet from the heavy dew, Kitty teetered on a narrow branch far beyond Margot's reach. Climbing the tree was out of the question. She stared up at the cat, wondering how to coax her down.

"Get Kitty! Please!" Billy's little body was shaking; tears fell from his sorrowful blue eyes. "I want to hold her."

"Just a minute, Billy. Try to stay calm. Let's see if she'll come down by herself."

"Okay." Billy's voice wavered. Then he picked up a small stick and threw it at the tree. "Why won't she come down?" He stamped his foot. "Nana got her down one time before. Kitty likes Nana."

"I know, honey, but Nana's not here right now. I'll try to help Kitty if she'll let me."

"I wish Nana was here." Billy's youthful voice cracked. He collapsed at the bottom of the tree in tears.

"Oh, Billy, I'm so sorry." Margot knelt down by the boy. She didn't know what to do first—comfort Billy or rescue the cat. Kitty crouched on a branch near the top of the tree and meowed a few times, then limb by limb, the cat slid down to the last big branch and meowed again. Finally, she jumped down, sashayed over to Billy, and swished her tail around his little legs. Rubbing her head against him, she acted as if nothing unusual had happened.

"She's down!" Billy pulled the cat to him, scooping up her long body with both arms. Kitty was a big load, but Billy hugged and squeezed her anyway. She purred and tucked her head into his neck.

"There," Margot said. "No harm done, huh, Billy?"

The little boy looked up and grinned, then carried Kitty out of the orchard. "I'm going to take her to Nana's. She likes it there." He turned his head toward Margot. "I don't want her to leave like Nana did."

"Yes, of course. Take her to the trailer." Margot sighed, relieved that at least this tiny crisis was over. She followed Billy up the trail to the Airstream. Halfway up, Billy put Kitty down and the tabby cat followed him, tail held high; within minutes, he was laughing and playing with her.

Now that Billy and Kitty were reunited, Margot stopped on the trail for a few minutes. Her mood turned somber as she watched the two toddle up the path. She couldn't help but wonder what this little drama, mixed with her personal drama, had been about. She had a niggling suspicion that Billy, Kitty, and the apple trees were involved. *But why?* She swung around and scrutinized the orchard for any obvious clue among the trees and meadow. But there were none. Still, Margot wanted to question Billy about Nana, but with care. The kid had enough trauma for one day.

"I have to go home now," Billy said when she reached the deck. "Can I come and visit tomorrow?"

"Absolutely." For a moment, Margot wondered if there would be a tomorrow for her here. She wasn't sure.

Billy sat on the deck stair and petted the cat. "Kitty has to stay inside so she won't run away," he said, and jumped up. "I have to go now. I hear Momma. Bye!"

"See you later, alligator!" Margot waved to him as he ran down to the edge of the trees. The instant the child disappeared into the dense forest, an epiphany hit her. Margot let out an elongated whistle that echoed down the field to the orchard. She knew the connection now—or at least part of it. Her encounter with Billy was a lead-up to something much, much bigger. All she had to do was wait. The answer would come.

"Woo. I think I'm getting this," she said, and walked into the trailer.

The land eased into the gloaming as the afternoon light faded. A soft pink haze washed across the horizon with a delicate hint of yellow backlighting the treetops in the orchard. Despite the extraordinary beauty, Margot suddenly felt woozy, distracted, her emotions churning. Holding her head with both hands, she dragged herself to the daybed and slid, fully clothed, under the comforter. She closed her eyes. "I need rest," she whispered, and then, everything went black.

From a distance, Margot sees Billy standing in the field about twenty yards in front of the trailer. He waves and beckons her to follow him. The sky is bright, and the air is warm. It appears to be an early summer day. Kitty walks right beside Billy as they head toward the orchard. Billy turns around to make sure Margot is following them. He waves again and smiles at her. Then he stops and stands at the entrance of the orchard. Kitty walks past Billy and into the orchard. She stops on the grass between two of the largest apple trees and sits, curling her long tail around her front paws. She looks at Billy and at Margot, then meows loudly. Billy points to Kitty and then runs into the woods. Margot walks toward Kitty. She feels cautious but keeps moving and stops beside the cat. Kitty meows several times, yawns, and looks up at Margot. Instantly, the cat vanishes. Panicked, Margot looks around the perimeter. Billy is gone, and the cat is nowhere to be found.

Margot snapped open her eyes and bolted upright. The pitch-black room felt cool and oddly familiar, but she couldn't pinpoint her whereabouts. "The dream—the dream! Remember the dream," an inner voice shouted. She shook her head. Her heart pounded so fast she couldn't get a full breath. Now she wasn't sure she'd heard anything. *What the fuck? What time is it?*

She reached for the light switch and knocked over the alarm clock. "Damn it. Where's the light?" Pawing the surface of the night stand, she found the lamp and clicked on the bright light. "Oh, God," she moaned and closed her eyes. Every muscle in her body ached. She dove under the comforter and covered her head, wanting the pain to stop. It must have been all that running down to the orchard, she thought. *Wait! Hold on a minute—what running?*

Margot's eyes popped open. Stunned, she threw back the covers. "Jesus!" she said. "I'm in California now." *How does this happen?*

After Margot realized she was home again in 2008, she sank onto the pillows. Confused and disoriented, she tossed and turned for a few minutes and then rolled out of bed. She grabbed her mother's crocheted afghan and felt her way along the dark corridor to the small living area. Dropping into her big upholstered chair, she pulled her legs up and huddled under the warm throw. She needed to think this thing through. *What was happening to her?*

A morose cloud settled over her as she curled deeper into the chair. Staring into the dark room, unable to push away maudlin thoughts, Margot lingered on the more dismal parts of her life since the new millennium.

There had been days when she felt she couldn't go on, couldn't tolerate another rejection notice, much less figure out how to buy food for the next week. On those days, it had been difficult for her to maintain an ounce of sanity. Wrapped womb like in the afghan lovingly made by her mother, Margot's heart flooded with regret. She wanted to cry, but instead forced herself out of the chair. "Enough of this," she said, mimicking her mother's voice. "Buck up, girl. Show yourself."

Dutifully, she extended her arms up, took a deep breath, and leaned down until her fingers touched the floor. "Up and down, breathe," she said again and again. Moving into the Warrior pose, she lunged back and forward, forward and back. Her feet wobbled as she struggled to maintain her balance. In the midst of her turmoil, she felt her mind search for an answer.

It was then she sensed another larger part of her being that remained free, tranquil despite her emotional uproar. This neutral, unconcerned part observed her opposing mental forces in a state of calm. As her left and right brain bickered back and forth, this non-partisan bystander watched with faint amusement as the two hemispheres fought for dominance.

Feeling a headache coming on, Margot moved out of the pose. "I need coffee and something to eat," she said, and busied herself in the kitchen to fix breakfast. But she couldn't stop thinking about her trip back in time to Georgia's trailer. As she buttered toast, her thoughts focused on Billy and Kitty. *Was it all a dream?* She wasn't sure.

Then the memory of an important discovery in Georgia's closet filtered into her thoughts. The suitcase. She'd almost forgotten about that.

After Billy left, Margot lingered in Georgia's trailer for a few more hours. The temperature warmed, so she selected a light, crisp white *Ship 'n Shore* blouse out of Georgia's closet instead of the heavy sweater she'd worn earlier. That's when Margot found the small suitcase resting on the floor of the wardrobe.

When she clicked open the case, she found a myriad of accessories: gloves, scarves, and a few leather belts. Curious, she picked through the accessories and pulled out a few scarves to try on. "Lovely," she said, and tied a colorful scarf around her neck. It was when she returned the scarves that Margot noticed the long, faded ribbon attached to a stained satin lid at the bottom of the suitcase. Margot gasped when she lifted the lid.

Underneath laid a thick, worn sketchbook. "Georgia's journal!" Margot caught her breath. The black book bulged with notecards and faded newspaper clippings. A few of Georgia's sketches fell out of the robust journal when she opened it.

Flush with excitement, Margot pushed the typewriter aside, sat down at the dinette table, and ferreted through the book. Handwritten at the top of the first page in neat uppercase letters were the words: *Adventures with Kitty*. Underneath the title was a black and white line drawing of a cat walking between two trees.

With an editor's eye, Margot turned each page, scrutinizing the writing. In a tidy script, the opening entry showed several book ideas outlined in vivid detail. Further in the book, a few notes were smudged and hard to decipher, but most of Georgia's concepts were legible and accompanied by preliminary sketches.

Georgia also enclosed several black and white snapshots of potential locations for her story ideas; thrown in, too, were a number of illustrated profile sketches for prospective characters. But the best and most astonishing part of the journal was the back section, entitled *Notes on Neom*.

Margot had just finished reading the first page of *Notes on Neom* when Billy came to the door a second time.

"Come in," Margot said.

The door opened. "Is Kitty here?" said a tiny voice.

"Billy! You're back. I was wondering who was knocking." Margot smiled at him. "Kitty isn't here right now. Do you want something to eat?"

"Do you have any cookies left?" Billy skipped into the trailer.

"There might be a few. You ate quite a lot of them."

"I know." Billy giggled. "Can I have some milk too?"

"Of course. Have a seat. I'm glad you stopped by."

Billy plopped down in a seat. He stretched his little body across the table and looked upside down at Georgia's journal. "That's Nana's book. She writes and draws in it."

"Yes, I found it in the closet. It has notes and drawings about story ideas in it."

"I know. When Nana draws in the book, I get to draw too. She has special paper and crayons for me over there." Billy pointed to a side drawer near the kitchen counter.

"Would you like to draw now?"

"Yes! Can I paint too? Nana lets me paint if I want to." Billy smiled. "I like black and red best."

Margot walked over to the drawer and got out paper, crayons, pencils, and a narrow tin container filled with small squares of watercolors. There was a well-used brush inside the tin. She held it up. "I bet this brush is yours, isn't it?"

"Yep." Billy's face beamed. "Can I have some water? In a glass."

Margot filled a glass with water and placed it next to Billy's paper. She wanted to quiz him about Georgia but didn't know where to begin or what to say without alarming the child. "Do you and Kitty go down to the orchard often?"

"Sometimes." Billy looked at his drawing paper. He laid down a wide stroke of bright orange and concentrating on his paints, sloshed the brush in water and then in another color.

"Nana said I can only go with her to the orchard. She says I can't go by myself."

"Yes, she's probably right."

Billy selected a new color and ran the brush filled with dripping paint down the vertical side of the paper. "Nana says the orchard has a secret. She says Kitty knows what the secret is." Billy shakily lifted the water glass and handed it to Margot. "I need clean water."

"Of course." Margot rinsed the glass. "Do you think Kitty would tell me the secret?" She filled the glass and then placed the clean water next to Billy.

"No." Billy looked at his painting. "But I know the secret too." Billy swirled his paintbrush in the water and dabbed the wet brush with red paint. "I like red. See."

"Very nice." Margot smiled at Billy and then glanced out the window for a few minutes while she tried to form her next question. "Say, Billy, do you think you could tell me the secret?" Margot let out a brief sigh and then sat back to wait.

Billy picked up a green crayon and scribbled it over the painted sheet of paper, up and down, making wild, chaotic lines. "Done." Billy jumped up from the table and put his jacket on. "I gotta go home now."

"Okay." Margot kept quiet. She knew children should not be forced into compliance with serious matters. They would supply the answers if not coerced. "It was so nice to see you again, Billy."

"Can you zip me up?" He walked over to Margot and stood still, waiting for her to zip his jacket.

"There you go," she said after zipping him up.

He stood looking at her for a moment, then cupped his little hand and whispered. "I saw Nana leave."

"Do you mean disappear?"

Billy nodded. "Uh-huh. In the orchard," His voice got very soft, "and then Nana came back real fast. So did Kitty!" Billy put his forefinger next to his lips. "It was between the apple trees." Billy ran to the door, twisted the doorknob, and turned toward Margot. "Bye!" he said.

Before Margot said another word, Billy hurried out, ran to the edge of the forest, and vanished into the woods.

Part Three

Back to the IN Road

2010

Margot slid into the passenger seat of the de Havilland and fastened her seatbelt. As the small plane's engine revved for takeoff, she nodded to the man across from her. "Going to Orcas?" he said.

"Yes." A swell of excitement rose within Margot. She realized then with all certainty, not only was she returning to Orcas, but she was going back to 1958 too. She felt it in her bones. In fact, the feeling was so strong, so deep, there wasn't an ounce of doubt. What rattled her at the moment—what she couldn't for the life of her figure out—was how. *How was she going to get there?* Her first few time travel encounters had been flukes. She still couldn't fathom how she'd stepped back so cavalierly fifty years into the past.

Margot turned in her narrow seat to gaze out the seaplane window as it soared along the coast. Off in the distance, puffy white clouds clustered around the densely wooded San Juan Islands. As the plane cruised above Puget Sound's massive waterway, she saw her life in California slip away, evaporate into the thin troposphere. At that moment, it felt as if her life there had never existed. She stared through the thick paned window and tried to grab onto a few snippets of her recent past. Wanting to recall any details of what she'd just left behind seemed important, especially when she had no idea what would happen next. *What if she was left in 1958 this time?*

Just ahead of the de Havilland's flight path was Turtleback Mountain. After that, she knew the village of Eastsound would come into view. Margot stared out the window, observing the land and water slip by. She thought about the miracle of flying and wondered why she resisted learning to fly. Dad had encouraged her to take after him.

All at once, the island seemed to reach up and signal to Margot. A ray of sun shot through the window, as if saluting her return. "Hello, Orcas," she whispered. Pushing thoughts of California aside, she sat back and listened to the pilot's flight chatter as the plane began its final approach. When the plane touched down on the tarmac, she calculated how many years it had been since she'd been on Orcas. Five, she guessed, or more if you counted the trips back to 1958.

Margot unfastened her seatbelt and glanced out the aircraft for Lisel, who she hoped would be there to pick her up. There had been no word from her sister before the flight took off, even though Margot had left a reminder via a quick email and topped it off with a phone message prior to boarding. Lisel seemed aloof and distracted of late. Her email messages were infrequent and sparsely written; that worried Margot, but she dissed the notion, rationalizing her sister's behavior by saying, "That's just Lisel." Over time, she'd learned to accept some of Lisel's behavior, especially after the hit-and-run accident years ago.

Late one October evening, a drunk driver hadn't seen Lisel walking down the road, then bam! His car hit her. In his drunken stupor, the man didn't stop. Lisel's twenty-year-old body buckled from the impact and was tossed off the road like a tin can. The sky had been dark and the temperature cold that night, and there was an early snow. Knocked over the snow berm where no one could see her, Lisel lay there for hours. By sheer happenstance and what Margot now presumed was an act of God, the high school principal saw Lisel out of the corner of his eye on the way to the prom. He stopped and called the police who came with an ambulance that took Lisel to the hospital. Both of Lisel's legs were broken, one in two places. She lay in the hospital in a body cast with one leg in traction for over two months. Lisel had been conscious through it all, even in the snow. After thirty years, the memory of the trauma still lived in her legs, but she rarely complained about it anymore.

Margot waved when she caught sight of Lisel and stepped down the ramp. The wind blew across the airstrip and caught her hair in an upsweep, swirling gray curls around her head, hiding her face. Brushing her hair back, Margot reminded herself, once again, to be more congenial to her sister.

At this stage in her life, Margot wanted to feel more centered and peaceful and had taken up a new strategy: meditating daily using visualization techniques. She planned to use it to create a more amiable rapport with Lisel, something playful, akin to the sisters' past camaraderie when, as little girls, they played dress-up or cut out paper dolls together. Lisel was Margot's only sibling, and the only living member of her immediate family. Margot wanted to treasure what little family she had left and vowed to be nice. Hold her temper—laugh it off instead.

"Well, Sissy, how was the flight?" Lisel said.

"Not too bad." Margot hugged her sister. Adjusting the strap on her heavy work satchel, she searched the nearly empty parking lot. "Where's the car?"

"Over there." Lisel pointed toward a small pickup truck. "I bought a new-to-me truck," she said, and reached for Margot's other bag. "Picked it up yesterday." They walked over to an older model Toyota pickup painted metallic purple with a matching truck canopy. The women circled the vehicle, inspecting it. The body had a few minor dents and marginal tires, but overall, the truck looked good. "How do you like it?" Lisel said.

"Wow, a new truck. Looks pretty clean," Margot said, knowing full well, in time Lisel would trash the vehicle with gardening tools, heaps of plants, and a load or two of horse manure—all occupational hazards of being a landscaper on Orcas Island.

Smiling, Lisel gestured to the bumper sticker on the tailgate. "And see! It even has my motto." In large white block lettering, the bumper sticker read, Crones Happen. Lisel winked at her sister and unlocked the pickup.

"Perfect!" Margot laughed. "The truck looks just like you too. How does it run?"

"There are a few things wrong, but it's all fixable." Lisel threw Margot's bag into the back and got in the driver's side. "Hop in," she said. "I have to make a stop before we get to the house. Do you mind?"

"No," Margot said. Lisel almost always had one stop, or more, before heading home. But for once Margot wasn't in a hurry. Her plans didn't start until tomorrow. She scooted into the cab. "How are the horses?"

"Sol is huge, of course, and Cody is doing better. He had a rough bout a few months ago. The farrier cut his hooves too close, and he went lame," Lisel said. "Sol has been stealing Cody's food again. I have to rope him off when I feed Cody. Sol doesn't like it."

"I can imagine," Margot said. Sol was a sweet horse, but he just didn't know how big he was. Half Percheron and black as night, he was a giant compared to Cody, a lithe, gentle thoroughbred. "Mutt and Jeff." Margot laughed. "What a pair! Just like us."

Lisel drove along the perimeter road out of Eastsound. The two sisters rode in silence for a while. Along the roadway, Margot noticed several more OPAL affordable homes had gone up, but the road had not changed. The same old potholes and bumps were there. Some things don't change, she thought.

Just then, Lisel hit a pothole. Without thinking, Margot snapped, "Yikes! Slow down. You still don't drive any better."

"Okay, Margot, I know," Lisel said, grinding the gears into third. "But we agreed not to bicker, didn't we?"

"Yeah, you're right. Sorry. No squabbling," Margot bit her tongue. Changing the subject, she said, "How's work anyway? Are you busy?"

"I've been *really* busy—still have a few jobs lined up too. But ugh," Lisel sighed, "I'm getting older. Sometimes my legs ache now and that makes it harder to work long hours." Lisel gripped the steering wheel, whipped around a corner, and gunned the truck up a steep incline. Margot grabbed onto the front dash, bracing herself. Not missing a beat, Lisel continued. "People keep calling, though, wanting me to work in their gardens. Where are they when I need the work in January?"

Tempted to make another comment about her sister's driving, Margot looked away instead. "I wondered," she said. "Your *communiques* have been marginal of late. You know I worry sometimes if I don't hear from you."

"I know, I know," Lisel said, and turned down a long driveway. "But I'm pooped at night. Too tired to do much but eat and go to bed." Lisel braked and screeched to a stop. Dust flew up from the loose gravel. "Here we are," she said. "I'll be right back."

Fifteen minutes later, the purple metallic truck sped down the double-lane paved road again and raced past the tall conifers and madrone trees indigenous to the San Juan Islands. Margot couldn't help but notice Lisel still had a lead foot despite two recent speeding tickets, but she kept quiet. She hung onto the armrest and tried to look casual, glancing out the window. They flew past plowed fields, some dotted with huge round balls of hay. "Just admire the pastureland," she told herself. "It's harvest time."

"Say, I'm thinking about walking around that private estate again. Anyone living on it yet?" Margot said.

"You mean the Swan place?" Lisel glanced sideways at Margot. "Uh, I'm not sure. I don't think so anyway." Shifting into second, Lisel made a sharp turn down a bumpy dirt road. "You know the old woman—the writer—is long gone, and her grandson doesn't seem interested in living there anymore. They say it's haunted. I don't know about that, but the last time I saw the place, the trailer was rundown. It looked like a dump, really overgrown. These days you can't see anything from the road."

Just as well, Margot thought, makes it easier to slip in and look around. "Haunted?" Margot said. "That sounds a little like Twilight Zone, doesn't it?"

"Yeah, I guess it does." Lisel laughed. Shrugging her shoulders, she leaned into the steering wheel and made another turn. "You know islanders, though, always gossiping about something or other."

"Oh, yeah, I *do* know," said Margot, and again reminded herself to keep the project quiet—even from Lisel. She didn't want it getting around Orcas that she was chasing ghosts or dipping into the supernatural, especially since some islanders thought the place might be haunted. The thought of controversy made her feel queasy. "What do you think?"

"Huh? Oh, probably not," Lisel said. "More than likely, someone saw a homeless person wandering around. That's all." She slowed the truck. Twenty yards ahead, a fawn and doe stood on the roadside. "Whoa, Nelly." The truck crept to a full stop.

"Wow," Margot said. They watched the deer cross the road in front of the truck. The fawn skittered after the mother, who leaped into the bushes. "Sometimes I forget there are deer on the islands."

"Yeah, they're out year round, especially in the gloaming time. I keep a watchful eye. God, I don't want to hit one! My neighbor did a few months ago. Terrible." The truck lurched as Lisel stepped on the gas.

"No, me either. You know, Lisel, you might be right—about a homeless guy, I mean. Someone could be squatting." Margot's voice trailed off for a moment. "I wish the dogs were still alive. Don't you?"

"Yeah, I miss Rascal," she said.

"I miss Karina too. What a dog." Margot flashed on Karina dashing around the large, daisy studded field years ago. That dog loved running and Margot loved watching her. She could still see Karina's petite Dalmatian body disappearing and reappearing in the tall grass and wildflowers. Karina would have known where to go.

As the truck cruised down the country dirt road, Margot fantasized about starting a new painting of Karina running in the field. She calculated the canvas size, the style she'd use, the color range, and which brushes she'd need. Before she knew it, the piece took form in her mind's eye. She envisioned contrasting abstract splotches of black and white against a bright, spring green landscape with vibrant splashes of orange and yellow wildflowers. It would be fun to use her painting tools again, she thought. Just thinking about it perked her up. Maybe she would work on it after this project—

"No!" she heard a voice say. "There won't be time."

Margot shook her head. "What?"

"I didn't say anything," Lisel said, and gave her an odd look.

"Huh. Oh, sorry. I thought I heard you say something." Margot glanced out the window. "What is a convenient day for me to borrow your truck?" Margot said. "I'd like to drive by the old estate."

"My truck and I are booked this week, but you can borrow Merlin whenever you want. He runs okay, but he's low on gas. Fill up before you go anywhere."

"Super. Thanks." Margot hesitated. "Okay if I use Merlin tomorrow?"

"Be my guest," Lisel said as they turned into her driveway. "Here we are, last stop."

Morning came too early for Margot the next day. She'd tossed and turned most of the night, feeling as if someone, or something, called her. The disturbance kept her awake, but she finally shrugged it off and collapsed for a few hours before sunrise.

Lisel kept the windows cracked at night, and by morning the damp Pacific Northwest air pervaded the tiny house. This morning was no different. Used to the hot, dry Sonoma weather, Margot shivered and zipped her fleece jacket. The cold, dark house put her in an edgy mood. Chilled, she threw on a down vest and tiptoed into the small kitchen. Ebony, Lisel's cat, meowed under her feet as she put on the kettle for hot water.

"Okay, girl," Margot whispered. "Just a second. Let me find the canned stuff." Ebony swished her tail and wound her long, fluffy body between Margot's legs. A rush of excitement filled Margot as she spooned cat food into Ebony's dish. This will be the day, she thought. *Today, I'll find it!*

Walking into the garden with a steaming cup of tea, Margot followed the path to the flower bed where Rascal was buried. A lingering mist hung over the raised beds and narrow walkways. A few purple asters and other late summer flowers still bloomed in and around where Lisel buried him. Margot stood in the hazy light and sipped her tea. Her mood simmered as she thought about Rascal. When he popped into her mind's eye, his big, chocolate brown face grinned. "Hello, old boy," Margot said. Chuckling to herself, she remembered what the Dalai Lama had once said about dogs.

Ten years ago, Margot and Lisel attended a large Buddhist venue for His Holiness, the Dalai Lama. During his long discourse, His Holiness made a comment that he didn't think dogs smiled. The sisters looked at each other and grinned. They knew dogs smiled, especially Rascal. He smiled a lot. People who didn't know him, though, thought he was growling when he loped to greet them with bared teeth. Margot and Lisel knew Rascal wouldn't hurt a soul unless, of course, you were a raccoon.

Revived after her tea and brief tête-à-tête with Rascal, Margot ambled back to the tiny hobbit house. She hummed a few bars as she passed the handcrafted wooden ladder leading to the loft where her sister slept. The cozy space doubled as a private meditation sanctuary and an extra sleeping area. "I need to focus on finding the IN road and that portal," Margot whispered.

Lisel turned over in her narrow loft bed. "Is that you, Margot?"

"Yes. I'm thinking about my day; headed toward the shower now. Want some tea first?"

"Hmm, yes." Lisel said. "With a little milk, please."

After Lisel left that morning, it didn't take long for Margot to get ready. Her backpack was packed. Suspecting her digital camera wouldn't work if she landed in 1958, she'd brought out her trusty Minolta XG-M from deep hibernation. Remarkably, the camera still functioned. After checking for extra rolls of 35mm film and another camera battery, Margot shoved her bag into the front seat of Lisel's Pathfinder and turned the key.

Right on cue, the old SUV started up. *Vroom*. "Geez, you weren't kidding about the gas, Lisel," she mumbled. The fuel gauge registered empty. Releasing the hand brake, Margot headed out of the driveway, excited to be on her way. She punched it down the road toward the gas station and the IN Road.

Thirty years ago, the Swan estate was legendary, a work of nature's art. Georgia Swan gained the property one parcel at a time. After her disappearance, Sandra, her daughter, remained on the property and used part of her inheritance to purchase additional land. Later, Billy, Sandra's son, added the final parcel in 1985, making the estate one thousand pristine acres. The IN Road, a single lane dirt road, led you to the estate property and the trail to Georgia's trailer.

Before her mysterious departure, Georgia hired workers to bulldoze and carve out two mile-long, narrow parallel roads. The lanes, separated by a strip of forest and wetlands, ran circuitously; one marked IN for ingress, the other OUT for egress.

Back in those days, the two roads were groomed year-round by an estate caretaker. For privacy and to maintain a sense of the Pacific Northwest wilderness, Georgia wanted the roads to remain as natural looking as possible, and that meant pruning be kept to a minimum. Sandra carried on the tradition, making sure the roads were detailed to look slightly overgrown. "No small feat in the Pacific Northwest," Lisel said.

Lisel loved working on the estate, but after a year of caretaking the Swan place, her landscaping business took off and there wasn't enough time for the estate job anymore, so she quit. Sandra moved away later and eventually, so did Billy.

Years later, Lisel told Margot she'd driven by the estate one day and found to her surprise a For Sale sign posted on the big Douglas fir near the entrance. But the property did not sell. The parcel was taken off the market, and the gates padlocked. Island murmur stirred around the mysterious closure. "But no one seemed to know much," Lisel said.

Margot turned into a small dirt pullout and stopped the car just outside the estate road. The heavy wooden gates, weathered over decades, were in terrible disrepair. The padlocks were gone, but the IN Road sign was still there. The land looked wild and free, as if no one had been on the property for a long time.

Grabbing her small backpack, Margot locked the car and headed onto the property. She walked down the IN Road about one hundred yards, then stopped. A rush of confusion swept over her. She felt lost. The surrounding topography appeared unrecognizable. The trees lining the road were much taller than she remembered. Years of accumulated undergrowth had overtaken the IN Road, disguising the area. The land was so unfamiliar, in fact, that it seemed to her she'd never been there before. "Lisel was right," she said. "The place is a wreck."

All at once, a slight chill ran down her spine. She felt shaky and unsure. "Don't be afraid," she said and took a deep breath. "There's nothing bad in here. You can do this." Scanning the perimeter, Margot didn't detect anything unusual. "The road is safe. Keep going," she said under her breath. Still, she had an uneasy, almost spooky feeling.

Above her, a deep green tree canopy unfurled. A splash of dappled lighting lay ahead on the road. Off in the distance, Margot heard the faint call of an eagle; the trill of happy birds chattered among the leaves overhead. Even with these blithe, reassuring sounds of nature, she walked down the road cautiously, casting a look around for anything that might suggest danger.

After a few tense minutes, Margot broke the moment by laughing out loud. She realized she'd imagined herself wearing military cami pants, her face black with grease as she darted in and out of the forest like a skilled ninja. She shook her head.

"Oh, dear God," she said. "Calm down, girl. Now, what am I doing?"

"Just follow the road," a voice shot back. Margot stopped and trembled. Unsure if she had heard anything, she cocked her head this way and that. Then came the distinct words. "Keep going."

Margot swung around. "Where are you?" she demanded. "Who are you?" But she saw no one and heard no answer. Nervous, she hurried down the narrowing dirt road, her heart pounding with each step, but she didn't turn back. Something pulled her forward, urging her on. She tried to dismiss the strong, irresistible compulsion, but couldn't. The feeling was relentless. Margot forced herself to remove any resistance, knowing deep within it was the dream calling her—the one she'd dreamt so many times she knew every nuance by heart.

The dream starts with a panoramic view of the orchard. She glides into the grassy field and stops at the vortex, the spot where she and Karina stepped into the portal and returned to the year 2008. Standing between the two apple trees, Margot waits. Soon the surrounding air blurs and shimmers like a mirage on a hot, paved highway. In a split second, she disappears in a tiny poof.

But there is a twist to the dream. Instead of arriving back in 2008 as she had in three-dimensional time, Margot finds herself transported to another place—a land that doesn't resonate with any earthly dimension she's ever seen.

Each time Margot awakens from the dream, the next instant the memory of it always vanishes, and she is never able to capture the details except for the exhilaration of dimensional travel. The sensation lingers for a while. Her body quivers with exhaustion as if she's been on a long overseas flight.

Margot has no reference point for the surreal landscape. The land and all it entails occupies her conscious thought like a paradox. It feels like a familiar memory, as if she's been there many times, yet she does not remember when or where.

Triggered by an intense need to get back on track and stay focused, Margot moved deeper into the property, pushing aside her unease and any thoughts about the dream. She willed herself to concentrate on her mission: locate the apple orchard and time portal and investigate the area around Georgia's trailer. Those were the key points for the day. But the strange voice unsettled her so much she couldn't quell her discomfort. Especially since the land and road had changed radically. She didn't recognize the terrain. In her confusion, she called out, "Where do I go?"

"Ahead. Just go ahead," the voice said.

Margot jumped and turned to look behind her. "Jesus! Stop that! Who are you anyway?" But she saw no one. A part of her wanted to turn around and run back to the car. *Hadn't Lisel suggested the place was haunted?* But a more powerful part of Margot's psyche held her. She struggled, unable to yield to either point of view.

And then, as if by rote, the left side of her brain sprang into action. Margot heard herself say, "Look for something familiar. Yes. Look for something familiar." Guided by her own words, Margot crept along, scouring the area for recognizable landmarks—anything that might help her locate Georgia's trailer and the portal. She took another deep breath and continued her stealth like trek, scanning the roadside for a sign, when unexpectedly she skidded down a steep, loose gravel incline and stopped.

Ahead, an old dead Douglas fir had fallen across the road. When the huge conifer toppled, it had taken a swath of willow bushes with it, and they clung to the tree trunk. Margot wrestled with the tangled branches and climbed over the decaying tree. On the other side, the road was empty of debris. She stood still for a few minutes and took stock of the area. It was then she saw something that looked familiar. *The mailbox! It's still here!*

She rushed down the road. Once at the mailbox, Margot cleared the undergrowth and brush away. She pushed aside the thorny blackberry vines that had crept over the mailbox and stepped around a large clump of stinging nettles. Bent and beaten up, the rusty turquoise metal box still had its red flag, and across the side, a faded name: Swan. "Yippee!" Margot yelled. The rusty door creaked as she pulled it open. It was empty, but that didn't matter. Just finding the mailbox was enough of a touchstone to keep going. Margot pulled out her camera, flipped the red flag upright and took several shots at varying angles to document her finding. "Okay," she said, and snapped shut the lens cover.

After she left the mailbox, the road and surrounding topography straightened. Walking became easier on the smooth grade. The rhythm of her stride helped Margot relax, and she savored the peaceful, natural setting enough to calm down. Along the roadway, she recognized a few giant, crumbling tree stumps and outcrops that had weathered time.

She strolled along feeling looser and more buoyant. She remembered the year Lisel was a caretaker for the property. Together, they had manicured the roads off and on that year.

One day, as a lark, Margot shot photos of the area. It had been fun, and later, when the property was on the market again, she mentioned her negatives to Lisel, who contacted the broker. He paid her for the film and developing and promised to use her services again—next time for a fee. Word got around and they offered her more photo opportunities. After hiring on as a photographer several more times, she felt comfortable adding photographer to her resume. Yes, those were the days.

Margot kicked away some loose gravel. Now she'd be lucky to get one freelance job. But that didn't matter anymore. She'd reinvented herself, and at age fifty-five, wrote and illustrated children's books and self-published them with some financial success. The small but steady income helped her retire early and enabled her to walk down the IN Road today.

Margot rounded a long bend. High above, she heard the eagle call. One hundred yards ahead on the right, she recognized the enormous maple tree she'd favored long ago. The tree rose like a monument, magnificent as before. The crisp fall weather had turned the leaves bright yellow. Off to the right of the maple tree, she spied the tiny trailer still sitting near the orchard.

As usual, Lisel was spot-on. From where Margot stood, the trailer, enveloped in years of unchecked underbrush, looked rundown, old, and forgotten. Dark cracks spotted the deck where cedar planks had fallen through the ramshackle porch. Margot leaned against the maple tree and sighed. She felt sad and knew Lisel would feel the same.

The field around the trailer was no longer pristine and picturesque. All the daisies and wildflowers that had once set the meadow ablaze had given way. Time and neglect replaced them with tall weeds, stinging nettles, and gnarly-looking brush. There were more apple trees in the orchard than she remembered. A few were damaged with broken or split branches hanging down; one large limb touched the ground.

On top of the tarnished Airstream, dangling in the breeze, hung an old tattered flag. Margot grappled with her emotions as she took in the sight. The land felt forsaken and disregarded, much like she had been. She forced herself to step onto the narrow game trail that led to the trailer.

Treading lightly up the wide steps, Margot tested each weathered plank as she traversed the deck, and like the ninja she imagined earlier, she slipped into the dank hollow of the trailer. The air smelled musty. Thick cobwebs filled the corners. The windows, frosted with layers of dust and bug marks, were intact. Only one was cracked. The interior space appeared to have been vacant for a long time. Still, there were a few things that remained: the hanging brass lamp and dinette table, a few tattered books scattered on the shelf. In the sitting area, a grimy divan upholstered with faded brocade stood near a worn leather footstool. Over the sink, several chipped cups hung from hooks. But that was all; nothing compared to the cozy warmth she'd seen in 1958.

Margot tugged on a cabinet drawer. Swollen from the damp air and disuse, the drawer was stuck. She wrestled with the knobs until she freed the drawer, then wrenched open the others. There was nothing of interest in them, just a few clothespins, one soiled, checkered dish towel, and an old, No. 2 pencil stub.

Next, she eyed the small clothes closet and unlatched the door. When it creaked open, something soft dropped on her shoulder. "Jesus!" Margot hopped back into a sticky veil of cobwebs. Twirling around, she saw a small, green tree frog leap onto the counter. The tiny creature hopped to the floor and vanished into a crack.

"Damn!" Margot bent over and coughed hard until she belched. Suddenly, she burst out laughing. "Good Lord!" she said, catching her breath. "Those critters!"

How many times had they startled her? Hundreds, she guessed. They'd been everywhere in the cabin she rented years ago; hip-hopping across counters, lolling in Karina's water dish, and scaring the shit out of her when they leaped off a shelf. She could still hear their loud croak. Margot had been so captivated and inspired by the harmless little amphibians, she wrote and illustrated a children's picture book about their pranks. The project had been a successful, if somewhat corny, kid's story.

All of this action happened in seconds, and for a few minutes, Margot felt bemused by her obvious blunder. Once her heartbeat came back to normal, she moved on to her original mission: the orchard and time portal.

She wiped the grimy trailer window with the dish towel and peered toward the orchard. With some dread, Margot scanned the fenced parcel to pinpoint the vortex. She had to go down there. This was the part of the trip she was most unsure of. Margot walked outside onto the rickety deck and stood for a moment.

Just as she stepped off the porch, a large tabby cat sashayed toward her. "Well, hello," Margot said. The cat stood for a long moment and swished her tail. She looked eye-to-eye with Margot, then skittered down the path to the orchard. "Wait!" Margot yelled, but the feline had disappeared. "Oh my God, I think that's Kitty—Nana's cat!" Margot hurried down the grassy trail toward the orchard.

It wasn't long before her pant legs were soaked from the knee-high, dewy grass, but Margot barely noticed the discomfort.

Her mind was on Kitty. She could not believe the cat was still alive, and so nimble too. She had to be at least thirty years old or more. *How could that be?*

About twenty feet ahead, around one of the narrow turns, she found the cat waiting for her. *Yes, that's her! She is alive.* Before Margot reached Kitty, the feline took off again. "Cats," Margot said under her breath and hastened along the trail.

Near a tall clump of willow bushes, Kitty sat on a mossy log cleaning her front paws. When she saw Margot, the cat leaped off the log and bolted down the trail. With her tail held high, she shot down the path as if playing hide and seek.

Annoyed and breathing heavily, Margot trudged after her. Winded, she stopped a few yards from Kitty, who sat perched at the edge of the orchard. "There. Those are the ones, aren't they, Kitty?" The cat twitched her tail but didn't move. Margot sank down next to the cat and gave her a long stroke. "Thank you, girl," she said. Purring, Kitty looked at her and then ran off. In seconds, she disappeared into the tall, variegated grass.

Hunched down, resting her middle-aged body for a few minutes, Margot stared at the two trees. Their elderly, twisted trunks were laced with lichen, a sign of age and decline. From the looks of them, the old trees had battled decades of island weather, withstanding the hellacious windstorms of the Northwest. Each had the broken limbs to prove their solidarity and valor. A large branch on one tree had snapped off with only the bark holding the limb to the trunk. Scattered on the ground were a few brown, shriveled apples left over from the summer. The trees appeared much older and larger than she remembered, but they had to be the right ones. Kitty led her right to them. A light breeze caught the aged trees, rippling the few leaves that remained. "Yes, these have to be the ones," Margot said. Her body jerked when she stood. She stumbled, almost losing her balance as she stepped between the two old guardians.

Margot took a deep breath, closed her eyes, and envisioned disappearing and re-entering another time period like she'd done in her dream. She opened and shut her eyes several times, but nothing happened. *What was she doing wrong?*

She stepped away and hunted around the trees for a clue— something that might jog her memory. Margot tapped her forehead, trying to relive her first time travel experience. But her mind was blank. "Well, what the hell? I'll give it another try," she said and kneeled down between the two trees. "I can do this," she whispered. The timber in her voice sounded weak, bereft as the old trees. She closed her eyes.

"You're trying too hard," the voice said.

"Too hard? For Christ's sake!" Margot barked. The sound of the voice snapped her out of lethargy. She frowned and clutched her backpack. "What do you mean?" She looked around to locate the voice. "Where are you?"

Just then, Kitty reappeared. The cat sashayed her soft body around Margot's legs. "Kitty! Where have you been?" Kitty meowed several times and scampered up the path toward the trailer. Heartened by the old cat's spry appearance, Margot said, "Okay, dammit, three's the charm," and shut her eyes.

For a few moments, she fought her jumbled emotions. *Had she made a drastic error by coming here?* Then bang! A full range of psychedelic colors burst into her mind's eye. Vibrant reds, greens, and blues ricocheted inside her head. Ping. Ping. Ping.

Stunned and unable to concentrate, Margot forced herself to override the internal chaos. Unclenching her jaw, she loosened her lips and moved her mouth around the primal sound of OM, projecting it outward. The vibrating sound relaxed her so that she slid into a meditative state. After a few minutes, a powerful force surged through her solar plexus. She felt dizzy, sick to her stomach, and opened her eyes. She gasped at what she saw.

The whole orchard, every single tree, looked different: healthy, younger, and smaller in girth. Only a few thin branches were damaged on the two younger apple trees she crouched between. Margot swung around and around, not sure if any of this was real. But she knew one thing—something *had* happened.

Rattled and woozy, Margot retraced her steps to the tiny trailer. As she tromped up the path, the crisp air and bright fall colors sharpened her senses and cleared her head. The entire landscape was no longer wild and unkempt, as it had been an hour ago. Part of the acreage had been mowed. The fence line was in good repair. *What the hell happened?*

A chilly breeze cut through her fleece jacket as she reached the deck. Margot turned, and for a few minutes, searched the area for Kitty. It was then she heard whistling coming from behind the trailer. She peeked around the Airstream. Twenty feet ahead was a man about the age of thirty, stacking split firewood.

"Hello," she said, and stepped into view.

The tall, thin, fair-haired man stopped stacking wood and popped straight up. "Geez, you startled me," he said, and squinted at her. "I didn't think anyone else was here." The man bent down to pick up more firewood. With a slight grin, he said, "Where did you come from?"

"Uh, I walked in. Took the IN Road. I was just down in the orchard looking at the, uh, the trees. I didn't expect to see anyone either." Margot paused and rubbed her arms up and down. "Brrr, it's cold."

"Yeah, those trees need to be pruned." The man nodded his head toward the orchard. Continuing to stack wood he went on, "But that's not my job. Guess I'll have to call the grounds man. I own the place. Come here once in a while to tidy up and make sure the trailer is okay. You look cold. Want some tea?"

Curious about this man, and most especially, what decade she was in, Margot shrugged and said as nonchalantly as she could, "Sure."

The man motioned to the trailer. "Come on in." Dropping an armful of split wood onto the deck, he hopped up. "Watch yer step," he cautioned, pointing to a hole in the floorboard. "The deck is old and kinda slippery. I'll heat the water. Pretty sure there are a couple of cups and some tea bags in here somewhere."

Shaking her head, Margot said, "Ah, I don't think there is—"

The young man gave her an odd look and went into the trailer. Just as Margot was about to enter, she froze. With one leg suspended over the threshold, she perched on the other. To her astonishment, the whole interior of the trailer—everything— had changed. Holding onto the doorframe, she gulped air and took in the scene.

The kitchen counter was now cluttered with unopened mail and periodicals. Stacked on the shelf above was a trove of colorful coffee mugs. A worn, but still charming, seating arrangement huddled at the end of the trailer. Wedged into the corner of the kitchen nook was Georgia's manual Royal typewriter, covered in dust.

The whole interior of the trailer had transformed since she'd been there a mere hour before. Reaching for the counter near the doorway, Margot gripped the surface to steady herself. Clearing her throat, she stepped in. "What's your name?"

"Billy. Billy Joe Swan," the man said and cocked his head at her. "What's yours?"

"Margot Anderson."

"Well, how do ya do?" The man smiled at her and took out a tea bag from the cupboard.

"Uh, er, fine, I think." Still unsettled, Margot looked around, wondering if it was possible that Billy recognized her. "Mind if I sit?" she asked.

"No, no. Go ahead, have a seat." Billy gestured to the dinette booth and pushed aside the mail to clear a small area of the table. "Strange, but you look familiar," he said, "a lot like my grandmother." Billy tipped his head to the side and stared at Margot for a moment. "She was a writer, you know. This is her trailer, but…she…she doesn't live here anymore." Billy turned on the burner and put the kettle of water over the heat. "She disappeared one day in 1958. I was five years old then. Maybe you read about it. We thought she'd come back, but she never did. No one knows what happened to her."

Margot watched Billy put a Lipton tea bag into a mug. "Oh, I'm so sorry," she said. "What was her name?"

"Georgia. Georgia Lee Swan. I come here once in a while to check on the place. I always hope she'll be here." Billy's voice dropped a notch. He shook his head. "Hope springs eternal, they say."

Margot looked out the small kitchen window. "Yes. Yes it does," she said. "What is the date today? Do you know?"

"Yeah, sure. It's September 7."

Margot looked past Billy and paused for a second. "What year is it?"

"Why, 1983," Billy said, and looked at Margot as if she weren't all there. Reaching for the steaming kettle, he poured hot water into her cup. "How did you get here?"

"Good question." Apprehensive about what to say next, Margot traced the veins in her hands. "Honestly, I'm not sure how I got here. I guess you could say Kitty brought me."

"Kitty? That old cat?" Billy handed Margot the cup of tea and then walked over to the doorway. "What's she up to now?" He stuck his head out the door and searched down the field. "I tell ya, that cat has *more* than nine lives! Where the heck is she?" he said, and stepped outside.

Margot sipped her hot tea and worked to calm down enough for logic to take hold. Worried about what to say to Billy, fifteen minutes went by before she realized he had not returned. Aware now of the surrounding silence, Margot jumped up and went outside to look for him. Billy was nowhere in sight. In fact, no one, not even Kitty, was there.

The air was humid, almost balmy. Along the horizon, a squall formed over the Sound. Near the trailer, a clump of unshorn grass danced in the stormy breeze. Margot trembled when a bank of damp, cold air hit her. Avoiding the rotten cedar planks, she walked off the deck and scanned the field toward the orchard, hoping to see someone—anyone. The wind tossed the sparsely leafed tree limbs back and forth, bringing with it a sense of abandonment. "Where is everybody?" she said. But there was no answer and Margot saw no one.

By now, it was clear she was alone. Even the birds had run for cover. She looked at her watch and then stopped in midair. "What the hell am I doing?" she said. "Jesus. This time thing is making me crazy." Margot dug into her backpack for her windbreaker. "I've got to get out of here," she murmured and zipped up her jacket. Verging in panic, Margot jogged up the trail toward the IN Road. "God, I hope Lisel's car is there," she muttered. Her heart sunk, thinking it might not be.

Halfway up the trail, Margot remembered her camera. *Dammit!* In her haste, she'd forgotten to take photos. Her original plan was to research and document the trip, but now she wasn't sure she had enough gumption to do it with all that had happened. "Oh, hell, never mind," she said.

"Buck up, kiddo, you can do it."

Startled, Margot stood still. The voice. She had forgotten about the voice. Leaning over to catch her breath, she said, "No. No, I don't think I can. I want to get the hell out of here—now!"

"Go back and take the pictures. You'll need them soon."

For some reason—one that Margot could never explain—she dug out her old Minolta and tromped back to the site. As if on autopilot, Margot shot a series of photos of the Airstream, porch, and woodpile where she'd met Billy. When she entered the trailer again, the interior was just as she had left it minutes ago. The books, her teacup, and still warm teakettle were there—even Georgia's typewriter layered in decades of dust.

Thank God, she thought. Relieved she wasn't losing it, Margot shot another sequence of photos, and her disquiet subsided. She felt centered, and like the professional she was, photographed images, shooting, and adjusting F-stops, taking time to focus on tight close-ups. Satisfied she had enough material, Margot hurried out and slammed the door.

She ran up the trail to the IN Road with the feeling she'd crossed a mysterious invisible barrier, somehow pushed through an undetectable wall much like Alice had in *Alice Through the Looking Glass*. But the reality was—and her sense of reality was in question at that moment—she didn't know where she would end up or what year it would be when she got there. In her panic to leave, all Margot knew was she had to get back on the IN Road—and post haste. *Heck, what was reality anyway?*

Margot hurried along the trail, figuring she'd seen just about everything. She had no way of knowing that ahead more would come to shake her to her core.

At the edge of the trail before the IN Road, Margot stopped when she heard a loud rustling noise behind her. She whipped around to see thorny vines and fall-colored foliage crawl across the dirt path. Long, dark tendrils crept along both sides of the trail and joined in the middle, weaving an elaborate, tangled gate just as it had in 1958. She watched in disbelief as the trail entrance closed, leaving no sign of the footpath. Unnerved, Margot jogged down the IN Road toward Georgia's old mailbox, thinking she'd seen it all. But there was more.

The hair on Margot's head rose when she found the metal door on the old mailbox hanging down. Someone had opened it, but she saw no sign of anyone. Still, Margot felt nervous when she peeked into the box. Inside were a mimeographed flyer, a few grocery inserts, and one white number ten envelope. The rusty door creaked when she pulled out the contents. She flipped over the envelope. It was addressed to Georgia L. Swan, Dolphin Bay Road, Orcas, Washington, and postmarked September 4, 1983—three days ago.

Margot hopped back and waved the envelope high above her. "Yes!" she shouted. "Thank God! I haven't hallucinated. I'm in 1983!"

Not a moment later, her jubilance shifted. "Damn," she said, and slumped over like a deflated balloon. "I'm in trouble." The postmarked envelope counted as a bona fide clue, but she was still caught between two worlds, two dimensions: 2010 and

1983. How would she get back? Margot groaned. "Dammit, I'm in limbo."

She stared hard at the postmark and toyed with absconding the mail. *Who would know?* Batting the envelope on the back of her hand, she thought better of it. "No. I'll take photos instead. I have a little film left."

Margot slipped off the lens cap and snapped her last two frames. She put the mail back, slammed the corroded door shut, and without another glance took off down the IN Road toward Dolphin Bay Road where she hoped Lisel's car was parked.

Relieved to see the old fallen Douglas fir ahead, Margot stepped up her pace. Before she reached the thickly-barked trunk, she glanced back. To her amazement, the daylight she'd just walked through had grown dark. The forest and road behind her were so veiled and out of focus, they appeared to be in a deep hollow. In front of the fallen tree was a bright forest lane lit up like theatrical stage lighting. She pivoted around several times to look in both directions. The old fir seemed to be a line of demarcation, an imaginary boundary that had been drawn between deep shadow and brilliant light. The eerie contrast made her uneasy. Her face paled. "Oh, my God."

"Not to worry."

"Easy for you to say," Margot quipped and scurried over the tree trunk. By now, she found it easier to converse with the voice.

Despite her anxiety about which dimension she was in, Margot kept her fears in check and headed toward Dolphin Bay Road. Her gait quickened. The physical movement forward quieted her inner turmoil. She tried not to think about what had just happened. She concentrated on Lisel's car, envisioning it parked, waiting for her.

Once she reached the heavy, broken-down gates, Margot exhaled a long sigh. Across Dolphin Bay Road sat Lisel's Pathfinder at the pullout where she left it. She whooped, clapped her hands, and crossed the road. "Thank you," she said, patting the metal fender. Her hands shook as she unlocked the car door. She slid in and sat without moving, her mind blank for a few minutes. Finally, Margot exhaled a long breath, and in slow motion, reached for the key.

When the old vehicle cranked right up, she settled further into Merlin's threadbare seats. The soft, shabby fabric comforted her. She let the motor run for a while and then shifted into first gear. "Okay," she said, "let's go, Merlin." The SUV crept down the road. The simple act of driving along the familiar dirt road felt cathartic—real. Rubbing the smoothed edges and tiny cracks on the steering wheel helped calm her nerves and peeled away her fears.

Margot swerved into Lisel's place thirty minutes later. Still a bit dazed, she almost missed the driveway. Languishing in the car, Margot rehearsed what she'd say to Lisel. Well, nothing, she thought. Maybe she would just say she went for a walk down the IN Road and leave out the part about Billy and the time warp. The whole thing seemed far-fetched anyway—almost delusional, even to her. Her sister was a practical, no-nonsense person. Heck, no matter what Margot said, Lisel wouldn't believe her.

"Well, where'd you go today?" Lisel said as they sat down to dinner.

"Oh, just down the IN Road for a walk." Margot stared at her food, hoping she sounded inconsequential, cavalier even.

"Why are you interested in the old Swan estate?"

"Ah, just curious about the place. I…I wanted to look around." Margot took a deep breath. "I'm thinking about renting the old trailer."

"Really?" Lisel's voice hung in the air. "I thought the place was a wreck. I heard it was run-down. Why would you want to live there? What are you thinking?" Lisel fidgeted in her chair and continued to pepper Margot with more questions. "What did you find? Is there *anything left* on the property? Don't you think it's strange you want to live there?"

"Not really." Margot reached for her wineglass. After taking a swallow, she continued. "The old mailbox and trailer are still there. It looked pretty sad to tell you the truth. Very different from when you were caretaking there." She cleared her throat. "I walked down to the orchard and listened to the eagles. I like the area. It's private. I think I need that kind of quiet environment now. That's all."

Looking long and hard at her sister, Lisel took a deep breath. "Well, whatever." She picked up her fork and stabbed at her baked potato. "I think it's a bad idea." Lisel squirmed, put her fork down, and crossed her arms. She leaned back in her chair. "You know, come to think of it, there has been a rumor that someone *might* live there. Maybe it's already rented. Did you see anyone?"

"Uh, no." Margot hesitated. "No one. Just the eagles and a few ravens. You're right, it's probably a rumor, one of those *island* rumors." Margot smiled and tipped her glass toward Lisel. "Anyway, it didn't look like anyone had moved in. There wasn't much there. The trailer was almost empty." Her voice faltered. She took a sip of wine. "Do you know whom to contact about renting the place?"

"I don't know." Lisel stared past her sister. "Well, wait. I heard that the family is putting up the entire property for sale again. It's a big estate now, as you know. The daughter bought that acreage next to the trailer after her mother disappeared, and later, Billy—you remember the grandson—bought that colossal piece in the nineties after I worked there." Lisel took a few bites of food.

Margot watched her sister process and shift her thinking. She knew Lisel would wind up supporting her idea. "Hmm. Try Windermere," Lisel said. "I think I saw a listing several weeks ago in the paper. I bet they want big bucks." Lisel raised her fork and pointed it at Margot. "They'll get it too."

The sisters finished their meal in near silence. In polite conversation, they circled around the subject of the Swan estate. After dinner, they stood on Lisel's deck and took in the cool fall evening, relishing the Sound's smooth, dark water. They watched the last ferry of the day slip out of the landing and cut through the sparkling water. In unison, both women sighed with relief. The tourist season was over. By now, the last tourists were sailing on that ferry toward the mainland. This meant the stampede of summer visitors was gone, and the island would once again be tranquil.

Later in bed, Margot reflected on the day. She thought about Billy and Georgia. *How could she find them?* She still didn't understand how time warp worked. Margot leaned over and scribbled a note to google multidimensional, "no woo-woo stuff, though," she added. What she needed were empirical, scientific facts with a definitive slant on metaphysics and time dimensions. "Look up string theory," she wrote. Somewhere she'd read that time warped and bent, and as a result made it possible to move through dimensions consciously. *But how?*

The next moment a vision came to her. This type of vision differed from her normal fantasies. These rare glimpses into the cosmos came into her mind's eye out of nowhere and were short, four-color vignettes that rolled like a movie sequence. Over time, she'd found these to be vital spiritual messages that often foreshadowed the future, containing layers of hidden meaning. This one was no different. It was about Billy, a much older Billy.

She walked into a recently refurbished gas station. It was closing time, and no one was around. The scene panned to the front counter and tracked in for a close-up of an old map pressed under a piece of thick glass. Illustrated on either side of the map were tall, green trees with reddish, thick trunks. A man walked out of the back of the garage. Margot knew the man was Billy. He was somewhere in his mid-fifties with graying hair and a small beer paunch.

Margot watched as Billy shut the lights off in the back and walked up to the counter where he stopped in front of her. He looked right through Margot as if she wasn't standing there and glanced around the front office; satisfied, he walked out the door and locked it behind him. Almost as a second thought, he turned around and peered into the window as if checking on something inside. Billy looked straight at Margot and stared at her for a long moment, then turned and left. The vision faded to black.

Before Margot could dwell on the meaning, she fell into a deep sleep.

Part Four

Georgia Lee Swan

1957

After months of publicity hype around her book, the hullabaloo proved too much for Georgia. The frantic marketing and public response boggled her mind. She had never expected all this fuss—not in a million years. The book she had labored over for years had become a surprising bestseller—almost overnight. According to current book reviews, her star was shining bright, and the public begged for more. When she was still working as a librarian, it never dawned on her she'd get this kind of reaction as a published author. Her quick rise to fame came as a shock and equal annoyance.

Today, feeling overwhelmed and stifled by all the media attention, Georgia sat rigid in front of her typewriter. She rubbed her forehead, back and forth, over and over. Her head throbbed just thinking about the hubbub around her novel. The recent promotional tours and publicity spillover had traumatized her. She wanted out.

The mounting demands of celebrity infringed on her privacy and peace of mind, making it impossible to write one compelling sentence. Georgia felt like a frightened child. Frantic to find a safe place, she yearned to be away from the hordes of people crowding her, knocking on her front door. They were even peering into her windows, for God's sake! And what about those inane reporters calling her at all hours? Georgia's blood boiled just thinking about it.

Revved up again, she stalked into the kitchen and gulped down two aspirin. She shook her head. "No! Dammit! Wait just a minute!" she yelled and marched over to the phone to dial the travel agent.

Even though her writing career started out as a lark, something to occupy her time when her daughter, Sandra, married and moved away, Georgia knew she had at least one good book inside her. So, at the tail end of a twenty-year career in library science, finding herself at loose ends with plenty of time on her hands, she made the leap to write. As it turned out, she was a natural.

When she told Neom, her faithful guide and counselor, she wanted to write a substantial piece of work, he replied, "Sit down and write every day until you can't write anymore. You have the talent. Discipline is needed now to finish the task."

At first, she found writing every day a challenge and for a few fledgling months squirmed in her chair, waiting for inspiration. Neom continued to nudge her into a routine. At his suggestion, she taped a bold reminder onto her Royal typewriter: *Write every day until you can't.* This written mantra seemed to solidify her resolve. Every day when she rolled the first sheet of blank paper into the typewriter, Georgia stared at the maxim for a few minutes, then typed her first word. Before she knew it, the text streamed onto the empty page.

Some days, writing was just plain hard. Many times, she had to maneuver around the wave of excuses that rushed forth. Make the bed, do the dishes, empty the ashtrays—even taking out the garbage seemed like a refuge from writing. On those days, she'd do just about anything to avoid the blank page. Yet, at the end of a year, she'd finished her first draft, a 250-page volume that shot off the literary charts. No one could have been more surprised than she.

The day Sandra called to say she'd given birth to a son was a landmark day for Georgia. Pounding words out on her typewriter, her head deep into the plot, she jumped when the phone rang. The news of a grandson thrilled Georgia. She put her work aside and rushed to her daughter and little Billy for a few weeks. The child was an absolute joy, but Georgia sensed unease within her daughter's marriage. So, it didn't surprise her when six months later Sandra informed Georgia that she and Billy were moving—alone.

What startled Georgia was their destination: a remote island in the San Juan Islands archipelago. Why would a city girl with a small child pick up and move to a tiny dot in the middle of nowhere? *What was Sandra thinking?* As far as Georgia was concerned, Sandra's move was a rash, outlandish decision, and she tried to persuade Sandra not to go. The Pacific Northwest islands were remote and untamed. "What about little Billy?"

she asked. How was he going to learn to read in the boondocks? That worried Georgia.

Despite her mother's caution, Sandra set off with little Billy in tow for an island in the archipelago called Orcas Island. According to Sandra's recent letter, things were working out. "Once I stepped foot on Orcas, good fortune showered down on me," she wrote. "I can't believe how my life has changed for the better, Mother. Things have just opened for me here. I bought an old truck yesterday with the money you sent. It rattles and burns a little oil, but it works!"

Within a few weeks, Sandra not only had a vehicle but a job too. She hired on as caretaker to a large estate. To sweeten the deal, the landowners included a quaint cabin on the land, rent-free. The property was about ten miles from Eastsound, Orcas's central village. Angled down Dolphin Bay Road, a winding two-lane gravel road, the large estate was accessible only by a single lane drive. One mile long, this narrow, unkempt country lane was often muddy and studded with potholes. But Sandra didn't care. To her, it was heaven.

A few months after Sandra arrived, she jotted off a short invitation to her mother, asking her to visit Orcas. Georgia leaped at the chance. Taking a trip meant escaping from the barrage of publicity, and she'd spend undisturbed quality time with her daughter and grandson. After calling the travel agent, Georgia readied for the trip, and within two days, she was on a plane headed to Seattle.

That's how life on Orcas started for Georgia—with a visit. Her plan was to spend time with Sandra and Billy far away from the crowds and explore the archipelago. It would be a relief, she thought as she waited for the ferry at the Anacortes terminal.

Her eyes searched the smooth waters of the Puget Sound for a reason, any reason, not to go back.

Clustered together near British Columbia, the San Juan Islands was a godsend and seemed like a perfect solution. Few people outside the Skagit Valley knew about the San Juans, and Georgia hoped it would remain that way. No one on the island except Sandra and Billy knew of her fame, and that's the way she wanted it.

Immediately charmed by the cozy island atmosphere, Georgia walked off the ferry and within two days became a part-time resident. "I'd like to live here," she said. "It's quiet and safe."

Overjoyed with her newfound privacy, Georgia put into gear all the mechanisms needed to set up residency. By sheer happenstance, she became a property owner almost overnight. A few days after arriving, she noticed a For Sale sign posted near Sandra's place. Georgia inquired about the property and by the end of the first week purchased the land from an elderly couple. The pristine twenty-acre piece sat next to the estate Sandra was caretaking and in close proximity to her little home.

One month after signing the papers, Georgia's new Airstream trailer arrived and was permanently parked near the old apple orchard on her property. Even though the abandoned orchard had been fallow and unproductive for years, it was a powerful selling point for Georgia. The instant she set foot on the property, she envisioned a flourishing orchard with apple blossoms in the spring and cider in the fall, and hired a local carpenter to deer fence the perimeter of the orchard.

The Airstream, the orchard, Billy and Sandra living next to her—all of it—afforded her the comfort, time, and space she needed for writing. She could write and be near her family. It was so perfect that Georgia felt ready to work again and returned to her sequel novel. Within a few months, the first draft came together. "Nearly done," she wrote Abe, her agent. He was happy and so was the publishing house.

The day she met her first friend on the island lit another beacon for Georgia. Distracted after a frustrating writing session, she ambled out to the road where the handyman was installing a postbox for her. She'd hit an impasse in the new story and needed a plot shift, but her mind had gone blank.

With the storyline in limbo, she stood mesmerized as she watched the handyman dig a narrow hole for the post. It was then she heard the grinding of gears and the loud roar of a truck coming down the road. When the vehicle rounded the bend, she gawked at the rickety mail truck bouncing toward her. The driver waved and stuck his head out the window as the truck rolled to a stop.

"Hi, I'm John, the mailman," the driver said. A half-smoked, gooey cigar stuck out of the side of his mouth. "You're new here, ain'tcha?" The truck backfired as he opened the door and got out. He tipped back his grimy captain's hat and exposed a pile of chaotic, graying curls. "I noticed you was puttin' up a new mailbox," he said, and smiled. He reached in the truck and pulled out a wooden folding measure.

Georgia nodded. "Yes, I've just arrived and bought this place."

"Well, uh, welcome!" John said. "I wasn't sure if you knew what the official *specs* were for mailboxes. That's why I stopped. I thought I'd help ya out so's you have it right. Regulations, ya know." John rolled the fat stogie around in his mouth.

"Sure. Go ahead. I want things to be right." Georgia studied his demeanor and had to admit the man had a certain charm, but she couldn't take her eyes off his cigar. It reminded her of Harry, her former husband. Even now, after all these years, her stomach turned when she thought about him and how hurtful he'd been. He also smoked cigars like the one John had. For a fleeting second, she wondered if he still did.

"Thanks! Well, uh, we don't deliver mail *every day,* but we do deliver!" John laughed and unfolded the wooden ruler. He measured the height of the postbox from the ground up. Squinting at the rule, he said, "Yeah, that's just about right. Gotta go by regulations, ya know." Folding the measure, he stuffed it in his pocket and grabbed a clipboard from the truck. Poised with a pencil in hand, he said, "Whatch yer name? So's I get it right."

Georgia glanced at his hands and giggled. His old gloves were so tattered the tops of the knitted fingers were gone. Deciding to play coy, she stepped back a little. "Georgia. Georgia Lee Swan." She winced and waited for him to recognize her name.

"Okay, then. Georgia Lee Swan," he said, pronouncing each distinct syllable. "Swan like the bird, right?" Georgia grinned and nodded. With deliberate care, John wrote her name. "Your address will be Dolphin Bay Road, Orcas, Washington. That's it. Okay?"

"Yes," she said. "Thank you."

"Happy to help." John threw the clipboard in the truck seat. "Ya know, we have swans that come here every year. There's a small lake down the road from you where they land." John pulled his cap down snug on his head and grabbed a few papers out of the truck. "Mind if I call ya Georgia?"

"Uh, no. That will be all right, I guess."

"Alrighty then. Here's some stuffers for ya. Just junk, but I have to deliver it. Mail, ya know." He moseyed over to his truck, got in, and turned the ignition key. The old truck fired right up. "See ya in a few days, Georgia!" he said, and winked at her.

Amused by John's quirky casualness, Georgia watched his truck jostle potholes, waddling side-to-side like a duck as it went around the bend. Standing there, she had a strong feeling that John would be a good friend, and that in the future she might just need one.

Georgia paid the handyman and walked back to the trailer. Well, that wasn't too bad, she thought. At the trailer site, she took a long look around, imagining her future life there and mentally added items to include in the outdoor setting. That's when the idea came to her—she wanted a deck!

A simple wooden porch would be an enjoyable addition to the exterior space. She could afford that now and splurging on it appealed to her. Flowers would be nice, too, she thought. She'd ask Sandra to buy some potted flowers the next time she was in the hardware store—oh, and two deck chairs. Humming, Georgia went into the trailer to start on the next chapter. At last, she knew where the story was going.

It wasn't long before the front deck took shape. The first draft to the sequel fell together right about then too. A daily writing regime was the right formula for Georgia, and again, she saw the wisdom in Neom's words. He had predicted she would complete the book before the year was out if she remained vigilant to a routine. Her muse was more congenial, too, when she sat down at her typewriter at the same time each day. Through the years, she'd found it didn't pay to ignore the muse. Her mystical wordsmith did not tolerate lateness and would nudge and nag her until she sat in front of her Royal typewriter, hands poised for the day's task.

With a flourish, Georgia typed *The End* on the finished draft and stubbed out her cigarette. Done. She pulled out the page from the typewriter and with librarian skill sorted and organized the sequel's pages into chapters, then combined the chapters together. Table of contents will come later, she thought. Cradling the manuscript like a newborn baby, Georgia laid the pages in a box and slid it under the bed.

She grabbed a fifth of Jack Daniels and walked outside, feeling satisfied the plot worked. She'd polish it later. Georgia sat on the steps of her new deck, relishing the moment, and took a swig of bourbon. This was another momentous occasion in a long line of fortuitous events this year. Georgia took a deep drag off her cigarette and gazed down her property toward the orchard. She could rest now and let the story simmer for a while. In about six weeks, she'd go through the pages again and do the rewrite.

Throwing back another shot of bourbon, she sighed. "Congratulations, girl," she said, and waited for the whiskey to work its magic.

Feeling warmer, looser, and more confident about the new book, she mentally released the project to the winds of fate as she had with her other stories. Energetically, she let the work go and thanked the muse and Neom. Dear old Neom, she thought. He had been with her for so long, she couldn't imagine life without him.

Now freed from the constant pressure of writing, she wondered if there were any ripe apples yet. With Jack Daniels in hand, she sauntered down the trail toward the apple orchard. A hint of an early fall breeze brushed past her as she wandered through the orchard gate and over to the immature trees she'd planted last fall. They had grown over the season, but there were only a few small apples on the slender limbs. The older, more established trees fared better, but the whole orchard needed at least another season to produce the bounty she foresaw in her vision.

In early spring, a neighbor suggested she put horse manure around the trees to enrich the soil. He had horses and plenty of manure, so she paid him to bring his tractor over with a load and spread it around. The orchard smelled rancid for a few weeks, but after it rained, as it invariably did in the San Juans, the manure leached into the ground and the odor dissipated.

Near the first row of trees in the orchard, Georgia stood for a few minutes, taking a long, affectionate look at her property. It was then she knew she had done the right thing by moving to Orcas. Living on her land with Sandra and Billy nearby gave Georgia the contentment she could not put into words. She had to pinch herself to believe that after all the years of disappointment, toil, and turmoil, she'd been elevated by writing a book—one simple story. Neom was right again, she thought. He had told her this would happen.

Georgia meandered around, lulled by a sense of peace, until she stopped at the two largest, oldest trees in the middle of the orchard. She didn't know why, but these two were her favorite. Planted about fifteen feet apart, they were a healthy distance from each other, but to her, they seemed too far apart. She wanted them closer together. Examining each tree trunk for deer marks, Georgia noticed there was a deep, odd-looking indentation in the ground between the two trees about three feet in diameter. It looked as if the ground had sunk at least six inches lower than the rest of the orchard. She had not noticed it before.

The instant she stepped into the sunken patch of grass, Georgia felt the ground rumble and quiver like an earth tremor under her feet. Then it stopped. Her heart flip-flopped. She lurched out of the sunken area and walked around the cavity, certain this sinkhole had not been there a few days ago. *Had she imagined the whole thing?* Those two shots of Jack Daniels must have gotten the best of her. Georgia grinned, shrugged off the incident, and headed back.

About halfway up the trail to the Airstream, Georgia saw Billy off in the distance. He was playing soldier in his yard, and from the looks of it, he was animating a battle of some sort. She heard him using verbal sound effects and random shouts as he shot his play guns at the bushes. Acting out two distinct characters, he moved back and forth between them with impressive ease. That kid is amazing, she thought. At four years old, he had quite a theatrical repertoire and could play-act just about anything. The other day, when he was visiting her in the Airstream, he squashed himself into his little toy box. Calling out to Georgia, he said, "Look, Nana, I'm an ice cube." She laughed out loud, remembering his happy little face.

"Billy! Come over and have a snack."

When he heard Georgia calling, Billy dropped his play rifle and ran as fast as he could across the field. Panting, he said, "Do you have any cookies, Nana?"

Georgia took his little hand. "Of course. Come with me. Let's see what kind I've got." Being a grandparent was something Georgia had never imagined until Billy was born. The warmth she felt when she was with him pervaded every cell in her body. There were no words to describe it. "I made these yesterday just for you." She opened the cupboard, took out a tin of cookies, and pried the lid off. "Take a couple."

Beaming, Billy reached into the tin. He knew she always had cookies for him. "Can I have some lemma-nade, too, Nana?"

"How 'bout please," Georgia said.

"Pweese."

"Okay. Here you go." Georgia poured fresh lemonade into a child-sized glass she kept for Billy. She had a variety of smaller utensils and dishes, too, plus a large array of educational toys in the toy box for him. There were also plenty of children's picture books stacked on the shelf, ready to read. At each visit, Billy pored over the pile of books until he found a few he wanted her to read. Some stories he knew by heart. Billy loved it, too, when Georgia would sit down without a book and invent a whopper of a story out of thin air.

When Georgia heard Sandra pulling into the driveway, she said, "Time to go, Billy. Momma is home." She waited for Billy to finish the last of his drink and then grabbed his hand, gently squeezing his chubby little fingers.

As they crossed the property, Georgia heard Sandra's muddy truck hiccup and backfire; then the engine died in the driveway. She frowned. That old rattletrap is a hazard and beyond repair, she thought. Georgia tried to encourage Sandra to buy a newer truck, something safe, and even offered to help with the down payment. But Sandra had done nothing about it yet. Determined to keep her family intact, she decided it was time to talk with Sandra again. She would tomorrow.

They planned to drive to Obstruction Pass and have a picnic lunch. Halfway around the island, the little sequestered beach was a quiet, lovely interlude, and the walk down to the water wasn't difficult for Billy. He loved it there and would run up and down the pebbled shoreline while Sandra sunned and she read.

"Hi, Mom, thanks for watching Billy. I had to run to the market for something. I saw you two go into the trailer, so I took off without letting you know. Sorry."

"That's okay. We had such a good time. That child is so much fun, Sandra." Both women watched as Billy ran into the yard and picked up a toy. "Well, don't forget, we're going on a picnic tomorrow."

"Oh, right. I almost forgot," Sandra said.

"We'll take my car and give that old truck of yours a rest." Georgia waved to Billy, who was shooting his toy rifle and playing soldier.

By the end of summer, the field grass had grown high, seedy, and often camouflaged stinging nettles. Taken in dried form, stinging nettles was a medicinal herb that claimed to help arthritic inflammation, but brazing a live plant with bare skin caused a nasty, lingering sting. On the way back to the trailer, Georgia spied a crop of nettles hidden within the tall brush and stepped around them. Georgia rubbed her left arm, remembering the intense burning sensation when she ran into a patch a few weeks ago. Those damn things, she thought. She'd have to warn Billy about them again.

The afternoon breeze kicked up as Georgia navigated across the field. The chilly air swept in from the Sound, churning dark clouds along the coastline. "Brrr," she said, and shivered. It was then she heard a faint meow. She stopped and cocked her head to listen. After a few seconds, she heard the tiny meow again. Georgia studied the perimeter. The field grass was so tall it was hard to see through the brush. She heard another weak cry and walked toward the noise. Just as she was about to take another step, she looked down to see a tiny kitten. "Oh, for gosh sakes. Where did you come from?" Georgia picked up the scrawny, flea-bitten feline, and held it close to her heart. The kitten's heart beat so fast she could feel the pulse through her heavy work shirt. "Where's your momma, little thing?"

Georgia cuddled the kitten and carried it into the trailer. "Let's get you some milk." She poured a small amount of fresh milk into a saucer and then set the kitten and milk down on the kitchen counter. Crouched by the saucer, the kitten lapped up the liquid in seconds.

"Here you go. Have some more." Georgia poured more milk into the empty saucer. Standing on wobbly legs, the kitten devoured the milk, then cleaned its milk splattered paws and meowed at her. In that instant, Georgia felt an immediate heart connection. She had experienced this before with other animals and had seen cats come out of nowhere and settle in before you could snap your fingers. "You can stay here, little thing," she said. "Billy needs a pet." Georgia reached for a clean, soft towel and arranged a small, cozy bed near the heater for the tiny thing.

The next morning, Georgia walked over to Sandra's with the little kitten wrapped in a warm towel. "Sandra, we'll to have to postpone our picnic this afternoon because—" Georgia held up the squirming bundle "we have a fresh addition to the family!" The kitten's head popped out when she opened the towel.

"Oh, my gosh, Mom. Where did you find it?" Sandra took the kitten and snuggled it close.

"It's for Billy. I thought he needed a pet."

"Billy! Billy, come and see what Nana found!"

Carrying one of his play guns on his shoulder, Billy darted down the hall and swung around the doorway into the kitchen. With wide eyes he said, "What, Momma? What?"

"Look, Billy, a little kitten." Sandra bent down and opened her hands to show her son. "Nana found a kitten for you!"

A few weeks later in Georgia's trailer, the frisky kitten played with Billy, who dangled a long string over a chair. Georgia watched them cavort, amazed at how fast the handful of fur had grown. The plump kitten's coat was coming in silky. Although she kept this to herself, Georgia was certain the kitten was precognitive. The tiny creature often looked transparent, almost ethereal, and acted as if she had extrasensory powers. Just the day before, Georgia was sure the kitten read her mind before she'd even had the thought.

Billy had taken to the kitten right away. He called her Kitty and the name stuck. Every morning, he ran over to Georgia's and romped with Kitty. The two of them were inseparable, like peas in a pod. Billy often went home with scratches on his hands because they played so rambunctiously.

"When can Kitty come to my house?" Billy asked one day.

"Let's give it a little time, Billy. Kitty is still pretty young to be crossing that enormous field. The eagles might get her."

"Oh." Billy frowned. "Will the eagles hurt Kitty?"

"Yes, honey, they will, and then we won't have Kitty anymore."

Billy looked at the little kitten stretched out, sleeping in the sun. "I would feel sad, Nana, not to have Kitty to play with."

Georgia knelt down and gave Billy a big hug. "Don't worry, Billy, I'll watch out for Kitty and protect her until she's bigger."

To take the sting out of the moment, she reached out her hand. "Come with me. Let's walk to the mailbox." Within minutes, they were walking up the trail singing a silly song, holding hands, and laughing. When they came to the road, Billy trilled at the top of his lungs, swung his arms, and raced to the mailbox. He pulled open the metal door, stood on his tiptoes, and peered inside.

"Nana, there's mail in here!" he yelled. His nimble fingers reached into the box and grabbed the bundle of letters and leaflets. He stood for a few moments and looked through the pile pretending to read. When Georgia walked over, he held up the mail and said, "Do I have mail?"

"Well, I don't know." Georgia laughed. "Let's see." She flipped through the stack. There were a few bills, something from the hardware store about her deck chairs, a letter from Abe, her agent, and one mysterious envelope from an unfamiliar return address in Grants Pass, Oregon. "Doesn't look like anything for you today, Billy. Sorry, but here's a newspaper you can carry." He grabbed the newspaper and ran helter-skelter up the road toward the trail, his arms flailing. That child is nonstop, Georgia thought as she glanced through the mail.

She opened Abe's letter. He wanted to know when he could expect to see her new manuscript. The letter was a gentle nudge. Her agent was smart enough to know she would not be provoked, but Georgia knew he was getting impatient. Using his diplomatic skills, he asked for an estimated completion date, something he said to appease the publishing company.

"Not yet, Abe. Not yet." She sighed. The last thing she wanted was to get in the limelight again. Her second novel needed to be well-written, not a book rammed through to mollify the public. There were at least six weeks of rewriting before she could release the manuscript, maybe more. Abe and the publisher would just have to wait.

The mysterious envelope was more complicated. She had a sense of dread when she slid out the letter and recognized the tight, almost illegible cursive. The hand scrawled note was from Harry. He'd seen the publicity about her, knew she was an accomplished author, said he'd kept up with her notoriety in the press. Now he wanted money and claimed she owed him. He was her husband, wasn't he?

"Well, no, Harry, you're not my husband. You *were* my husband. We're divorced. Remember, Harry?" Georgia whispered.

There was still a blood connection between Harry and Sandra, and little Billy, of course, but Harry had never taken the time to engage with Sandra, much less Billy. As far as Georgia was concerned, there was nothing left between them. She had not a trace, not an ounce, of feeling for him anymore. In fact, she hadn't thought about him for years until she saw John the postman smoking that stogie.

Claiming she owed him didn't surprise Georgia, though. Harry had always been an opportunist. He could smell opportunity from miles away. Hadn't he connived situations to his advantage before? Georgia chided herself again for ignoring her instincts long ago. Harry hadn't changed. He was still trying to manipulate her.

"Heartless Harry," her mother called him after he skipped out. Weeks after Harry left, Georgia received a cryptic note from him saying he was sorry he left, but that was how it had to be. That was all. He left no forwarding address—nothing. He didn't even ask about Sandra. Georgia cried for days and was inconsolable for months. In the end, she picked herself up, went back to school, and a few years later received her degree in library science. Without the support of her parents, though, she wouldn't have made it. "No," Georgia whispered, "I don't owe you anything, Harry, not one red cent."

Years ago, she made sure Harry had no legal claim to anything belonging to her when she divorced him. Still, his demand was unnerving. What gall. Once again, she was grateful she'd taken steps then after the lawyer cautioned her. He had advised her that Harry might come after her in later years. So, Georgia paid the lawyer extra to protect her interests in every legal way possible.

After that, she did not want Harry to know her whereabouts or anything about her—forever more. But now he'd found her. *How did he know?* Only Abe and Sandra knew.

Georgia escorted Billy home and then walked back to her trailer. On the way, her thoughts swirled as she puzzled what to do. Should she have her lawyer contact Harry or just let this foolishness go? If she didn't respond, it's possible Harry would drop his demands, give up on this ludicrous idea—well, maybe.

Kitty meowed and swished around Georgia's legs when she stepped into the trailer. "Want something to eat, little girl?" She poured dry food into the kitten's bowl and patted Kitty's head. "I'm going down to the apple orchard now," Georgia said. "See you in a bit."

The sun faded to the gloaming before Georgia stepped into the orchard. Dusk was her favorite time when the light between day and night took on a mystical sheen. Dimensions blurred and dissolved into subtle lighting, making it possible to glimpse fairies and nymphs as they crept out of secret hiding places. Once she was sure she'd seen a tree gnome stare down at her from a giant Douglas fir. No, it couldn't have happened— and yet. Georgia shook her head. "No, it couldn't have," she whispered, and hurried toward the apple trees in the middle of the orchard.

She wasn't sure why, but she felt an urgency. Her stomach churned. She could feel something about to happen. When she reached the sunken area between the trees, Georgia suddenly felt jittery. Her heart beat faster. Cautious, she put one foot and then the other into the shallow area. Out of nowhere, Kitty hopped beside her. Georgia jumped. "Oh! Kitty, you scared me."

The instant Kitty entered the concave space the air shimmered around them. A strange whirling sensation gripped Georgia. Dizzy, her mind spinning like a top, she clenched her stomach and forced herself to stand still. Everything—the trees, the ground, Kitty—shook, vibrating back and forth. Nauseous, she closed her eyes and then opened them, hoping to stop the jarring movement, but the vibration did not stop. Then she heard a popping sound like a BB gun going off. To steady herself, she looked down. Kitty sat beside her. Her small body pulsated along with everything else. "What's happening, Kitty?"

Before Georgia uttered another word, the whirling and dizziness stopped. The atmosphere, now hazy, resembled an out-of-focus photograph. She shook her head and closed her eyes. When she opened them again, Georgia was no longer in the apple orchard, but standing near a gas station—an old, rundown gas station. Kitty was nowhere to be found.

Georgia tittered backward. In disbelief, she rubbed her eyes and scanned the surrounding setting. *Where was she?* The environment was unrecognizable. The decrepit gas station, cloistered by tall, giant-sized trees, looked abandoned. Attached to the station was a small building in disrepair. Both buildings must have been painted white once but were now a dappled gray. Chards of discolored paint peeled down the sidings. A dim light glowed behind dusty, smudged windows crowded with torn posters.

Off to the left of the station, a beat-up tilted highway sign marked a redwood grove. Georgia knew from past research that redwood trees were communal and grew in groves within forests. There were only a few areas with the climate for the redwood groves, Northern California being one. California! That's where she was. The area was known for redwood timber. *Why was she here?* Georgia pivoted around and tried to make sense of her surroundings. *Where was Kitty?*

A few minutes went by before a logging truck roared past and pulled into the wayside a short distance away. When the cab door popped open, a heavyset man dressed in rugged work clothes jumped out. Georgia gasped. The man looked like her ex-husband, Harry. He was older, more ragged and weather-beaten, but from his familiar swagger, she was certain the man was Harry.

A minute later, another truck pulled behind Harry's truck. Harry waved and strolled over to the other driver. Reaching inside his jacket, he pulled out a flask, took a drink, and then offered it to the other driver. Georgia walked toward the two men and heard them talking.

"Yeah, she's famous now—my wife, an author. Whodda thunk it?" Harry said. "There's an article about her in *Newsweek.* Did ya see it?"

"Hell, no. You think I've got time to read?" The driver took the flask and gulped down a swig. "This old truck breaks down on every run. I ain't got time for nothin' but fixin' and drivin'," said the other man. He wiped his mouth on his jacket sleeve. "Who cares anyway? I thought you were divorced."

"Well, shit, *I* care, Denny. She's still my wife—and by God, she's got money now. She owes me, don't she? I helped her get her start. Yes, sir, I did." Harry turned and walked toward his truck. He checked his load, pulling on the thick ropes tied over the giant logs. Reaching in his shirt pocket, he pulled out a pack of unfiltered Lucky Strike cigarettes and lit up. Exhaling, he hollered at the other man, "Think I'm gonna write her, ya know. Tell her I want my share." He sauntered to the end of the truck. "Yep, that's what I'm gonna do!" He kicked the back tire.

Georgia scowled. Fuming, she walked toward Harry. "You son of a bitch," she said under her breath. She was about six feet away from him when he looked straight at her—or rather, through her.

Taking a long draw on his cigarette, he exhaled the smoke toward Georgia. "She damn well better gimme some of that dough," he said, and pointed his finger in Georgia's direction. "Yes, sir, she better—" Harry's voice trailed off. He threw down his cigarette and stamped it out.

"You dip!" Hot anger coursed through Georgia's body. "That will be the goddamn day when you get anything more from me, Mr. Harry Swan!"

Harry didn't flinch. Hiking up his jeans, he tightened his belt and strutted to the front of his truck. It was then Georgia realized that neither Harry nor the other man could see or hear her. Enraged, she shook her fists at Harry as he climbed into his truck. "You bastard!"

Harry started the truck, revved the engine, and adjusted the big side mirror. "So long, Denny," Harry shouted over the engine noise. "Beat ya to the pass." He cackled, lifted his flask at Denny, then flipped him the bird. Dust billowed behind his rig as he lurched onto the highway.

Shaking, Georgia watched as Harry's truck disappeared down the road. She heard the gears grind as he double-clutched and shifted into high. "Good God, he hasn't changed much, still an egotistical asshole," Georgia muttered.

Denny gunned his engine and pulled out. Georgia jumped back before he sideswiped her. Dust and gravel scattered. She coughed and wiped her eyes. Waiting for the debris to settle, Georgia realized she'd forgotten about Kitty. At that moment, she had an intense need to find the cat. *Where is she?* Her eyes skimmed the highway, searching for Kitty. Dang. No sign of the cat.

Georgia felt sick. Her mind pinged with incessant chatter. *What just happened? Where am I? How am I going to get back to Orcas? Where the hell is Kitty? I can't leave her here. Goddamn it, Harry.*

In turmoil, Georgia flashed on an old movie scene in *A Christmas Carol* where Ebenezer Scrooge is visited by the Ghost of Christmas Past and whisked to a party at his nephew's house. He hears the partiers talking about him. No one knows he's there; no one can see or hear him. No one knows I'm here either, Georgia thought.

Stranded at the roadside, she realized she had no physical means to get back to Orcas, to Sandra and Billy—to her life. She didn't even know where she was. This realization startled her so much she stopped looking for Kitty. Breathing deeply to quell a fresh wave of panic, Georgia marched toward the gas station.

A faint light glimmered inside. The front door was ajar. She pushed it open and peeked into the room. A gray haired man sat in a rocking chair near a small wood stove reading a book. He raised his head and smiled. "Howdy, can I help ya?"

"Yes, you can." Georgia cleared her throat. "I think I'm lost. Where am I?"

The man chuckled. Curling his fingers around grimy suspenders, he said, "Well, yer near Oregon." He snapped his suspenders. "At the edge of the redwood forest, just up from Crescent City on Highway 199. Yer on yer way to Grants Pass,

Missy." His response sounded as if he'd answered this question many times before.

"Grants Pass? You mean Grants Pass, Oregon?"

The man nodded. "Yep."

Georgia's mind went numb. "I'm near Oregon?" She stumbled across the room and grabbed onto the corner of the front counter to steady herself. "How far is it from here to Grants Pass?" she said, squinting out the murky window.

The man sighed. "Well—I'll show ya." He closed the book and hefted his large frame to a standing position. He limped over to the front counter. Setting the book down, the man pushed his glasses up on his nose and pointed at the road map underneath the dirty, thick glass on the counter. "Here's where we are." He moved his gnarled finger along the map. "Ya take the highway all the way up here. Parts of it are nice. The Smith River runs throughout here. The road's winding, though," he said, snickering, "but we like it like that." The man looked Georgia up and down. "Anythin' else?"

"Uh, no. Well, I mean yes, just one more thing." Georgia tapped the glass. "I was wondering—uh, do you like the book you're reading?"

"Huh? Oh, yeah, it's pretty good." The man nodded and patted the book. "Takes some gettin' used to, though, but it's not bad. Written by some woman author—famous, they say. But I haven't heard of her before." The man paused as he glanced at the book. "I'm a reader, though," he said. "I kin get used to just about anythin' with words."

"Well, thanks for your help, sir." Georgia pivoted toward the door. "Oh, wait!" She pointed to her forehead. "What's your name?"

"Gus. Gus Abbott. This here's my station. Bought it from my dad some years back."

"Yes, well, thanks again, Gus." Georgia deliberated for a moment, wondering if she should shake his hand. Deciding against it, she said, "Oh, by the way, I'm Georgia Swan." She pointed to the book cover. "That Georgia Swan." Before Gus could say another word, Georgia dashed out of the station.

Within minutes, she stood in the exact spot where she had first seen Harry. Her eyes searched the roadway for Kitty. "I...I don't understand. How can Gus see and talk to me and not Harry?" she said. Georgia turned around and around, scouring the roadway and perimeter. "Kitty? Where are you?" Then she heard a quiet meow and looked down to find Kitty standing at her feet. Purring, the young cat peered up at her and swished her tail. "There you are!" Georgia bent down to pet Kitty. "I was worried about you. How are we going to get home, girl? Click our heels together?" Georgia exhaled a short, nervous laugh. The idea was so absurd, so obtuse that it somehow appealed to her, especially since she had no clue how to return to Orcas and her authentic life. Kitty meowed and skittered over to the other side of the road. "Come back, Kitty! We need to stick together right now." But Kitty scampered into the tall trees and disappeared. In a panic, Georgia followed her.

The moment she entered the redwood grove, the filtered shadows and coolness of the forest felt reassuring. As Georgia searched for Kitty, her confusion and stress slowly dropped onto the earthen floor. Fifty feet into the dense woods, she paused and leaned back to stare up at the immense redwoods. Their presence comforted her. Dwarfed by the majestic canopy, she felt like a small child wandering, searching for a place—a way home, but she saw only fragments of blue sky filtered through the massive branches, nothing that might suggest an opening or vortex.

Georgia walked around rich green sword ferns and underbrush. Some of the redwood trees had charcoal lined cavities at the base, their innards burnt by fire decades ago. She touched the charred wood and marveled at the ancient trees' resilience. Georgia knew redwood trees protected themselves from fire and disease. Legend had it, too, that they were once miles high. These grand old conifers had seen centuries in the making, knew secrets she would never know. Tall and stately, they had been growing for hundreds of years, some more than a thousand.

As she went deeper into the grove, Georgia relaxed. Engulfed in the forest rhythms, she wandered, her senses comfortably numb. After about thirty minutes, an incredible sense of loss hit her, and panic ensued. Georgia willed herself to concentrate on the peaceful forest, soaking in the silence, hoping to sense anything that would lead her home. She desperately wanted Neom. *Where was her wise guide?*

Right before razor-edged fear took hold, Georgia came upon a small clearing. A shaft of sunlight beamed into the center of the clearing. It was then she heard Neom's familiar voice. "Go stand in the light."

"Thank God," she whispered and pressed forward. When she came to the sunlit area, Georgia glanced up at the bright cerulean blue sky peeking through the treetops. The dazzling sun shaft and its reflected light almost blinded her. Shading her eyes, Georgia moved to the center of the clearing. When she stopped in the middle, she heard a whirling sound and a BB gun pop. For a minute, everything appeared blurred like it had in the orchard. The trees and vegetation pulsated around her.

Underneath her feet, Georgia felt a pressured movement as if she were being lifted in an elevator. Queasy, she closed her eyes. "Please. Please, take me home." Then everything went black.

Georgia opened her eyes, surprised to be kneeling on the sunken grassy area between the two apple trees. She stood up and looked around the orchard. How long had she been gone? The sky had grown dark. A damp, chilly breeze swirled around her, warning of an impending storm. "Better get home," she said, and let out a sigh. Georgia rotated her sore body. "Where is Kitty?"

In an instant, Kitty appeared at her side. Meowing, she wrapped her svelte little body around Georgia's legs. "There you are! We're home, Kitty," she said. "Thank you, and thank you, too, Neom." Georgia picked up Kitty and ran her hand over her soft, furry coat. The kitten purred. At the edge of the orchard several island deer grazed as a dense fog bank rolled in off the water. "We better hurry," she said and rushed up the trail.

Inside the cold Airstream, Georgia grabbed the Jack Daniels bottle and poured herself a stiff double shot, then filled the tea kettle and turned on the burner. Waiting for the water to boil, she checked the clock: 7 p.m. She hadn't been gone that long. Georgia lit a cigarette and sat down to think.

There were so many unanswered questions rumbling around in her head, she felt scattered, her body still numb. Georgia drummed her fingers on the table and slugged down another shot of bourbon. She'd traveled back in time, but *why*? Why was Harry there? What was he going to do?

She grabbed her notebook and jotted down a few notes. At first, details of the trip came in bits and pieces. Then images poured out. Her hand couldn't move fast enough, so she pulled over her trusty Royal typewriter and hammered out more text. Half an hour went by before she stopped typing. Most of what she had written read like a jumbled, fragmented mess. She reread the material. Three questions glared at her.

One: How had she gotten to the gas station from the orchard?
Two: Why could Gus see and talk to her but not Harry?
Three: What was Harry going to do next?

Part Five

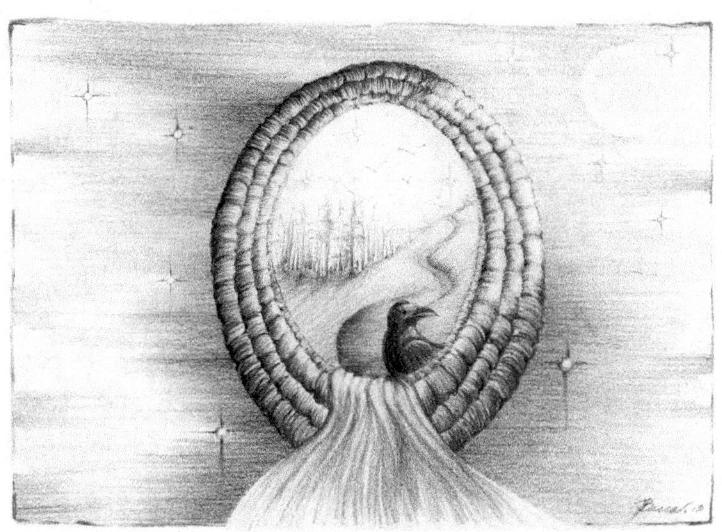

Neom and The Group

By the time Georgia was a toddler, her parents boasted to close family and friends about Georgia's remarkable behavior. "We think she has unusual sensitivities—mystical," they said. In private, though, they were often befuddled by their daughter's strange talents.

Advised by doctors they would be forever childless, the birth of a baby girl came as a welcome surprise. Beautiful, petite, and perfectly formed from the moment of her birth, Georgia's parents showered their only child with love and adulation. Although impoverished at the start of Georgia's life, her parents gave her everything they could. Their unconditional love and support set up a powerful alliance that would one day help Georgia achieve international acclaim.

From the start, Georgia's mother coddled her infant child. Swaddled in soft cotton, her tiny face haloed with platinum blond curls, the child slept through the night quite early and rarely cried. "She's a treasure," her mother told friends. "Georgia is very special, and we are so grateful she is with us. We cherish her." Hugging and kissing her daughter, she would then whisk her child away to the safety of her frilly bassinet.

It was true Georgia was exceptional. Early on, her parents realized she knew things, otherworldly things. She showed a strong tendency toward precognition and the paranormal at a young age. Many times, her mother found Georgia making unique sounds, carrying on cheerful, nonsensical conversations with what she assumed were imaginary friends. Sometimes she caught her little daughter staring with a blithesome expression into space, pointing and jabbering in childspeak across her little table to an empty chair. This behavior fully manifested when Georgia was around three years old. It came as no surprise when at the start of her fourth year, Georgia announced to her parents her imaginary friend's name was Oma.

After that pronouncement, Georgia chattered to Oma almost nonstop. She carried on long conversations, played dress-up or pretended to serve tea to her new friend. When tucked in every night, Georgia made a space for Oma in the bed, snuggling and whispering to her invisible friend as if she were next to her.

This behavior startled Georgia's parents. Still, they regarded their child as an exceptionally bright youngster. They did not interfere with Georgia's imaginary friendship and allowed her the freedom to play with Oma. They told themselves their daughter carried on this way because she was an only child; playmates were few, and without Oma to play with, Georgia would be lonely.

Her parent's devotion enabled Georgia to carry on her relationship with Oma throughout her formative years. When she was around other children, though, Georgia hid her private friendship, and if confronted, covered up her conversations by pretending to talk to the air, trees, or forest creatures. Georgia did not want to share Oma with anyone. Oma was hers and hers alone.

The year Georgia turned seven, Oma introduced her to a community of ravens. One winter day, a small, noisy flock of ravens flew onto an enormous tree outside Georgia's bedroom window. The silhouette of the dark tree and coal black birds were a stark contrast against the winter white. Mesmerized by the flock's raucous sounds, Georgia watched the ravens in childlike wonder as they cackled in the leafless tree. She asked Oma what the ravens were doing.

"Why, they've come to introduce themselves," Oma said. "The raven bird is one of your totems. You can call on your raven totem anytime." And so, Georgia did.

Deep in the night, Georgia dreamt she saw a large, silky, black raven perched on the end of her bed. Cocking his sleek head this way and that, the noble bird said to her in a throaty voice, "I am Jedediah, your guide and friend. I am here for you."

Surprised to hear a bird talking even in a dream, Georgia nodded in wonderment, and in a split second, he was gone.

The next morning, she woke tucked in her bed with her mother standing over her. "Georgia," her mother said, "are you all right? You've been sleeping so soundly. I thought you might be ill."

"No, Mother. I'm not ill. I'm fine. Where is Jedediah? Have you seen him?"

"Who is Jedediah?" Georgia's mother looked around the room. Thinking one of her daughter's stuffed animals might be Jedediah, she pointed to a little pile of stuffed toy animals on a chair. "Is he over there?"

"No," Georgia said, rubbing her eyes. "Jedediah isn't a toy, Mother, he's a bird."

"A bird? What would a bird be doing in your room, Georgia?"

"He's not just a bird, Mother. He's a raven, a really big raven." Georgia slid out of bed and put on her robe. "Oma told me he's my totem."

"Oh. Well, I don't know about that, dear, but come downstairs. Father is leaving for a week, and he wants to say goodbye."

And so, it went. Through the years, when she called on Jedediah, he came to her in a dream state. Then one day, her dreams of Jedediah stopped. When Georgia queried Oma about the raven's whereabouts, she asked, "Where did Jedediah go? Will he come back?"

"Do not worry," Oma reassured. "Jedediah has been called away, but he will always be near whenever you need his help. One day he will assist you, and you will be glad to see your friend," Oma counseled.

It never dawned on Georgia that Oma might leave, too—until the day it happened. On the day she started her menses at age twelve, Oma stepped back into the ethers. That morning Georgia woke early, lying in a pool of blood. When she called to her friend, who had always been there, Oma did not answer. Georgia called again and again, but it was her mother that rushed in to comfort her. Without warning, her childhood and beloved friend Oma had slipped away in the night. "It will be all right, Georgia," her mother said, stroking her daughter's hair. "Oma still loves you."

Oma's departure was a tremendous loss for Georgia. She felt as if she'd been dropped into an icy vat and left. Deeply saddened and angry with Oma for abandoning her, Georgia shut down the spiritual side of herself. Ashamed, thinking she had done something wrong, Georgia nullified the other ethereal realities she had grown so fond of, and withdrew. She called them silly, childish fantasies.

Forced to seek new friends, Georgia spent most of the next year and all her waking hours struggling to fit in with school peers. She curled her hair, wore lipstick, spent hours in front of the mirror, and chatted with her new teenage friends. These behaviors aided her efforts in numbing down her psychic, sensitive internal world and made it easier for her to close the dimensional doors she once shared with Oma. Soon her secret worlds disappeared into the ethers; and for a time, she forgot them.

By the start of grade eight, Georgia had stowed away all her intuitive sensibilities and learned to act normal. Her school friends accepted her as long as she mimicked them. Only late at night, when she woke from a deep sleep to find her room spinning around like a merry-go-round, did she remember she was not ordinary. Georgia kept all of her abilities hidden, not understanding then that these supernatural gifts would one day save her life.

With her spiritual side tucked away, Georgia concentrated on a life she considered socially acceptable, and her marriage to Harry Swan solidified her commitment to normalcy. From the first moment she saw him, Georgia knew life with Harry would be about him, and she accepted her new existence. He did not know about her spiritual side, and that was the way she wanted it. During the day while Harry was away, Georgia coached herself on how to be a good wife. She read etiquette books and devoured periodicals that preached proper, traditional, married life. Georgia welcomed this made-up external world as if there had never been another; that is, until Harry left.

Shocked and stricken with indescribable grief, Georgia spent countless nights dwelling on Harry's abandonment and the wreckage of her short-lived marriage. How could he leave her? What had she done wrong? How was she going to manage? The day the creditors removed the sofa and easy chair, she called her mother. Bereft, her infant Sandra crying in the background, she sobbed to her mother. "They've taken everything, Mother. I need your help." That's when her parents suggested she move in with them for a time and go back to school.

Lying in bed in her old childhood room with Sandra snug in a crib, Georgia cried every night until there were no more tears. On one sleepless night, she lay wide-awake, pondering for the umpteenth time how this had happened when she felt something familiar tingling within her. Brought on by great sadness and emotional vulnerability, this tiny crack in her hardened psychic veneer allowed other worlds to trickle in.

At first, she had only the slightest sensation. But before long the impressions grew so strong she felt dizzy, sick to her stomach. Georgia clamped her eyes shut, squeezing them tight to quell the nausea. "Go away," she said. Still, the images continued to enter her awareness. Sparks of vivid color came from a great distance and whirled around inside her head, expanding, growing until the energy enveloped her in a swath of vibrant hues.

Layered over the brilliant color were translucent, human-like faces—male and female. One by one, the likenesses faded in and out, sometimes overlapping one another. Bewildered at first, Georgia did not acknowledge the beings until thick waves of healing energy wrapped around her. In a cradle of love, she felt safe and unafraid. Georgia realized then that the faces were friendly, much like Oma. "Thank you," she sighed. Relieved, she fell into a deep sleep, and from that moment on, the door to her inner world remained open.

Over time, as she embraced her psychic abilities again, Georgia's emotional distress lessened. Renewed by a surge of positive energy, she handled her waking three-dimensional life with aplomb, especially when she knew a special event awaited her at the end of the day. Busy with work, Sandra, and school, it was only late at night when she felt free enough to enter other dimensions. She'd stare spellbound into strange portals with her new friends as if watching a blockbuster movie.

Then another unforeseen phenomenon occurred.

Having no particular pattern, Georgia's late night trysts to other worlds materialized at random and usually with no forewarning. The only constant was the time: 3 a.m. The instant the clock struck three, her eyes popped open. Wide-awake, she knew it was time to tiptoe through inner worlds. Thrilled with a sense of wonder and purpose, she welcomed the psychic escapades. When a group of intraterrestrial beings knocked on her spiritual door early one morning, she ushered them in.

At 3 a.m. sharp, Georgia woke from an intense dream to find a group of beings standing at the end of her bed. She studied their vague, outlined forms. In the semidarkness, she could only make out their long, stylized robes—none of their facial features. Knowing intuitively these beings were androgynous, Georgia peered down the bed, intrigued by the glowing, arched halo surrounding the group. A pervading sense of peace filled her bedroom. She was not afraid and knew intrinsically these beings were of a gentle, high spiritual nature. One being was very tall and appeared the leader of the group. Georgia stared in silence at the visitors for a while and then drifted off. When she reopened her eyes, the beings had vanished. Later, she wondered if she'd imagined the entire event.

A few weeks went by before Georgia had another visitation. Again, she woke at 3 a.m. and found the same beings at the end of her bed. Without a sound, each held out a hand and together they beamed a strong ray of light toward her. The energy rushed to the bottom of her feet and sent a powerful wave of gold light up through her torso and out the top of her head. The jolt put her into an unconscious state. The next morning, she was healed of any residual heartache or physical pain.

Writing in her journal that night, Georgia described the experience as being touched by the hand of God. It was then she knew there was no going back. She had to live an authentic life now and could no longer hide behind the cloak of normalcy.

As time went on, the number of visitations increased. Two to three times a week, she expected a 3 a.m. visit from The Group as she called them. No words were spoken by the beings during these visits. In the dark silence of night, the luminous figures transmitted their messages through mental impressions. Georgia felt or saw their intentions as written words, pictures, or feelings. They guided her through wormholes, portals, and dimensions, using cryptic symbols and rudimentary images.

Exhilarated by The Group's presence, she wandered with them through other worlds embellished with brilliant kaleidoscope colors; met exotic creatures as they strolled in expansive, mystical landscapes that led into still more dimensions. Sometimes she walked on soil that sparkled as if alive with consciousness.

During her waking hours, Georgia remained in an earthbound world: working, studying, and tending to Sandra and household chores. She knew she lived a dual life. But as her rich internal world became more and more active, she could no longer contain her robust inner realm, and it bled into the physical, three-dimensional world.

While attending a creative writing class, Georgia composed a short story about a memorable late-night episode with The Group. The instructor was so intrigued by her paper he wanted to meet with her after class.

"I found your short story captivating," he said. "Can you tell me more? Have you had out-of-body experiences before?"

Skilled by now in hedging delicate spiritual matters, Georgia hemmed and hawed. "Uh, no. I…I don't think so. I just made the story up. It's make believe—fiction," she said, and backed out the door. After that slight brush with scrutiny, she avoided any personal contact with her professor, and he never brought the subject up again.

This confrontation caught Georgia short. She'd made a mistake by opening herself up to human conjecture. Vowing to be more careful, she found a private outlet for these psychic adventures by purchasing a large moleskin journal where she jotted down her thoughts and experiences, writing the indelible scenes in detail. She transcribed everything she remembered, made tedious side notes, and often added pen and ink sketches to further illustrate a late-night incident. After finishing each entry, she hid the notebook in a small suitcase her mother had given her. Never again would she divulge her secret life to anyone.

Journaling her out-of-body experiences helped stabilize her life and created a pillar of believability she clung to. The process helped clear her thoughts and focus on normal three-dimensional life. Little did she know then these entries were the beginnings of several fantasy novels that would one day make her famous.

In time, Georgia grew comfortable traveling to other dimensions with The Group. A sense of wonderment often lingered for days after a multi-dimensional trip. More and more, she preferred the lightness of the ethereal to the drudgery of dense three-dimensional life. With The Group's help, Georgia entered realms no one she knew had dared to imagine. Thrilled to be wandering down long, multi-dimensional corridors, she told herself, "Who wouldn't want to go to Wonderland?"

Intellectually, Georgia understood the concept of time travel, but she had only walked in and out of dimensions with the aid of The Group—never alone. These adventures piqued her curiosity so much that she wondered, "Can I go myself? How does it work?"

Through a series of symbolic visions, The Group suggested she reflect on any fear she may have before going alone. "Fear would inhibit or block dimensional travel and stifle a solo attempt, making it dangerous," they said.

Yes, she had to admit, she was afraid. What would happen if she got lost and couldn't return? What would happen to Sandra? That worried her. Her guides continued to encourage her to overcome any fear and advised her that meditation would help clear any conflicts.

Georgia tried, but she fixated on worrisome probabilities too much and became frustrated, fitful, and unable to sleep. She dragged herself to work, put off her studies. Tired and agitated, she snapped at Sandra and her co-workers. "I…I can't do this myself," she admitted. "I need help." In the end, it was Sandra's childish logic that proved to be pivotal for Georgia and helped rein in her unruly behavior.

After scolding Sandra for spilling cocoa on the furniture one evening, Georgia collapsed on the sofa in tears, her nerves shot. Sandra ran over to her sobbing mother. "I'm sorry, Mommy, it was a assident. Don't cry." Sandra patted Georgia's hand. She looked into her mother's tearful eyes. "Mommy, you need someone to talk to."

Georgia stared at her daughter as if she was an age-old sage and nodded. "Yes, honey. I do." She let out a long sigh. "I'm sorry I yelled. Thank you."

This short, poignant scene shook Georgia. She knew Sandra was right; she needed a confidant. Someone nonjudgmental, someone with whom she could have frank, supportive conversations about otherworldly subjects—someone like Oma.

After putting Sandra to bed, Georgia sat down to meditate. She tuned in and sent out a call for a spiritual guide, a higher being she could trust and converse with.

The next afternoon, she and Sandra walked to a local park. The day was a warm, early spring day. As she sat in the sun watching Sandra play, Georgia heard a quiet voice inside her head.

"Hello."

"Hello?"

"Yes, hello. This is Neom speaking."

"Oh! Neom." Startled by the suddenness and clarity of the voice, Georgia swiveled around to the other side of the park bench, expecting to see who was talking. "Where are you?" she said.

"You cannot see me, but I have come to be your spiritual guide as you requested. At present, we are communicating only through telepathy."

"Oh, I see." Georgia laughed. "I mean, I can't see, but I see—the telepathy part, that is." Georgia shivered. Her stomach felt queasy. Was he one of The Group?

"Do not be afraid. I am here to help as you requested."

"Help how?"

"With your work, your real work."

"What do you mean, my real work?"

"It is the nature of birth on the planet Earth to do work, but do not confuse the meaning. I do not mean physical labor but work in a deep spiritual way to enable your authentic life mission—your purpose. Do you understand?"

"Uh, yeah, sure. I mean, I think so." Georgia closed her eyes and looked inside. She saw nothing, only dark shadows.

"I will reveal myself to you soon. Now we will communicate through the use of telepathy. We will talk in conversation at a frequency comfortable for you, to get more chummy, if you will."

"Chummy?"

"Yes. This is a word you know. Is that correct?"

"Well, yes. I know what chummy means, but the word sounds funny coming from someone, uh, without, well, without a body."

"Yes, I understand. May we proceed?"

"Who is we?"

"Allow me to explain. We are a group of five who have come to communicate with you. We are skilled in various venues of spiritual progress and thought."

"You want to do this now?" Georgia said. "I can't possibly do it now. I have to take Sandra home, feed her, and put her to bed. Can we do this later? At the normal time—say 3 a.m.?"

"As you wish. Please indicate when you feel capable of communicating. We are familiar with your concerns and routines. We have been visiting you for some time now."

"It *is* you! Sheesh. At last, I can hear your voice!" Georgia squirmed and looked over her shoulder. She did not want to be talking like this in public. Good Lord, someone might think she's loony. "You know, I absolutely cannot talk right now. I'm in a park. People are watching."

"There is no need to fear. You requested additional guidance in auditory form. We are making ourselves known. We will return when you are in private."

"Yes, yes, thanks. And, uh, Neom?" Georgia said. "You're right. I need to talk. Thank you." Georgia scanned the playground area. It was nearly empty. "But I have to go now. We'll speak later, okay?" There was no reply.

A short distance away, Georgia saw Sandra swinging on a swing set with another child and the child's mother. Georgia grabbed her purse and hurried over to Sandra. "Come on, sweetheart. Time to go home."

"Who were you talking to, Mommy?"

"What?"

"I saw you talking to someone."

"You saw him? Oh, honey, I don't know—just someone." Georgia ruffled Sandra's hair, reached for her little hand, then stood for a moment, hesitating. "Sandra," she said, "what did the man look like?"

"He was big."

"Anything else?"

"He looked nice, Mommy." Sandra smiled and looked up at her mother. "Can I have some cocoa when we get home?"

That night Georgia paced the floor and tried to reevaluate her situation now that Neom had come forward. Excited to have a real spiritual guide at the helm with a name, Georgia sorted through childhood memories of Oma, trying to remember what it was like to converse with a trusted friend. Georgia had repressed those experiences for so long that her recollections remained vague. Oma had been a perfect guide as a child, but she could not picture her secret friend anymore.

Her desire to digest complex realities compelled Georgia to further embrace her latent mystical abilities. She wanted to expand her otherworldly experiences, learn to time travel, reach new dimensions alone. This was no longer kid's stuff. She decided to do a little homework and research telepathy, out-of-body beings, and time travel. At the library, she pored over any book she could find during her lunch break.

A few days later, girded with well-sourced material, Georgia put out a telepathic call to Neom and The Group. With fresh perspective, Georgia hoped she wouldn't freeze like she had in the playground. She felt ready, armed with enough foreknowledge to ask specific questions.

Filled with expectations, Georgia slept fitfully that night, waking up every hour. Her long, restless night left her agitated and frustrated; disappointed and confused too. Why had there been no contact with The Group? *Had she done something wrong?*

It would be another week before she felt Neom come in. She would discover then that contact with spiritual entities can happen anywhere, at anytime.

"Neom here."

"Neom. Yes, well, uh, fancy meeting you here." Georgia's face turned bright red. She hoped he couldn't see her on the toilet reading the latest *Coronet*. "I was wondering when I would hear from you again, but I…I didn't think it would be now. I mean, here."

"Yes. We thought this would be more private for you."

"Uh, I think the word is awkward."

"As you wish," Neom said. "We are here to give you information about your books."

"My books? I haven't written any books. I've barely graduated from college."

"You will write more than one book. We suggest you take notes for future reference."

"Now?"

"If you wish, yes."

"Well, uh, I think I'll wait on the notes if you don't mind. I can't get up right now. Will this take long?"

"Not within your concept of time and space. The information we will give now you will find useful later. With your permission, we will begin the download. We will proceed now."

"Yes, of course." Georgia slipped the periodical on the floor, shut her eyes, and sat still. A moment later, a subtle, gentle wave enveloped her body, quieting her mind. A soft light funneled down through the top of her head, into her throat, settling in the area around her heart.

Within her mind's eye, she saw shimmering, white gold, almost translucent, energy fill her entire body from the inside out. At once she felt a great peace. Lulled by the sensation, she wondered if this light, a quiet yet vibrant feeling, was what The Group called downloading, a terminology she was unfamiliar with. *I'll ask Neom about it later*, she thought, and brushed the thought away. She sat for a while, for how long she did not know, transfixed by the still presence inside her. Then Georgia detected a slight disconnect, a gentle release as if pushing off from the edge of a swimming pool. She knew then the download was over.

On instinct, she got up, flushed the toilet, and went to lie down. Stretching out prone on her bed, Georgia felt relaxed and unafraid. Her mind was alert, but her body felt as if she had worked all day and into the night. Yet, she felt renewed. Georgia curled up. Pulling a light crocheted throw over her, she closed her eyes and drifted. "Neom?"

"We are here."

"Are we done?"

"Yes. The first session is complete. We will answer your questions later, after you rest."

Drowsy, she said, "Must I be on the toilet then?"

"If you wish."

As luck, or providence, would have it, Georgia didn't connect with Neom the next day. Sandra's weekly dance class was scheduled for the afternoon. Running late, Georgia scooped up her daughter at school and rushed her to tap dance class. There was no time to think about Neom and The Group. It wasn't until much later, after a hectic week, she had time to reflect on Neom and her first download.

During the week, she ignored any thoughts about the download and silenced any judgments. There wasn't time to reflect or even acknowledge her feelings or any turmoil, and at night, she dropped into bed and slept hard. Now that the week was over and Sandra was asleep, she had time to think.

Georgia slipped under the covers and leaned back. She scrolled through her memory like she would a rolodex and sorted through her initial impressions of the download. Setting aside her jumbled emotions, she reviewed any red flags. The process was tedious, but in the end, two big, alarming questions arose. What had she gotten into? *Was she ready for this?*

Her angst interfered with her effort to organize the data floating around in her head. It seemed impossible. Overwhelmed, she picked up the Saturday Evening Post. Before long, her eyes fluttered. When she reached to snap the light off, a large, semi-transparent figure appeared at the end of her bed. She gasped and threw back the covers.

"Do not fear. It is I, Neom."

"Neom? Jesus! You scared the crap out of me!" Georgia took a long, stern look at him. "You, uh, well, you look different from what I imagined."

"Indeed, I am different. I have gone to a higher level, causing my vibration to change. I am sorry to startle you, but you have been unavailable. We wish to connect with you now."

"Yes. It's been a very busy week."

"We are busy too. Much is happening in the universe. Some of The Group are transforming just as I have done. Therefore, you will notice changes amongst us when we visit in the future. There is no need to fear. These are vibratory changes and need not be alarming. As these transitions occur among us, it will be necessary to meet only when we, The Group as you call us, can gather. We will then contact you and download more information and answer questions if you need assistance. Do you understand?"

"Sort of—" Georgia paused. "Is the information you are giving me that important?"

"Not at present, but later you will find the information helpful."

Georgia laid her head back and sighed. "Okay," she said. "Sorry to sound so discouraged, but I'm just scared. I feel funny about all this. It's much different from what I expected. I don't know where it's going, and besides, I haven't even had time to think about what you call the first download. What is that anyway?"

"We are giving you information that will be beneficial to you and others later. Think of it like an internal library of reference material you can access when you need it. This might be difficult to comprehend now, but later you will appreciate the value. Now we will begin."

The downloading process this time was different. Into her mind's eye flowed transparent letters and strange cuneiforms. The matrix streamed into and through her so swiftly there was no time to linger on any imagery. Brilliant, transparent colors whirled at top speed. Humanoid figures floated around her interior landscape; mixed in were purple and green smoky forms near the peripheral corners of her internal vision. She could not make sense of what she saw. The dizzying sensation had no apparent continuity or logic.

Georgia opened her eyes several times to get her bearings, only to find her drab, messy bedroom. The contrast between her inner and outer realities startled her. Still, she closed her eyes and continued watching the mind-boggling scenes, which were far more appealing than her dreary room. I like this, she thought. When the light show was over, she fell into a deep sleep.

Days passed before Neom came through again. This time Georgia contacted him. "Neom? Neom, can you hear me? I have questions," Georgia whispered.

Silence and then, "Neom here."

"Where have you been? I've been waiting to hear from you. I thought we were supposed to meet."

"Yes, you are correct. However, we felt the last session contained a great deal of information and that you needed time to process what was given. We were waiting for you to approach us when you felt ready. You may proceed with your questions."

"Yes. Well, first, how will I use this information, and then, how do I know it is right?"

"The information that has been given, and that will be given, comes from the Akashic records—from all that is. The Great I Am. You will know when you need to access this information. You will know these records hold the truth. It will resonate within the deepest part of you. There will be no doubt. That is all."

"Okay, but Neom, is that all?"

There was no reply. Neom's advice seemed cryptic, obtuse, but Georgia quickly wrote them down. Pausing, she waited for more. Soon came the now familiar calm and peace that foretold of another download. With a deep sigh, Georgia leaned back on the sofa and fell into a heavy sleep.

Hours later when she awoke, Georgia felt different, not uneasy or ill, just different, as if something inside her had changed. Her mind, always sharp, burst with active neuron impulses she had never used before. Her head, filled with new syntax, felt as if it would explode. She'd been given an enormous sheaf of information, more than she could comprehend.

Georgia sensed a congregation of beings who had monitored her progress during the download. She'd seen them inside her head. She stared into the vacant room for a long time. Her surroundings had taken on a new quality; everything vibrated as if it were alive. When she stood up, Georgia almost tipped over. Her joints were stiff. Her body felt puffed up like a balloon, her brain thick as if stuffed with cotton. She waddled toward the bathroom. Holding her head. she called out. "Neom, what is happening to me?"

Neom's spiritual consultations and subsequent downloads continued several times a week for the next six months. By the end of the year, Georgia was exhausted and overwhelmed. Consumed by her dual life, she wanted to put a hold on things for a while and end the sessions for a short time. But she kept this to herself and did not voice her discomfort to Neom and The Group for fear of losing her new friends, just as she had Oma. This emotional push-pull syndrome left her feeling conflicted; one day she wanted the association, the next day she didn't. Then, just as suddenly as the encounters started, they ended.

Late one night, Neom came to her alone. He announced that their mission was complete. He and The Group would discontinue the sessions. His words were gentle but definitive.

"But Neom," Georgia said, "what if I need you? What if I get lost? How will I get back?"

"We will be available," Neom said. "Think deep thoughts and imagine my whereabouts, then project yourself into that sphere. This is time travel as well."

"Well, okay," Georgia said. "I'll try. But you know, Neom, truth be told, I am happy to be rid of those damn downloads. My mind is stuffed. I feel like an enormous walking encyclopedia." Georgia laughed. "But Neom…I will miss our sessions and you especially. Truly, I will."

"Little one, know that we are always together. Meditate on this and you will find us." With that, Neom was gone.

For the third time in her life, Georgia went into a dark emotional tailspin. She had not realized how saddened she would feel by the loss of her otherworldly friends. Their unexpected departure crushed her to the bone as it had when Oma, and then, Harry left. Perplexed and burdened with safeguarding channeled information taxed her grieving heart. *What was she to do?*

During the first months of those early morning visits with Neom and The Group, Georgia had grown fond of, comfortable, living a dual life. She considered their relationship sacrosanct. Although she tired of the early wake-up calls and surge of esoteric information, living without it left a deep hole. She felt empty, alone, and found it difficult to shake her grief. As a result, Georgia moped for weeks like the injured child she had been when Oma departed.

Several times she woke early in the morning thinking she'd heard Neom's voice. She strained her ears to hear him, but only the quiet space of her bedroom surrounded her. Unable to return to sleep, she would let her thoughts float and with idle curiosity, observe the channeled information. Still uncertain of the meaning, Georgia probed her vast mental library and marveled at the strange flowing matrix inside her head.

One compelling segment of information had to do with multi-dimensions and how to travel within them. This was what she had asked Neom for long ago. Georgia went over and over the data until it was rote. To her astonishment, she discovered time travel to be a broad subject and was thankful Neom had culled the material into something understandable.

Using an ancient cuneiform he had taught her, Neom outlined how to move through the vortexes, wormholes, and dimensional spaces. He detailed his guidance using animated visuals, which showed her where and when to travel. Neom's technique was sophisticated and diverse, different from her childhood experience with Oma, who taught her to use enhanced imagination. Her sporadic childhood ventures had been simplistic and often confusing for her then. Now they were dim memories.

Neom and The Group presented challenging stuff, and Georgia did not feel comfortable experimenting alone. She hesitated to take the first step by herself. If she didn't have it right, she might not return. Thinking she needed additional hands-on support in case something went wrong, Georgia leaned on an old childhood fail-safe for help and called on her totem raven, Jedediah.

"Yes. Jedediah. I don't know why I didn't think of him before."

This spark of inspiration gave Georgia confidence, and she developed a tentative plan. With his help, Jedediah could guide her to the right portal and from there, using Neom's instructions, she'd slip into a vortex, down a wormhole, and out to another dimension without mishap. When she wanted to return, she'd signal for Jedediah to help her through the vortex, and, voilà, she'd be home safe.

One night before bed, Georgia felt particularly brave and cavalier. "Okay, I'll try it," she said, and put out a call for Jedediah. He appeared right before she drifted into sleep. A flash and nod of his sleek head showed he'd heard her call, and together they slid into a dream sequence.

Wrapped in a gossamer-like mist, they soared through a blue-black space. Soon, they met a small flock of ravens. Jedediah motioned to the other ravens and Georgia to move toward an oval-shaped portal. A strange bland, opaque wall surrounded the portal. Georgia dabbed at the substance. It felt supple, almost flesh like. On the other side of the orifice was a brilliantly lit landscape. In awe she said, "I have seen nothing like this before."

Jedediah flapped his huge wings and beckoned her to follow. "Once through the doorway, you can go where you want," he said.

She stood back and observed each raven as they showed the shape-shifting technique. Through osmosis, she felt her body shape-shift too. Her arms turned into black wings, her torso lined with downy feathers. Before she knew it, Georgia had shifted into a birdlike body.

Jedediah flapped his shiny wings in approval and signaled to her and the other ravens. One by one, they flew through the portal. Georgia leaned forward to follow, but before lifting off, she stopped. The instant she held back, the dream broke, and she snapped back into her body.

For a few minutes after she jerked awake, a sensation of winglike appendages ran down her arms. She felt the distinct bone structure and feathers of raven wings. Sweat rolled down her back as Georgia worked to shake the feeling. In drenched bedclothes, she lay in bed and imagined shape-shifting back to her body over and over until certain she was in her body again.

Early the next morning, fueled by angst, Georgia questioned herself. She grappled with fierce emotions, as if wrestling with a mighty dragon. "Why had I stopped? What the hell was I doing?" she chided.

The fact was she would have gone with the ravens except for her daughter, Sandra, the most important person in her life. Georgia couldn't shake her guilt feelings. What if she'd entered the wrong multi-dimension and had been unable to return to Sandra? How foolish.

It was then Georgia shelved any further notions of time travel and multi-dimensional explorations until her daughter, who was entering junior high school, graduated from college. No sense losing what she had worked so hard for—not now. No. She'd wait.

Part Six

The Trouble with Harry
1958

The very thought of seeing Harry again put Georgia's teeth on edge. Her stomach felt queasy. She let out a formidable belch when her ex-husband's face popped into view. "That rogue," Georgia said. "How dare he."

Decades ago, she put Harry out of her mind. As difficult as it was, once she accepted the fact he was not coming back, Georgia forced herself to stop thinking about him. But now, after reading Harry's letter, Georgia couldn't stop thinking about him. How ludicrous his demands sounded. What gall! She was sure Harry was up to no good, and despite all her precautions, she couldn't shake the feeling she'd see him again. Yesterday, after reading his inane letter one last time,

Georgia ripped his terse words into tiny bits. "Dammit!" she hissed. "What an ass."

Panic and a sense of foreboding churned inside her as she waited in the car for Sandra. She wished she hadn't been so hasty to tear up the letter. Georgia rehashed what she could remember of his hand-scrawled demands and forced herself to calm down. Her hands shook. "Think. Think, girl, think," she said. Switching to the left side of her brain, she took a deep breath and concentrated on gathering her wits. She needed rational thought to cope but instead blurted, "That scoundrel. How did he find me?"

"Look at the postmark."

"What? Oh, for God's sake, I don't know what you're talking about."

"Look at the envelope."

"*Yes, of course!*" Why hadn't she thought of that? The postmark will show his whereabouts. At once jubilant, she searched her purse. An instant later, Georgia sank. "Dang," she said, "It's in the trailer."

"Use your skills."

"Yes," Georgia whispered, her breath shallow. "My skills." She leaned back and scrubbed through her memory for the clairvoyant technique Neom had taught her years ago. It didn't take long before she saw the rudimentary images he'd given her. "Yes, now I remember."

"Breathe deep, then proceed."

Georgia fidgeted for a few minutes before centering her attention on a pastoral scene. The Airstream was in plain sight at the forefront of the setting. With her eyes closed, she imagined walking into the scene and into the trailer. She held her breath until the interior of her tiny trailer came into sharp focus.

There. The envelope was right where she left it on the kitchen table. Shifting all her attention now, she honed in on the postmark. The printed words were faint but legible. Like a movie camera, Georgia tracked in on the lettering. At first, out of focus, and then she saw: Grants Pass, Oregon. She gasped, her eyes popped open. The vision snapped shut.

Grants Pass. So that's it. Now she understood the strange dream she'd had at Gus's gas station. Yes, that was Harry! *He had been there!* She lit another cigarette.

Drumming her fingers on the steering wheel, Georgia thought about the man she'd married so long ago. She didn't trust him. *What was he up to?*

Thirty years ago, Georgia was sure her life was over the day Harry left. Her grief deepened to total despair after discovering she had no money, no visible means of support. Unbeknownst to her, Harry had played the stock market, and when it crashed, he lost everything—the house, the car, everything. Left alone to sort out her future, Georgia was frantic. *What was she going to do?*

The day after Harry departed, her mother drove over to see Georgia and found her destitute and forlorn. Georgia sobbed in her mother's arms until there were no tears left. "Why did Harry go, Mother? How could he do this to us?" She wiped her eyes. "How am I going to take care of little Sandra?"

"Don't worry, dear," her mother said. "Your father invested in land and has plenty of resources. He's willing to help." That afternoon Georgia packed the rest of their belongings, swaddled her infant daughter in a soft blanket, and moved into her parent's home. A month later, she registered for secretarial training.

Since that day, her life had radically changed. She'd studied, worked hard and made something of herself. Thank God, Georgia thought, and slid open her cigarette case. She took out another cigarette and pressed the elegant silver box shut. Trying to make sense of the unsettling development, Georgia clutched the slim, engraved container as if it were a talisman. It had been the first thing she'd purchased with her royalty money, her money, not Harry's.

She tapped the unfiltered cigarette on the case and lit it. Exhaling a long stream of smoke, Georgia could not stop thinking about Harry. She searched for any residue of love for him. Nothing.

Long ago, when they first met, Harry had swept her off her feet. Even through all the hardship and years of disappointment, she still remembered that day.

A week before high school graduation, Georgia strolled down Main Street with two girlfriends. Excited, they chatted back and forth about the graduation ceremony and the summer ahead. Georgia boasted about going to college in the fall. Her parents had arranged an interview. Absorbed in their conversation, the girls walked by the local dry goods store without noticing Harry Swan, who stood near the window stocking shelves. Tall and handsome, Harry was the local heartthrob, the smoothest guy in town. All the high school girls swooned over him.

Harry took a long look out the window as the girls walked by. The minute he saw Georgia, he dropped the bolt of fabric and rushed out of the store. The heavy glass door swung open and startled the girls. Slipping back and out of her new wedge shoes, Georgia lost her balance. Harry grabbed her as she was about to fall and lifted her into his arms. "Hel-lo-o, beau-ti-ful," he said.

That was it. In that split second, they'd fallen for each other. Later, Harry told everyone he had been struck by a thunderbolt of lightning.

As Georgia remembered it, that first moment of embrace seemed incredibly romantic. She was so enamored by his sudden admiration that her mind swirled for weeks with fantasies about how she and Harry, her Prince Charming, would live a charmed life, complete with a spacious home and darling little children. Two months after they met, Harry asked Georgia to marry him and, deciding to forego her college education for him, she agreed.

Though it seemed innocent then, deceit trickled into the marriage from the start. Just as Georgia had camouflaged her psychic abilities, her new husband led a double life as well. Filled with lofty ambition, Harry wanted to be rich. So, in order to make a quick buck, he gambled and invested in some shady back door deals. During the day, he worked as a general store clerk, but at night and on the weekends, he bet heavily at the races, played craps in the alley, or when he could, romanced a sweet real estate deal. He wanted to make a big win, so he doled out more cash to invest in the rising stock market too.

Each time Georgia queried him about the sudden influx of cash money, their new car and finery, Harry came back with stories about how he was working extra hours and made a few good investments. That's all. Georgia went along with Harry and ignored her instincts, trusting him to build their future as her father had done.

For Georgia, part of that future included having children, and within a year she was pregnant. That was when the real trouble began.

What was keeping Sandra? Georgia craned her neck, searching for Billy and her daughter. She took one last drag off the cigarette and stubbed it out. Once again, she had misjudged Harry. The tone of his letter was shameless. His audacity never ceased to amaze her. Harry wanted—no, demanded—money, and claimed she owed him his share.

What share? There was no sharing with him. He's a fool, she thought, and leaned back. Truth be told, she had been a fool then, too, and it had taken a long time to forgive him—and herself.

"Hop in," Georgia said to Sandra as she slid over to open the passenger door.

"Hi, Mom. Thanks for picking us up. The truck will be ready late tomorrow afternoon. He has to put in a new transmission. It will be expensive." Sandra sighed. "Just one more thing—"

"Momma, can I have a popsicle?" Billy wiggled into the middle of the front seat.

"Yes, honey. When we get to the store. But right now, hush, Billy. I'm talking to Nana."

"Don't worry, Sandra. I can help you out with the repair bill," Georgia said. "You should think about a new vehicle. That old truck is in rough shape."

"I know, Mom. But it's what I have and besides, having a truck is handy for lugging around my tools. Shovels and pitchforks don't work in a sedan."

Georgia smiled at her daughter and thought about all the times her parents had helped her. They hadn't been wealthy, but somehow, they always had enough to give her when she was in trouble. She was happy to do the same for Sandra and little Billy.

"Sometimes I wish I had a man to take care of things like money and cars." Sandra looked straight ahead. With a long sigh, she continued, "I guess we're not destined to be married, are we, Billy?"

"What's married, Momma?" Billy asked.

"Married is when two people vow to love and cherish each other. They have children and live together happily ever after."

"Oh," Billy said. "Are we married, Momma?"

"Well, Billy, in a way we are." Sandra gave Billy a quick hug. "I'm happy living with *you!*" she said and gave him a kiss on his head. Sandra loved her son's youthful innocence. Billy was always asking questions, curious about the ways of the world. She guessed it was getting time to explain to Billy about his father, but not today. Later, she promised herself she'd sit down and tell Billy the complete story.

Sandra sat for a few minutes as her thoughts segued to her own father. What about her father? *Was he still alive?* She knew her mother had divorced her father years ago, and remembered the day her mother told her about him. She was five years old. According to her mother, her real father had disappeared and wasn't coming back.

Even after their conversation, Sandra wanted to believe her father would return. She waited. When it looked like her mother was right, she gave up and switched her full attention to her grandfather, who, as early as she could remember, had been her real father anyway. Kind and generous, Grandpa told her funny stories, took her for walks in the forest. She still missed him after all these years. No, she hadn't thought about her birth father for decades, and had long since gotten over the need to see him. She wasn't sure she ever wanted to now.

"After I drop you two off, I have to run down to the hardware store," Georgia said. "There's something I need for the trailer. I want to check on those building materials for the deck. Did you order those pots?"

"Yes, Mom. They should be here now," Sandra said.

"Good. I'll pick 'em up too." Georgia laughed. Winking at Sandra and Billy, she said, "I sound like a real island hick, don't I?"

Gilliland's Hardware near Eastsound doubled as a building supply and general store for islanders. Bustling with commerce, the store was a saving grace for everyone who lived on Orcas. Georgia loved the down-home feeling of Gilliland's and as a new local, preferred to patronize the island merchants. Her needs were simple, and it didn't take long before she relinquished any desire for mainland life. Gilliland's and Templin's Grocery, the neighborhood market, stocked almost everything she needed. She'd mail-order anything else and John the mailman would deliver the package.

Heading inside the hardware store, she bumped into John. "Hey, Georgia girlie! How are ya?" John said with a wide grin. For once, he didn't have a stogie in his mouth. He looked scrubbed and clean-shaven too.

"Fine, John, just fine, and yourself?" Sizing up John's appearance, Georgia caught herself wondering how old he was, if he was married.

"Absolutely couldn't be better," John replied. "Say, Georgia, I left a small package for you at your trailer. Should be okay right now." He pointed up at the clear blue sky. "Don't see no rain overhead," he joked, and pulled out a small cigar box from his shirt pocket. "Hey! You want to have coffee and a donut sometime?" He stood back and lit a match. "They've got real good ones down at the café in West Sound."

"Well, maybe, John." Georgia hesitated. "When were you thinking?"

"How 'bout tomorrow? I could pick you up after my route. Say, ten o'clock tomorrow morning?" John took a few puffs off his cigar.

Georgia stepped out of the cigar smoke. "Sure. That's a good time. I'm finished writing by then."

"Great! See 'ya in the mornin.' So long, Georgia girlie." John slid into his truck and put the old jalopy in reverse. A few sticks of lumber jostled in the truck's bed as it rattled down the road.

Suddenly, Georgia's knees felt weak. Both feet wobbled as if the earth trembled under her. She braced herself against a lumber display and bent over to clear her head. It was then she realized the ground hadn't moved. It was John's sudden invitation that shook her. She shot up ramrod straight. "Oh, good Lord, Georgia. You're acting like a silly schoolgirl. Stop it."

Watching John's beat-up truck disappear down the gravel road, Georgia wondered if having coffee and a donut with a man constituted a date nowadays. "No, definitely not," she mumbled. Coffee and a donut was not date material. Besides, she rationalized, she needed a little male coaching. She wanted to probe John's mind, ask him a few questions about the island. He seemed to be a conduit for what went on around Orcas. Since she'd received Harry's letter, she had the persistent feeling he might make his demands known again—this time in the flesh. If so, she might need some help.

The village of West Sound is a mere pinprick, a tiny nib on the map, but by Orcas's standards, the popular locale held great allure—especially the West Sound Café, an island favorite. The small, unincorporated community near Deer Harbor housed the tiny café, renown for good food and friendly hospitality. Each morning, delightful scents of fresh baked goods wafted throughout the small eatery. The day John and Georgia walked into the café was no different.

Across the long bank of windows, a clear, Dutch boy blue sky brightened the café. White, puffy clouds furled over the peaceful blue-green waters of West Sound. "Beautiful," Georgia said when they entered the bustling café. She sat at a small table next to the windows and waited for John to bring the coffee and donuts.

"Yeah, it's a beauty, Georgia girlie," John said as he sat down at the table. "There ain't nothin' like it nowhere."

"It's exceptional this morning, John." Georgia dismissed his choice of words and reached for a donut smothered in rich, dark chocolate. "Thanks," she said. "These look so fresh."

"Made this morning! It's their specialty. I love 'em." John sipped his coffee and bit into a large, glazed donut. "The cinnamon twists are great too. Have one!"

Georgia grinned. "Thanks. I just might." She was glad she had accepted John's invitation. From the first day they met, she knew he was a genuine fellow, and now it appeared he would be good company too. Before taking another bite, she asked, "How did you come to live on Orcas, John?"

"Oh, that's easy, Georgia." John wiped his mouth with a napkin and took a long drink of coffee. "My folks were farmers. They ended up here after their farm went bad in Oregon. They worked real hard trying to make a living there, and then things went bad, so they gave up and moved here. My dad liked to sail and took up repairing boats at the boatyard in Deer Harbor.

He worked there for years. I used to help him out when I was growing up. Heck, I was practically raised on a sailboat."

"Really," Georgia said, surprised. "That must have been quite an upbringing."

"Sure was. It taught me a lot about the water, weather, and living in small spaces." John chuckled and then gave Georgia a serious look. "My folks were real strict and made me learn a lot about sailing, just in case I got caught out by myself."

"That seems wise." Georgia reached for her napkin and dabbed the icing off her mouth.

"Turns out it was." John put down his cup and stalled for a moment. Georgia sipped her coffee and waited. "Well, when I was a teenager, I got caught out in a sudden storm, alone in my skiff, and nearly capsized." John gulped down his coffee. "That was quite an experience and if I hadn't known what to do in bad weather, I wouldn't be here today." John picked up another donut and took a deep bite. His eyes went distant.

"Sounds scary. I'm not sure I would have known what to do," Georgia said.

"Well, my parents taught me well and when you're in trouble, you do things you never thought you knew how to do." John exhaled and then downed the last of his coffee. "Anyway, that's enough about me. What brought you here, Georgia?"

"Well, that's simple, too, John," Georgia said. "I followed my daughter, Sandra. She moved to Orcas with my grandson, Billy. We're a small family and I wanted to be near them."

"You write books, don't ya, Georgia?"

"Yes. Yes, I do, John." Georgia looked away, hoping to skirt the subject.

"What are some of 'em? I like to read, you know. Maybe I've read one."

Georgia hesitated. She fidgeted with her napkin, trying to decide if she liked John enough to tell him about her notoriety. She had been enjoying her anonymity on the island. "Well, the most popular one right now is a novel called *Down South*. It's a mystery having to do with the Negro culture and segregated attitudes during the forties in the South. There's a spiritual, well, psychic slant to the story."

"Hmm. Don't know much about that, but I always like a good story. Maybe I'll pick it up."

"No need, John. I have an extra copy you can have. My gift to you." Georgia paused and then gave him a playful look. "But only if you invite me for more of these *delicious* donuts."

John laughed. "Sure thing, Georgia girlie. Sure thing," he said and blushed. "Well, I guess we'd better be goin'. Whadda say?" John picked up the check and held the chair for Georgia.

On the drive back to Georgia's trailer, John chatted about his early life on Orcas. Along the way, he pointed out various land parcels, telling her who owned the acreage. With cool disdain, he showed the parcels owned by wealthy mainland landowners who rarely came to the island, and gushed over smaller agricultural plots, which were working farms run by local pioneer families.

Georgia listened and waited for a lead-in to her question. She wanted to know if police protection was available. She wanted to know who to call if she needed help.

"Say, John," Georgia gulped and then exhaled. "Is there much crime on the island?"

John laughed and winked at Georgia. "Now that's a joke, Georgia, isn't it?"

"Well, I was just curious." Georgia wanted to sound casual. "I haven't seen a police car here yet. Is there a police station nearby?"

John looked at Georgia again. "Yeah." Sensing her serious tone, he studied her. "But the primary station is in Friday Harbor, the county seat. You 'spectin' trouble, Georgia?"

"Well, no. Not really. But if there *was* an emergency, who would I call?"

"Well, there's Roy Palmer here. He's our guy on Orcas. Roy's got a small office in Eastsound right near the post office. But he's usually not there. He's in his car, cruising. Haven't you seen him yet?"

"I guess not." After mulling over the information, Georgia said, "Hmm. Just one cop on Orcas?"

"Yeah, but Roy doesn't enjoy being called a cop. He prefers Sargent." John snickered. "It's an inside joke 'tween him and me. Roy and I go way back. We went to school together."

"I see," Georgia said. "Glad to hear that." At least there was someone here to uphold the law, she thought, and made a mental note to call Roy Palmer and have a talk with him. "Do you have his telephone number?"

"Sure, Georgia. I have it memorized. It's easy: 3344—say, do you have a phone now?"

"Well, no, but I'm thinking about getting one." Living without a telephone had been pleasant and kept the press at bay, but with Harry looming nearby, Georgia thought she better get a telephone—and soon.

"A phone is always a good idea, Georgia. You need a phone," John said. "My buddy, Ralph, installs 'em on the island. I'll call him for ya. I know just about everyone and everything happening on Orcas."

"Yes, you do, John. Thanks. I appreciate that." Once again glad she'd met John, she was even happier that he volunteered to help with the phone. Yep, John will be a good friend, she thought.

Over the last few weeks, Harry had worked himself into a frenzied lather. He felt restless and bored sitting around all day doing nothing. He was broke, too, and his body ached so much he could hardly move since the accident. That damn Joey, he thought, and poured himself another scotch.

They'd had a few drinks at a rest stop before bringing in their loads. Nothing wrong with that; all the guys did it. But this time, when Harry dropped his truckload, he tripped getting out of the cab and fell. Hard. To break his fall, he landed on his left wrist and wrenched it. "Feels almost broke," he told the medic. He also threw his back out when he landed. The doc said he was lucky he hadn't broken his hip or been paralyzed.

Right about then, the little luck Harry possessed ran out. When Joey let it slip about having a few beers with Harry the day he fell, the boss fired Harry. The foreman claimed he was drunk on the job. But Harry knew it was because the company didn't want to pay workers compensation. *Those shit-for-brains cheapskates.* He hadn't been drunk—not then! Now he couldn't find work. Where was he going to get the money?

Stopping at the gas station with his last load, he mentioned the mishap to Gus. "Hey, Gus, this here's my last ride. I'm being laid off."

"What I heard was you got fired." Gus put his book down and laughed.

"Yeah, maybe," Harry said. "Joey shit on me." Harry pounded his fist on the counter. "That son of a bitch!" That's when Harry saw Georgia's book. He couldn't believe his eyes. Printed in bold letters on the cover was Georgia's name.

"Holy shit!" Harry pointed. "That's my wife! Who'da thunk it?"

"Georgia Lee Swan is your wife?" Gus scoffed. "Hell, I thought you were a free man, Harry. Didn't know you were married to a famous author."

"Yeah. There's a lot you don't know about me."

Gus frowned and leaned back. He picked up the book. "This here's a bestseller." He flipped to his place. "So long, Harry." Gus didn't look up when Harry stomped out.

Less than a minute after Harry left the station, the seed of a plan formulated in his mind. Within a few strides, he had the perfect scheme: he'd get money from Georgia. *That's what he'd do!* He'd write her and demand some of that book money. "Yeah, that's it!" he said. "She's a famous author, ain't she? She has money. Hell, she's probably rollin' in dough. Besides, I'm her husband. She owes me, by God. I have rights, don't I?"

"What about the divorce?" a voice whispered in his ear. Harry glanced over his shoulder. Unsteady on his feet, he held onto the truck door handle and glowered at the station. He knew it wasn't Gus's voice. Gus was reading Georgia's book.

"Shit! She's *still* my wife. Who the hell are you anyway?" Harry tugged at the truck door. "Divorced," he mumbled. "God knows I haven't forgiven her for that! Just because some judge signed a few papers don't make it right. Divorce is a sin, ain't it?"

Harry cranked the truck engine, but it misfired. He pumped his foot on the gas pedal and the motor roared. "That damn woman has some nerve." He revved the engine. "Left me without a red cent. Wouldn't even let me see my kid. She sure as hell *owes* me. I have my pride. They don't call me Harry Smooth Swan for nothin'." Harry shifted into gear and the truck rumbled down Highway 199.

Mid-morning Georgia woke to the sun streaming into her trailer. She stretched and rubbed her eyes. The day felt lazy, the air damp. She draped her sloppy chenille robe around her body, fastened the sash, and moved a few steps into her tiny kitchen. "Coffee," she said. "Nothing better on a fine, sunny morning." She loved the outdoorsy taste of camp coffee and spooned coarse grounds into the pot. Waiting for the water to percolate, she pushed the lacy curtains aside and peered out. Kitty was sunning on the new deck. "What a cat you are." Georgia sighed. "You never miss an opportunity for warm weather."

With freshly brewed coffee in hand, she stepped outside to greet the morning. The clean air smelled sweet. She walked over to Kitty and stroked the cat's warm body. Half asleep, Kitty rolled over and purred. "Good morning, girl," Georgia said.

Sipping the hot, rich drink, Georgia glanced at the cluster of potted begonias on the shady part of the deck. The hybrids she'd ordered in the spring had flourished, and their blossoms were voluptuous. She stared at them, admiring the scarlet petals; heavy droplets of dew still lingered on a few. In the distance, Canadian geese honked, and the resident eagle signaled for his mate. Georgia lit a cigarette and drank her steaming coffee. *Life is good here.*

In the tranquility, she contemplated her encounter with the local policeman, Roy Palmer, last week. The sergeant assured her that living on Orcas was safe and if there was trouble, he'd be there to help. "Thanks, Officer. Here's my new phone number," she said, and handed him a piece of paper with her name and number. She explained how to get to her trailer down the IN Road.

"Aw, I know right where that is," said Roy Palmer. "I used to play down there when I was a kid; fished with my dad off the shore there sometimes too." He went on about how he and John had pulled some pranks on the old neighbors around there. Georgia smiled. She could see those two as young boys hunkered down, whispering to each other about what to do next to the mail truck when it came down the road.

Despite her gut feeling, Georgia ignored Harry's letters. The second one, short, brusque, and demanding like the first, had arrived yesterday. It mystified her how he'd gotten her address until Abe, her agent, enlightened her during their conversation several days ago. Abe's secretary had given Harry the address. Harry had tricked the woman, convincing her they were still married.

"That's a terrible mistake, Abe. Damn, I wish that hadn't happened." Abe was apologetic, but it was too late. Harry had her address. Now he could find her. Georgia squeezed her fist into a ball and hoped Harry would stay away, but deep down, she knew he wouldn't.

Like it or not, Harry was in her life once more, and she would have to deal with him. Even though he had always been a handful, mean and arrogant sometimes, she wasn't sure he had the gumption to harm her. He could be downright nasty, though, and she dreaded having another scene with him. Unease circled around Georgia as she remembered that last awful day.

It had been early morning when she walked into the bedroom holding little Sandra, who had settled down after a fitful night. Exhausted, her face drawn, Georgia had not slept. Harry stood by the bed and was throwing clothes into a suitcase. "What are you doing, Harry?" she said. Harry didn't respond. Frightened, she said again, "Harry, what *are* you doing?"

Harry whirled around and slapped her hard. She reeled back and held Sandra close. Her face stung from the blow. She burst into tears, and so did Sandra. Harry called her a fucking bitch and told her to shut up. He slammed his suitcase closed, grabbed his hat, and stalked out.

Georgia told no one about the abuse she endured—only that Harry left. The farewell drama, etched in her memory, still hurt. For years, she wondered what she had done wrong. *Had it been her fault?* Knowing Harry might surface again, a feeling of disquiet surrounded her; the old pain squeezed her heart until she couldn't breathe.

Harry had always been unpredictable, constantly scheming and lying to get ahead, and in the end, abandoning her and Sandra. If he came to Orcas, she needed a plan—an escape. Jumpy and on edge, Georgia thought of little else. She contemplated calling Roy or John for advice, but in the end, decided against it. "No. I'll handle it another way," she said.

Georgia rushed home after a quick trip to Templin's in Eastsound. She unlocked the trailer door and hurried inside. Bursting with ideas, she pushed the groceries aside and grabbed a pencil and notepad. Using old shorthand skills, her hand moved swiftly across the paper, organizing random bits of inspiration. Like a crazed woman, she wrote every thought, every nuance down, attempting to refrain from judgment. From time to time, she lifted her head, squinted at the time portal in the orchard, and studied the area, then jotted down a few more notes. Finally, she sat back and reread her work. Everything she'd written pointed to the vortex. *Was this her most plausible escape route?*

Georgia lit a cigarette and glanced again at what she'd transcribed. "I wonder," she said, and pointed to the vortex. "Can I direct myself to another dimension from that portal? And come back using deliberate intention?" The key word, of course, was *deliberate.*

"Yes," she said, and stamped out her half-smoked cigarette. "I'm sure it's possible. If Harry saw me disappear, that would scare the shit out of him, wouldn't it?" All of a sudden, an image of Harry popped up in front of her. Georgia burst out laughing when she saw the horror on his shocked face. "I just might do that!"

"But seriously, Georgia girlie," she said, mimicking John's voice, "it could happen." If she figured out how to pinpoint a location and time frame, she might transport herself somewhere out of Harry's reach if he threatened her. Once he was gone, she'd come back. It sounded almost too easy. "Dang, I wish Neom and The Group were around."

It was then she heard a familiar voice.

"Neom here."

Georgia jumped. "Oh. I was just thinking about you, Neom. Listen, I need your help."

"Yes. We sensed your vibration."

"Thank God, er, I mean, thank *you*! I think I might be in trouble, Neom. Can you help me?"

"We are here, little one."

"Well, uh, you know I have a time portal in the orchard." Georgia hesitated.

"We are aware of this vortex. We have been waiting to advise you about its use."

"Really? I mean—would you, could you do this *now*, please?" Georgia sighed. "I think I'm going to need help and right away."

"As you wish. The vortex is a time portal where one can egress and ingress, move into and out of dimensions. We must warn you that entry can be dangerous."

"Yes. Yes," Georgia said. "I've already used it once before. But…but I didn't know what I was doing. I still don't. Can I move in and out of dimensions freely? I mean, disappear, and reappear *with intention*. Is…is that possible?"

"Yes. It is possible. What you suggest is a form of interdimensional travel."

"Will you show me how, Neom? I mean, *right now*?" Georgia slapped the table several times. "I need to do this now!"

"As you wish. There is time, child. You need not worry. If you follow my instructions, you will be safe."

Georgia exhaled and took in a deep breath. "Thank God, you're here, Neom. I've been so worried."

"This ability has always been within your power, but you must have full and unequivocal pure intention *before* departure and re-entry. That means you, the soul, must vow to do no harm. Should your intention be unclear or impure, there may be damage to your passage."

"I see. No harm," Georgia muttered and searched her motives for any internal conflict. "Hmm, yes, I…I think I can do that."

"Very well. We will download the information. If you follow the guidance, you will be transported safely. Please be still now. When the download is complete, meditate on what you wish to know, and then rest with it. The instructions will enable you to return at will. That is all."

"Thanks, Neom and, oh, if I need further help, will you and The Group be around?"

"As you wish. We are here."

Within seconds, Georgia felt the surrounding energy brighten; the familiar stream of warm light flowed down through the top of her head, into her spinal column and out her feet just as it had many times in the past. A golden, transparent light circled her body and back up to the top of her head, down and around again, over and over, until the light became a fluid, continuous flow. Cocooned in a velvety substance, Georgia floated through space and soon fell into a deep trance.

The instant she woke the next morning, Georgia knew the channeled information Neom had given her was the boost she needed for her escape hatch—the vortex. *Now she had a plan!* Still, she worried about her intentions. Did she have any guilt or regret, any lingering desire for vengeance? Rolling this over, she wasn't sure how pure she had to be, but one thing she was sure of—she had a getaway, a place where Harry could not go. Georgia's head ached, thinking about him.

She shook her head and put her attention on creating an exit strategy. *If she had to escape, where would she go? What kind of dimension did she want to land in?* She pondered and searched inward for inspiration. After a while, when nothing came, she glanced at Kitty sleeping in the sun and shrugged. "Well, I guess it's time to chop wood and carry water, Kitty." Georgia threw on her flannel jacket and went outside to gather kindling. Neom said she would have time.

The sound of a foghorn woke Georgia late in the night. She listened to the deep, mournful sound echoing down the waterway as if calling her. When it grew faint, she fell back to sleep. In the morning, a thick fog lay atop the ground. The moist, opaque air hovered around the trailer like cotton stuffing.

By the time Georgia dressed and entered the orchard, the fog had burned off. The sun glowed on the big droplets of heavy dew that hung on the tall grass as she moved toward the vortex. The sunken area between the two apple trees glistened as Georgia stepped into the sacred space.

Kitty leaped into the area behind Georgia. "Oh! You surprised me, Kitty. I didn't see you." She squatted down to pet the cat. "You're wet, girl. Stay out of the way while I try this." Kitty looked up at her and meowed. With her tail up and twitching, the cat sauntered out of the perimeter and disappeared into the wet grass at the edge of the orchard.

In the middle of the vortex, Georgia stood with her eyes closed. As per Neom's instructions, she entered a meditative calm, opened her thoughts to a higher frequency and imagined moving through time. She visualized walking into a beautiful field of wildflowers where the sun shone. The blue sky above brimmed with white, puffy clouds. She heard birds chirping in the background. "Yes, that's where I want to be," she said. *"Right there, right now."*

No sooner had the words left her mouth than Georgia felt the ground under her feet tremble. For a moment, her mind went blank, and she saw only darkness. Then a flash of light came at her from a great distance and zoomed past like a comet, almost blinding her.

To her amazement, when she opened her eyes, she stood in the center of the field she'd visualized. The sun was so brilliant she shaded her eyes. Birds by the hundreds were soaring and swooping above. Their songs were almost deafening. The field ahead was as she had imagined; colorful wildflowers stretched as far as she could see. In the distance, perched on a gradual knoll, sat a large bench. "Wow. I've done it!" she shouted. Her voice echoed down the field.

Taking in the full thrust of what she'd done, Georgia turned around and around, stretching her arms wide. So far, her experiment had succeeded. Now, all she had to do was get back. Neom had already coached her about the return. "Going back in time might be a challenge at first," he said, and advised her to concentrate on the return destination, emphasizing that she needed to hit the right moment, the instant after she'd departed. This part was critical and would be her only safe entry. If she could not enter at the right moment, she might find herself in another time zone and place. Neom also stressed she must not allow fear into the equation. Any sense of trepidation would bring in a negative field and affect her travel and ultimate destination.

Since her return was the biggest challenge, Georgia planned to depart right away. She didn't want to jinx her success, so she concentrated on quieting her mind. Willing the loud bird chatter and outside distractions into silence, she envisioned her trailer, the orchard, and conjured as much detail about her home and surrounding land as possible, taking care to visualize the exact moment she departed, including the time of year and season. "Okay." She took a deep breath. "Let's go back."

In an instant, she found herself back in the orchard. Georgia reached out to touch a tree for validation. She was in the exact spot where she left. Her body was solid, and her clothes were still fresh from the morning. It appeared all was well, and that she had arrived with everything intact. She'd come back safe and sound, all with intention and of her own volition. Relieved, she glowed. "Thank you, Neom," she said, and skipped like a child back to the trailer. She wanted to double-check the time and date.

Over the next week, Georgia practiced and perfected her time travel technique until she felt confident she could move in and out of designated time portals with relative ease. She also experimented with time and location, using the sequential methods Neom had taught her, and pinpointed her landing with some success. These clandestine explorations put another level of excitement into her life, reminiscent of her childhood when she dabbled with her psychic talents while alone in her bedroom. With a lilt in her voice, she hummed and daydreamed about her renewed psychic abilities.

There were a few setbacks, though. On two occasions, finding herself lost between dimensions, she became confused. Once, Jedediah, the old, wise raven from her childhood, came to guide her through a portal. Another time, Neom's voice brought her home. The most delicate moment occurred when Billy saw her reappear.

While she was exploring another dimensional realm, Georgia heard Billy's faint voice call for her and Kitty through the ethers. Thinking he was in trouble, she panicked and quickly returned. The moment she appeared in the vortex, Billy saw her. He stood at the edge of the orchard. His five-year-old face lit up with wonder when he saw her appear. "Nana!" he yelled.

"Billy, I heard you calling."

"Where have you been, Nana?"

"Just away, Billy, on a little trip. Somewhere you can't go right now. Little boys like you have to stay here and play." Georgia laughed and brushed his hair back. "Let's get some cookies. Whadda ya say?"

"Yeah!" Billy said.

"First one there gets the biggest cookie!" she said. Billy grinned at his grandmother and then took off running up the trail.

With arms crossed, Harry propped up his bad leg on the dash and waited in the ferry line at the Anacortes terminal. He hated waiting, but he had gotten used to it, driving a truck. To kill time, he reached for the San Juan Islands map again. After he had it in his head to send off those two demanding letters to Georgia, Harry couldn't wait to get the money. He drove like a wild man out of Grants Pass straight to Anacortes, stopping only for coffee and a few sandwiches when he needed pee breaks. He hardly slept. It had been a long trek, but he was a seasoned driver and used to traveling great distances. Even with his injury and long involuntary furlough, he could still handle the long-distance stress.

Spreading the map over the steering wheel, he inspected Orcas's horseshoe-shaped terrain. His finger traced the road from the ferry dock to Killebrew Lake Road. "At the White Beach Y, take a left on Dolphin Bay Road and drive down past Diamond Hill," he said. He didn't know how he knew these directions, but he was sure it was right. His finger moved over the map to a small lake labeled Diamond Lake just on the other side of Diamond Hill. Dolphin Bay Road continued to wind around until it ended at McNallie Lane. If he took the shortcut from McNallie Lane to Horseshoe Highway, it led into the village of Eastsound, the midway point on Orcas.

Harry examined the map, moving his finger back and forth along Dolphin Bay Road as if dowsing for water. Finally, he zeroed in on what he was looking for—the IN Road. He had a hunch where Georgia's place was and drew a big X on the map in the approximate vicinity. Harry knew he'd find her. He had a hunter's instinct and was an excellent tracker.

Confident he could locate Georgia, Harry closed the map and leaned back to take a short snooze. It would be another hour before they loaded the cars onto the ferry and then longer to get to the island. He had time, lots of time.

Georgia stood at the edge of the IN Road and waved goodbye to Sandra and Billy as they drove off to the ferry landing to board the Chelan headed to the mainland. Sandra needed supplies and to shop for Billy. He wanted some special paper and crayons for his first day at kindergarten, and Sandra needed some hard-to-acquire gardening tools. Since they were on a shopping spree, Georgia asked her to pick up a few things for her. Sandra planned to stay overnight with friends on the mainland and return the following evening. She also promised to take Billy to a Walt Disney movie. He was beside himself with excitement.

"Nana, I'm gonna see *Snow White and the Seven Dwarfs*. It's a cartoon with dwarfs!" Billy twisted in his seat to look at his grandmother.

"I know, Billy. Won't that be fun?" Georgia leaned into the truck to give him a farewell kiss.

"I'll tell you all about it, Nana, when I get home. Bye!" Billy waved his little hand as Sandra pulled out of the driveway.

"I can't wait, Billy. Have a great time." Georgia stood by the roadside and continued to wave as Sandra's truck disappeared down the road.

Once her daughter and grandson were out of sight, an unexpected feeling of foreboding came over Georgia. She couldn't shake the nagging sense that something was about to happen—something big. Worried for her family, she said, "Keep them safe, God," and headed toward the apple orchard and the vortex, her escape route.

She liked to think about the time portal in those terms. Who would have thought she could disappear and then reappear like magic? "Bada bing bada boom," Georgia said, using one of John's favorite expressions.

At the last minute, right before turning down the trail to the orchard, she stopped by her little Airstream home. When she stepped up on the deck, something told her there was trouble ahead. She took a quick look around the area but saw nothing out of the ordinary. Georgia shrugged and walked into the trailer.

"Hell-o-o, Georgia," Harry said, and flashed her a big smile. Hunched over the kitchenette table with her new manuscript spread open in front of him, he winked. "Looks like you've got us another bestseller, Georgia."

"Leave that be, Harry. What are you doing here?"

"Just thought I'd stop by, see how you're doing." Harry gave her a sly, cunning side look. "And check on our enterprise."

Georgia walked over to the table and snatched the manuscript. She put it back into the box and slammed the lid down. "There is no enterprise. You don't belong here, Harry. Leave."

"Now, Georgia, that's not very nice. I've come a long way. We haven't seen each other for quite a while. Sit down. Let's have a drink. I noticed you had some whiskey in the cupboard. Pour us a drink, honey."

"*Don't* call me honey." Georgia walked to the cupboard and pulled out the bottle of Jack Daniels. Her hands shook as she poured the drink. "Harry, why are you here?"

"I haven't heard from ya, so I came to *personally* check on our enterprise."

"We don't have an *enterprise*, Harry. You know that. Drink your drink and then go." She shoved the shot glass over to him. "You're trespassing."

"Why, sure we do, Georgia. We have Sandra and you write books and owe me my share. Don't cha, honey? We are husband and wife. Remember?"

"That's over, Harry. You know that. Sandra is an *adult* now. She lives on her own. And…and…" Georgia glared at him. *"I don't owe you anything!"*

"Well, we'll see about that now. Won't we?" Harry slugged down the whiskey and pushed up from the table. "I'll be going now, Georgia, but I'll be back. We need to talk about what you owe me. 'Cause you *do* owe me. You know you do." Harry limped past Georgia. "I'll be around."

"Don't come back, Harry. You're not welcome here." Georgia watched Harry walk out the door and down the trail. She gripped the neck of the Jack Daniel's bottle and took a long swig. Their pithy exchange shook Georgia to her bones. She lit a cigarette and puffed a long stream of smoke out the door. Harry would be back. She was certain of that. A shiver ran through her, and she hugged herself.

Georgia was glad Sandra and Billy had gone to the mainland. She didn't want them involved in this. Right now, she had a few things to do—and fast. Georgia was certain Harry would be back soon and try to coerce her. He was a powder keg. All it would take is one false move. She had to be ready.

Shivering, Georgia grabbed a sweater. Cold to the bone, she took another swig of Jack Daniels and opened the manuscript box to begin prepping the pages for shipping. Her editor hadn't seen the final yet, but Abe had a copy. They were planning a fall publishing preview, and Abe had begun preparations. He had already scheduled a few radio interviews. Now, Harry's appearance complicated things. She wasn't sure if she'd make the tour.

Georgia looked at her wall clock. Ten o'clock. If she hurried, she could give John the package. As was his habit, he stopped by around ten thirty every morning. Georgia dashed off a quick note, stuck it in the box, and wrapped the whole thing in brown paper. She was labeling the package when John knocked on the door.

"Hey, Georgia girlie, how's it going?" When she heard his voice, Georgia let out an involuntary sigh of relief. "Have anything to mail today?" he asked. John stood at the door and took a long look at Georgia. Her face was ashen, her hands trembled. "Everything all right?"

"Yes. Fine, John, I'm…I'm just in a hurry," she said. "I need you to mail this *today*." Georgia's hands were still shaking as she handed him the box.

"Sure, Georgia. Can do. You're right on time." John looked at his watch. "Any coffee left?"

"No, John, not today. I have to go somewhere in a few minutes. I don't have time to chat. Sorry."

"No problem, Georgia. We'll make it another day. Okay then, I'll be off. Take good care, Georgia, and I'll see you tomorrow." John winked at her and walked out the door.

Georgia lingered for a few moments in the doorway. "Thanks, John," she said. He waved and walked down the trail. As she waved back, an uneasy feeling came over her. This might be the last time I'll ever see him, she thought. Georgia shuddered, went inside, and sat at the kitchen nook. Brushing cigarette ashes off the crowded table, she lit another cigarette and rolled a blank page into the typewriter.

Late into the night, Georgia woke with a start. Her sleep had been restless, her body drenched with perspiration. "Damn menopause," she swore. Unable to go back to sleep, she switched on the light, walked into the bathroom, and changed into a fresh flannel nightgown. She wrapped her robe around her and sat at the kitchen nook. Swathed in warm chenille, she crinkled her half-typed letter to Sandra and Billy and reached for her fountain pen. She wanted to write her message in cursive. The pen-to-paper ritual calmed her.

If things went awry with Harry, Georgia wanted Sandra and Billy to know how much she loved them—especially if she missed the moment of return. Deep down, Georgia suspected she might not make it back. It had occurred to her that even with all the preparations she'd made, something might happen. She didn't know what.

In careful longhand, Georgia told her daughter and grandson how much she cared for them, how she would miss them, and advised Sandra not to worry about anything. She had seen to it they were well cared for, and instructed Sandra to contact Abe for details about her will and the estate.

After sealing the letter, Georgia sat in the dim morning light and reflected on her life, her daughter, and precious Billy. Yes, she would miss them, but what would be would be. She'd made it this far through the grace of God, hard work, and perseverance, despite a few rough years. Whatever happened would be all right.

Georgia set the sealed the envelope on the counter, then she dressed. In flannel-lined dungarees, a wool shirt, and her trusty jean jacket, she walked down to the orchard. The air was crisp. Dew sparkled on the grasses and tree limbs. Intricate spider webs stretched across the game trail. Their dewy gossamer threads shone like diamonds in the morning light. She marveled at how a little spider could make such elaborate netting in one night.

Midway down, Georgia came to a halt to admire the shimmering meadow and orchard. Kitty was at her feet. "Hello, girl." She reached down to pet the feline. "Beautiful morning, isn't it?" Inhaling the clean air, Georgia knew it didn't get any better than this.

She smoothed the cat's soft fur, stroking her silky back; her underbelly glistened from the morning dew. She would miss Kitty too. "Kitty, you can't go with me anymore. Stay here and take care of Billy. He would miss you too much." Kitty purred and wrapped her tail around Georgia's arm. "Scoot off now." After the cat scampered away, Georgia felt a tinge of sadness ripple through her.

Just as she entered the orchard, Harry leaped out of the brush and grabbed her elbow. "Gotcha!" Startled, Georgia turned around to find Harry leering at her with a crooked grin. His tall, heavyset body heaved. She smelled alcohol on his breath. "Where ya goin', bea-u-ti-ful?"

"Let go of me, Harry!" Georgia wrestled her arm free. "Get away!"

"Now, Georgia, I told ya we had to talk." Harry made another grab for her, but Georgia stepped back out of reach.

"Leave, Harry!" Frantic, Georgia looked around. She was about thirty feet away from the portal. "Get out of here. You don't belong here." Georgia tried to steady her voice as she crept backward. "If you don't leave, Harry, I'll call the police."

"The police?" Harry laughed. "Hell, Georgia, there's only one cop here, and he's miles away sleeping in his car. I just passed him. Besides, the phone line is down."

"You're evil, Harry. Plain evil. You won't get any money. Not like this."

"Oh, yeah? We'll see about that. We're husband and wife, ain't we?"

"Not anymore, Harry. You know that. You left me—and Sandra. We're divorced!" Georgia's voice climbed a few decimals higher, her heart pounded. She could feel a wave of fear surfacing. Her head throbbed. *"Run!"* said a voice.

Harry made another lunge toward her. "Now, Georgia—"

With one quick movement, Georgia sidestepped Harry and took off toward the vortex. She ran like she'd never run before. Surprised at Georgia's agility, certain she had no place to go, Harry stood and watched her, amused for a moment.

It was enough of a stall to give Georgia a lead. She kept running and didn't look back. Out of breath, her heart pumping, she jumped between the trees and into the vortex. She closed her eyes. Georgia struggled to keep the fear away. She searched for a safe place in time. The next instant, she saw an image and locked on to it.

Stiff and clumsy, Harry willed himself to sprint toward Georgia. Puffing hard, he labored to catch her. With just a few paces between them, he stretched his bulky arm to grab her by the shoulder. In the split second before his rough hands touched her, Georgia vanished. Poof!

Part Seven

Billy

1995

Billy yanked down the tattered posters from the grimy front windows. Dust billowed in the stale air. He couldn't see out and was sure no one could see in. He waved his hands back and forth to clear the air and then picked up a crumpled paper towel to wipe a window. When he peered through the smudged windowpane, he could barely see Gus's old sign. He'd have to change the name of the place, of course, and have a new sign installed.

Billy moved through the interior of the old shop again and studied the antiquated layout. Long cobwebs stretched across the doorways. Old, worn tires and broken machine parts had been tossed across the pitted cement floor that was spotted with oil like a Dalmatian's coat. Rodent nests huddled in the corners amid rancid food scraps; a few outdated car parts sat on the shelves.

Effective this morning the disheveled station was no longer the legacy of Gus. Billy was the proud owner now. A few days ago, he signed the final bank papers. Standing in the middle of mayhem, he surveyed the huge cleanup job before him. *What was he getting into?*

"A very smart buy," the real estate broker assured him when they toured the property. "Great location, good road access," the agent said, and slipped into a spiel about the highway up to Oregon and Washington. "Highway 199 is attracting road travelers interested in a more scenic route these days," he said. "It's a perfect time to purchase the property. As owner, you'd get in on the early stages of the tourist trend."

Nearing the age of fifty, Billy didn't care about all that. He just wanted to own something, have a working investment, and build his long-held dream. He had the money. His grandmother left him half of her estate, and he'd saved most of the gift until now. Besides, he was finished with Orcas and island living anyway. He and his mother still owned Nana's land on Orcas, but the island was getting too crowded, and Billy long ago lost interest in the community.

Some of his friends had already moved away, including his mother. Five years ago, she retired and moved to Ashland, Oregon. Billy promised her he'd stick around Orcas to handle the estate property and be on hand just in case word of his grandmother surfaced. After his mother left, Billy drifted, living island style, but a sense of wanderlust he couldn't ignore set in one day. Something called him to hop on his Harley and cruise down the highway to find what he was looking for—a new life.

Very early in his teens, Billy had taken a liking to motorcycles. His mother hated the idea, but placated her son's obsession by offering to buy him a small moped when he was fourteen. He buzzed around the island on it until he handled the motorcycle like a master. The next year he sold the moped and upgraded to a larger, more powerful machine. Each year or two after that, Billy upgraded his bike habit until he bought his first Harley Davidson. Along the way, he discovered a natural inclination for mechanics. Absorbed in his hobby, he spent hours tinkering, learning all the intricacies and nuances of maintaining a motorcycle. On the way, he discovered an interest in restoring old bikes. This led him to believe he might, one day, like to have a commercial shop where he could specialize in cycle repair and restoration. Perhaps he'd even have a showroom for retail sales.

In the past when he could no longer set aside his yearning for boundless freedom, Billy would strap on his leathers and roar off the ferry on his Harley. He loved the thrill of road trips. For him, there was nothing better than riding on the winding roads of the backcountry. That's how he'd happened upon Gus's old garage and gas station. The minute he saw the For Sale sign, Billy knew this was his dream come true.

Right after Billy passed *Gus's Guzzlin' Gas Stop,* something told him to "go back." He circled around and stopped alongside the highway across from the old station and studied the buildings. Certain this was the place he'd imagined so long ago, he parked his bike and poked around the abandoned site. He roamed around the perimeter several times and inspected the structures. Overall, they were solid, in ill repair, but sound. After wandering around, he booted a few dented, empty pop cans away from the front door. Bolted shut, it wouldn't budge.

He brushed off the crusty front window. When he peeked into the main room of the station, the interior instantly lit up. There it was—*his showroom!*

Startled, Billy backed away from the shabby building and walked over to the old gas pumps. He fiddled with the rusty mechanisms for a few minutes to clear his thoughts. One of the pump gauges read $0.96 a gallon. "I'll be damned," he said, and chuckled. "Look!" But there wasn't a soul around to respond. In fact, he hadn't seen a car pass since he stopped.

He kicked a few rocks out of the way and ambled over to the side of the road. At the highway's edge, he stood for a few minutes, deep in thought. He looked up and down the country road. Billy swung around and took a long, discerning gaze at the station, and burst out laughing. As unkempt as the station was, Billy loved it. This *was* the place where he would start his new life, right here at Gus's old station on Highway 199. He was sure of it.

Billy exploded with excitement. "Yes!" he shouted. He pulled the For Sale sign off the wall and jammed it into his back pocket. In less than a minute, he was winding down the back road toward Crescent City to meet with the real estate company.

Twenty-four hours later, he'd signed the contract agreement to buy the old station. The agent told him the purchase would close in less than a month, and Billy would be the official owner. He was ready.

On the day he signed the final papers, Billy tucked the notarized Deed of Trust into his saddlebag, turned the key on his Harley, and headed out of Crescent City. Before he hit the freeway, his mind surged with remodeling plans. Skillfully taking the tight corners, Billy cruised on autopilot while his imagination, primed for just this moment, projected his long-held dream in vivid color. Moving faster than his Harley, an elaborate vision streamed into his thoughts.

First, he saw three shiny chrome Harleys sitting in a freshly-painted showroom. Behind the brand new motorcycles, a well-stocked mechanic stall stood ready for use. The vision rolled on and on until everything he had fantasized about for years presented itself in precise detail. Billy grew more excited as he careened up the road. He could not wait to get started.

When Billy arrived at the old station, he stopped in front for a few minutes and scanned the abandoned buildings with sonar-like vision. Within seconds, the old complex magically transformed into the remodeled structures he'd envisioned. "What the—" He blinked several times and took another look. Sure enough, the newly constructed buildings were right in front of him: the showroom, the repair shop, and even the café he'd always dreamed of owning.

Tacked onto the side of the building, the extra stall and storage area had morphed into a small country café. Here was his cozy breakfast spot that offered a menu of pancakes, waffles, bacon and eggs, with coffee—and pastries too. Every detail was as he'd imagined years ago, the day his mother told him about his inheritance.

As suddenly as the daydream manifested, it vanished, leaving Billy with a profound sense of gratitude toward his grandmother. He knew without her this wouldn't be possible. From the time he first saw Gus's station, Billy was certain his grandmother approved of his purchase, and often silently thanked her for her generosity. He could have sworn she was there the day he signed the contractual agreement at the real estate office.

Now standing in front of his new property, he said, "Thanks, Nana." The next moment, a thought came to him that it might be time to have a steady girlfriend too. "Yeah," he said. "I'd like that."

"That's the spirit!" said a familiar voice. Billy turned, half-expecting to see his grandmother behind him.

From the moment he discovered the property, he sensed her guiding presence. Sometimes he heard her voice out loud. On those occasions, Billy felt, without a doubt, she was standing beside him.

Knowing she was there, sensing her strong, loving presence, comforted him. He knew, too, she guided his every move, especially when a wave of ideas poured into his imagination at the right time. Already, she'd helped him select the exterior paint and urged him to line up a painting company. Yesterday, he hired a sign painter to work on his new sign and logo. *Billy's Place* was the name he decided upon. He liked the sound.

Time whirled by once the remodel began. Billy constantly teetered on overwhelm. As a general contractor, his hands were full. He hired a few local carpenters with enough skills to follow the architect's plans and worked alongside them during the day. After a long day of pounding nails and deciphering architectural diagrams, Billy popped open a cold beer and flipped through tool catalogs and Harley Davidson brochures.

Wanting to start small in the repair department, he ordered new tools and equipment for one mechanic stall. He'd carry a few of the more popular Harley models to test the market, and asked his lawyer to work up an application for a Harley dealership.

With so much on his mind, Billy hardly slept. Most days he trudged home exhausted. Still, his excitement grew as his dream took shape. Then one day, as if with a snap of his fingers, he looked around, astonished to find the bike shop and repair stall ready for business.

The fresh paint on the building exterior mimicked his vision so perfectly he had to walk over and touch the wall to make sure the finish was real. Inside the café, the carpenters were putting the final touches on the interior of the new restaurant. The place looked as he'd imagined years ago.

Now, he needed to find a talented baker and short-order cook for the café, but he wasn't worried. Late one night, after reviewing the last of his paperwork, his grandmother's voice popped into his head. "Don't worry, Billy, the right person will come. Run an ad in the local papers." Once again trusting Nana's guidance, he placed an ad in the Grants Pass and Crescent City papers. Today, several applications sat on Gus's old front counter, waiting for the interviews. He'd scheduled the first one for 9 a.m.

Truth be told, Billy was nervous about interviewing. He didn't know what to expect, or what was expected. Heck, he had never owned a business before, much less interviewed anyone, and he was jumpy. Billy tried to shake the feeling and took a few minutes to go over the list of questions he'd compiled. Sweat rolled down his back as he skimmed them. *Was the list too long?* He wasn't sure. He didn't want to come off too strong. Chiding himself for acting foolish, he checked his watch again—almost time.

Anxious, he glanced at the applications on the counter and wished his mother or grandmother were here to help. Billy focused his energy on the counter's familiar nicks and grooves. Just looking at its scratched glass top and scuffed sides brought him back to earth. He had kept the original front counter with the map under the glass, the rocking chair, and the old wood stove in tribute to Gus. They added a touch of local flavor and nostalgia to the place. Nana suggested it.

"Come on in," Billy said when he heard a knock on the door. He rattled some paperwork and pretended to read it as the door opened. "Have a seat," he said. Billy continued to rifle through the documents for a few seconds and then tossed them in the wire basket. "What can I do for you?" he said and stared at the applicant. The words stuck in his throat. Thunderstruck, Billy couldn't speak. In that instant, he knew the person across from him was *the one*.

"Hi, I'm Gloria Thomas. I'm here for the baker and chef interview." She smiled and handed him a typed sheet of paper. "Here's my resume."

Gaping at the typewritten words, Billy's heart skipped a few beats as he pretended to scrutinize the paper. He scarcely read Gloria's qualifications. It didn't matter. Billy already knew he'd hire her even if she couldn't cook an egg.

"I brought you some glazed donuts I baked this morning," Gloria said, and set a small paper bag on Billy's desk. "Do you have any fresh coffee?"

"Yeah!" Billy jumped up out of his chair. In his excitement, the chair flipped backward. He tripped over a chair leg and hopped over to the coffeemaker on the counter. Pretending to act nonchalant, he picked up the coffeepot and smiled, hoping she wouldn't think he was a complete klutz. "Would you like some?" he asked.

"Yes, thank you." Gloria grinned. "Black, please."

On the way back to his desk, Billy steadied the two full cups of coffee in his hands. "Well, I'll have one of those samples you brought." Billy passed Gloria her coffee, and pulled a donut out of the bag. "They look fantastic. Glazed donuts are my favorite. How did you know?" He handed her the bag. "Would you like one?"

"Oh, good! They're my favorite too. And yes, I'd love one." Gloria peeked into the bag and selected a fresh donut.

Billy took a big bite of his pastry. "Hmm. *Delicious.*" He brushed the glaze off his mouth and beamed. "You're hired!" he said and licked his lips.

Gloria nodded and gave him a warm smile. "I thought the donuts might help with the interview."

"Perfect," Billy said, and took another big bite. "Just perfect." Billy caught himself staring. He shook his head, blinked several times, and picked up the resume again. He glanced down at his questions and cleared his throat. "Uh, how did you hear about the job, Gloria…it's Gloria, right?"

"Yes."

Billy took a quick slurp of coffee to steady his nerves and reformed his question. "Uh, yes, Gloria, I mean, how did you find out about the job?"

"Oh. I saw the ad in the paper."

"Uh, ah, well, I put the ad in two papers last week. Which ad did you see?" Billy knew he sounded inane, stupid. He gushed. He couldn't help his attraction to Gloria—her name, her dimples, her fair complexion, not to mention her baking skills. It all seemed right to him. To get back on track, he shook his head again, and coughed. "Excuse me," he said.

Unruffled, Gloria ignored Billy's jittery behavior. "In the Crescent City paper, the ad…the ad caught my eye."

To break his trance, Billy jumped out of his chair. He grabbed a few paper towels and handed one to her. "Here."

"Thank you." Gloria blotted her mouth. "I'm *very* interested in the job, Mr. Swan."

"Billy," he said, waving his hand. "Call me Billy, please." He grabbed a pencil and tapped it on his forehead to stay focused. Then he put aside his list of questions. "Uh, listen, I know our location is a little out of the way. Will that be a problem, uh, Gloria?"

"No, I don't think so." Gloria smiled. "I don't live far from here, just a few miles away. The location is *very* convenient for me. I just moved here a few months ago." Gloria looked into Billy's eyes. "I came up here to stay with my mother and raise my young son." She gestured to her resume. "I'm qualified to fill the position. As you can see on my resume, I was a pastry chef in Sonoma for nine years."

"Oh, uh, yes." Raising his eyebrows, Billy perused the resume again. "Yes, I see that now. *Very* impressive." Billy crossed his arms, looked down at the remains of his donut, and over to Gloria's resume. "You make a great donut, Gloria. Would you like the job?"

"Yes. Yes, I would, very much, uh, Billy."

"It's a deal then." Billy stood up to shake hands.

"Thank you, Mr. Swan! Uh, I mean Billy." Gloria extended her hand. "You won't regret it!" They shook hands.

Blushing and relieved the interview was over, Billy grabbed a few papers. "Would you like to see the café, Gloria? The interior is almost finished," Billy said, and spewed out a progress report. "The painters are coming next week. They've installed most of the kitchen equipment. The chairs haven't come yet, but we have all the tables, linens, and tableware. They came a few days ago. We're waiting for a few more things, though."

He drew in a deep breath, opened the front door, and ushered Gloria out. "Sorry," he said, "I guess, uh, I'm excited about this. I just want you to know where we are on the project.

Construction-wise, we're almost there." Billy continued to prattle on as he escorted Gloria over to the café. When they stopped in front of the building, he pointed up at the brand new sign. "They just put the sign up yesterday. Whadda ya think?"

Gloria stared at the painted sign for a long minute. "Looks great!" she said with a nod of approval. She read the logo out loud. "*Billy's Place*," she said. "You know it kind of has a friendly quality. Comfortable. I like it." Gloria turned and looked Billy in the eye. "When do I start?"

The next day Gloria walked into *Billy's Place* at 9 a.m. sharp, bringing with her a gust of fresh energy and brisk professional efficiency. With seasoned authority, she took on all the café duties, arranging the kitchen, cooking tables, grills, pots, etc. to her liking, and then moved to the seating area, rearranging the dining tables, and unpacking the chairs when they arrived. She inventoried the linens and tableware and handled countless other details Billy had neglected. After a week under her tutelage, the café hummed with pre-opening activity.

Overjoyed and relieved that he'd hired her, Billy watched this part of his dream take shape. "Gloria, you're fantastic," Billy said as he peeked out the café window a week later. A crowd of locals, curious about the growing activity, gathered in the parking lot. "Looks like the locals are sniffing around," he said. "I better go check it out."

"Sure, but come back. We still have to talk about the opening." Gloria continued scraping the paint residue off the windowpanes as Billy walked out of the café. She sprayed the windows with cleaner and kept one eye on Billy as he shook hands with several of the men out front. For a few minutes, she stopped and observed the activity as three of the men walked to the showroom with Billy.

The men crowded around the motorcycles, pointing, gesturing, and nodding to one another. Laughing, one man leaned down to squint at the mechanical features as Billy continued his Harley sales pitch. From the looks of it, a few of the men were more than a little interested in the new machines. Gloria was sure the man leaning down was a buyer.

Billy burst into the café after the men left. "Boy! That was easy. I just made my first Harley sale." He grinned with boyhood exuberance. "He'll be coming by tomorrow with a check."

"Congratulations, Billy! I had a feeling about it," Gloria said. "Want something to eat?" She put a fresh donut on a plate and filled two cups with coffee. "Have a seat. We still need to talk about the opening."

Billy winced and sat down. "Gosh, Gloria, I don't know." He spooned some sugar into his cup. "I'm almost too excited to talk about the opening right now, but I'll try."

"Good boy." Gloria sat down, pushed some paperwork aside and then, in a business tone, laid out her plan. "Now, we'll need a month or two for the shakedown before the grand opening." Chewing on the end of a pencil, Gloria checked the list she'd made. "You still have to hire a waitress, and the menus need to be printed. And you need to think about advertising the opening. We'll need a few banners, too, offer some prizes or—I know, let's have a drawing!"

"Wow! You're good, Gloria. I hadn't thought about banners or prizes." Billy gazed out the café window toward the showroom and sighed. "You know, I might call that other applicant to see if she wants the wait job. I felt bad about canceling her interview when I hired you. What was her name?"

"Suzy." Gloria rifled through some papers and handed him Suzy's application. "Looks like she has lots of waitress experience. She lives close by too."

"Great. Thanks, Gloria. I'll call her after we finish up here."

"Okay. That's settled then. Now, back to the opening." Gloria handed Billy an old ad clipping. "Here's an idea about the opening we had a few years ago in Sonoma. It went well. We could do something similar. We need to get people up here so they can see what you've got, taste the food, and give 'em a reason to come back."

Billy scrutinized the clipping. "Good idea. Let's do it! I'd like to offer a drawing for mechanical service. Maybe feature a Harley accessory like saddlebags, leathers, something like that."

"Okay, just tell me what you want, and I'll have the newspaper work up an ad." Concentrating on her list, Gloria jiggled her pencil back and forth. "That's about it. Everything else is done. We could have a soft opening in a week or two. I'm just waiting for the food delivery. Then I can stock the pantry and order the fresh produce and dairy." Gloria got up to reach for the coffeepot. "More coffee to go with that donut?"

Billy rubbed his stomach. "Sure! But if you keep this up, I'll have to buy bigger pants. Those waffles you made yesterday hit the spot. I love waffles, how did you know?"

"Oh, you look like a waffle man." Gloria filled his cup with coffee. "Bacon and eggs too."

"Well, I guess I am." Billy blushed. He always seemed to blush in front of Gloria. "Heck, that's the reason I wanted to own a café." He chuckled to himself. "Say, bring your son over. I'd like to meet him. You know, my mother and grandmother raised me too."

"Oh, I didn't know."

"Yeah, I don't remember my father, but my grandmother came up to the islands when I was a little boy. She lived right next to us. I used to spend a lot of time with her." Billy stared out the window and fell silent.

Noticing the change in Billy's mood, Gloria's voice softened. "Oh, Billy. Is your grandmother still living?"

Billy sat quietly for a few moments. "Yes, I suppose she is, somewhere, but I don't know where. She disappeared when I was five. No one knows what happened to her."

Gloria reached over to Billy and touched his shoulder. "Oh, Billy. I'm so sorry."

"Me too." Billy patted Gloria's hand. "Thanks, Gloria. She meant a lot to me, still does. She's the reason I have this business." Billy pushed his chair back. "Well, think about bringing your son around. How old is he now?"

"Jeffrey turned six last month and starts school in the fall. He's pretty excited about it."

"I remember my first day. Mom bought me new crayons and paper, plus a notebook and satchel. I couldn't wait for school." Billy glanced outside for a few moments. "It seems like yesterday—" Billy's voice drifted off, then he perked up. "Hey," he said, "maybe Jeffery would like a short spin around the parking lot on my bike when he's here. Would that be okay?"

"Well, I guess, but only the parking lot, Billy." Gloria's voice took a stern note. "He's too young to be going out on the highway."

"I'll be careful, Gloria, I promise. No highway riding." Billy knew Gloria was protective of her son. So far, he'd asked no questions about her private life, and resolved not to unless Gloria brought up the subject. It was none of his business anyway, and he knew it. Still, he was curious. He'd wait, though, and let the story come out organically.

When it came to business, Billy didn't have to wait long for things to heat up. Local interest exploded at *Billy's Place* from the first day the café opened. At 8 a.m. that morning, half a dozen breakfast customers came in. Before noon, the place was packed. Suzy, the new waitress, was a gem. From the moment she started, she had control of the dining area. With Gloria dishing out steaming hot food by the plateful and Suzy delivering delicious cuisine with casual ease, they made a great team. After the first week, the coffers were almost full. More than pleased at closing that first Saturday, Billy beamed. "Well, ladies, it's been quite a week, hasn't it?"

"I'll say," Suzy chimed in. She was wiping down the front counter. Gloria stuck her head out of the kitchen and nodded approval too. She was doing the last of the cleaning and prepping for the Sunday brunch.

"I'm bushed," Billy said. "Let's go down to *Sullivan's* and have a beer to celebrate. Want to? Drinks on me! We deserve it after all this effort."

Gloria and Suzy cheered in unison. "Sure!"

"Okay, I'll meet you down there in about twenty minutes. I have to close up the station. Get a nice table by the river. See you two in a bit." Billy walked out of the café whistling.

Cleaning and closing up his shop at day's end was a satisfying routine for Billy. This chore seemed to put the final touches on a busy day. He liked to keep things neat and had learned the art of organization with the help of his mother. Meticulous about his tools and work area, he made sure everything was in its place for the next day. After straightening up and putting away the last of his wrenches, Billy lingered in the shop area for a few more minutes and admired what he had created. Lost in thought, giving silent thanks to his grandmother, he didn't hear the door open.

"Hello. Anyone here?"

Billy swiveled around. "Yes, in the back," he called out. "I'll be right with you." He snapped off the overhead lights and walked to the front. "How can I help you?"

"I'm looking for the owner."

"I am he," Billy joked as he wiped his hands with a fresh shop rag. Adjusting his baseball cap, he said, "I'm about ready to close up for the day. What do you need?"

"I was looking for an older gentleman, someone by the name of Gus. I understand he owned the place."

"Not anymore. I bought the place from Gus about eight months ago. He retired. I believe he's in a retirement home, but I'm not sure. Do you need to reach him?"

"Well, I'm looking for some information. I wanted to find out something he might remember, something that happened a long time ago. My name is Margot Anderson."

"Yeah, well, I have his mailing address. I can give it to you. Just a second." Billy rummaged through his rolodex and pulled out a card. "I'm sure you can reach him at this address. Need a pen?"

"No thanks, I've got one right here." Margot pulled out a thin black marker. "I'm a writer and artist. I've always got a pen or pencil." She jotted down the address in a small, tattered notebook and shoved it back into her bag. "Thanks. I appreciate this."

Margot turned to leave, then stopped and took a long, careful look around. "Say, the place looks great. It used to be a mess when Gus owned it. Well, I mean…uh, I imagine it was, uh, a mess, I mean." Margot stepped back a little. "What I mean is, uh, I drove by once. I guessed it was a shambles, you know, from the way it looked outside." Changing the subject, she asked, "Have you remodeled?"

"Yeah, we opened this week." Billy took off his baseball cap and scratched the top of his head. "We've been busy."

"I notice you have some antiques over there." Margot gestured toward Gus's rocker and the wood stove. "And this map. Looks like it's been around quite a while." She pointed to the highway map under the glass counter. Her finger traced the highway up to Grants Pass on the glass.

"Yeah, all this stuff belonged to Gus. I kept Gus's relics in honor of him and the local clientele. He owned the station for a long time. You might remember he called it *Gus's Guzzlin' Gas Stop*. They say he used to sit by the stove in that rocker and read to pass the time. I guess he read a lot when business was slow."

"Sounds like an interesting guy. I bet he has lots of stories to tell." Margot turned to leave. "Well, thanks," she said. "I won't keep you. Oh, and congratulations! The place looks super."

"Thanks. Uh, what did you say your name was again?"

"Margot. Margot Anderson," she said, and opened the door.

"Right. Well, so long, Margot." After she left, Billy walked over to the door and stood in the doorway. A nagging sensation came over him as he leaned against the doorframe and watched Margot cross the parking lot. Stopping at the edge of the highway, she turned around and waved. He waved back and then shut the door. He wasn't sure what, a vague memory, perhaps, kept gnawing at him. He couldn't help thinking he'd met Margot before, but when he turned around to take another look, she was gone.

On the way home from *Sullivan's Bar and Grill*, Billy reflected on his first official week as a business owner. Up to today, it had been quite a ride. He felt exhilarated, like he used to feel flying down the highway on his Harley. The two beers had helped, too, but he didn't care. He had enjoyed himself. The women were good company, especially Gloria. The three of them laughed and joked and saluted each other with high praise. He felt flattered and tired at the same time. It was a good tired, though.

Billy fell into bed, exhausted. His last waking thought was about Margot Anderson. He wondered what she wanted to talk to Gus about. He couldn't shake the sense he'd seen her before, *but where?*

Part Eight

Moving to the IN Road

2010

Mid-morning passed before Margot peeked out from underneath the comforter. She had struggled with the thumbnails for her project until after midnight and then dropped into a deep sleep. Groggy, Margot stretched her arms and grabbed the alarm clock: 10:30 a.m. "Dang, I sure could use another hour of sleep." She ran her fingers through her hair. "But you have too much to do, girl. Better get up." Margot groaned and rolled out of bed.

Lisel, always an early riser, had left the house hours ago. Half asleep, Margot vaguely remembered hearing her sister pack a lunch and walk out the door earlier that morning. Lisel's probably up a ladder pruning trees by now, she thought.

Margot threw on a scruffy down vest over her rumpled pajamas and padded around Lisel's petite kitchen, fixing a late breakfast. When the phone rang, its urgent ring cut through the house like a fire alarm. The piercing sound ignited a powerful force inside Margot, which shook her out of her mid-morning reverie. Jolted by the sound, she tipped over her coffee mug and spilled the hot liquid onto the counter.

A mysterious internal cogwheel, locked tight for eons, broke loose and surged inside her giving off a signal that something significant was about to happen. Margot picked up the receiver, not knowing what to expect. "Hello?"

"Hi, this is Janet Smith at Windermere in Eastsound. I'm trying to reach Margot Anderson. She left a message for me yesterday about renting the old Swan place."

Margot crossed her fingers and took a deep breath. "This is Margot."

In a brisk tone, Janet got right to the point. "Yes, well, listen, Margot, technically, the Swan property isn't available for rent. The family has put it up for sale again and I'm not sure they'd agree to a rental situation. The place is a little rundown anyway. There could be a liability problem for the owner."

Margot's heart sank. This was not what she expected. "I see," she said. But something nudged her to keep going. "Well, would you be willing to contact them to see if they might reconsider? I'm a writer and photographer, looking for a secluded place to live and work for a while. I'd like to rent the spot for short-term, you know, maybe for, uh, six months. In all likelihood, it would be less than a year."

Janet hesitated. "Hmm, well, I don't know." With a hard edge to her voice, she continued. "The place has been empty for quite a while, Margot. I'm sure there will need to be repairs before it's livable. I know there's electricity available, and the well works. Can't say for sure, but I think there might even be some firewood left—" Janet's voice trailed off.

"That sounds perfect," Margot said. "I'm *very* handy, and I don't mind roughing it. Do you, I mean, would you contact the family to see if they'd be willing to rent the property?"

"Well, I suppose."

Margot felt an internal nudge again, so she talked it up. "It's such a wonderful spot. I'd love to live there for a while. I'd keep a watch, you know, take care of the place until it sells."

"Well, I guess I can call the owner and see what he says. The property has been on and then off the market several times. Maybe they'll reconsider." Janet sighed. "It's a long shot, but I'll try it. The executor of the estate has the final say, though."

"Yes, I'm aware of that, but I appreciate you trying, Janet."

"Sure. I suppose it wouldn't hurt. I'll give the owner a call. See what he says. He lives out of state and might be out of town now too. It could take a little time to hear."

"I'm not in a hurry."

"Renting would only be temporary, you understand," Janet said, "Until the property sells."

"Oh, I know it's temporary. That's all I want. I'd appreciate it if you'd let me know as soon as you find out, either way."

"Of course."

"Thanks so much, Janet. Goodbye." Pulsating with excitement, Margot hung up the phone and sat down to finish her breakfast.

Despite her doubts, she had done what the voice had told her to do. A week after she'd made the exploratory trip on the IN Road, Margot heard the voice again. One morning, the words, *Call the agent*, echoed in her ear. At first, Margot thought she imagined it, so she ignored the words. The next day, while taking out the garbage, she heard the prompt again, only this time it sounded like a definite command. "Call the agent now," the voice said. She'd been toying with living in Georgia's trailer anyway, so Margot dialed the number and left a message.

Still, she did not know how things would turn out. She had a good feeling about it, though. Even with the agent's reticence, Margot had a distinct intuitive sense that things would work out. "Don't worry," the voice told her.

As puzzling as it was, she couldn't help but wonder about the voice, and why—just why—she had done what the voice commanded. For reasons she could not comprehend, Margot sloughed off any doubts and obeyed, trusting the voice as if it were her own. Over a lifetime, she had learned to trust her own still small voice, and now it seemed she had faith in this mysterious one too. "Just do it," she told herself.

With the writing project in its formative stages and gaining momentum, this was no time to shy away, she reasoned. "Pull up your bootstraps, girl. You can do this," she coached, and forced herself to concentrate on the reason she'd come back to Orcas—to write the book about Georgia Swan.

Although thinly developed and sketchy so far, she knew writing about Georgia Swan's mysterious disappearance had the potential to be an intriguing read. Ahead of her was plenty of tedious grunt work, though. With only a few dangling leads, she needed a firm baseline to cinch up her hypothesis and flesh out the narrative. She hoped the research photos she'd taken last week at the trailer would provide more fodder.

Margot slipped on her clothes, plucked the film from her camera, and stuffed it into her pack. "More grist for the mill," she said and swung her backpack over her shoulder. When she walked out the door, her body hummed with renewed certainty. Whistling a lively tune, she hopped in the car. "Things *will* work out," she affirmed.

The winding ten-mile drive to the village of Eastsound zipped by so fast Margot suspected she'd been teleported. Laughing about the absurdity of it, she nearly missed the turn. At the last minute, she cranked the wheel hard to the right, almost clipping the signpost. "Whoa, girl. Watch yourself," she said and slowed. Easing onto Prune Alley, she found a parking spot and headed to Ray's Pharmacy to drop her film.

Picking her way through the crowded store, she navigated the narrow aisles, left the film, and then cut across the street to the Library Park. On the far side of the small, tidy garden, Margot climbed the steep steps made of old creosote railroad ties and headed to the library.

Warm air greeted her when she opened the heavy wooden doors to the Orcas Island Library. Margot grinned. The library, with its elegant wood interior, was a comfort for her, a reassuring space with cozy alcoves, cushy chairs, and classic green reading lamps. This was her sacred space and second home now.

Perched above the village center, the library housed a small, refined collection of literature. Each time Margot stepped through the massive glass doors, she knew she was among fellow islanders hungry for literary nourishment. A busy hub, the library catered to the locals who milled around the aisles every day pursuing current periodicals and newspapers. Some gleaned new releases and old favorites from the well-stocked bookshelves. The library also touted free computer service. Margot moved toward the far wall where four tables stood, each with a computer setup for Internet use. Anyone could walk in, sign up and use an available free computer to get online for up to an hour.

Familiar with the routine by now, Margot walked over to the front counter to sign up. She scanned the list. There were several people ahead of her on the sign-up sheet and about twenty minutes to wait, so she moseyed over to the Pacific Northwest writers' collection where she hoped to find one of Georgia's three novels. Up to now, none had been available.

From the left, her hand traced the hardbound spines along the shelves. When her fingers stopped on the first of Georgia's books, she gasped. Next to it was another of Georgia's award-winning novels. Margot stared at the books for a few seconds. "Thank God," she said. "Finally!" Feeling conspicuous, wondering if anyone had heard her outburst, she slid the books out. Her hands trembled as she glanced at her watch—fifteen more minutes.

Cradling the books, she sat in one of the reading alcoves to examine the novels. Each hardbound title of Georgia's legacy comprised roughly 200 pages, scant by current publishing standards. Margot knew Georgia was known for her sparse but poignant writing style, and called by some book critics a female Hemmingway. Before her disappearance, she had also received several national book awards.

Margot leafed through the books, thinking she might ferret out a morsel, some forgotten clue regarding Georgia's disappearance. She studied the book flaps, table of contents, and a brief biography in the back of each book. There didn't seem to be anything unusual, except the bio photo, which caught her attention. The publishing house had used the same photograph of Georgia for both books. It was also the one she'd seen at a party. "Hmm, I wonder," she murmured.

Comparing both photos, she took in every detail. It was the same haunting, poetic shot—a stark black-and-white image of Georgia sitting at her writing table smoking a cigarette. The photographer caught the artistic swirl of cigarette smoke as her arm leaned against a Royal typewriter—the same typewriter Margot had seen in the trailer. Familiar, too, were the curtains in the background. In fact, the entire scene was a replica of the trailer where Margot had been in 1958. "Now we're talking," Margot whispered.

"You're next," the library attendant said as she touched Margot on the shoulder. Breaking from her semi-hypnotic state, Margot looked up at the woman. "Thanks. I'll be right there." She stretched her arms and rubbed her eyes. Closing the books, she clutched the hallowed volumes, carried them to the computer, and logged in. When the browser window popped up, she stared at the screen and tried to remember why she had come to the library. "Oh, yeah," she muttered. "Time travel." Holding her breath, Margot typed the words into the search window.

It didn't take long for the search engine to come up with a wide range of websites about time travel. Amazed at the vast trove of information on the web, Margot's face lit up at the options in front of her. *This will be easy*, she thought, and scrolled down. She picked a likely link and clicked on it.

The instant the website opened, Margot balked. "Ugh," she said. Her shoulders dropped. The dark purple background glared back at her. She felt the sickly sheen of the LCD screen on her face. The site, amateurish and poorly designed, displayed crude pixilated images of pharaohs and obelisks running down each side of the window. "Terrible," she said under her breath.

The header was ghastly too. In fancy, almost illegible script, the words read: *Going Back in Time, Secret Channeled Messages from Ancient Deities.*

Margot ignored the gross misuse of graphics and scrolled down to the smaller print. She didn't have to go too far. In tiny yellow type on a black background, the first paragraph told her what she already knew: the site was a bunch of bunk. "No," she whispered, "too woo-woo." She tried another website, but that link was just as convoluted as the first. What she wanted to find was esoteric information offering real, scientific equations or diagrams that might help her evaluate and understand time warp, time travel, and vortexes.

Though she did not have a natural inclination for science or mathematics, Margot had a fascination and aptitude for sacred geometry. In fact, early in her life, she found geometric forms and their construction so captivating she took time to study the subject under her father's tutelage, a man who had been a WWII fighter pilot and an avid student of physics. With his guidance, she learned to follow simple scientific theories and geometric diagrams, and still used the golden mean in her work. She had the knowledge to extrapolate the scientific theories she needed, if only she could find some.

Margot typed a different set of search words: time warp and then multi-dimensional travel. Scrolling through the pages, the links grew increasingly obtuse, filled with overblown verbiage about precepts and techniques she would never, ever consider. Some of them bordered on sheer fantasy; there didn't appear to be much in the way of rudimentary, factual information on time travel. *Who writes this stuff?*

Feeling pressured, Margot glanced up at the clock. Her hour was almost over. "Dang. I need more time," she said. "Definitely more than an hour." Frustrated, she logged out and trudged to the front counter to check out Georgia's two novels.

Outside the library, Margot met with sultry air. She glanced upward to overcast skies and frowned. The dark, gnarly clouds threatened rain, which reinforced her foul mood. "Go ahead, rain, dammit," she said. On cue, a few big drops splashed on top of Georgia's books. Margot dashed to the car.

On the road to Lisel's, she wondered if her sister would get Internet service so she wouldn't have to drive into Eastsound every day. It wouldn't be an easy sell. Lisel was behind the times with certain modern conveniences, especially computers. She preferred a simpler lifestyle and resisted any new electronic technology, including cell phones.

"How'd it go today?" Lisel said.

"Oh, all right, I guess." Margot sighed. "A little slow."

"How so?"

"I did some research at the library's computer this afternoon. I only had an hour on the Internet, which wasn't enough."

"Oh. That's too bad." Lisel sliced fresh cucumbers for the dinner salad. "We're having fish tonight. Okay with you?"

"Yeah." Margot sat watching her sister make the salad. "Do you think you would ever consider opting for Internet service here?"

"Why would I? I don't have a computer." Lisel pushed her glasses up on her nose.

"I know—but I do. You could get a computer. They're not that expensive anymore and now they're so much easier to use. You'd like the convenience once you saw the benefits."

"I don't know, Margot. I don't want a computer." Lisel chopped more greens for the salad. "They're not healthy. Heck, I don't even have a TV."

Certain she would get nowhere with Lisel about technology, at least tonight, Margot forewent any more electronic discussion. She felt depressed about her progress anyway, so she moved on. "I heard from a real estate agent this morning, about renting the Swan place, I mean." Her voice took on a note of optimism. "She's going to call the owners and see if they'll agree to rent the property."

"You really want to do that?"

"Absolutely." Margot shot Lisel a look of defiance. "Why not?"

"Just asking." Lisel reached for the olive oil to mix the salad dressing and ignored Margot's edginess. She didn't want an argument tonight. She wanted to relax. Her day had been full of cantankerous clients. To distract Margot and skirt any altercation, she handed Margot the corkscrew.

"I bought a nice bottle of Sauvignon Blanc. Pour us some wine, would you? I could use a glass. It's nice and warm out. Let's eat on the deck tonight. Would you set the table?"

Dinner passed quietly. Both sisters stayed within their own thoughts, evaded eye contact, and avoided confrontation. Margot, still distracted, cleaned the kitchen, and then gathered her books and backpack. She hugged Georgia's novels to hide the titles from Lisel. "I think I'll turn in early and read."

"Sure." Lisel looked up from her cluttered desk. She was going over some landscaping estimates. "See you tomorrow then."

"Okay."

Lisel put down her pencil. "Oh, uh, Margot? Listen, I do hope things work out for you, truly."

"Thanks. See you sometime tomorrow. I've got a bunch of stuff to do, but I'll be home before you. Good night."

Margot couldn't keep her mind off Billy Swan. Lying in the dark, he bounced in and out of her thoughts. She'd feigned ignorance to the real estate agent. Of course, she knew Billy was the executor of the Swan property, but wanted to hold her cards close just in case the voice was wrong. Still, she couldn't get Billy out of her thoughts.

Deep in the night, Billy came through in a dream. In this one he was much older and lived somewhere other than Orcas. Behind him in the background, she saw a forest with gigantic trees; across the road sat an old gas station. In the dream, Billy told her about his grandmother. He described how they had played together when he was a little boy; how she had told him wild, funny stories; how she always had cookies for him at her trailer, and that he missed her very much.

Just before dawn, Margot woke to a half-dark, chilly room. Her eyes fell on the eerie, languid shadows across her bed. She groped for the light switch. As was her habit now, she grabbed her notebook, and before losing the dream thread, jotted down everything she could remember. Unable to stay awake, she collapsed into a deep sleep.

When Margot's feet touched the carpet later that morning, she felt another internal rumble. This time a tremendous swell of excitement grew in her belly. There was no mistaking the enumeration: Billy *would* let her rent the trailer. She was so sure of it that she started packing and organizing her belongings. How could it be otherwise? How else would she know what happened? *She had to go there!*

Despite her enthusiasm, one thing still puzzled her. *Why was she involved? How did she fit into the picture?*

"Hello, Margot? This is Janet Smith with Windermere again."

Lighthearted, thinking this was it, Margot said, "Hi, Janet! What's up?"

"Listen, I've heard from the owners of the Swan property." Janet's voice sounded clipped and businesslike. "They're not keen on renting the place. They just want to sell it and think a renter might complicate matters."

"Oh, I see." Margot's heart sunk. She was *so sure* it would work out. Disappointed, she willed herself to maintain a neutral stance. "Would it help if I contacted the owners myself and gave them a rundown of what I envision?"

"It might help." Janet paused. "You could try."

"Great! Do you have a good address where I could reach the owners?"

"Well, normally we don't give out that information," Janet hedged, "but since the property has some unusual history and the buyer's market is down now, I think it might be all right."

"Okay! Just a second. Let me get a pen." Margot scrambled through her backpack and grabbed her pen. She flipped to a blank page in her notebook. "Sorry. Who did you say the executor was now?"

"Billy Swan. He is also part owner. You can reach him at 3329 Redwood Lane, Crescent City, California."

"Is there a zip code with that?"

"Oh, sure. It's 95531."

"Do you have a phone number as well?"

"Hmm, we're not allowed to give that out, but I bet he's in the phone book. He owns a small café and garage up Highway 199. It's called *Billy's Place.*"

"Perfect. I'll look that up." Margot snapped her notebook shut. "Thanks a lot, Janet. I'll let you know what happens.

Bye for now." Margot sprung out of her chair and, defying her middle-aged body, clicked her heels together. She couldn't wait to get to the library.

When Lisel came home that night, the house was dark and quiet. "Margot?" Lisel called down the darkened hallway. "Margot?" she said a little louder. Lisel heard a drowsy moan from the back bedroom.

"Hmm, what? *What?* I'm in bed. What time is it?"

"Just after ten o'clock," Lisel whispered. "You're in bed early. Are you feeling okay?"

"Yeah, fine. Just tired. It was a busy day." Margot turned on the lamp and squinted. She patted the comforter for her glasses. Scattered around the bed were photos, library books, and her notebooks.

Lisel sat on the corner of the bed. "What are you doing? Working on another book?"

"Uh, yeah." Margot hesitated. "I'm onto something interesting, but…I can't talk about it yet."

"Yeah, I know." Accustomed to skirting creative issues with Margot, Lisel didn't push. Her sister's work always included a time of silence and quiet deliberation. She often forbade anyone to ask about her projects when starting out, claiming that it would release the energy and ruin the effort. But Lisel couldn't help herself tonight. "What are all these pictures for?"

"The new project. I just got them developed today. I was looking at them and I guess I fell asleep."

"This one got bent." Lisel picked up a photo and tried to bend it back. "Where is this trailer?"

"At the Swan property, the place I want to rent."

"Wow, the old Airstream looks pretty shabby, Margot. Are you sure you want to live there?"

"Honestly, Lisel, don't worry," Margot snapped. "It will be fine. I can fix it up. Besides, I won't be there that long anyway, just a few months, maybe six at the outside. I don't really want to talk about this right now, okay?" She leveled her eyes at Lisel, snatched the photo from her, and collected the rest.

"Well, okay." Lisel backed out of the bedroom. "I'm hitting the hay for now. Remember, I'm leaving real early in the morning. I'll feed the horses before I go and then I'm heading off the island for a couple of days. There's a workshop I want to attend. You said you'd feed the horses while I'm gone."

"Sure, I remember. No problem. Don't worry. I'll take care of the horses. Goodnight, Lisel."

"Okay then, goodnight."

Disgruntled with Lisel's prying, Margot frowned and turned her attention to the photos. She stacked them in a neat pile, picked up the top photo, and studied the lighting and general composition. The definitive shadows and stark whites had the right ambiance she was after. Black and white photography fascinated Margot and was the main reason she had chosen that palette to document the Swan property. The spare, grainy technique enabled her to catch the tone of the fifties era and help carry the story. She wished she had salvaged the photos she'd taken in 1958, but these would work. She flipped through the photo images. Each one had sharp angles and contrasts and was professional-looking enough to soften her hard-edged demeanor. "Good job, Margot," she murmured.

After stumbling, or rather falling, into 1958 and Georgia Swan's life, Margot's original plan was to craft a short essay about Georgia's disappearance, one that mimicked the old

Newsweek article she'd found in the trailer. But as things germinated, the piece took an unexpected turn and expanded into a larger theme. Before she knew it, the story ballooned to a full-fledged book. Now in the formative stages, Margot jousted with timelines and multi-dimensions, unknown characters, and mysterious plots. She needed new, meaty threads regarding Georgia's unsolved demise, if there were any.

At first glance, she'd imagined an inquisitive, factual spin using police reports and court records, plus personal interviews. But after rethinking her brief experience with time travel, a new angle occurred to her and was now the current springboard for the story. She switched the narrative to historical fiction, focusing primarily on the mystical overtones of time travel and multi-dimensions. If there were any obvious gaps, she'd insert a few poignant black and white photos with long captions, and maybe use her illustrations with descriptive fill.

After her own baffling multi-dimensional experience, it seemed to her the actual basis for Georgia's strange, unexplained disappearance was beyond the physical realm. So far, Margot could not nail down what that meant, but the more she explored Georgia's life, the more convinced she was that something extraordinary happened—something otherworldly. These were only gut feelings and unsubstantiated. She scrambled for data about what happened to Georgia. There seemed to be little physical evidence—next to nothing.

Most of the islanders who may have remembered the incident were deceased or had moved off the island. The biggest stumbling block, however, was the fact that there was no trace of Georgia; they never recovered her body. According to all reports, she had literally disappeared. This made Margot wonder if, in fact, Georgia was dead. Was it possible she had amnesia and might still be alive, living somewhere? That was one option. *If so, where was she?*

Determined to find out, Margot turned off the light. Drained from the day, she fell into a heavy sleep. Her last waking thought was about contacting Billy Swan. *How could she convince him to rent the trailer?*

During the night, Jedediah, the majestic raven, appeared in Margot's dream. With piercing black eyes, he explained he'd come to teach her the nuances of time travel, instruct her about vortexes and wormholes, and offered to show her how to move through dimensions. An excitable flock of ravens huddled around him as he spoke.

Surrounded by Jedediah and his gang of corvids, Margot was tempted, but something held her back. Deep inside, an intuitive force warned her not to go. She shook her head. "No, I can't," she said. The giant bird tipped his head sideways, then back and forth several times, his beady eyes questioning her. It was then the dream ended.

When Margot woke the next morning, she found herself enveloped in the oddest sensation, one she'd never experienced. Shaped like a large winged creature, a part of her floated above her body, dangled by a transparent strand. Another part— her solid, three-dimensional body—lay in bed. Conscious of the two separate dimensions, she was also aware of another part, which existed between the two. This part observed the phenomenon with omnipotent detachment. With her eyes barely open, Margot glanced at her human form lying prone, and felt her winglike arms—large, black, shiny raven wings. In her mind's eye, she saw the x-ray form of the feathers and boney wing structure. As perplexing as this was, her awareness of being connected and separate at the same time left a powerful impression, one she would remember for a long time.

Margot waited for the sensation of wings to dissipate and for her body's mobility to return. After massaging her arms for a few minutes, she reached for her notebook to jot down as much of the dream as she could recall. With numb fingers she drew a loose sketch of the time portal Jedediah had shown her. Although the shape seemed familiar, she couldn't fathom where she'd seen it, or if she had.

Afterward, Margot stepped into the shower. Bracing her hands against the wall, she let the warm water run down her body until she felt the dream and the last remnant of the raven wings drain away.

Dripping wet, she wrapped a beach towel around her and stomped into the bedroom to make ready for a trip to Eastsound and another round of Internet exploration at the library. Dreading the tedium, she tried to talk herself out of going, but then she heard, "You'll find it." The voice. There it was again.

Margot shook her head. "This is spooky. Quit it," she said, and slipped into her clothes.

Still feeling zombie-like and distracted, Margot slid into the car. She took a deep breath, turned the ignition key, and leaned her head against the steering wheel. Sluggish and exhausted, as if she had done a full day's work, Margot listened to Lisel's old SUV engine run. She knew she was in a fog—a dense, mental bog. She concentrated on the engine noise, imagining the warm oil moving through the car, lubricating the metal. After a while, Margot raised her head, put the car in gear, and popped the clutch.

The car shot out of the driveway. Margot gripped the steering wheel and slammed on the brakes with both feet. "Whoa,

Nellie!" she said. The car stalled broadside in the road. In a panic, she looked around for approaching traffic. Her heart pounded as she reached for the key. Grinding the ignition, she pumped the gas until the engine coughed and sputtered, then ignited. "Thank God!" she said. With shaky hands, Margot shifted into reverse, and backed up. Her heart still pounding, Margot straightened the wheels and put the SUV in first gear. It lurched forward. The next moment, an old pickup truck honked and whizzed past. "Jesus!" she said. Gripping the steering wheel tighter, she crept forward.

Once the car gained cruising speed, Margot let out a heavy sigh and relaxed. The shock and panic of near disaster cleared her head. Everything around her brightened a few notches. With her dour mood gone, she drove down the winding road with a bizarre sense of tranquility. Strange as it was, she couldn't help but laugh. It all seemed so ludicrous! In her mind's eye, Margot relived the reckless moment as she slipped the SUV into overdrive. Good 'Ol Merlin must have known she needed to be first on the computer that morning. Margot chuckled at the thought. "You're right, old boy," she said, patting the front dash. "There's a lot to find out before I call Billy Swan."

"Billy's Place."

Margot's voice caught in her throat. "Uh, er—"

"Hello?"

"Uh, yes…uh…" Margot searched for the right words. "Oh, I'm sorry. Uh, what are your hours?"

"We open early, ma'am," the woman said, her voice cheerful. "Seven o'clock for breakfast and we close at 4 p.m. Those are our winter hours."

"Okay. And, uh, yeah, where are you located?" Stumbling over her words, Margot knew she sounded like a complete idiot, but she couldn't help it.

"Up Highway 199, ma'am, about halfway between Crescent City and Grants Pass. We're right on the highway. There's a big sign—*Billy's Place*. You can't miss us." The woman sounded upbeat but a little impatient. Margot could hear noise from the café in the background. "Can I help you with anything else? Burritos are our lunch special today. We start serving around 11:30 a.m. Come on in and join us."

"Thanks. Uh, listen, I was trying to reach Billy Swan." Margot's heart beat faster. "Is he available?"

"Billy? No, he's not here right now. Out of town until tomorrow. He just got married."

"Oh, okay. He'll be there tomorrow afternoon then?"

"Yeah, sure. They'll both be here. Can I take a message?"

"No, thanks. I'll call back." Feeling like a fool, Margot hung up. "Christ! What the hell am I doing?"

The minute Margot hung up, her energy plummeted. Her silly blunder plunged her into despair. She felt moody, like an idiot. In her turmoil, she heard her sister's voice. "Are you *sure* you want to do this, Margot?"

"No. I'm not sure, Lisel. I don't know what the hell I'm doing. Stop it."

Later that afternoon, Margot climbed out of her melancholy long enough to head to the horses. When she reached the crossroad, she pulled over to contemplate her next move. Maybe Lisel is right, she thought. Maybe she didn't want to live in an old, beat-up trailer. Why not check out Georgia's place again, just to be sure? Margot made a U-turn onto Dolphin Bay Road and headed toward the IN Road. There was enough daylight to take another look before feeding the horses.

At the turnout across from the IN Road, she parked and stared across at a new gate. The old, dilapidated gate she'd crawled through was gone. Now, a metal latch and shiny padlock secured the entryway. Tacked to the new lumber was an orange fluorescent sign that read: Posted. No Trespassing. "Holy shit," Margot said. "Who did that?"

She jumped out and inspected the blockade. There was room to squeeze through the new timbers, but she thought better of it and, instead, retrieved her camera. She took a few quick photos and huffed back to the car. Peeved about being locked out, Margot roared down Dolphin Bay Road to the horses.

Margot trudged to the hay shed in a quandary. "I can't think about this now," she said, and clipped the plastic bands around a large hay bale. She stacked two thick leaves of Timothy and hefted them over to Sol's fenced area. Sol nosed her shoulder and pawed the ground as she tossed and spread the hay. Twenty minutes rolled by as she walked back and forth from the pasture to the tiny enclosure. The rhythm and motion helped shake her angry mood, but something still troubled her. It bothered her, of course, that someone locked the gate, but that wasn't what nagged at her. *What the hell is it?*

She thought about her work and the book's burgeoning synopsis. Surely, she had enough material. After sorting the time travel research, there would be plenty of data. She shook her head. *No, that wasn't it.* Something important was missing. Margot drifted over to Cody's corral and stroked the old horse's nose as he chomped on his feed. "What is it, Cody?" she said, and slipped him a carrot. "What's missing?"

That night, Margot had another vivid dream. This time she walked down a narrow, winding highway. On the left, giant redwood trees lined the roadway. A steep cliff hugged the right side of the road; a river below gushed around a winding rocky riverbed. There was no traffic and no sound other than the roar of the water. When she walked around a long bend, she noticed several buildings less than a quarter of a mile ahead. Painted on the roof of one building was a gigantic sign that read *Gus's Guzzlin' Gas Stop.* The instant she saw the words, Margot found herself at the wayside near the station. A moment later, several logging trucks pulled in. The drivers, dressed in heavy work clothes, hopped out and greeted each other. She moved closer to listen to their conversation.

"Yep, she's a famous writer," said one man. "Gus told me the other day. That's how's I know. I don't read much myself."

"She was your wife?" said the other man.

"She's *still* my wife. We're divorced but that don't make no difference to me. I married her and as far as I'm concerned, we're still married. Yep, that's for sure."

"What are you going to do?"

"Thinking about seein' her, talk to her 'a course. I'm gonna need money. This here's my last load. They're lettin' me go. You know, Joey snitched on me. That son of a bitch."

"Yeah, I heard. Well, hey, man, sorry. Listen, uh, I got to get goin' now. Good luck."

"Sure thing, Rudy," the man said. "Hey! Don't do nothin' I wouldn't do!" He laughed and limped toward the main building.

Margot watched as Rudy plucked the logging ties on his load and climbed into the hub of the big truck. The old vehicle clanged and clattered as the engine roared out of the wayside and scattered gravel onto the highway. She saw the other man go inside.

Transported again, she landed in the back aisle of the station near the snacks and pop machine. An older man stood at the front counter ringing up a sale. "Thanks, Gus," the man said as Gus handed him a receipt. "This here's my last load, you know."

"Yeah, that's what you said, Harry. Too bad." Gus gave Harry a sly smile and picked up a paperback book. "Say, I've just finished Georgia Swan's latest. I'm done with it; you want it? It's a bestseller and I gotta tell ya, it's a goodun."

"Uh, no, Gus. I don't read much." Harry moved to the door.

"Well, you should. Sounds like this one is about *you*."

Harry stopped and turned. "What?"

"Yeah, the main character sounds *a lot* like you. The guy's got a bit of a nasty streak. A real bad ass, just like you." Gus chuckled. He could tell he had Harry at last. That son of a bitch is sweating bullets now, Gus thought. He didn't like Harry much and sure as heck didn't trust him. Not after he tried to lift some pop and chips from the shelves a while back. Gus caught him red-handed and made him pay up. After that, he didn't want Harry inside the shop, but Harry worked for the local logging company and bought gas on the company's account, so Gus *had* to tolerate him on account of business.

Gus moved to the wood stove and raised a bushy eyebrow at Harry. He couldn't figure out what in the hell Georgia Lee Swan ever saw in him.

"Well, er, gimme that book." Harry hobbled over to Gus and grunted. "Yeah, maybe, uh, I better have a look at that."

Gus handed him the book. "Okay. Here ya go. There's a few dog-eared pages and a corner torn from the cover, but all the words are there. It sure was good. Read it twice! I hear she's coming out with another one soon. Sure like her style."

Gus bent down, stoked the fire, and then sank into his rocking chair and sighed as if bone-tired. "Got me another book now." He picked up a brand new paperback and waved it at Harry. "Pulp Fiction." He opened it in the middle, cracking the spine. "Hope this one's as good as hers." Gus glanced up and nodded a dismissal. "Well, so long, Harry."

"Yeah, see ya around." Harry stormed out and slammed the door.

Margot jumped. Her eyes popped open. Certain she'd heard a door slam, she rubbed her eyes, and frowned. No. *It was the dream!* The noise came from the dream. Every ounce of her wanted to go back. She closed her eyes tight and tried to fasten onto the last sequence.

Margot drifted through the dream and filtered out what she remembered. Finally, she saw the scene, the setting, Gus and Harry's conversation, their subtexts and underlining meaning behind the conversation. Keenly aware of the subtle conflicts between Gus and Harry, she saw each man's backstory animated with translucent layers that surrounded each man and highlighted their reactions toward one another, much like a hologram or matrix the eye cannot see. There were two, possibly three—she wasn't sure—vignettes for each of them within the dream; these were layered on top of one another, synced yet running independent as if they were separate movies within a movie. Margot found the whole visualization intriguing. She had never seen a vision with so many discernible levels of meaning.

When she could no longer hold on to the dream, Margot rolled to her side and looked out the heavy glass door leading to the deck. The hour was early. In the yellowish hint of morning light, she heard the first ferry docking down at the landing. Margot switched on the table lamp and reached for her notebook and pen. She wanted to get this down. Harry and Gus. *What part did they play in all this?*

Margot puttered around Lisel's little hobbit house, sorting and packing. Her thoughts lingered on the dream. All morning she had mulled over the scenes, rewinding and reviewing again and again. She couldn't help but wonder about the significance of each multi-dimensional player. What did it mean? *Who were these people? Harry and Gus. How could she contact them?*

She had no clue how to locate Harry. He seemed like a complicated character: stubborn, irascible, and likely a bully, she speculated. His image seemed to loom large, almost foreboding. *Was he still alive?* Just thinking about him made her uncomfortable. It was no small wonder Georgia divorced him. Margot pushed the thought of him aside.

That left Gus. He was a lesser character, but he might be easier to locate and interview if he was still alive. Her guess was he'd be cooperative and might fill in some backstory too. Margot examined Gus as a candidate and wondered where he lived, what he might look like now, and what he might say.

On a hunch, she opened her notebook. Brimming with post-its, she flipped through the pages and came across a brief entry labeled GUS AND BILLY. The two paragraphs dated months ago described a dream sequence, one she'd forgotten about. According to her notes, she walked into Gus's old gas station and talked with Billy. He had given her Gus's whereabouts.

Margot read the entry again. Apparently in the dream, Billy told her Gus was alive and staying at an assisted living home somewhere in Oregon. *Addie Meedom something.* She couldn't make out the full name; her scribbled cursive was almost illegible.

"Oh, my God," she whispered. She had no memory of this. But it must have happened. She'd written it in her notebook. *How bizarre.*

Puzzled about the journal entry and the connection to her burgeoning story, Margot busied herself for another trip to the library. She'd been there so often in the last few weeks she was on a first-name basis with the librarian.

Margot tapped her forehead. "Good grief, I almost forgot—I need to call Billy." After her embarrassing conversation with the waitress, Margot waited a few days before attempting another call. "God, I hope that woman doesn't pick up."

After she dialed *Billy's Place,* a man answered, but the line was so scratchy Margot barely heard the voice. "Hello? Uh, hello?"

"Oh, sorry. Our phone doesn't seem to work this morning, just a second." There was a moment of silence and then a click. "Can you hear me now?"

"Yes. That's much better."

"*Billy's Place.* What can I do for you?"

"Well, I am looking for Billy Swan," she said. Her heart palpitated. "Is he available?"

"You're talking to him. This is Billy Swan."

"Great. Uh, I mean, hi." Margot took a deep breath and started with the script she'd rehearsed for the last few days. "My name is Margot Anderson and I'm calling from Orcas Island. I'm interested in renting your Airstream trailer on the property you have there. Would you consider that?"

"Well, uh, I don't know." Billy hesitated. "Did you say your name is Margot?"

"Yes. Yes, it's Margot. Margot Anderson."

"Well, Margot, I'm living here with my wife now and we won't be going up there much. I want to sell the property. The place is kind of rundown and we don't want to own it anymore. What is it you had in mind?"

"I understand the property is listed and will sell, Mr. Swan. I'm a writer and artist, looking for a quiet place to live temporarily, maybe six months or so while I'm working on a book." Margot glanced at her script. "The area is familiar to me. My sister was a caretaker for the property some years ago." The words spilled out of her mouth. Margot took a big gulp of air and continued, "Uh, er...I'm also handy and can take care of the trailer for you. Plus, someone living there might be good staging for a prospective buyer. Don't you think?"

"Well, you made some good points here, Margot, but I don't know. I'd rather not." Billy paused. "Tell me who your sister is again?"

"Lisel Bridges. You met her when you lived on Orcas. She was a caretaker for your mother's estate a few years back. She's been on the island for over twenty-five years."

"Lisel? Wow! Sure, I remember her. What's she doin' now?"

"The same. She's caretaking property and landscaping for several people." Margot let out a deep breath and felt hopeful for the first time.

"Does she still live near the ferry landing? I used to see her walking her dog all the time down by the store."

"Yes, she still lives there. But her dog died a few years ago." Okay, Margot thought, *I'm in!*

"Oh, that's too bad. He was a good pup. Well, Margot, I'll give your proposal some thought. Give me a few days. I want to call the real estate company and talk to them a bit more. The property belonged to my grandmother, and I've been watching over it since my mother left Orcas. We used to live there in the house, one property over from the trailer. That's our land now too. My mother bought it after my grandmother left."

"Oh. I didn't know that." This was a little white lie, but Margot couldn't help herself. "Is your mother still living?" she asked.

"Oh, yeah, she's retired now and living in Ashland, Oregon. Nice place right near town. She loves theatre."

Margot threw out another hook. "What was your grandmother's name?" she asked.

"Georgia Lee Swan. You might have heard of her. She was a best-selling author in the fifties." Billy's voice broke slightly.

"Wow. I think I've read one of her books. She was an interesting writer. Wasn't she an artist too?"

"Yes, and a good one," Billy said. "I have some of her drawings. My mother has some too. Look, Margot, I'm gonna need to cut this short. Getting a lineup of customers here."

"Oh, sure. It was so nice to talk with you, Mr. Swan. When do you think you might have an answer to this?"

"Call me Billy. Give me a few days to think about it, Margot. I'll have Janet Smith, the real estate agent, call you." Margot could hear some commotion in the background. "Listen, I've gotta go."

"Okay, bye for now, Billy…and thanks." Sighing, Margot laid down the receiver, crossed her fingers, and said a silent prayer.

It never ceased to amaze Margot how much she could accumulate in a short period. Lisel teased her about being a magnet for clutter. Sure, she had a lot of stuff, but it was all part of being an artist and writer, wasn't it? She had years of work packed away; a storage locker full of paintings, photos, art supplies, and paraphernalia, not to mention outdated electronic equipment now considered antiques.

Hefting another bulging box out to the car, she wedged the heavy cardboard container into Merlin. There. Finally. The last load was packed and ready to go to the Swan property— her new home for the next six months. Maybe longer if things went well.

Three evenings ago, Margot found Lisel's scrawled note on the kitchen counter. "Janet Smith from Windermere called and said thumbs up on renting the Swan property," the note said.

Hallelujah! She was in. There were a few stipulations on the lease, but overall, the agreement worked. According to the contract Margot needed renter's insurance, have the propane stove certified and order automatic fill. Other than that, she was free to fix up the place and move in whenever she wanted. Billy had been kind and more than generous with the rent too. He kept the monthly rent affordable and required only a nominal fee for the security deposit.

Yesterday morning Margot signed the rental agreement and paid two months' rent, plus the deposit in advance. Janet told Margot that Billy's heart had softened because his grandmother had been a writer and artist and he wanted to support her past efforts.

With the last load packed, Margot was ready to live on the IN Road. All that remained was to get settled, and then she could dig in and focus on the book again. Easy peasy.

"Addie Meedom House. How can we help you?"

"Hello. My name is Margot Anderson. I understand Gus Abbott is living there. Is he available?"

"Just a moment, please. I'll ring his suite."

"Hello." The male voice sounded gruff and hollow, as if the speaker were coming from a tunnel.

"Is this Gus Abbott?"

"Yes. Who's this?"

"Hi, Gus. My name is Margot Anderson. I'm a writer and I am doing a story about someone you might have met a long time ago. I was wondering if I could ask you a few questions."

"Well, I haven't got a lot of time." Gus coughed. "I guess you might say I haven't got too much time left. At least, that's what the doc tells me." Gus chuckled and then coughed. "What do you want again?"

"Questions. I have a few questions."

"Oh, yes. Well, give it a try. I hope I can help ya some."

"Do you have time for a brief interview? I'd love to visit you."

"Interview? What's this about?" Gus snapped. Then, in a guarded tone, he said, "Is there trouble?"

"No. No. Of course not," Margot said. "I'm writing an investigative book about Georgia Lee Swan, who was a writer and artist. You may remember her. She disappeared some years ago. That's what my book is about. I heard you met her once."

"Georgia Swan?" Gus paused. "Ya mean the writer?" He laughed. "'Course, I remember her. I might be old, but I'm not demented. Well, I *do* have a few cobwebs, but the memory's fine, at least what I can remember of it." Gus laughed at his own joke and then coughed again. "This darn emphysema. It's going to be the death of me yet." Gus chortled, then wheezed and coughed again.

Margot waited for him to stop hacking. She wasn't sure how much time the old guy had left. "Can we set up a time for the interview now? When would be convenient to come by and see you?"

"Anytime. Anytime at all," Gus said. The tenor in his voice turned jovial. "You live nearby?"

"Well, I'm up in Washington right now, but I'm planning to make a road trip down there. It'll take a few days."

"Come on down! Glad to have the company. What's this about again?"

"A book. I'm writing a book about Georgia Swan."

"Aw, yeah. Nice gal. Met her once." Gus's voice wound down to a whisper. "Her ex was a son of a bitch, though," he said.

"That's one of the things I'd like to know, Mr. Abbott. I'd like to talk about that when I get there. Would it be all right if I call you when I get to Crescent City? I think I can leave here a few days from now."

"Sure. Give me a call. I'll be waiting for you. There's not much else to do here except wait. I'm good at that. Yes siree Bob. I got a stack of books here just begging to be read."

"Thanks, Mr. Abbott. See you soon. Bye for now." Margot clicked off her cell phone and picked up a pen to make a list. She would have to ask Lisel if she could borrow her car. Merlin wouldn't make the two-day, 800-mile drive down and back, and she better get right on it too. Gus didn't sound good. The old man had to be in his late nineties.

After an expeditious trip to Crescent City and back, Margot was certain she was onto something big. The interview with Gus had gone well. His input gave the book more character and expanded Harry's barbarous personality another level. No wonder Georgia left him.

Gus, still a fascinating, intelligent guy, had an excellent memory and sense of humor, considering his age. He told her one heck of a story. "Yep, she came to the station one day, right after her ex drove up," he said. "I saw her with my own eyes standing in front of him, yelling. He acted like he couldn't see her. It was strange, you know, him not seeing her like that."

"What was she yelling? Do you remember?"

"Couldn't quite hear it. My hearing is bad, ya know. Bad then, too, but I guess it didn't matter because Harry just walked away from her. Ya know, like she wasn't there."

"Did you talk with her?"

"Oh yeah, after Harry left, she came into the station. Asked me where she was. I showed her on the map."

"Then what?"

"Well, this is where it gets stranger. She thanked me and told me she was Georgia Lee Swan, the author of the book I was reading. Then she scooted out the door before I could say anything, which is unusual, ya know, because I always have plenty to say." Gus chuckled and blushed. "It's true. I've been known to carry on a bit—" He coughed hard and blew his nose. "Sorry, can't help the cough…where was I? Oh yeah, like I said, I didn't have time to say anything to her before she skedaddled." Gus coughed again and struggled to clear his throat. "Dang," he said. "Sorry. Now what was I saying?"

"Georgia Swan hurried out the door."

"Yeah. Well, I went over to the doorway and that's when I saw her walk to the edge of the road…and disappear! She vanished right in front of my eyes." Gus clapped his hands.

"Just like that. Never saw anything like it before or since, for that matter."

"Did you see a cat nearby?"

"Cat? No, no cat." Gus took a long drink of water. "Well, wait a minute. Maybe there was a cat but…aw heck, I don't know. My memory is fading."

"Well, you're probably tired, Gus. We've been at this for a while. I should go."

"Yeah, I could use a nap. Though God knows I sleep enough as it is."

"Okay, well, thanks, Gus. I'll let you know how things go." Margot packed up her equipment and walked toward the door. "Get some rest now. I'll be in touch," she said and closed his apartment door.

When she pulled out of the assisted living residence, Margot began cataloging the triad as her vehicle moved into the long I-5 corridor. "Georgia, Harry, and Gus," she whispered. *How did it all fit together?* She'd have to think about Gus's information and listen to the interview a few more times to get a sense of things. Margot smiled. She'd struck gold.

She turned on the radio and thought about Georgia and Harry. She'd been right about Harry. He was incorrigible, a cad. According to Gus, Harry was a kleptomaniac and a liar too. "Yep, that guy could lie smiling, I tell ya! I saw him lift a few things from the store twice. The second time I called him on it, he lied, said he hadn't done it, and then hightailed it out the door without paying. That's when I called his employer to complain. I knew his days were numbered."

Margot turned off the radio and hummed a nonsensical tune to the rhythm and beat of the tires as the car rolled along the highway. Hypnotized by the long stretch of asphalt ahead, she imagined herself floating over the dark pavement toward the San Juan Islands. The miles and hours flew by.

After two days on the road, she boarded the Orcas ferry. During the hour-long crossing, exhausted yet exalted, Margot resolved to make this project superlative, a work of art and prose—Georgia's magnum opus. She was not a fatalist, but she had the distinct feeling this would be her last contribution to the literary world. She wanted the work to shine and Georgia's work revitalized. It was time.

Margot stared into the blackened horizon as the ferry chugged closer to Orcas. She thought of her sister and made a note to invite Lisel for dinner the next evening to christen her little abode. It would be her only foray into hospitality before deep diving into the abyss of writing.

Margot lit the propane oven. Delighted with her handiwork, she glanced around her refurbished living space. All her hard work had paid off. Several weeks before she left to interview Gus, Margot enmeshed herself in cleaning, painting, and general repair of the Airstream in preparation for the deep dive into Georgia's story.

After two fortuitous trips to the Exchange Thrift Store, the little trailer burgeoned with gently used household items. Stocked with an eclectic collection of kitchenware, lamps, shades, and linens, Georgia's trailer exuded the quaint, cozy style Margot savored. She knew Lisel would be pleased too.

In the trailer less than ten minutes, Lisel began to nose around the tiny space. "What's in here?" She pointed to the small closet near the entryway of the old Airstream.

"Oh, just a bunch of old stuff I found. Take a look," Margot said. It did not surprise her to see Lisel rooting around in her things. She expected it. Her sister had a strong curious streak, especially if anything seemed intriguing. When they were small children, she got into Margot's belongings and mussed them as she went. Her constant inquisitiveness had been a source of many childhood arguments.

Inside the closet, Lisel wrestled around and brought out a few items. "Looks like these are almost antiques," she said, holding up an old, tattered umbrella. The wooden handle was carved into a parrot's head. "Where did you find this?"

"Under the trailer. There was a lot of treasure down there. I pulled stuff out for days. I'm amazed no one bothered about it all these years. Most of it is not usable anymore." Margot walked over to the closet and pointed. "But look in that old suitcase. It looks like one Grandmother had, doesn't it?"

Lisel hauled out the little suitcase. "Wow, it sure does." She opened the case. "Geez, whose scarves are these?" Lisel held up several long chiffon scarves. She wrapped a faded peach colored one around her neck. "Can I have this?"

"I think they belonged to Georgia Swan, the woman who lived here, the one I'm writing about. Remember her? She disappeared, and no one knows what happened to her." Margot looked over at her sister. "Take whatever you want."

"Yeah, I remember that story—the famous writer, Sandra's mom. I worked on her estate, or Sandra's by then. Have you written anything yet?" Lisel took off the scarf, picked up another one, wrapped it around her neck, and walked over to the bathroom mirror. "Whaddya think?"

"Nice. I like that one too." Margot said, slicing up tomatoes. "I've just started writing, barely passed the note taking stage.

Next, I have to transcribe an interview I conducted with a man who met Georgia before she disappeared. Gus. The guy I went to see in Crescent City. He's in his late nineties, but still sharp, and gave me some good information. He actually met her."

"Really? I wondered why you went to Crescent City." Lisel turned her attention to the suitcase again and reached for a few more items. She shook a wrinkled silk scarf out and smoothed some creases. "I like this one too. Can I have these?"

"Sure. I won't wear them and I'm pretty sure Georgia won't either." Margot set the fresh salad on the table and sorted through the table linens. "Here," she said, handing Lisel napkins and placemats. "Can you set the table? I left the candles in the car. I'll be right back."

Lisel folded her cache of scarves and placed them near her purse. When she was about to close the suitcase, something caught her eye. To one side, she noticed the crumpled end of brown satin. Thinking it was a stray silk remnant, she pulled the end, but the fabric didn't budge. When she lifted out the scarves to take a better look, she saw a secret panel at the bottom of the suitcase. Underneath the faded satin panel was an old, worn sketchbook. Margot walked in just as Lisel was about to open the book.

"Look what I found!" Lisel's eyes blazed. "A secret compartment in the suitcase!"

"Oh, my God!" Margot rushed over to Lisel. "I've been looking for that book. Jesus! I knew it was somewhere. This is incredible!"

Lisel looked down at the sketchbook. "What is it? Is it important?"

"Good God, yes! It's Georgia Swan's notes, her book ideas, and sketches—there's all kinds of stuff in here. This is what I've been missing. Bless you, Lisel!"

"Here." Lisel handed the book to her as if it were a sacred document. "You better take it."

Margot grabbed the book. "Half my story is in here! Thank God!" Hugging the sketchbook, she twirled around, then caught herself and plopped down next to Lisel. "There's one portion that is the most important," she said, leafing through the pages. "Channeled information about time travel. Georgia experimented with time travel and planned to write a book about it." Margot smoothed the pages and pressed them open.

"How do you know that?"

"Uh, I dreamt about it, I think."

"Wow! How cosmic." Lisel leaned closer to her sister and peered at the handwritten notes. "Huh. *Notes on Neom*. Who's Neom?"

"I'm fairly certain Neom was Georgia's guide, the one who channeled information about time travel and all mystical things. She mentions him in one of her books. Oh, this is fabulous." Margot hugged the pages. "I've been looking for this. Thanks, Lisel. You just made my day *and* my life easier!"

Margot slammed the sketchbook shut and put it down. "Let's stop. I can't look at this now. I need to study it." She walked over to the kitchen counter. "I'm starving. Aren't you?"

"Well, not really. I want to look through the book some more."

"No," Margot said, her voice sharp and firm. "I need to take my time and read everything—later, when I'm alone and my stomach isn't so jumpy. Let's eat. The food is ready. Pour the wine and light the candles, will you? I'll carve the lamb. Let's celebrate!"

During the meal, Margot tried hard to contain her excitement. At last, she'd found Georgia's notebook. The missing link! She couldn't wait to explore the pages, but with Lisel there, it was impossible.

Lisel quizzed Margot throughout the meal, wanting to know more about Georgia's notebook. She peppered her sister with questions. "How did you know about the book, Margot? Can't we look at it after we eat? Come on, aren't you curious?"

Her insistence forced Margot's hand. She had to tell Lisel about the time travel incident last year. She skirted a few key details, leaving out John the mailman, little Billy, and the crawling vine gate. But Lisel kept after her sister, not satisfied with vague answers. "*If* this happened, Margot, how did you get back? I mean, if you've never time traveled before, how did you know what to do?"

"Well, uh, I don't know how I got back. It just happened. One minute I was there, the next I was here. Well, in California, that is."

Truth be told, Margot still knew little about time travel. That's why Georgia's notes were so important. She knew venturing into other dimensions was dangerous if you didn't know what you were doing. The whole thing seemed complicated and so rich with intrigue she wanted, needed, to do more research. To feel safe, she needed time to investigate—if only Georgia was here.

After Lisel left that evening, Margot stacked the dishes and settled deep into the easy chair. She focused on *Notes on Neom,* rereading the time travel entries and jotting down a few notes and questions. Then she flipped to the middle of the book, where she found a section containing diagrams and sketches by Georgia.

Georgia's rudimentary drawings of Neom's concepts reminded Margot of Michelangelo's scribbled explorations she'd seen years ago. "Find a book about Michelangelo," she wrote at the top of her notes.

It was well after midnight by the time she finished examining Georgia's sketchbook. By then, she had compiled several pages of notes, all extra research she needed to do before writing. Relieved, Margot sighed. She felt comfortable about writing a strong, definitive narrative now that she had Georgia's notes. She also sensed the book had the potential to be a blockbuster— gilt in gold.

Margot laid the sketchbook down for the night and took a few deep breaths. *Had it been by chance she'd gone back to 1958?* She was beginning to think nothing was by chance.

In her dream that night, Margot conversed with Georgia. The author sat by her old Royal typewriter and lectured about the intricacies of time travel. She warned Margot to be careful, very careful. "One could get stuck in another dimension," she said, "and find returning difficult."

According to Georgia, that was what happened to her when Harry chased her in the orchard. In her panic, she'd been suspended between dimensions. "It felt like being in *The Twilight Zone,*" she said. "A real one, not one made for TV."

Part Nine

Working on the IN Road

2010

Margot cradled her favorite coffee mug with icy fingers. The steaming cup warmed her hands as she stepped onto the old deck. Early morning light, saturated by fine mist, glistened down to the water's edge far below. Margot breathed in the chilly sea air, glad to be alive. She was about to dive into something much larger than she first imagined. Last night after finding Georgia's sketchbook, her project took a quantum leap, and the realization set Margot's mind humming. She couldn't wait to get started. A buzz ran through her body as she stared at her slippers wet with heavy dew.

Invigorated, Margot wiggled her toes in anticipation and then scanned the sky. Off to the left of the horizon, a squall, seeded by dense clouds, skimmed over the dark gray waters of Puget Sound, heading straight toward her. Whitecaps churned in the distance, ruffling the water. Clouds swirled with congested fervor. The roiling turbulence disturbed her. *Was it a sign?*

When Georgia appeared in her dream last night, her image was so clear, so striking, Margot wondered if she might still be alive. She imagined meeting Georgia, having a conversation with her in present time, and ran through a hypothetical script. *If they spoke, what would she say?*

The instant she initiated this thought, Lisel's comments barged in obliterating the dialogue. Margot's mind went momentarily blank. She knew she'd tipped the scales of sanity as far as Lisel was concerned, and as much as she tried to diminish her own doubts, she couldn't help dwelling on her sister's last words before leaving. "This sounds like a pretty crazy mission, Margot. Think about what you're doing. You're messing with something that sounds dangerous. *Please* be careful."

Tossing out the last few drops of coffee, Margot crossed the threshold into the trailer. Snippets of Georgia's handwritten comments in *Notes on Neom* popped into her mind as she dressed, reinforcing her resolve. She nodded to the sketchbook sitting on the table and reminded herself to honor Georgia's dedication and stalwart belief in Neom's sagacity. It occurred to her that Lisel was right about one thing. She was on a mission. She felt compelled to write Georgia's story. There was no backing out or reversing the project, even though it was too soon to know the outcome.

Contemplating the precipice she was about to leap from, Margot plugged in the computer and shimmied like a wet dog, shaking off any negativity clinging to her. She pushed aside

Lisel's precautionary words. Today was the day to move ahead and dispel counterproductive thoughts. With newly acquired information in her grasp, she was determined to prepare for the obvious next step: a trip back into the past. The thought came, too, that she might come face to face with Georgia Swan.

Margot couldn't pinpoint the moment she embraced traveling back in time. She suspected the unconscious decision must have happened long ago. *Hadn't that been her intent after all— to time travel?* But until last night, she'd fumbled along with little clarity. Finding Georgia's sketchbook had revamped her haphazard notion and broken things wide open.

From the moment she woke this morning, she felt consumed by the prospect of journeying to the past again, this time using conscious intent and control. Her mind spun with options. *What should she do first?*

Sitting on the edge of her seat waiting for her computer to key up, Margot poured over the sketchbook. She flipped to *Notes on Neom* to review Georgia's keen perceptions and studied her handwritten precautions about moving through time. Margot wanted to be doubly sure she had the instructions down. She had no desire to end up drifting, lost somewhere else in time, especially after Georgia's warning.

Margot's previous serendipitous jaunts into the past had been unplanned. She assumed these were sheer happenstance, directed by an outside source for some unknown reason. There was no skill involved on her part. She still didn't have the foggiest notion how she arrived at Georgia's trailer in 1958 or what predicated the adventure. But she was sure about one thing—she did not want to be stuck in a time warp. That much was clear.

Jittery from too much caffeine, Margot hunched over and grabbed her gut. Panic struck her. "What are you doing, Margot?" she groaned. She hobbled over to the daybed, rolled onto it and curled into an embryo shape. Margot closed her eyes and worked to brush away random, fearful thoughts. Searching for a realm of peace in the deepest part of her soul, Margot focused on the simplest shape she could conjure—the sphere. One by one, her apprehensions melted away as she concentrated on the circular shape and the nothingness of being.

After a few minutes, the mind chatter dissipated. Margot sighed and let her anxiety go. She stretched her body and wiggled her toes. It was then a brief paragraph from *Neom's Notes* popped into her mind's eye. The passage written in Georgia's neat handwriting clearly read: *Center yourself, free your mind, maintain a sense of confidence, don't step beyond your level of understanding and ability.*

"Okay, fine," she whispered and broke her meditative state. "That seems simple enough. Let's do it."

The next thing Margot remembered was a short blast of white light. Her eyes popped open. The surrounding space was pitch black. She couldn't see a thing. She must have slept through the afternoon. Margot shot up into a sitting position. "What time is it?" she said.

Her head ached. The pain felt like someone had hit her with a sledgehammer. Margot gasped and with both hands grabbed her pounding head. Keeping one hand on her forehead, she eased upward, feeling the wall for the light switch with the other hand. She clicked on the overhead light. Her mouth dropped open in astonishment. She braced herself against the wall. "Oh, my God," she said. "Where am I?"

To her left hung a clutch of washrags above a sink cluttered with pans. By the door stood a broom and dustpan. Next to that was an old 1930s vacuum. Standing in what looked to be a large storage closet, she murmured, "Where is this place?"

Then she heard voices.

"Harry? Harry, are you there?" a woman called out, her voice wavered. "Honey, where are you?"

"Over here, Georgia. I'm outside stacking wood. Come here."

Margot cracked open the door. She held her breath and inched toward the woman's voice. With her head still pounding, she stood in the hallway and stared in disbelief. A young woman wearing a flimsy day dress and brightly colored apron walked out of the miniscule kitchen and down a short flight of stairs to the backyard. Instinctively, Margot knew this had to be a younger Georgia Swan, and the man, a handsome and younger version of her husband, Harry.

"Harry, can you open this for me?" Georgia held up a large mason jar of canned fruit. "Mother really sealed these jars when she canned last fall. I can't get it open."

"Of course, Georgia. I'm your man, ain't I?"

"Don't say ain't, Harry. It's not a word, remember?"

"Aw, Georgia. Honey, I'm only kiddin' ya. I know that! Haven't you told me a hundred times or more?" Harry took the jar and twisted the lid off. "There ya go, sweetheart. How 'bout a little kiss before lunch?"

"Sure." Georgia smiled and gave Harry a quick peck on the lips. "I have to finish making lunch. It will be ready in just a few minutes."

"Okay, sweet pea. Gimme a whistle when it's done."

Frantic, unable to figure out her next move, Margot ducked underneath the hall stairwell into the shadows. She did not know if she was dreaming or if this was, in fact, real. Regardless, she didn't want to be seen. Barely breathing, Margot studied Georgia as she moved around the small kitchen preparing the meal.

Huddled in the dark, she watched Georgia as she brought the dinnerware into the dining area to set the table. Margot estimated Georgia to be in her late teens or early twenties, a beautiful young woman with poise and grace beyond her years. From the looks of the tableware, linens, and candles, she'd prepared lunch for some kind of special occasion.

Georgia stepped back to admire her handiwork. Satisfied, she took off her apron and walked over to the back door. "Harry, honey!" she called. "Time for lunch!"

With an air of youthful confidence, Harry strode into the house. Ruggedly handsome, shirtsleeves rolled up past his elbows, he brushed the wood shavings from his vest. "There, doll, you should have enough wood for the stove while I'm gone," he said, and went over to the kitchen sink to wash his hands. "Summer's just about here anyway. You won't need much. 'Sides, I'll only be gone a few days. Before you know it, I'll be back." Harry sat down and surveyed the table. "Saaay, this looks great! Is this a special occasion?"

"Maybe," Georgia said, smiling. "It is Sunday, you know. Would you like some roast beef, Harry?" Georgia handed him a large platter filled with carved meat.

"Baby, this looks great." Harry tucked a napkin into his shirt collar and piled meat onto his plate. "Hand me the gravy and potatoes, will you, doll?"

Margot stared in silence as Harry and Georgia ate, but she couldn't hear them. Mindful of staying in the shadows, she crept closer to the dining room to hear their conversation.

"Harry, I have something *very* special to say." Georgia put down her fork and clasped her hands together.

"Yeah, baby, what's up?" Harry grabbed the butter dish and buttered another corn on the cob. "This sure tastes good, Georgia."

"Harry, I've been thinking—"

"Yeah? What about, baby?" Harry chomped on the corn.

"Well," Georgia said and paused. "Well, honey, I've been thinking we're going to need a bigger place. Something with an extra bedroom." Georgia smiled slightly. She looked over at Harry and blushed.

"What? We don't need a bigger house, Georgia—" Harry stared at her as if not comprehending her words. "Uh, what? What are you saying, Georgia?"

"Well—"

Harry cocked his head. Then things clicked. "Are you telling me you're gonna have a *kid*?"

Georgia grinned broadly and nodded her head. "Yes, we are. Isn't it wonderful?"

Harry gulped. His face went ashen. He slammed down his corn and looked away. "Oh, Jesus! Not now." When he turned back to Georgia, his face was bright red. "I'm just startin' out, Georgia!" The timber in his voice amplified. "We can't afford another place, not now. I just made a big investment in the stock market. Christ!"

"But Harry—"

"You can't have a baby now, Georgia. I won't allow it. I don't have the cash. You should have asked me. I'm your husband, ain't I?" Harry ripped off his napkin and stood up. "Damn it, Georgia, not now."

"But Harry—" Georgia's voice faltered. "I...I thought you'd be pleased. Happy about the baby."

"Well, I'm not." Harry puffed his chest out and unbuttoned his collar. "I mean, maybe later. But not now, Georgia, we're broke." Harry turned and yanked his jacket off the hook. "I'm goin' out," he said and stamped out of the room. Georgia jumped when the door slammed. She put down her head and sobbed.

Margot was so caught up in the scene that without thinking, she stepped forward into the dining room near Georgia, who was still crying. She wanted to comfort her. As Margot reached out to touch her shoulder, Georgia glanced up. She wiped her tears and turned toward Margot. Realizing her mistake, Margot shrank back, but to her surprise, Georgia acted as if she had not seen her. She stood up, walked past Margot into the kitchen, and dialed the phone.

Loud, chaotic chirping noises woke Margot from a dense, meditative state. She moaned and turned her body. Margot tried to rub her eyes but could hardly lift her arms so she let them collapse on the daybed and rotated onto her back. Not fully conscious, she kept her eyes shut and groaned. *Why am I so stiff?*

Despite her grogginess and physical impairment, Margot's internal world throbbed. Patterns of sound vibrated inside her head like clanging bells. Florescent green and purple colors swirled toward her from a great distance, moving closer and closer until a merry-go-round of psychedelic colors filled her head. Blinded by the brilliant, spinning kaleidoscope, she wanted to blink, but instead squeezed her eyes tighter.

Seconds later, vague impressions of faces she didn't recognize faded in and out of the internal light show. Details of an old memory filtered in and then receded like an ocean wave. She felt odd, disjointed, and fearful. Yet deep within her, Margot sensed a circle of calm. Surrounding the center of peace was a mishmash of irrational thoughts that pounded at her fragile countenance, frightening and confusing her. *Fucking fearmongers,* she thought.

Through the chaos, she felt the left part of her brain search for a reason—an antidote to combat the strange occurrence. *Why was she feeling this way?* No sooner had the thought left than the light show inside her head dimmed, and a vision of a young, tearful Georgia Swan walked through her mind's eye.

Of course! She'd done it. She'd gone back in time!

With a start, Margot opened her eyes. The immediate space around her resembled a dull blur, having no definitive lines or dimensions. She lay still for a few minutes to get her bearings. As far as she could tell, her body was suspended in a sort of void, a no-man's-land, stretched between timelines, as if she were stuck in the middle of the past and the present, similar to the foggy celluloid between photographic frames. *Where am I? What decade is it?*

"Get up." The harshness of her voice surprised Margot but she obeyed the command. When she swung her legs off the daybed, the room cleared, sharpening into a crisp, recognizable dimension. Margot checked her whereabouts. Her eyes roamed around Georgia's trailer and landed on her alarm clock. The large Helvetica numerals glowed 10 a.m. Without thinking, she grabbed her cellphone and flipped it open. 2010. "Thank God," she said.

Numb and achy, she spread her hands and fingers wide, inspecting each digit. She stretched her arms over her head, wiggled her fingers and toes, and extended her body upward. Margot leaned over and touched the floor. She took a deep breath and walked over to the kitchen nook to switch on her computer. When she heard the familiar start-up gong of her laptop, she let out a long sigh of relief. "Okay. I'm back."

On the way to Eastsound two days later, the rain pelted Merlin as if punishing the old rig for having the audacity to be on the road. The windshield wipers squeaked in an erratic rhythm. Large maple leaves and broken fur boughs lay scattered along the slick pavement forcing Margot to drive slowly. She didn't care. The storm and windy turmoil matched her mood. With a tight grip on the steering wheel, she weaved the SUV through the falling debris.

Margot couldn't stop thinking of her recent trip back in time. The more she maneuvered through the storm rubble, the more confused and disoriented she felt. Once again, she questioned reality. *Was any of what happened real? Was Georgia real? What about Harry?*

Feeling mixed up and topsy-turvy, Margot constantly checked her watch, unsure what day, or time—or year—it was. She knew she teetered on the brink of disaster and had nearly lost her grasp of the physical plane. *Had she lost her mind too?*

Yesterday, the voice said, "Thane will help."

"Okay," she said. "I'll call him." This casual response to an unknown, invisible entity seemed almost normal now. As each day passed, Margot found herself more and more comfortable with the voice. "Yes, maybe talking to Thane will help," she said, and searched for his number.

The rain stopped and the wind mellowed as the SUV crept into Eastsound. A patch of sky cleared. Across Fishing Bay, a large shaft of sunlight cut through thick, gray clouds. When she passed the quaint white Episcopal Church, Margot imagined a giant, luminous hand reaching through the dark clouds and lifting her out of the doldrums into bright light. "That's what I need," she said. "A lift."

Recommended by one of Lisel's friends, Thane Wisen, a well-known spiritual channel and healer on Orcas, was an authority on psychic abilities; someone who studied time dimensions and other phenomenon. Headed to his office this morning, Margot hoped he'd lend insight to her predicament, reassure her, and smooth her frayed nerves. Anything would help, she thought as she pulled into the parking lot.

Thane's office looked unexpectedly homogenized, plain, and sterile compared to what Margot thought she'd find. She had envisioned tie-dyed drapes, exotic feathers, incense, and candles burning. But when Margot walked through the door into the small foyer, she found two straight back chairs and a side table piled with periodicals. There was no receptionist, so Margot sat in the diminutive waiting room and glanced through a New Age magazine.

Nervous, thumbing through the pages, Margot heard murmuring behind the closed door. *What are they saying? Was everyone having psychic experiences these days?* She chuckled at the thought and conjectured about the conversation on the other side of the door. Several hypotheses flashed through her mind, then she froze. *Oh, God, what will I say? What will he say?*

"You're just nervous," the voice said.

Margot jumped. She stopped her mental fidgeting and whispered, "You're right, guess I am." It was then Margot realized she had entered a new phase with the voice. They had segued into back and forth conversations now. Margot threw out another line of dialogue. "Well, I'm glad we're having this conversation." But she did not hear a response. "Are you there?" she whispered into the tiny room.

The doorknob to the private office turned. When the door opened, Margot closed the magazine and sat up straight. A man in his late thirties walked out. To her surprise, he looked refreshed and somewhat relieved. Without a word, the man nodded to her and went out the entrance.

Within minutes, another man came out. "Hello," he said, and stepped into the reception area. "Sorry to keep you waiting. I'm Thane Wisen." Making eye contact, he offered Margot his hand. "Please come in."

Thane's eyes were so clear, so ice blue, that Margot gasped as she shook his hand. She had never seen eyes cast with that color or with such loving intensity. His gaze bored a hole right through the dark cloud surrounding her.

Thane ushered Margot into the small office. "Can I get you something? Tea? Water?"

"No. No, thank you. I'm fine," Margot said. "Just a little nervous."

"Please have a seat."

Margot appraised the room. There were two overstuffed upholstered chairs positioned four feet across from each other. A Queen Anne table stood next to one chair. On the small antique table sat a decanter of water, several glasses, and a box of tissue.

Thane motioned for her to sit in the chair nearest the table. Off to the side of the companion chair, Thane's chair, was a low wooden table with a tape recorder and a few tapes stacked next to it. The room's ambience had a pleasant, comfortable feel. Margot relaxed as she sat in the cozy chair.

"Is this your first reading?"

Margot nodded. "Yes." Her face turned several shades of red.

"Don't worry," Thane said. "There's nothing that will harm you here."

Still anxious, Margot squirmed. "Thank you," she said, and slid farther into the cushioned chair. The brash part of her wanted to rush forward and prod Thane with questions; another part was ready to leap out the door. But she pressed her lips together and made herself sit still. Thane's calm demeanor helped Margot relax and within minutes, she felt at ease.

Thane smiled as his sparkling eyes gently probed Margot's auric field. "What can I do for you today?" he said.

"Well, uh, I think I need some help." Margot let out a long sigh; her body slumped. "I've been having some psychic experiences I don't understand. Someone told me you were an expert in this kind of thing and I, uh, well, I need some clarity." Margot didn't want to say too much. She didn't want to give him any sign that might suggest she was having a psychotic break, even though she thought she was.

"I do what I can," Thane said. "Let's try to see what I can do for you."

"Okay."

"First, let me ask if you want this session recorded? I have extra blank tapes if you do."

"Well, I guess."

"Some clients like to hear the session later to reflect upon it. It is unnecessary, but if you want, I can tape the reading."

"Sure. I'd like that. Thank you."

"Very well." Thane slipped a fresh tape into the recorder. "Please say your full name out loud three times. I need to hear the vibration and that will help me tune into your energy and present situation. Rest your hands lightly on your legs. Please do not fold your hands together. Now we will start. If you will, please repeat your name three times." Thane closed his eyes, sat back, and waited.

"All right." Margot coughed, cleared her throat, and laid her hands on her thighs. She had a tremendous urge to bolt out of the session. The reading felt too intimate. She was dangling on the edge of her sanity. *What on earth was she doing?*

Her throat clogged before she could say a word. Margot grabbed a tissue and blew her nose, then concentrated on Thane's face. Warmth washed over her and enveloped her in a renewed sense of calm. She made a concerted effort to keep her hands quiet. In a weak voice she said, "Margot Lee Anderson. Margot Lee Anderson. Margot Lee Anderson."

The next instant, Thane went into a deep trance. The air surrounding him softened. His rugged, chiseled face smoothed. A penumbra of blue light formed around his head. "We are ready for your questions now," he said.

The inflection of his voice startled Margot with its robust strangeness. His general mannerisms seemed different too. He appeared more elevated and androgynous, making her wonder who was talking.

Thane opened his ice blue eyes and said, "Proceed."

"Uh, well, uh." Margot fidgeted and let out a short cough. "Uh, well, right now I'm working on a writing project about a woman who disappeared from the island fifty years ago." Sweat rolled down her armpits. She looked at her hands. They were shaking. She tried not to clasp them.

"I'm, uh, I've been having all kinds of strange experiences. Vivid dreams, visitations, and visions—you name it. I think I've been, uh, I've been—" Margot took a deep breath. In quick succession, the words fell out. "Well, I think I've been traveling through time too. I need help. I'm very confused." Her voice broke. A tear streaked down her face. "I don't understand what is happening to me."

There was a long pause, and then Thane said, "Yes. We see you now. Please say the woman's name."

"The woman?"

"Yes, the woman you are writing about."

"Oh." Margot hesitated. She couldn't form the words. "Uh, Georgia Swan. Georgia Lee Swan."

Still uneasy, Margot wanted to clasp her hands together and run out of the room. Then she heard, "Yes. We see her. She is in a wormhole, a tunnel between…between what you call time dimensions. We see her moving back and forth, in and out of time, through various stratospheres. She says she wants to talk to you. She is asking for that."

"Well, yes." Margot paused. "I want to talk to her too. How do I do that?"

"She has been communicating with you, but you are unaware of her." Thane turned his head at an angle and put his hand up to his ear, as if to amplify his hearing. "You call it the voice, but it is she who is talking to you. She wants a clearer connection with you. She says she has many things to discuss."

"Sure. Okay, how do we do that?" Margot twisted in her chair. Sweat rolled down her back. "I don't know how…how do I do that and keep myself sane at the same time? All of this is making me crazy, crazier than I already am!" Margot laughed.

"One moment, please." Thane closed his eyes. Poised as if listening, he said, "Yes. We can help you with that. Do you know about automatic writing?"

"Hmm, yeah, sure. Well, sort of—"

"We recommend you communicate with her using that method."

"But…but isn't that a little too elementary?" Margot said. "I mean, if I already hear her voice—"

"This practice encourages your own voice and opens a channel within. We recommend you write at the same time each day. Write what you hear inside your head. She will contact you through that method until you are at ease, more comfortable communicating with someone from the other side. This will help create a repertoire between the two of you and give you a written and dated reference point for your research and eventual book. Do you understand?"

"Yes."

"Will there be anything else?"

"Yes." Margot sat for a moment working on her question. "Is this real? I mean, sometimes, I feel like I'm going crazy. What can I do?"

"Yes, we see your confusion. It is real, but not a three-dimensional reality—the reality you are familiar with. You are confused because you are not yet familiar with working in other dimensions on a conscious level. We also see you have gone into other dimensions without making the proper preparations. We recommend you do grounding exercises. This will help you stay centered so you can handle contact with other dimensional beings. We recommend you do grounding and breathing exercises *every day* to stay focused and in your earth body. Do you understand?"

"Yes. All right. I know what grounding is…and…and I certainly know how to breathe—" Margot felt sheepish. She had done none of her grounding work or yoga breath practice for weeks. With the excitement of the last few months, she had neglected the very thing that kept her sane. Was that all she needed to do? *Was it that simple?*

"Do you have any further questions?"

Margot thought for a moment. "I do. One," she said. "Uh, I'm not sure how to phrase this, but—" Margot held her breath. "Well," she said exhaling. "I feel like Georgia is contacting me for a reason. What does she want from me? Why is she contacting *me*? Why am I involved?" This was the most pertinent question she wanted answered. *Why her? Why not someone else?* "I need to know."

Thane closed his eyes. It appeared to Margot he was listening to an elaborate conversation from somewhere above the ceiling. When Thane opened his eyes, he said, "She says you are connected to each other, and that is why she contacted you. She says she wants to help you tell her story—the *real* story—and will explain everything once you are better able to communicate with each other. That is all."

Part Ten

Meeting Georgia

2012

"He wasn't *always* an asshole, you know."

Margot froze. She was standing in her tiny kitchen preparing dinner for Lisel, whom she expected within the hour. Unsure if she'd heard a voice or if it was more of the incessant mind chatter that had bombarded her all day, Margot cocked her head. "What?"

Margot sensed an unmistakable presence behind her. She grasped her kitchen knife tighter. She didn't want to turn around. Instead, she said, "What did you say?"

"Yes, at first I thought he was wonderful. It was the baby and going broke, you know, after the crash, that changed him."

Margot loosened her hold on the knife and slowly pivoted. She hadn't expected it to start this way, meeting Georgia face-to-face. But there she was—sitting in the easy chair across the room, relaxed, smoking a cigarette. Centered within an etheric orb of diffused light, Georgia smiled and nodded. "Hello, Margot."

Margot caught her breath. "Hello," she whispered. She couldn't help but gawk. The enormous sphere surrounding Georgia vibrated with a peculiar frequency, as if jettisoned from another world, another universe; each molecule, every particle within the space, shimmered and quivered. Encircled by this energy source, Georgia, the chair, and the surrounding space pulsated. In fact, everything, even the cigarette smoke, throbbed. Margot watched, spellbound. She had read about such things but had never seen the phenomenon.

The next moment, Georgia exhaled a stream of cigarette smoke toward Margot, and the gyration stopped. "Yes, Harry was a great husband at first. Very romantic and loving."

Wispy bits of blue smoke spiraled around Georgia's head and then evaporated into the ethers. Strange, Margot thought, I can't smell the cigarette smoke. Unable to speak, she continued to gape while Georgia stubbed out her cigarette in the plant saucer next to the chair. "You've done a marvelous job fixing up the place," Georgia said. "I liked living here."

Clinging to the counter, Margot stood transfixed, not knowing what to do or say next; all she could do was gaze at Georgia in the luminescent orb. Finally, she said, "Is this real?"

"Yes, in a sense, this is real. However, if you're comparing it to your basic third-dimensional reality, then it is not— really real." Georgia chuckled. When she rose out of the chair, the energy field around her dissipated. "Honestly, Margot, you could not see me this clearly if we were *just* in the third dimension." Georgia fluffed the chair pillow and walked over to the bookshelf. "You have a nice selection of books. I see mine are here too."

Margot's eyes followed Georgia to the bookshelf. "Yes. Yes, well, uh, where am I then? I mean, if I'm not *just* in the third dimension, where am I? And where are you?"

Trying to stabilize her thinking, Margot struggled to underplay her emotions, but she couldn't help feeling a firestorm erupting inside her. Her stomach jumped. She felt dizzy and afraid. Meanwhile, her left brain searched for a logical explanation, something that would make sense. No, it can't be true, she wanted to say, but instead she heard herself say, "You look so real."

"Yes, of course, my dear, I am real! I'm as real as you are. Like I said, it's just a matter of dimension—the perception—you're in. Everything you can think of is real. It's difficult at first, taking it all in. What to believe and what not to believe. Believe me, I know." Delighted with her choice of words, Georgia giggled like a little girl. "Take that space over there, for instance." She pointed to the chair where she'd been sitting. "The area around the chair transformed into a higher order of molecules in order to create an entryway for me, enabling me to download and appear on a lower frequency—your three-dimensional reality. That's why it looked more vibrant and alive when I came in."

"H–how…how did you get here in…in that thing?" Margot stuttered. "I mean, well, er, is that a *spaceship*?"

"That?" Georgia looked behind her. "Oh, no. That's just the remnants of a portal, an energy field. It doesn't last long, just long enough to travel through."

"Oh." Margot didn't quite get the full significance of Georgia's explanation, but the idea intrigued her. For a minute she tried to imagine going through a dimensional portal, then she caught herself. *No, wait, am I making all this up?*

"No, Margot, you haven't made it up. You aren't delusional, for heaven's sake," Georgia said. "I'm as real as you are, just in a different molecular configuration. *And* let me remind you why I've come. I'm here to help you with the book you're writing, just as Thane indicated. Remember?" Georgia sat down again and lit another cigarette. After taking a deep inhale, she said, "Shall we start?"

Margot stood motionless. "I guess."

"Good. Now first, I like your idea, but you've got some facts wrong." Georgia looked into Margot's eyes. "I want to set the record straight—straight as a pin."

"Facts? I'm writing fiction. I don't know what you mean." Trying to calm down, Margot exhaled. Suddenly tired and confused, she said, "Can you explain?"

"Of course." Georgia sat back and took a draw on her cigarette.

Woozy, feeling out of her element, Margot said, "I...I don't feel well." She massaged her forehead and limped over to the daybed, then collapsed face down onto it.

"Do try to relax, dear." Georgia inhaled and blew out a long gust of smoke. "Gawd, I always loved to smoke. You can do it in the ethers without worrying about getting cancer. Did you know that?"

In slow motion, Margot rolled on her side toward Georgia. She still couldn't believe this was happening. "Uh, no. I didn't."

"Well, FYI, you can." Georgia took another drag off her cigarette.

Margot watched the smoke vanish as if it had never existed, which technically, Margot knew, in three-dimensional reality, it didn't. Heck, she couldn't even smell the smoke.

"Let's see now. Yes, I was telling you about Harry," Georgia said, striking a thoughtful pose. "Back then I would have described him as *gallant*." Georgia elongated the word, making it sound more like gul-lawnt. "When I was a young girl, I had been quite taken with him and all his promises. Yes, I guess that was the *real* problem between us. Life with Harry turned out to be *only* promises. I was innocent then, too, but soon hard reality set in after I became pregnant. Harry didn't like that idea. Nope. Not one bit. He got mad, you see, said the timing was off, threatened to leave me and then—" Georgia paused. "And then he did."

Margot shook her head. Her throat felt dry and scratchy. "I…I know," she said, barely able to cough out the words.

"I know you know, dear." Georgia stamped out her cigarette and stood up. "I *did* see you that afternoon, but I was so stunned, so hurt, I couldn't think. So, I pretended I didn't see you and called my mother instead. She came right over."

Georgia brushed a few ashes off her shimmering garment. Still glowing, she walked over to the window. "He came here, you know," she said, looking toward the small orchard. "When I found him here. *Right here* in this very trailer," Georgia pointed to the floor, "I could tell nothing had changed. Neom had warned me about him, and he was right. Harry *was* still angry—and broke too. He acted so distressed that I thought he might hurt me." Georgia twirled around and looked at Margot. "But I'm getting ahead of myself."

She picked up a small crystal objet d'art on the table and looked at it. "They interviewed him after my disappearance, but nothing came from it. The local paper posted a small article about him, a photo too. Look it up. You'll see." Georgia put down the sculpture piece. "I'm glad you're here, Margot," she said. "I'm glad it's *you* that will tell my story because the authentic story needs telling. You're an important part of it, you know." Georgia smiled and waved. "Tootle-do," she said. Then her body faded, and in seconds, she was gone.

Speechless and stunned by Georgia's sudden departure, Margot's mouth hung open as she watched Georgia disappear into the ethers. She went over to the easy chair and looked at the planter where Georgia had put out her cigarettes. There was nothing in the saucer. No ashes. No cigarette stubs. Nothing.

"Good God," she said. "Did this happen?" Afraid she was losing her grip again, Margot didn't dare answer her rhetorical question, but went into the bathroom and splashed cold water on her face. Her heart quickened and beat erratically. She took several deep breaths, sat down, and tapped her sternum. She continued tapping until her heartbeat came back to normal.

Still on edge, Margot leaned back and took a few more breaths. Had she imagined Georgia sitting here? *What about the cigarettes, her smoking, for God's sake? Why couldn't she smell the smoke? Where are the butts?*

Once her heart slowed to a steady pace, Margot picked up the objet d'art Georgia held only minutes before. She grasped it and thought about her step back in time the previous year. How mind-blowing that had been! At first she hadn't believed something like that was possible, but yet, it had happened. Or at least she thought so. Margot clasped the art piece tighter and with firm resolve said, "Yes. Yes, it *did* happen. I know it did!"

It was then she heard footsteps on the deck. "Shit!" Margot jumped up. "It's Lisel! Jesus, I forgot!" In that instant, she vowed to keep Georgia's visit a secret and not jinx things. Besides, Margot rationalized, Lisel wouldn't believe her anyway. *She could hardly believe it.* Georgia's visitation was so surreal, so incredible she might not be able to keep quiet. Tapping her pounding heart, Margot opened the door.

"Heeeyy," Lisel said, holding up a gift-wrapped bottle. "I brought you something!"

"Wh–what is it?" Margot cleared her throat. "I mean, how did you know?"

"Know what?" Lisel gave her sister a puzzled look. "You look weird. Are you okay?"

"Th–that we needed something to drink! And yes, I'm fine." Margot managed a smile and reached out to give her sister a big hug. "Good to see you," she said.

"Well, you *said* we were celebrating something, but you wouldn't tell me what over the phone. Here." Lisel handed her the package. "It's a nice bottle of red wine. Go ahead. Open it. Looks like you could use a glass." She threw down her keys and shrugged off her coat. "What's the big mystery anyway? What *are* we celebrating?"

"Huh?" Margot took the wine and with a blank expression turned toward the easy chair where not five minutes ago Georgia sat. "Oh, right. Yes. Yes, we are celebrating." Margot brushed her fingers over the Beringer wine label, an excellent vineyard in Northern California. "Life." Margot grinned at Lisel. "That's what we're celebrating." She reached for the corkscrew. "To life. Long live us!"

Several days later, Margot found herself at the Orcas Library again. "Well, Margot, hello," said Beth, the head librarian. "We haven't seen you here for quite a while. We've missed you."

"Thanks, Beth. I got hooked up with DSL service so I'm busy at home now. But I'm here today to do special research for my writing project. I need to look up some stuff in your archives."

"Be my guest." Beth gestured toward the research computer. "The station is empty."

"Thanks. Gotta go. Sorry," she said and waved. Margot liked Beth. The librarian had been very helpful months ago, and she enjoyed their interaction, but there wasn't time today. Without another word, Margot logged onto the research computer and began searching the newspaper archives.

Margot hated research. Although a necessary aspect for any writing project, scrolling through old files was a lesson in tedium for her and took a concerted effort on her part to forage through dusty, forgotten material. But today was different. Egged on by a well-developed, persistent sense of curiosity, she flipped through the microfilm, eager to find the year 1958. "There it is," she said. The article. She checked the date— one week after Georgia disappeared.

The short piece landed on page five of *The Orcas Islander* with a photo of Harry embedded within the article, just as Georgia had indicated. Margot scrutinized the image. Harry looked nothing like he had when she first saw him. He was no longer the handsome young man with a powerful jaw. The news photo showed a much older, balding, somewhat stocky guy; and from the looks of it, the years had been unkind to him. His facial expression was one of a broken man, someone who might be desperate and demanding enough to threaten Georgia—someone who might hurt her. "Wow," whispered Margot, "what the hell did she see in him?" She took some notes and jotted down several questions to ask Georgia the next time they talked, if there was a next time.

Intent on cross-referencing as much as possible, Margot enlarged the news story on the screen and perused the article.

Scanning the blurry type for points of interest, she scribbled a few more notes. According to the reporter, the police questioned Harry, and at first, considered him a person of interest just as Georgia had said. Since they found no clues or physical body, the authorities had little to go on, so they released Harry. At the end of the story, the reporter coined Georgia's disappearance as an island mystery.

Margot continued scrolling through more editions, hoping for more information. That's when she found a short news clip written several months later. In the follow-up article, Georgia's daughter, Sandra, insisted that her mother was merely missing, not deceased, and was quoted as saying she was sure her long-lost father, Harry Swan, had nothing to do with her mother's disappearance. Since the local police investigation had no clear evidence, the authorities determined there was no foul play, and the investigation fell away. Margot searched further through the archives, but found nothing more about Georgia. She hit the print button for a hard copy and logged out.

Driving home, Margot found it hard to concentrate on the road. On autopilot, her mind reviewed the newspaper articles. "Georgia was right," she said, swerving around some road debris. The clippings had filled in a few blanks. Harry *had* come to Orcas just as Georgia revealed. Margot thought it might have been Gus who told Harry where Georgia lived. The news snippets also validated Georgia's appearance in the trailer. She had not been hallucinating. The visitation had been real.

But what about Harry? After he left Orcas, what happened to him? Where did he go? Had he disappeared too? *Was she missing something?*

She mulled this over and realized she was more confused than ever. "I need to sort things out. I need a timeline—an outline—something," she said. Laughing at her outburst, she downshifted Merlin and pulled into the turnout. What an idea! She had been in such turmoil she'd sidestepped a basic, fundamental writing approach to any story: the outline. *What a dope.*

Later, as night set in and the world around her little trailer grew dark, Margot sat at the kitchen nook underneath the bright beam of the hanging lamp and labored on a timeline, the precursor to her outline. On a long, narrow scrap of poster board, she drew a straight thin line across the paper about twelve inches in length, then laid down short vertical lines along the horizontal line. Above each vertical line, she neatly wrote a year: 1908, 1920, 1926 and so on, up to 1958—the year Georgia disappeared. Underneath each year's vertical line she printed, in an abbreviated style, entries of Georgia's known activities, i.e., when and where she was born, the day Georgia and Harry married, the approximate time when Harry left, Sandra's date of birth, etc. She figured these were the most significant dates in Georgia's life. Margot worked with quiet intent for a while until she heard, "You don't have to do that, you know."

"Yes, I do." Margot glanced over to see Georgia sitting in the easy chair. Not surprised to see her, she laid down her pen. "I wondered when you would stop by again," she said.

"I can give you all that information. Just take notes." Georgia cupped her hands to light a cigarette.

"I want to do it this way. It gives me a visual, something to refer to," Margot said. "I need a timeline to give me a sense of chronological order. I was getting confused and thought it would help." She picked up her pen and finished writing. "I will do an actual outline later, but for now, this seems like enough. See." She held up the narrow poster board to show Georgia her work.

"I like your handwriting, very legible and calligraphic. It looks a lot like mine did. You saw the notebook, didn't you?"

"Yes! What a surprise!" Margot put her pen away. "Lisel found it. She read very little of it, though. I hid it soon after. I thought it was important."

"Very." Georgia walked into the kitchen. She rotated on her heels around the small space. "The decorative styles now are certainly different from when I lived here," she said. "I'm glad you fixed the deck and kept the little deck chairs. I like the color you painted them. Looks fresh and peppy."

"Thank you."

Georgia leaned on the table across from Margot. "Just so you know, I hid the notebook before I left, but I suppose you figured that out already. Later, when Billy was older, I suggested to him in a dream he stash the suitcase, the one you found underneath the trailer, for safekeeping and, bless the dear boy, he did. Ahead, I saw someone would find my story and write it. I just didn't know when or that it would be *you*."

Margot crossed her arms and frowned. "What do you mean?"

"Take a closer look at Notes on Neom. There's some interesting stuff in there."

"I have."

"Well, look again. You'll see what I mean. Bye for now."

Before Margot could say another word, Georgia vanished like mist evaporating in the hot sun. Margot stared at the vacant space where Georgia had just been. "Goddamnit, Georgia! Explain yourself!"

In a fury, Margot grabbed the notebook and rustled the pages. "Why all of this hunt and peck work?" She squirmed and threw down her pen. "Oh, what the fuck," she hissed. "Why am I talking to a ghost anyway?" Margot stomped to the easy chair, flopped down and flipped through the pages to *Notes on Neom*.

"Come on now, slow down. Take your time."

The room appeared empty, but Margot knew Georgia hovered nearby. She swiveled in the chair. "Oh, be quiet," she said. "I'm reading."

When she'd first examined Georgia's notebook weeks ago, Margot concluded some material had to be strict dictation, written information channeled from Neom and transcribed by Georgia. Other passages were obviously Georgia's own thoughts and the result of her discoveries after she experimented with various out-of-body techniques. From the gist of her writings, Georgia tried many of Neom's suggestions, but not all had successful outcomes.

Even though Neom indicated moving through dimensional portals was relatively easy, Georgia had serious concerns. According to Georgia's notes, some of her attempts failed. Rescued several times by Neom and once by Jedediah, she realized dimensional travel was tricky and should not be treated lightly. She also alluded to a rising fear of being stranded in another dimension without a secure way to return to the present time. If she could not pinpoint the exact place at the critical moment, how would she get back? It was clear from her journal entries that Georgia feared the consequences of any error that might affect Sandra and rearrange both of their destinies.

It was well after midnight before Margot finished sifting through the Neom material. Chagrined after her earlier outburst at Georgia, she was glad to have taken the extra time and had, in fact, earmarked several critical pages for future reference. *Notes on Neom* contained some fascinating, thought-provoking stuff, and she had to admit that Georgia was right. She'd missed a few important notations. She'd have to apologize the next time they talked.

A section she overlooked centered on soul connections. Georgia maintained it was possible to have relationships with other dimensional beings while living in a third-dimensional body and world. She claimed she had alliances with aliens from other universes and called them relatives of another sort.

Margot stared into space and let her mind circumnavigate the concept of alien relatives. This was an aspect she had not considered before. Was it possible she might be connected to aliens too? Margot closed the book and laid it aside. Her mind brimmed with too many strange and new possibilities. She couldn't sort it out. So she dismissed the thought, turned out the light, and fell into a deep sleep.

"Ever heard of the Philadelphia Experiment?" Margot said to Lisel, who was ahead of her on the trail. They were taking a leisure walk around Mountain Lake. The four-mile walk in Moran State Park was a favorite of theirs, especially during the warm summer months. Today the sky was clear; the air was fresh and alive with the sound of birds.

Stark shafts of light ran across the trail ahead. Twenty feet beyond, the trail disappeared into the thick forest as the wide path narrowed into sharp switchbacks heading up the steepest ridge. There will be dappled lighting there, Margot thought as her hiking boots crunched on dry pine needles.

"Uh, it sounds vaguely familiar." Lisel looked down at her sister as she turned the sharp corner of the first switchback.

After climbing for a few more minutes, she waited for Margot. "Didn't that have something to do with quantum physics?"

"Something like that, yes." Margot passed Lisel on the trail. "There's a lot more to it."

"What do you mean?"

"Well, as I understand it, there are many fields of consciousness. Like the human body, for instance. Your body is one field of awareness. According to the quantum physics theory, matter, the body, can move from one spot to another without moving through intervening space. Bing!" Margot snapped her fingers. "Just like that." She shrugged her shoulders. "That's my understanding, anyway."

"Really? How so?"

"It takes a bit of imagination following this logic, I know. Take thought forms, for example. Like when you're thinking about someone and then they call. How many times has that happened to you? That's simply information, another field of awareness, moving instantaneously across a vast distance. According to Neom—and Georgia—it's all about probabilities. Life is a series of probabilities."

"Tell me about it." Lisel hastened her gait and followed close behind Margot. "How do you know? I mean, about the Philadelphia Experiment." By now, they were almost halfway up the ridge. "Let's stop up ahead for a minute, okay? I get winded on this trail sometimes. I'm out of shape. Just getting old, I guess."

"Yeah, me too." Margot stopped, took in a breath, and continued her hypothesis. "I was doing research on time travel and came across some information on the Philadelphia Experiment. It's roughly based on Einstein's unified field theory."

"Time travel? Good grief, Margot, what are you up to now?"

"Oh, relax, Lisel." Margot gave her sister a stern eye. "I was just doing some research for my book."

"Okay. Yeah, sure." Lisel bit her tongue and pursed her lips.

"The other day while I was poking around online," Margot continued, "I found a few things on time travel, inter-dimensional travel, that is." Margot studied the pathway in front of them for a moment. They were almost to the top now, a few more tight corners on the steep grade and they would be there. "Yes. Yes. I believe that's the current catch phrase." Margot closed her eyes. "Inter-dimensional," she repeated. "I can't quite see it."

"See what?"

"Inter-dimensional. I'm trying to see what it looks like." Margot shook her head and opened her eyes.

Lisel stared at her sister. "Honestly, Margot, you're getting nuttier every day. I'm worried about you."

"Oh, never mind," Margot said and waved away her remark.

Pacing themselves, the two women hiked up the trail again in silence. When they reached the top, Margot turned to her sister and proceeded with her narrative. "Anyway, the Philadelphia Experiment was supposed to be about cloaking. You know, like the Klingons did in *Star Trek*. The experiment was to be used for war purposes, so it wasn't *exactly* time travel. Ultimately, *they* claimed the whole thing was a big hoax. Didn't happen." Margot shrugged. "I don't know if I believe that."

"Why?" Puffing hard, Lisel leaned over to catch her breath. "What makes you say that?"

"Because I'm beginning to think things like that are possible. I've been reading Georgia's notes in her book. You know, the notebook you found in the suitcase when I moved into the trailer." Margot fumbled around in her backpack and pulled out a water bottle. She struggled with the lid. "Damn it!" she said and wrenched off the cap.

"Georgia believes the Great I Am, as she calls it, is *pure consciousness*—the energy source that organizes everything in the universe. She discovered that probability when she began experimenting with time travel. Neom coached her, of course. Georgia talks about it in her notes, and according to her entries, *she did it.* Traveled through time, I mean." Margot took a long drink.

"Seriously? That sounds pretty crazy if it were true." With a hint of sarcasm in her voice, Lisel said, "Exactly *how* did she travel? In a spaceship off to the Great I Am? Really, Margot, this sounds like *The Wizard of Oz.*"

"Oh, don't be funny, Lisel. I'm serious." Margot handed Lisel the bottle of water. "Want some?"

Lisel took a big swig and then another. "Thanks," she said. "I'm serious, too, Margot. How *did* she do it?"

"Well, I'm not sure. She doesn't give exact instructions, just general information about purity of intention. There's some stuff about vortexes too." Margot reached for the water bottle and took another draw. "Anyway, a lot of Georgia's notes contain channeled information. She wrote everything down in that book years ago, before we were born. There's an entire section on time travel in the notebook. I'm still trying to decipher it."

"Wow. That's creepy. I'm getting goose bumps." Shivering, Lisel rubbed her shoulders.

"I don't think it's creepy. I think it's interesting, fascinating." Margot handed the bottle to Lisel again. "She even had a guide named Neom. Well, there was a group, really." Margot put her hands on her hips and twisted her body left, then right, stretching. "Neom was the leader. Because of his level of spiritual advancement, he could channel down into Georgia's vibration. That's how it works. You channel up, they channel down."

"Here." Lisel smirked and handed Margot the water bottle. "I'm channeling this to you."

"Laterally?" Margot laughed and stuck her tongue out at her sister. A sudden chill filled the air when a dark cloud slid over the sun. Margot realized the conversation had deteriorated to folly, so she dumped her sunglasses and water bottle into the pack. "Come on, let's get going. I'm cold."

From Margot's research, she gleaned there was no pat answer or safe path to move through time dimensions. The more she delved into the information, the more she found Neom's dissertation on the subject to be the most succinct and believable of all the source material she encountered. Much of what she gathered seemed irrational, flimsy, and downright convoluted. Neom's hypotheses, however, came across as thoroughly developed; his matter-of-fact tone and simple directions garnered confidence in her. Enough to assure her that she might have a safe, multi-dimensional journey if she stayed out of what Alice A. Bailey referred to in one of her books as the glamour or human ego. Following Neom's specific instructions seemed the safest venue.

According to Neom, one had to be very conscious of intention and practice using protective shields. The primary ingredient was clear intention. One had to push aside self-centered ego. Neom emphasized it wasn't imagination as much as it was a *knowing*. Successful time travel required one to go within and then go without. He also advised that because there are a multitude of different or potential realities, clarity of purpose was essential to set a true course.

Margot had no trouble believing time travel was possible since she'd experienced the phenomenon several times in the past. When she worked in Alaska, a friend there confided that he knew Russian Orthodox monks, who lived on Kodiak Island, teleported. In fact, he'd witnessed the event more than once, and said the monks knew what they were doing. One minute they were there; the next, somewhere else.

Although Margot time traveled before, she had never traveled on her own volition. Even now, she didn't know how she arrived at Georgia's trailer in 1958. Somehow she'd catapulted into a time continuum, arrived and returned by—well, *who knew?*

Margot knew mastering conscious time travel required a new awareness, and that she needed to become more evolved, more proficient with quantum concepts before attempting such a venture alone.

In her notes, Georgia stressed the need for clarity, and had earmarked a brief passage underscoring the need for mindfulness. If the soul had not prepared, or grown spiritually, then *conscious* travel might be fraught with danger or be impossible.

This had concerned Georgia so much that Margot couldn't help feeling skeptical and cautious. If she managed to time travel on her own and was ill-prepared, she might find herself out there without a lifeline, wandering the corridors of multidimensions with no recourse, unable to return. She did not want to get caught between worlds. Deep down, Margot knew the biggest obstacle she had to overcome was fear.

"Do you want to try it?"

Lost in thought, Margot jerked back from the kitchen sink when she heard the words. She shouldn't have been startled. Earlier that day she'd had an intuitive hit that Georgia would pop in again soon. Her visits were expected now. Margot finished rinsing her hands and didn't turn around. "I don't know. Maybe," she said, and reached for a towel.

"I can ask Jedediah to come and help you with the first one."

"Why can't you do it?" Margot turned toward Georgia. As usual, she was sitting in the easy chair, smoking.

"Tricky," Georgia replied. "Remember what happened to those sailors on the *Philadelphia*? Some of them melded into the metal. Awful." Georgia exhaled a stream of blue smoke.

"Was that real? The Philadelphia Experiment? I mean, do you think that happened?" Margot walked over to Georgia, sat down, and watched her smoke.

"Yes, it *was* real. They tried to cover it up, though—a chancy, doomed experiment that went bad. Real bad. Sloppy job all the way around I'd say."

"If Jedediah were to come and guide me through a portal, where would we go?"

"I've got the perfect place." Georgia waved her cigarette. "You'll love it. I can talk with Jedediah and ask if he and his group will help you with conscious intention. Then you won't be afraid."

"I'm *not* afraid."

Georgia shot a dubious glance at Margot. "Really?"

Margot's stomach dropped, her face flushed. "Well, it's that I don't know what to expect—that's the part making me feel anxious. I'd still like it if you came with me."

"Hmm, I see." Georgia strolled over to the door. "Let's go outside," she said, and walked out. Margot followed and stood beside Georgia on the deck. She felt like a scared five-year-old child. "Remember when you lived in Hawaii?" Georgia gestured down the acreage toward the orchard. "When you used to lie on the beach and fantasize about things?"

Margot narrowed her eyes at Georgia. "Yes."

"I was there in the fantasy with you, Margot. I could see through your eyes, feel what you felt. Didn't you sense something, uh, someone else there with you?"

Margot flashed on Kauai where she lived for a few years in the eighties. Somehow she'd scraped up enough cash to semi-retire in her late thirties and lived near Hanalei. Going to the beach every day was the best part of her life there. "Well, I guess so. Uh, yes, maybe I did, come to think of it. I just thought I was imagining things. I spent a lot of time on the beach then, imagining stuff."

"Yes, I know." Georgia grinned. "It was delicious there, wasn't it? I love Hawaii, don't you?" Georgia stepped off the deck. "Let's go down to the orchard. I want to show you something. We need to hurry, though. I think my time here is about up." She walked down the path with Margot following close behind.

Zelda, Lisel's new puppy, was in the trailer yipping to get out. Lisel had left the dog with Margot for the weekend. "Oh, leave the puppy there," Georgia said. "She's okay. You won't be long."

In a matter of seconds, the women stopped just short of the two apple trees. The trees in the small orchard were laden with ripe apples; a few red apples had fallen to the ground and had been nibbled on by deer. Georgia touched the trunk of the closest tree. "Aren't these trees beautiful?" she said. "I remember when I planted them. Seems like yesterday—"

Even though she was enjoying the moment, Margot couldn't help but wonder how they got to the orchard so fast. Georgia leaned back on the tree trunk and laughed. "Oh, that? That was just a teeny, tiny teleport. I love alliteration. Don't you?" Georgia pushed away from the tree. "Let's walk into the vortex together, shall we?"

A shock ran through Margot. She gulped. "Well, uh, I haven't prepared, you know, with the right intention and all. Uh, how 'bout we do this another time?"

"No." Georgia reached for Margot's hand. "Just take my hand and we'll go in together. I think it's better this way." Reluctant, Margot offered her hand. Georgia squeezed Margot's fingers. "Come with me."

In perfect sync, both the women stepped together between the two apple trees. "Let's stand here for a few moments," Georgia said. Margot glanced at their hands, fingers entwined. She was surprised to feel actual pressure and warmth from Georgia's hand. "I'll signal you with a nod when we're ready to go. We'll be there in an instant. You'll see."

Margot waited for the cue. She forgot to ask where they were going, but before she could say anything, Georgia squeezed her hand, then nodded. All at once the surrounding air whirled. Margot's vision blurred. She felt dizzy. In an instant, they were gone.

The next thing Margot heard was the husky sound of Georgia's voice in her ear. "How are you feeling, Margot?" Georgia peered into Margot's eyes. "Are you afraid?"

Margot held her breath. She struggled to exhale. "I don't know. Where are we?" Her voice bellowed. The sound of her words echoed for miles. Margot gawked at Georgia and buckled over. For a few seconds, she couldn't move.

Georgia touched her head. "Look ahead, Margot," she said. "This should take your mind off things." In front of them lay an immense pristine field brimming with colorful wildflowers. Above, a cloudless cerulean blue sky hung snug to the horizon line like a theater backdrop. Faint, warm, almost tropical breezes wafted around them. Everything seemed idyllic, picture perfect.

"Oh, my God," Margot whispered. "It's strange, but I think I've been here before."

"Yes, I thought you might recognize it. I love this spot, don't you? It's special. I come here when I'm worried and need some peace."

"I…I like it very much. Thank you." Mesmerized by the lush surroundings, Margot relaxed. Then a sudden pang surged inside her gut. Her heart palpitated. *What rabbit hole had she fallen down?* Inhaling short, gasping breaths, she signaled to Georgia. She held up her hands like a keystone cop. "Stop!" Margot patted her chest and concentrated on slowing her heart. "How'd we get here?"

"Oh, through a safe portal, the usual one I use."

"*Usual?*" Margot's body stiffened. She shot Georgia a disgruntled side-glance. "Good God! Did I come here on your personal jet stream? Your *cosmic freeway?*" Margot sputtered. "Are there *cosmic* traffic jams too?"

Georgia burst out laughing. "Thatta girl!" she said and clapped her hands. "Now you're coming to your senses! No. No. Margot, it's nothing like that." Georgia shook her head, still chuckling. "I was absolutely certain you'd be able to come through the portal with me, so I brought you here to my favorite place. You can't see a portal, at least not in three-dimensional reality. You have to *know* where it is and where it goes."

"Oh? Exactly *how* does one know—through cosmic osmosis?"

Shaking her head again, Georgia said, "No. No. It's not like that, Margot. You're getting too worked up about this, you know. Calm down." Georgia crossed her arms and stood thinking for a moment. "Listen, don't worry about *how* we got here right now. We'll get to that later. But I can tell you one thing, it *wasn't* by osmosis." Taking a few steps away Georgia said, "Anyway, see how easy it was!" She spread her arms out wide. "You've just traveled to another dimension, Margot. How do you feel?"

Realizing she had not thought about her body except for her rapid heartbeat, Margot looked down at her hands, arms, and torso to see if she was intact. Wiggling her fingers she said, "Uh, well, okay, I think but—" Margot frowned. "How do I get back? I mean, will you help me? That's what I want to know."

"No need to worry, Margot. Kitty will take you back. Won't you, Kitty?"

"Kitty?" Margot hadn't thought about Kitty for days. The cat had scampered off when Lisel's puppy came to visit. She looked down. There was Kitty swishing her tail and sniffing the edge of a blade of grass ever so carefully. "My God! Where'd she come from?"

"Oh, Kitty's smart—a class act. She knows how to move through time pretty smoothly. She taught me a few things way back when." Georgia leaned down and stroked Kitty's back. "We work together from time to time; Kitty's good company. Are you ready to go back now?"

"Not yet. Can we walk around a little?"

"Come with me." Georgia took the lead. Walking past Margot, she motioned for her to follow. Ahead of them, the breeze rippled in sequential waves along the field. The tall grass and flowers swayed back and forth, opening a path for them as the women moved through the pastureland.

Dazed by the resplendent environment, Margot strolled along, lingering among the wildflowers. The wild flora moved this way and that, folding rhythmically as she wove through the field. "This reminds me of something biblical," Margot said, "kind of like the Old Testament's parting of the water."

Georgia laughed. "*Cool*, huh?" She turned and waited for Margot. "I like to use slang," she said. "It makes me feel, well, cool." Giggling, Georgia pointed off into the distance. "Let's go up there and look around. The view is stupendous."

Following Georgia's line of sight, Margot saw a long, gradual trail that led to a large, emerald green grassy knoll. At the top was a small clearing. She could just make out the silhouette of a bench. Margot had not noticed the knoll or bench before. In fact, she was sure neither had been there a few seconds ago. Georgia winked at her. "Just like magic," she said.

The two women roamed through the field for a while before reaching the trail that led to the top of the knoll. "What a beautiful image," Margot said. From her vantage point, the enormous bench, backlit by a pastel peach and cream horizon, resembled something out of a fairy tale. The elaborately-carved ancient throne appeared to be large enough for several people to sit together. The handcrafted detail along the legs, back, and armrests appeared to recount stories of old. "I wish I had my camera to get this," Margot said. Then she caught herself. "What am I thinking? This is total illusion, isn't it?"

"Now you're getting it. Everything is an illusion, you know, Margot, here and on the IN Road too. Wherever you are is an illusion of sorts—*your* illusion, *your* dream. And the best part is you can conjure this idyllic spot anytime, anywhere, and it will appear."

"Is anything real?"

"Yes and no."

"Great."

"We can explore the subject of illusion another time, Margot. How about making that bench our meeting place? What do you say? Come when you want, and I'll be here. We can chat, talk things over." With that, Georgia headed up the trail at a quick pace.

"*Wait!* What? What do you mean?" Margot said. "Am I supposed to come here *by myself* from now on?" Margot watched Georgia walk up the trail. "How am I gonna do that?" she yelled. Her voice, riddled with agitation, bounced back. The full force of her anguish doubled her over. Margot groaned. "I don't even know where we are, for Christ's sake." Georgia didn't answer but moved up the trail. Her skirt bellowed in the wind.

Filled with a flood of raw emotions, Margot stumbled and fell to her knees. "How the hell am I going to do this?" she hollered. Georgia continued walking and did not turn around. "*Damn it, Georgia!* Why aren't you answering me?" Margot glared at Georgia's back, willing her to stop and hissed, "*Goddamnit!*"

With fierce resolve, Margot picked herself up and brushed the soil off her scraped hands. In seconds, the new scratches on her palms healed. A few moments later, the stinging pain from her knees disappeared too. Despite her emotional angst and inner turmoil, her body felt light and energized as if she could fly.

Now, Georgia stood near the bench on the hill. Her incandescent, nearly transparent silhouette waved to Margot, urging her on. Feeling foolish, Margot put one foot in front of the other. Dread nipped at her heels as she trudged up the trail, trying with all her might to mimic Georgia's confident stride.

When Margot approached the bench, Georgia motioned for her to sit down. A meditative quiet enveloped the women, and they sat in silence. After a long pause, Georgia said, "They call this the Contemplation Bench. It has been here for all eternity. Only the Akashic Record Keepers know who carved it or how it came to be. I come here as often as I can. I find it helps me remain peaceful."

Margot's breathing returned to normal. Her heart calmed. She had to admit she felt more peaceful. Soon, she let out a grateful sigh. It was then Georgia turned to face Margot. In a soft, yet commanding tone she said, "I want you to go back to the year 1929. Look around. Find Harry and our house. That was the year Sandra was born and things changed for me, and for Harry and Sandra too."

Immediately, Margot's heart pumped faster. Her face turned red. She peppered Georgia with questions. "How do you expect me to do that? How do I know where to go? Where did you and Harry live? Do I just dial up the address and push a button? Good Lord, Georgia, what else?"

"Really, Margot, you worry too much." Georgia patted Margot's hand. "I'll ask Jedediah to help you. He's good at gauging time warps and portals. I must go now. My time is over. See you soon." In an instant, Georgia vanished, leaving Margot sitting alone on the Contemplation Bench.

"Wait!" Margot said, but it was too late, Georgia was gone. Shaken by Georgia's sudden departure, not knowing how to return home, tears streamed down Margot's face. She couldn't stop crying. This was too much, too much. Her nerves were shot. Any resolve she might have had dissipated the instant Georgia disappeared. Margot felt like a lost child who wanted to go home. More than anything she wanted to go back to *her* life—her real life.

In the midst of her torrential breakdown, Margot heard a faint meow. Wiping tears away, she found Kitty at her feet and reached down to pet the cat. "Hello, girl," she said. Kitty leaped on her lap, and in an instant Margot snapped out of her doldrums. Strange as it was, it did not surprise her to see the cat again. The feline fit perfectly into the surreal setting and odd course of events. "I'm glad you're here," Margot sighed. Kitty nosed her arm.

"Will you help me?" Kitty raised a delicate paw and with her svelte head nudged Margot's arm. Georgia was right, Margot thought. Kitty is good company, a comfort. "Come on, girl, take us home," Margot said. "This doesn't look like Kansas anymore."

In a nanosecond, Margot found herself back in the orchard standing between the two trees with Kitty at her feet. The surrounding orchard was drenched from a recent downpour. "Thank you, girl," Margot said, and stepped out of the vortex. She steadied herself on the slippery terrain. Kitty hopped over the rain-splattered grass and with her tail twitching, slithered into the tall, variegated brush.

Again, Margot did not know how she shifted from point A, the orchard, to Point B, the Contemplation Bench, and back to Point A. This remarkable leap from one dimension to another made Margot wonder if any of the phenomena had happened. *Was she making this up?* It seemed very dreamlike; even the scenes she remembered now seemed bizarre and conflicted with her long-held sense of three-dimensional reality. Yet she found this memory, if it was a memory, extremely compelling.

More than a week went by before Margot stopped thinking about her trip to the Contemplation Bench. In fact, she could not think about anything else. Her mind stirred a phantasmagorical pot studded with conversations with Georgia. The rational normal side of her brain, churned and festered, puzzling out each tiny detail. *Was the Contemplation Bench real? Had she gone to another dimension with Georgia?*

Each day she played and replayed every scene, enumerating her dialogue, adding in comments she should have said, rehearsing one pertinent question after another. She was curious why Georgia wanted her to go to 1929. *If she went there by herself, would she be able to return?*

Then, as if that wasn't enough, while sleeping, Margot dreamed about traveling through time. Wandering through the mystical folds of Dreamtime, she basked in her seasoned ability to roam through multi-dimensions, hopping from one dimension to another with ease; that is, until morning. The minute her eyes opened, and she hit the solid floor of the Airstream, Margot was back to pondering the validity of psychic phenomena and doubted the esoteric side of herself. This relentless day and night clash went on for over a week.

Margot knew she was living a dual life and that battling these irreconcilable differences was paralyzing her psyche. She fumbled around the trailer unable to think straight and often woke numb and bewildered at her three-dimensional surroundings. She hardly spoke.

When Lisel called later that week, it was evident she needed a rest, a way out. Lisel thought so too. "Margot? You've been kinda quiet. What's been going on?" Lisel said. "I've left a few messages, but you haven't called back."

"Well, uh, I've been busy, very busy. The book, you know." Struggling to keep her balance and sanity, Margot hesitated to tell her sister much. "I can't seem to think about anything else, day or night. I'm a little messed up."

"Maybe you should stop working so hard. Take a break."

"Yeah. Maybe."

"Why don't I come over? We can take Zelda for a walk."

"Naw. Thanks anyway. My place is a mess. I need to put the work away. The first draft is finished. I've been thinking about camping in Oregon and then driving over to Ashland and take in some Shakespeare."

"Shakespeare? I thought you hated Shakespeare."

"I do, but I thought it would change the order of my thinking. You know, give me another perspective, another point of view. Shakespeare is good for that. He's all melodrama and mystery, blood and guts theatrically. I could use something to distract me like that, to take my mind off, well, you know."

"Sure. Okay. Do what you want. When are you leaving?"

"Pretty soon. I'll let you know."

Despite her determination to put Georgia's project aside, things promptly backfired. The day she shelved the finished draft, Margot tossed and turned all night. Just before daybreak, she bowed to her nocturnal restlessness, threw on her clothes, and tromped outside to catch the sunrise. She found little solace in the dull, overcast dawn. Margot wandered listless like a zombie through the heavy dew, circling the acreage and down to the orchard.

Staring at the two trees from a distance, she felt empty, her mind blank. Nothing seemed to make any sense—at least nothing she had known before meeting Georgia. "What am I going to do now?" she shouted out into the mottled gray morning. But there was no answer, only the piercing cry of an eagle in the distance.

For the next few days, time seemed to meld together into one seamless dreamlike state. Margot found it hard to control a rogue temper, which broiled inside her. She smashed lids on pots and pans, deliberately dropped her favorite plates and bowls in the sink, then stared mindlessly down at the chipped, broken pottery, perplexed at her aggression. One day, she slammed the mailbox door shut, snapped the rusty hinge in two, then kicked the mailbox's wooden post in frustration. "What in the hell am I doing living in an old beat-up trailer in the boondocks anyway?" she grumbled.

Fumbling with her mail on the way back to the trailer, she tripped over a clump of tall grass and fell to her knees. Crouching, holding her shins, she burst into tears and sobbed like a child. It was at this crystalline moment that Margot knew her sense of reality had slipped away. She'd lost touch with her former world, and the fear of having a serious psychotic break seeped in.

When she could think, Margot tossed around the meaning of reality like a cat batting at a catnip toy. In her notes, Neom had coached Georgia and claimed there were many potential realities. *If there was more than one, how many were there? Could you choose a distinct reality and go there—stay there?* She guessed that's what Georgia had done.

Embedded in mind-numbing upheaval, Margot knew better than to go anywhere near the vortex or attempt to return to the Contemplation Bench. Instead, she kept to the comfort of the trailer and only ventured out to get the mail and smoke cigarettes. Since moving to the IN Road and meeting Georgia, she had picked up the tobacco habit again.

Sequestered in her tiny environment, unable to do any productive writing now that she'd shelved Georgia's book project, Margot spent most of her time sketching. One image she concentrated on was a rough likeness of herself tiptoeing on a tightrope above a deep fissure. As she continued doodling along that theme, Margot drew a series of connected gestures, shaky lines twisting and turning a frail body forward and back; some images dangled over the crevice, almost falling. Each time she pressed pencil to paper, she contemplated the bizarre language of her drawings and as her pencil crept across the page, toyed with the idea of plummeting, knowing if she did, she'd be lost.

Several times over the course of her reclusion, she called out for Georgia, hoping to hear her voice, wanting her to materialize in the safe space of the Airstream. There, she felt certain they could talk, hash things out. "Georgia, please. Please come here," she said. But Georgia did not come.

This longing for Georgia's companionship brought up more surprising behavior for Margot. In an act of childish defiance, she pulled out reference books she'd stuffed in every nook of the trailer. Smashing them down on her nightstand one by one, she piled them high until she could not see the reading lamp. If Georgia wouldn't come, dammit, then she'd find her own answers. And so, for the next few days Margot did nothing except plow through the pile of research material again, hoping for more insight. The more she read, the more she wondered if any of what she'd experienced had been real. *Had she hallucinated? Was it that simple?*

When she could sleep, her sleep patterns were irregular. She read until morning and then fell into a deep slumber until late afternoon. Then one day waking early after a late night reverie, Margot let it all go.

As early morning light crept into the room, Margot woke crumpled on top of the bed, wedged between several thick volumes. She sat up and shouted, "I've had enough!" Research books strewn on the bed fell to the floor as she threw back the covers and stomped into the bathroom. "This is nonsense. I can't stand it anymore," she said, and slammed the door.

After a cold shower, she stood on the deck and gulped down morning coffee. Leaning toward the apple orchard, she yelled at the field and signaled to the two trees as if they were live beings. "I made it up, dammit," she said. "Yes siree, you know I did. I made the whole *damn* thing up. So there." She crossed her arms, exhaling a lengthy sigh. "I'm done. I've conquered my Mt. Everest."

More convinced than ever she'd made the whole thing up, Margot felt ashamed. Lisel was right. She'd been a fool to conjure those trips back in time, Georgia, the Contemplation Bench—every single bit had been pure delusion. *What had she been thinking? Was she out of her mind?* Whatever it was, she knew she'd come to her senses. She had let go of her fantasies! Margot grabbed her keys and hopped into her car. She needed something good to eat.

Dining on a thick rib eye steak and drinking an entire bottle of robust Italian wine brought Margot crashing down to earth. She toppled into bed. Tipsy, full, and tired of coping with a false sense of reality, she wanted nothing more than to sleep. Sleep, that's all she wanted. Margot stretched her body prone and dropped into a languid slumber.

The dream began with a huge, blue ocean wave. Floating on the crest of the wave, Margot spotted Georgia standing on the water near the shoreline with a being she knew to be Neom. Surrounded in sea foam mist, their shimmering silhouettes were some distance away. Sun rays beamed through semi-transparent azure bubbles and engulfed the pair as they skimmed across the water toward land. The surrounding air sparkled. Blinded by the brilliance, Margot watched as the two glided to shore. As the wave washed her toward land, she called out to them, but by the time she reached the sandy beach, Neom and Georgia were gone.

Margot woke from the dream, her body dripping wet. Half-asleep, she thought she'd just come from a shower, but then realized she'd been dreaming about an ocean wave. No. Wait. That wasn't real—*or was it?* Her skin felt feverish, salty to the touch. She went into the bathroom and looked in the mirror. Deeper, darker circles had formed under her eyes; her hair, snarled and matted, looked as if she had the beginnings of dreadlocks and—*there was sand on her cheek!*

Shocked, Margot brushed the grit off and turned on the bath water. She took a quick, hot shower and put on fresh pajamas. Still unnerved, she grabbed the extra down comforter and stumbled to the daybed. The instant her head met the pillow, Margot fell into another dream sequence.

This time she walked along a dark corridor. There were doors on either side of the passageway—some cracked open, some closed. "Choose one and walk through the door," a voice echoed down the hall. Margot looked around but saw no one. She continued walking, inching along at a snail's pace. The air around her felt lifeless, as if she was in a void. Yet she could breathe easily and felt no fear.

"Keep going until you find the right one for you," the voice said. Heeding the command, Margot crept down the lengthy hallway until she found a door that seemed right. The massive, ornately carved door was cracked open. She saw light coming through. Margot hesitated before entering. Her hand hovered over the doorknob. She exhaled all the air in her lungs, took a deep breath, and grasped the carved wooden knob.

Once over the threshold, she stopped at the top of a wide marble staircase. Lined on either side of the staircase were vivid fuchsia sprays of bougainvillea. Below was an enormous turquoise circular pool sequestered in the middle of an expansive, beautifully landscaped garden. Captivated by the sheer elegance of her surroundings, Margot walked down the stairway into the garden and over to the pool. Without thinking, she dove in.

She swam the length of the pool. Gliding through the crystal clear warm water felt luxurious. Her body moved without the slightest effort. Refreshed, Margot climbed out of the water and went down another short flight of stairs to a lower level of gardens. These were equally impressive and grand. The sun shone bright along the path toward the middle of the garden where there was an extravagant fountain.

With her nightclothes still wet and clinging to her body, she strode toward the center of the garden. Birds tweeted and sang among the tall, flowering trees and bushes surrounding the fountain. Margot wondered if it was spring, and then knew instinctively that there were no seasons here. There was no time, only the present, and the present was what you thought and projected outward. She knew and felt the truth of this.

On the other side of the fountain stood Neom. "Welcome," he said.

Amazed at how tall Neom appeared, words stuck in her throat. She nodded. He must be at least seven feet tall, maybe taller, she thought. His large, round, penetrating eyes looked into and through her. Embraced in his auric field, she felt his loving presence envelope her. He held out his hand, and she took it. "Come with me," he said, and led her into another part of the garden where there were other tall beings.

There were at least twenty other beings in the vicinity, and all wore long flowing, colorful gowns. These remarkable entities reminded Margot of old Atlantean drawings she'd seen. Their robes, made of soft fabric, appeared sheer, almost translucent, yet opaque at the same time. Margot inherently knew these souls were androgynous and kind.

Neom led her through an alcove in the garden that opened to an immense structure with many levels; each had a set of stairs leading up to an arched entryway. There were no walls on the upper levels. The curved, thick adobe-like archways were made of a smooth, plaster-like substance finished with an opalescent sheen Margot did not recognize. She wondered what the substance was and touched an archway as they walked by.

Neom led her up a narrow staircase and onto a platform where other beings had gathered. "We have been waiting for you," Neom said.

Margot woke feeling as if an outside force had shaken her awake. A stark emptiness filled the trailer. There was no sound; not even Kitty was around. Drowsy, she checked the clock: 11:55 a.m. The sky was a predictable dismal gray, but it was light so she knew it must be near noon and not midnight. Again, her body was drenched in sweat. "Damn menopause," she murmured, and staggered to the bathroom.

She hated this part of aging—that, and the insufferable broken sleep patterns that haunted her nightly existence. But she couldn't blame menopause for her restless sleep now; most of her fitfulness had to do with her obsessions: her fantasies, the book, Georgia, and those damn multi-dimensional trips. That had more to do with her chaotic sleep patterns than menopause.

"Stop it! Stop thinking about this!" Margot yelled and peeled off her soaked pajamas. Trading her wet clothes for a pair of dry sweats and a clean T-shirt, she slid into fresh clothing. "That's over!" she said.

Margot splashed her face with cold water. As she toweled off, animated sequences of last night's dreams exploded in her head. She took in a quick breath, leaned on the bathroom counter, and buried her face in the towel. She didn't move and labored to end the series of dreamscapes racing through her head. But the mind chatter and psychedelic visions wouldn't leave. The dizzying scenes paralyzed her. They were so real, so vibrant that she could feel the texture of the walls, ocean spray, and sand on the beach. When she opened her eyes, Margot stared at the mirror. Tapping her fingers on the surface of the bathroom counter, she said to her reflection, "It seems so real, as real as this."

She wondered, too, if Georgia, wherever she is, had moments of disbelief. *What would Georgia say when she told her the book project was over?*

"I understand you met Neom," Georgia said. Margot nodded and walked over to the Contemplation Bench. Kitty, who had picked her way up the knoll through the tall spring green grass, jumped up on Georgia and began kneading her paws on her lap. "Good girl," Georgia said, caressing the cat. "I've missed you too."

Margot was not surprised to find herself at the Contemplation Bench. Neither did she question her arrival but sat next to Georgia. "Yes, I liked Neom," she said, "and the others." The two women met eye to eye, and so as not to break the spell, Margot whispered, "They are so tall. I didn't realize—" She reached over to pet Kitty who purred. "Only Neom spoke out loud though. Everyone else used telepathy."

"Yes, I know." Georgia grinned. "Neom is the spokesperson for The Group. He's been with us for a long time." Georgia turned toward the valley beyond the knoll and waited for a few moments. "You haven't gone to 1929 yet," she said.

"No." Margot shook her head. "No, I haven't, not yet anyway." She ran her hand along Kitty's furry spine. "It...it seems like I'm waiting for something." Margot followed Georgia's line of sight down the valley. "Courage, maybe."

"There's nothing to be afraid of, you know."

"Well, everything is happening so fast. I can't keep up. The dreams. Our talks. Everything. I feel a little crazy."

"Yes, Neom warned me—"

"Why are you pushing me then?"

"Let's just call it accelerated learning. I'll explain later." Georgia patted Margot's hand and looked at her. "Harry's not a monster even though you might think so. He's just angry about life, unfortunately."

"I don't know. I...I don't know if I want to do this anymore, Georgia. It's getting too complicated for me and, and...I don't like Harry very much. He seems downright mean, heavy-handed. I don't want to see him."

"Well, yes, perhaps, but he wasn't always like that. That's why I want you to go there. See for yourself."

Margot stared at Georgia for a long minute. "What do you mean by us?" she said, changing the subject. "You said Neom had been with us for a long time."

"Hmm. Yes, I did. Well, we can talk about that another time too." Georgia sighed. "Right now, I want you to go to 1929 and find out what Harry was like for yourself. I'll be waiting for you here. Kitty, too."

The next thing Margot remembered was waking before dawn the following morning. It was pitch black outside. In the distance, she heard the mournful sound of a foghorn. She lay under the warm covers and listened until the noise grew faint, then rolled out of bed. Flicking on the lamp, Margot wrapped a thick terry cloth robe around herself and went into the kitchen to start the propane stove.

As she filled the teakettle with water, her mind suddenly flooded with words; waves of text surged within her. *The muse!* Her fingers twitched. All that bottled up energy begged to be released. She had to write, or she'd implode.

"Right, write," she heard herself say. "Get it down, let it out." The thought of tackling a blank page after her self-proclaimed hiatus frightened her. Margot stretched across the counter, grabbed a cigarette from her pack of Marlboro Lights, and lit up.

She cracked the window and blew a stream of tobacco smoke into the foggy air. For a few moments, she twirled the cigarette between her fingers, contemplating her next move. "Yes." She sighed and immediately relaxed. For her, smoking was a form of protection. The act of inhaling and exhaling grounded her, gave her a sense of clarity, something to hold on to, and *damn*, she needed that, especially now.

Taking a deep draw, Margot held the smoke in for a few seconds. She did not move to the computer, but prolonged the moment. "Just wait a minute," she said, her voice curt. Determined to work on her terms, she exhaled and took another drag on her cigarette. In that instant, Margot understood why Georgia enjoyed smoking. It gave pause.

She knew, too, that forestalling the inevitable would be impossible. The muse wouldn't allow it. Although she no longer had the gumption to walk away from the book project, Margot was reluctant to begin. After taking one last puff, she plunked down in front of the computer. "Okay," she said stubbing out her cigarette. "Let's get started."

Typing begrudgingly at first, she roughed out a few paragraphs as if on autopilot, but it didn't take long before a stream of consciousness spilled forth, and in no time at all Margot filled ten pages with polished text. Once more the project had taken on a life of its own, and she marveled at the fluidity of the work. She was a channel, a vehicle for the prose, and as long as she didn't think about it too much, Margot felt almost normal, writing—typing, that is.

When she finished transcribing the material, the next step would be to delve into the work and scrutinize the text, proofread, correct typos, punctuation, etc. During each copyediting session, an unsettled feeling enveloped, leaving Margot feeling flat, almost lifeless. The material, razor-sharp. laced with scientific theories and analogies, always transformed her three-dimensional world, skewed it beyond recognition. In the beginning, she did not expect to feel so discombobulated and out-of-balance. The information today would have been unfathomable then. Even now, she needed to pause. "I need to stop for a few minutes," she said. "Can I take a smoke break?"

At her request, the word flow stopped in mid-sentence. Margot grabbed the pack of cigarettes and lit one. "Thanks," she said, and walked outside. She knew it was best not to think too deeply about what she was writing. That would come later. Overthinking the material would cut off the source, and now that the channel was open, she did not want to stop.

Besides, she was almost certain her source was Neom—by the strength and quality of writing. Although he did not introduce himself today as he usually did, she was sure the counsel came from him, and having an innate affinity for Neom, she trusted his input. Margot stood for a moment thinking about Neom, remembering her encounter in the dream. "Yes," she said. "It has to be him."

Outside in the fresh air, Margot felt more like herself. That's why smoking helped. Smoking was about the only thing that felt halfway human. Refreshed, she shook off any further resistance, walked into the trailer, and sat down at the computer. "Okay," she said, "let's continue."

"How'd it go?" Georgia said when Margot sat down next to her. She had come to the Contemplation Bench, knowing Georgia would grill her about 1929 again. But this time she was ready. Although Margot had stalled as long as she dared before dipping back in time, she had finally ventured to 1929.

The event had gone smoothly. Granted, she had worked herself into an anxious lather before attempting to time travel alone, in the end she was surprised to find it had been easier than imagined. The practice voyages with Kitty had paid off! By choosing the right portal, she'd made it to 1929 and back without a hitch and was overjoyed at her new ability. The trip had not changed her opinion of Harry, though, and she was still unclear why Georgia wanted her to see the younger version of him.

"I went to 1929 just like you wanted, Georgia. I couldn't believe how easy it was," Margot said. "I went there and back *by myself!*"

"Good for you! I knew you could do it."

"Sorry to say this, Georgia, but I can see why you left Harry." Margot toned down her jubilance. "What an ass."

"Well, hmm, *he* left *me*. Remember?" Georgia waved her hands and pushed her remarks away. "Oh, what am I saying?" she said. "That doesn't matter anymore. Tell me how far back did you go? Were you able to see him *before* the crash?"

"Yes, but I haven't changed my opinion." Margot scowled. "I hate to say this, but I still don't like him. I've seen guys like that. You know, men who think they're *God's gift*. Good grief. I don't know how you missed that about him." Margot turned away from Georgia.

"Try not to be judgmental." Georgia gazed down the valley. "It was a very patriarchal atmosphere back then. Men were in charge; few women had the courage to go out on their own."

"You did. You went back to school, worked, and raised Sandra, made something of yourself; that takes courage."

"Yes, but I could not have done it without the help of my father—my parents. They took us in, fed and clothed us until I graduated. I'll always be grateful to them for that."

"Listen, I can't talk about this anymore—at least, right now." Margot walked behind the bench. "Look," she said, rubbing her forehead. "I went back to 1929 just as you asked me to, and I still don't see the point."

"Maybe you need to go back a little farther, earlier in the year. He started out so loving. That's his true self. You'll see."

"I don't know, Georgia—maybe I need another break instead." Margot grimaced. "I feel like I'm losing my mind. I don't know where I am or what I'm doing half the time. Besides, I've finished the writing. Well, most of it—" Margot's voice drifted; she felt the blood drain from her face. *Dang.* She was beat up.

A long pause arched between the two women. Then Georgia faced Margot. "Certainly," she said. Standing up, she bowed slightly in acknowledgement. "As you wish, Margot."

Another chasm of awkward silence separated the two women. Breaking the tension, Georgia let out a strained sigh. "Neom thought you might want time away. He cautioned me to be careful. I guess my enthusiasm got the best of me. I'm sorry."

"Thank you," Margot said. Tears ran down her cheeks, but she would not budge. She could not go on. She had to quit. Her sanity was at stake. "I need a break," she sniffed. "I'm planning a trip down the Oregon coast. The change of scenery will help me sort things out. Please understand."

Margot took a few steps away from the bench and studied the valley below. A warm breeze came up. The tall grass and wildflowers studding the fields moved rhythmically in the wind as it had on her first trip to the Contemplation Bench. "I'm leaving the project, but only for a while," she said. "I *do* want to finish the book. Really, I do."

Georgia sat down. "Yes." An apologetic smile registered on her face as she slid to one side of the Contemplation Bench. Motioning to the space next to her, she said, "Come. Sit. Let's commune together for a few minutes, and then I must go."

Margot took her time before she returned to Orcas. The first three days of her vacation, she wandered along the deserted Oregon beaches at Coos Bay, breathing in the salty air. Cloistered near the ocean felt freeing, restful. The rolling waves washed over her boots and swept her pent-up stress out past the horizon. Her mind often went blank as she observed the glory of the vast sandy shoreline.

At the end of her stay, Margot stashed her tent and camping gear in the car and drove to the quaint town of Ashland. Next on her recreation list was another distraction: Shakespeare!

Driving through town, she warmed to the theatre bustle, registered at a hotel, and settled in for a few days.

She'd planned a side bonus in Ashland too. Sandra Swan lived on the outskirts of town, and Margot wanted to meet and interview Georgia's daughter, if she was willing. Sandra's input might unlock the project's stalemate and motivate her to finish the project.

After throwing her suitcase on the bed, Margot hurried to the theater. On the way, she called Lisel.

"Hey, Sissy! Having fun?" Lisel said when she heard Margot's voice. "When are you coming back?"

"Well, that's what I'm calling about. I'm down in Ashland right now taking in a few Shakespearean plays. I'm gone for another week. Not sure yet of my timing. And yes, I am having fun. *Lots* of fun…and rest. I'm feeling more like myself now. Thank God."

"Wow, that's great! See any cute guys down there?" Lisel laughed. The sisters, in their mid-fifties now, had arrived at their crone era and often joked to each other about how invisible they felt. On the island, available men in their age bracket were almost nonexistent.

"Just the usual gray-haired old geezers. There are a few 30-year-olds that aren't bad, though, but hey, they're all taken. Dang it." Margot chuckled. "Can't imagine what dating would be like anymore, can you?"

"Nope. Dating seems like something from the distant past." Lisel chortled. "So, when do you think you'll be on the island again?"

"Oh, I'll be back around the fifteenth, maybe sooner. I'll call if that changes."

"Sure. Okay. I was just at the trailer yesterday. Everything looks good at the IN Road. Your kitty misses you, though."

"Kitty? You saw her? Wow, I can't believe you saw her, Lisel. She's elusive."

"Well, she came right up to me. I didn't know you had a cat. She sure acts like she owns the place."

"Yes, well, in a way she does." Margot laughed. "I'll be glad to see her. Jeez, I can't believe Kitty came right up to you."

"I'm not *exactly* a stranger, you know. I've been over to the trailer a bunch of times," Lisel said. "She seemed happy to see me and let me pet her."

"Yeah. If you see her again, tell her I'll be back soon."

"What's that noise?"

"Theater noise," Margot said. "Listen, I've got to go. My phone is almost out of minutes and the play is just about to start. See ya when I get back." Margot flipped her cell phone closed and hurried into the darkened theater. The curtain was opening for Act One of Macbeth.

"We missed you, you know—Neom, The Group, and I," Georgia said. With a wide grin, she held out her hand when Margot approached the Contemplation Bench.

Clasping Georgia's hand in both of hers, Margot said, "Thank you," and sat alongside Georgia. A big smile crossed Margot's face. She realized things were good between them again—and she had regained her balance. The old, nagging pressure was gone. Margot squeezed Georgia's hand. "I missed you too," she said, and leaned into Georgia. "I didn't think you'd notice my absence—I mean, being in the upper realms and all. I thought spirits were beyond that."

"Oh, of course, we are," Georgia said, meeting her gaiety. "*Way, way* above and beyond. The Tao, you know." Georgia touched Margot's arm. "I missed your presence and our congenial talks. I like you, Margot. You are very much a part of me, did you know that?"

"Is this the *us* you were talking about?"

"Something along those lines, yes," Georgia whispered. Her face brightened. "Oh! There's one important thing I forgot to tell you. I don't know what I was thinking. It slipped my mind." She walked around to the back of the bench. "See this carved disk in the center?" Georgia pointed to the circular piece near the top at the back of the bench. The handsome carved disk had semi-precious gems fashioned around a large hole in the center. Margot remembered seeing the workmanship before and thought the carving looked like an elaborate, oversized donut. Georgia pointed into the center of the opening. "See that?"

"See what?"

"Look closer."

Moving in, Margot squinted. In the center of what looked like a translucent space was an almost imperceptible small hole. She could just make out the aperture. She hadn't noticed it before. "That?"

"Yes. If you look into this tiny eye from behind the bench you'll see the future. If you look into it from the front, where you are now, you'll see the past." Georgia motioned to Margot. "Try it."

Peering into the miniscule opening, Margot said, "I can't see very much."

"Try again. Remember, you're looking into the past from that side."

Narrowing her eyes, Margot focused again. Unable to get a clear picture of anything, she moved back, blinked several times, and repositioned herself. Her nose almost touched the delicate shield stretched taut across the circular hole. This time, she saw a few blurry shadows and some unrecognizable figurative silhouettes; the images appeared skewed, more like an optical illusion. "Not much," she said. "But what I can see looks surreal, like something Salvador Dali would paint."

"Slow down. Give it a chance," Georgia said. "Don't forget you're looking at the past."

"Okay, but—" Margot rubbed her eyes and crouched down to get a better view. A few minutes went by. In frustration, Margot pulled back. "I can't see a damn thing that makes sense," she said. "Why am I doing this anyway?"

"Take it easy." Georgia laughed. "I thought you'd like to see your distant past. That's all. It's supposed to be fun, interesting."

"Oh." Margot faced Georgia. "Maybe I don't want to remember where I've been. Maybe I don't care. What's the point anyway?"

"Well, *maybe* this isn't the right time," Georgia said. "I just thought you'd enjoy this facet of multi-dimensional complexity, looking into your other lifetimes. As you know from your research on the book, your past is happening right now."

Margot nodded. "Yes, I've learned a few things about simultaneous time."

"Good. Here's an opportunity to see just that. Through this disk you can watch your past lives transpiring—just as it is happening. You can also see your future, which is happening too. I thought you might use this tool—later, I mean."

"Maybe." Uneasy, Margot paused. "Maybe I don't want to know."

"Well, you *might* another time. Just remember it's there for you if you need it." Georgia gave Margot a side-glance and changed the subject. "Do you think you're ready to work on finishing the final draft of the book?"

"Yeah, I think so." Relieved to be talking about something less ambiguous, Margot reached into her pocket and fumbled for a cigarette. She pulled out an empty packet and crinkled it.

"What's your present status on the book?" Georgia raised her eyebrows and smiled slightly. "Can you encapsulate what you've done so far? I'd like to hear your perspective on the project too."

"Sure." Margot cleared her throat and sat alert as if prepping for an interview. "I've completed the first draft as you know. I've also gone through the written material and made notes, marked edits. Sandra offered a few insights too."

Georgia nodded. "Good."

Softening her demeanor, Margot touched Georgia on the shoulder. "I think it's a moving story, Georgia. One I'm sure most women can relate to, even now. But you need to know—" Margot patted Georgia's hand for emphasis. "In this century, we call a man like Harry abusive, greedy, and self-absorbed. Narcissistic, if you will." She stared into the fields below. "He's not a killer, though. That's what puzzles me. Did you think he would kill you when you disappeared?"

Georgia pulled out two cigarettes from her pocket. "No." She lit both cigarettes, handing one to Margot. The women exhaled smoke in unison. Georgia's eyes followed the smoky swirl as it drifted toward the valley. "I wanted to frighten him. I wanted him to know that I was no longer in his power, and I *wanted* him to see me disappear."

Georgia took another deep draw on the cigarette and exhaled. "It was pure vindictiveness, but I couldn't help it. Neom had told me I might have to escape. That Harry would come and try to extort money. That he might try to threaten me—" Georgia stamped out her cigarette. "As usual, Neom was right. I did not want Harry to get the better of me."

"Why didn't you come back? That's the other thing I'm not clear on. What happened?"

"Simply put, I got lost. I know that sounds silly—especially now—but it's true." Georgia blushed; her face turned a bright pink. "In my haste, I missed the tunnel to the 1958 portal and ended right smack dab in the year 2012. Big mistake." Georgia sat for a moment, thinking. "It took me a while to find my way back and by that time, it was too late. According to the newspaper and police report, I was dead—or at least, missing. They thought it involved Harry. Remember? Well, in a way, he was involved, but he didn't kill me. Hell, he couldn't even find me."

"What about Sandra and little Billy? When I met with Sandra in Ashland, she mentioned how shocked she was when you disappeared, and that Billy was beside himself with grief. Didn't you want to be with them?"

"Of course! But for many reasons I didn't want to live on the third plane either. Back then, I had just finished my last book and rewritten my will. I felt complete—finished somehow. Neom had advised me earlier that I might leave and suggested I get ready for a quick exit—a more *permanent* departure. I was prepared and as backup, I sent a letter to my agent, giving him the power of attorney, and asked him to be executor of my estate just in case. With my steady royalties coming in, I knew Sandra and Billy were taken care of and out of harm's way. Besides, I was ready to go. I guess I didn't figure how much I would miss them—or them, me." Georgia sighed and looked away. "A few months before I disappeared, I started time traveling again and enjoyed the out-of-body experiences. For me, it was delicious exploring all the upper realms of conscious thought. I was fascinated by what I discovered. That's how I found you!"

"What do you mean found me? Did you know about me before we met?"

"Yes, in a way—" Georgia stopped talking. She turned toward the vista to gather her thoughts. "When I was looking through the disk," she said, and gestured to the hole at the center of the bench, "trying to figure out how to position myself for a return, I stumbled across your existence. When I mentioned you to Neom, he told me we were connected. I guess you'd call it that, though it's much, much deeper, and more involved than just being connected in a human sense."

Georgia turned toward Margot. With both hands she grasped Margot's shoulders. "This is what I've been waiting for, Margot. What I've been wanting to tell you for…for such a long, long time." Sighing, she looked into Margot's eyes. "Neom said we are connected because, well, we are the *same*, part of the same soul, that is."

"What? What do you mean?"

"Yes, that's right." Georgia released her hold on Margot. "I'll put it in simple terms because this is how Neom explained it to me. Imagine the spokes of a bicycle wheel. Using the hub and spoke concept, think of the hub as the soul with a myriad of spokes coming off its center." Georgia made a wide circle with her arms. Then, she thrust her fingers outward from the imaginary center.

"You and I are two of the spokes—the expressions—if you will, of our soul, each living separate but connected lives. There are others connected to the hub too. Other spokes, I mean. There's one soul, and like a bicycle wheel the soul has many spokes attached, spreading out and then reconnecting on an invisible level. These spokes have different lives in different linear time zones and are connected and influenced by the center soul—and by the other spokes too. Conversely, our soul is a spoke connected to a larger soul that is a spoke connected to an even larger soul. On and on it goes into infinity. Fabulous if you think of it."

"Uh, this is not making sense to me," Margot said. Her face turned pale. "How can that be? I...I don't understand." Squirming, she waited for an answer.

"Yes, I can see your difficulty with this," Georgia said. "I, too, was unclear for a long time. I'll try to explain further." Georgia stood up and walked around to the other side of the giant bench. She put her hand on Margot's arm. "You understand simultaneous time, right?"

"Yes, of course."

"Well, as I understand it, time as we know it isn't straight or linear. It warps, stretches, and folds much like pulled taffy, yet is translucent, invisible to the human eye. Occasionally, and somewhat randomly, some spokes meld together because of a fold or warp in the energy fields."

Georgia could see Margot was still confused. A dense cloud had formed around her. "Stay with me on this, Margot," she said.

Margot stared at Georgia. "Yes, I'm sort of following your train of thought."

"Well, these spokes, or lives, can *fold* into or come very close to one another, or touch, even though each life may be centuries apart in linear time. Sometimes, two spokes can experience the same lifetime. In our case, we were just fifty years apart. The year you were born was the year I disappeared. But for a few months, we both experienced the same lifetime. See? The depth of the connection depends on the conscious intent or skill as to what a spoke does or doesn't do within the existing dimension or possible fold. In our case, our lives crossed and, because of your spiritual practice and evolution of thought, we could meet again after I found you. Am I making sense?"

"A little."

Georgia withdrew her hand and sat next to Margot in silence. She watched Margot's reaction as her words sunk in. "As I mentioned, Margot, each spoke makes conscious choices, lives a different life, forms different ideas, has unique experiences. Because we are connected to the same hub or soul, we can, and usually do, impact other spokes—or sometimes, all the spokes of the hub by the choices we make within our life experience. Through an energetic bleed of sorts, a spoke can know another spoke's experiences. This happens through an out-of-body occurrence or remembrance of a past, present, or future life. Our meeting and subsequent collaboration is an example of this phenomenon. You and I are, right now, cohabiting with each other and other parts of our self, our soul self."

"Yes, I see that," Margot said. "That sort of makes sense."

"The crux of it," Georgia went on, "is that all the spoke experiences are happening at the same time, simultaneously, right now in the present. The only time there is." She pointed to the grassy surface beneath her feet for emphasis. "Most of us are unaware of one another. Meanwhile, the hub knows all its countenance and is guiding the evolution of each spoke, all while maintaining a space where there is no time; floating in the Tao, connected to other souls, other spokes, flowing, moving up, up the continuum of infinity. Understand?"

"Kind of—" Margot blinked, closed her eyes and looked within for a few minutes to transform Georgia's words into something she could comprehend. "Go on," she said.

"Good." Georgia smiled. "To evolve, as all souls must do, our soul, the one you and I are part of, communicates to us as needed during our life spans—advising, helping us by intuitive thoughts to move on and up for the good of the group, so to speak. You call this soul the higher self. Isn't that right?"

"I guess—"

"Well, yes, that *is* right." Georgia pulled out another cigarette and offered one to Margot. "Since you and I are spokes on the same bicycle wheel, I can come into your timeline, and we can commune."

"Amazing." Margot stared at Georgia and took the lit cigarette. "I wondered."

"Neom is a spoke from our wheel, too, but is far more advanced than we are, and as a result, on a higher plane of thought."

"No wonder he's the spokesperson." Margot laughed. "Was that a deliberate play on words or what?"

"Now you're getting it." Georgia nodded at Margot. "Neom comes from the Atlantean era; that was his last earthly incarnation. He told me he had had several very long lifetimes back then. Apparently, people lived much longer in that millennium, hundreds of years." Georgia paused for a few minutes, extinguished her cigarette. "He lived in the time of a catastrophic polar shift when much of the cultured world sank. You have heard of Atlantis, haven't you?"

Margot pursed her lips and nodded.

"Well, that continent was real, and it sank into the ocean. But the event didn't happen all at once. Neom said the devastation took generations to occur. According to him, there were numerous migrations before the land vanished under the water. Neom was part of the mass migration to Egypt. His group followed *Ra*, a leader who evolved into an Egyptian deity. The Atlanteans were a highly intelligent, technological civilization, and that was their downfall. Those that migrated to Egypt had more of a spiritual bent."

From the look on Margot's face, Georgia sensed she teetered on overload and softened her voice. "There are records to validate Neom's claim, Margot. Take your time to think about what I've said. Read Edgar Cayce. He wrote several channeled books that mention Atlantis. One speaks about the fall and the migrations." Georgia pulled out another cigarette. "Want another?"

"No, thanks," Margot said. "Keep going."

"Okay, this is the last cig though." Georgia lit the unfiltered smoke and leaned back. She studied the valley below. "It was a time of tremendous learning and spiritual advancement," she said, exhaling. "That's why Neom evolved quicker. Through his enhanced learning and because of his evolution of thought, his earthly path was complete, so he chose not to return to human form again. All that happened eons ago in our timeline. Neom is androgynous now; he carries both genders. Well, technically, because of his evolutionary growth, he's beyond gender. Long ago he asked me to use the masculine form when referring to him for ease of conversation. He has defined his mission to be one that acts as a mentor, an elderly brother if you will, and is committed to helping us—all of us—grow up, you might say."

"What happens when, or should I say, *if* we do?"

"I don't know how it will work," Georgia said. "But what I know is we *will* grow. And, more importantly, our soul will grow! It's all part of The Plan, the universe's plan, with a capital P." Georgia chuckled at her quip and stamped out her cigarette. "Growing spiritually is difficult, as you know. It will take some concerted effort for *all* our spokes to evolve in order for our soul to move up, as it must. *This* is what is happening here, the main reason I'm sitting here telling you all of this. There are a few of us, a few spokes in our wheel, who are not as welcoming to this concept of family." Georgia chuckled again. "Let's just say that Neom, The Group, and I are working on a reunion of sorts." And with that, Georgia's image began to fade.

"Wait!" Margot reached for Georgia, but it was too late. "Don't leave me! Come back, Georgia. I need more!"

Margot sat for a long time on the Contemplation Bench waiting for Georgia. She tried to digest all of what she had been told but had no idea what to do with the information. *How could she go back to her old life, knowing what she did?*

After a while, it was clear Georgia would not reappear. Shaken, Margot's vision blurred. She wanted to cry but couldn't. Exhausted, she had a tremendous desire to go home, to somewhere safe and familiar. Margot called out for Kitty. The instant she spoke, the old feline appeared at Margot's feet.

She leaned down to pet the cat. "Let's go, girl," she said. "Let's go home."

Together they returned to the year 2012.

Part Eleven

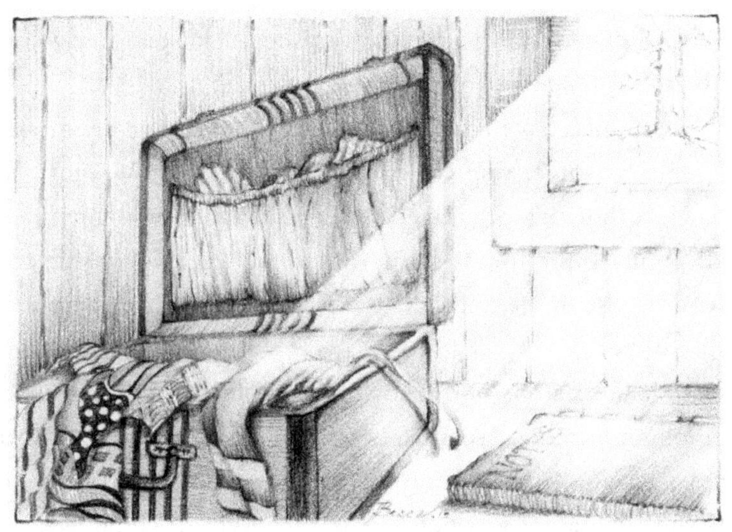

Lisel Speaks

2013

Journal entry, Orcas Island, May 2013

Lisel Bridges here. I'm Margot Anderson's sister. Right now, I'm sitting in Margot's trailer writing a follow-up to her personal journal. I write with trepidation mainly because Margot can't write. She's gone. *Where did she go?* I don't know. I keep rolling that question over and over in my mind. Why would my sister, one of the most creative, adventurous people I know, disappear? It pains me to say I don't know.

Here's what I do know.

Several weeks ago, I dropped by the tiny trailer Margot rented on the IN Road and discovered that my sister had gone missing, and I mean she vanished. I looked everywhere. There is still *no* trace of her. She's just gone.

The police have searched for her too. I called them after I realized something must have happened to Margot. The local authorities organized a search party and sent out an all-points bulletin. At their direction, scores of my friends scoured the estate and half the island, but so far, there is no sign of her.

To make matters worse, I had to call Billy Swan, her landlord. His grandmother, Georgia Lee Swan, disappeared fifty-three years ago under similar, mystifying circumstances. After I told Billy that Margot was nowhere to be found, he couldn't talk. I mean he went dead silent.

His wife took the phone from him, and in a whispered voice, told me they'd call back. It's been ten days now and I haven't heard a peep from them. Maybe he'll call. Who knows? What could he say? His grandmother went missing, too, and her disappearance remains a mystery to this day. I can only conclude that it must be hard for him. I know it's hard for me.

But, I digress.

Let me catch you up on what has happened so far—at least as much as I've discovered. I've gone over all Margot's notes and jotted down what I can remember of our past conversations about her mental health and what she was working on, as the local authorities suggested. There is the police report, of course, but when there is no evidence of malice, or a body, there is not much to report. Here's what I know the police don't: Margot was transfixed—well, obsessed is a better word. Yes, obsessed, that's it. She couldn't stop thinking or working on her book project, the one about Georgia Lee Swan. Maybe that's why she disappeared. I wouldn't be surprised if she couldn't take it anymore.

Personally, I think she was tired of living between worlds. In fact, she told me she needed to get away several times, said she felt crazy and depressed from working on the Swan book. She also said she couldn't stop. I don't know why, but the unknown held a compelling mystique for Margot. Even as a child, she gravitated toward the edge, to make-believe, and to other worlds.

I was never into New Age stuff like she was; I'm too close to the earth for that. But I know she delved into esoteric minefields even when she said she didn't, and I always knew when she was sneaking around hiding things from me. She wasn't fooling her ol' sis. Nope. Not me. We're sisters, after all—or at least, we were.

Again, I digress.

Now, here's the story, or as much as I know: several months ago, around the first of January, Margot came over one night for dinner. She was tired and looked out of sorts. Her eyes were bloodshot, and she looked as if she'd been up all day and night working. She seemed worried about something, said she needed to talk, and rambled on quite a while about the book—Georgia Swan's sketchbook—the one I found in the old suitcase a few years ago. Margot said she was experimenting with time travel and having a lot of vivid dreams about Georgia, the woman she was writing about. According to Margot, Georgia had materialized in her trailer. "More than once," she said, "and we had many interesting conversations." Margot went on and on about Georgia and their connection.

She also talked about an out-of-body being named Neom, and told me she had traveled to other dimensions, met other beings like him. All I could do was listen. When she finished, I didn't know what to say or think. But I knew she was headed for a breakdown, so I invited her to stay the night and get some rest. Thankfully, she did.

I was so worried about Margot, that late in the night I got up to check on her. When I went into the back bedroom, Margot was gone. The bed hadn't been slept in. I walked outside and called for her, but there was no answer. I grabbed a flashlight and searched all over the garden, but Margot wasn't there. Her car was still parked in the driveway, so I knew she had not driven away. I can tell you I was even more concerned. As I was going inside the house to call the police, I saw Margot standing by the door.

"What's going on?" she said.

"I was looking for you. Where did you go?" I tried to keep the concern out of my voice, but honestly, I trembled.

"I was just outside in the garden."

"Margot, come on. I was just out in the garden *looking* for you. You weren't there!"

"Yes, I was."

"No, you weren't. Why are you lying to me?"

"Well, I was smoking. I didn't want you to know."

"Smoking? You're still smoking?" I couldn't believe she'd taken up smoking *again*. It was so hard for her to quit the last time.

"Yes, well, Georgia got me hooked." Margot turned away and wouldn't look at me.

"Hooked?" I laughed. "A ghost got you hooked on smoking? That's rich, Margot. Come inside. I'll fix some tea." I can tell you at that moment I was more worried about my sister's welfare than I'd ever been. *What was happening to her?*

We sat facing each other with our hands cupped tight around hot mugs and talked for several hours. Or, should I say, Margot talked. I asked a few questions, but mostly listened. Margot was full of information that made little sense to me. I tried to understand what she was talking about, but her words sounded incomprehensible, more like gibberish, mumbo jumbo. I still don't understand it.

According to Margot, her turning point with the project came after her last meeting with Georgia, the very last one at the Contemplation Bench. Margot told me she had just finished the second draft of the book and set it down to percolate—her words, not mine. I knew what she meant, though. Margot's typical work habit was to set her draft aside for a while before ripping into it again and making revisions. She always did that; said the gestation period was a nice hiatus that gave her enough time to take a brief vacation if she could afford one.

Anyway, Margot went into a tailspin after she realized Georgia would not meet with her anymore. The thought that she may never see Georgia again disarmed her. She became deeply depressed, sullen, and almost uncommunicative. She stopped going into town and left cryptic messages on my phone asking me to shop for her, things like that. Then, for several months, it looked like she might snap out of the doldrums. During that time, she started the rewrite, but I don't think the work helped much. After a while, it seemed to depress her even more. Well, that's what I thought. I know my sister and she could have mood swings even on good days, but it looked to me like Margot was sinking into a serious depression. Now I'm sure of it.

After that night at my house, I attempted to connect with my sister as often as possible. If I couldn't talk to her on her cell, then I'd leave a message or email her every day. I sent all kinds of cheerful messages, hoping something might lift the dark cloud she was under, but nothing seemed to melt her melancholy.

A few weeks before Margot disappeared, I stopped by early one afternoon unannounced. Margot was typing furiously at her computer. She barely noticed me. When I walked in, she held up a hand and cautioned me to be quiet. In a voice as clipped as her typing, she said, "Hi. Let me just finish this thought. Sit down, have some tea." I wondered what was so important she couldn't stop, but I nodded and went over to the stove to heat the water.

The kitchen was an absolute mess, dirty dishes stacked all over the counter. There wasn't a clean dish or utensil in sight. Margot had piles of books and magazines scattered on the floor and on top of the table where she was working. Clutter was everywhere, *and* she was still smoking. Her ashtray overflowed with cigarette butts.

Shocked at this messiness, which was so out of character for her, I knew Margot was in trouble. My sister was a neat person—to the point of being fastidious. I used to tease her about it. But this…this chaotic jumble worried me. It took all I had to hold my tongue. I couldn't think of anything else to do, so I washed the dishes.

"Don't do that," Margot snapped without looking up. "Just wait, I'll do them later." Then she went back to typing again. I watched her fingers fly over the keyboard.

"I just wanted to help," I said when she finished. "How are you? You look awful."

"Geez, thanks, sis. I can always depend upon you to tell the truth, even if it's bad." She huffed into the bathroom. "What time is it anyway?" she asked, splashing water on her face.

"A little after twelve o'clock. I brought some food. Do you want lunch?" I pulled fresh Thai food out of a bag, and then reached for the two clean plates and cups I had washed.

"That's sounds perfect. Thanks, I *am* hungry." Margot came out of the bathroom and sat down. "I just finished a new section on Harry. I've changed my mind about him."

"Oh, how so? I thought you didn't like him."

"Well, I didn't, but now I understand him better. I finally met him." She raised her eyebrows and gave me a little smile. "We had a conversation—"

By the way she looked at me, I sensed Margot was calculating whether to go on with her story. She must have decided to continue because her face brightened. "I went back to 1929 again, a little earlier in the year this time. Georgia urged me to take another look. I wasn't that wild about the idea then, but after stewing for a while, I decided I had to see for myself *why on earth* she married him."

"Oh." I opened the cardboard containers and dished out the food. "Do you want something stronger than tea?" I laughed, trying to make a joke, but frankly, I contemplated a stiffer drink for myself. I had the feeling I might need it.

"No. Tea is fine." Margot mellowed at the sight of food. "Listen, can we go outside and eat? I'd like a breath of fresh island air." Before I could say anything, she gathered up her food, paper napkin, and the teapot, and went out to the deck. Once we settled in the chairs with heaping plates of Thai food on our laps, Margot sighed. "This is more like it," she said. "I'm exhausted."

"Yes, I can see that." I ate a few bites of food and cautiously eyed her. "Tell me more about Harry. What's his story? Why did you change your mind?"

"You will not believe this—" she said.

Margot was right. I put my fork down and did not touch my food until she finished her story.

According to Margot, she did, in fact, arrive earlier in the year 1929 as planned. As luck would have it, she landed in an idyllic phase of Harry's life, although Margot claimed it wasn't luck that brought her to that moment. Back then, it appeared young Harry *was* romantic and very devoted to Georgia. He came across as a perfect gentleman, the kind that brought flowers home, cooed at his wife, took her out dancing, made wild, sensuous love—all the stuff that would enamor a young woman. Margot understood then why Georgia loved Harry so much. She found him very charming and loving.

Yet, Margot said she couldn't ignore her sixth sense about him. Even without hindsight, she knew something was a little off. It didn't take a genius to see what he was up to—sneaking around, bargaining and scheming behind Georgia's back. She sensed his deceptive behavior would eventually lead to disaster, and it did. Margot speculated Georgia had ignored her inner voice. As a young, impressionable wife, she was too naïve, and in love, to see what was coming.

As I mentioned, Margot claimed it was not by accident she and Harry met at that juncture in time. According to Margot, it was her superconscious mind—her soul, if you will—that set up the encounter at the precise moment. Later, once she returned to the present, she realized why.

"Really? Why?" I said. I didn't see the significance.

"I believe it was ordained, sanctioned by my higher self," she said with aplomb. "Harry and I met at an important point in time, but it wasn't clear to me then. I only figured that out later."

"Why was it so important? What did that have to do with anything?" I asked.

"Just wait," she said. "Let me finish the story."

"Okay, but what is the superconscious mind? I mean, I've never heard of that." Margot frowned at me as if I was an ignoramus and went on with her story.

Once Margot landed in 1929, she found herself at the intersection on Main Street near where Harry worked. Margot said she was sure it was the same street where Harry originally met Georgia. Curious and amazed at the exactitude of her arrival, she walked around for several blocks in a daze until she circled back to the dry goods store. It was then Harry rushed out the door and bumped into her.

"Oh, sorry, Miss. Excuse me!" he said, and tipped his hat.

"Uh, that's okay." Margot looked down at her clothes and brushed herself off. She didn't know what to say; it all seemed like such an incredible dream.

Harry took her arm and escorted her out of the entryway. "Can I get you anything, doll? Do you need a ride home?"

"No. No, thanks, I'm walking."

"What's your name, honey? You're new here, aren'tcha?" Harry pushed his fedora back and looked into Margot's eyes, waiting for her to say something.

"Yes, uh, very new." Margot said she felt tongue-tied and didn't want to tell him her name. "I, uh, I was looking for a hotel. Something reasonable. Can you recommend one?"

"Sure! Right over there." Harry pointed to a two-story Victorian structure on the corner. In Black Gothic lettering, the sign read *The Marqueen Hotel.* "They have great food too. I take my wife there for dinner sometimes. Say! You look a lot like her—"

"Uh, thanks. Thanks, I'll try it." Margot said her heart was pounding so hard she had to get away. She pivoted and hurried toward the hotel. She didn't want Harry to scrutinize her too close because she thought he might notice her out-of-era clothes and sneakers.

"Hey, Miss, wait!" Harry caught up with her. "You thinkin' about living here? It's a great town." He smiled and pulled out a business card. "Here's my card. I work at the dry goods store here most days, but I have a side business selling real estate. It helps pay the bills, ya know." Harry laughed. Margot stood back and stared at him for a moment. She said she thought he laughed a little too giddily, which made her wonder what he was up to, so she played along.

"Great, uh, thanks. Let me think about it. I might call."

"Well, I can give ya a helluva deal! There are some lovely bungalows available now for cheap. Give me a call tomorrow. I'm free. I'll take you for a spin," he said, and pointed toward the polished sedan parked across the street.

"Sure. Thanks. Maybe I will."

Nodding, Harry smiled and touched the brim of his fedora. "Well, then, lookin' forward to it." Margot watched him hurry to his shiny Cord convertible sedan and speed off in a car too expensive for someone on a clerk's salary.

At this strategic point—and this was an important aspect, something that helped change Margot's mind—she saw Harry at the top of his game, at a pinnacle where he could do no wrong, or so he thought. She surmised his expansive living and youthful success gave Harry reason to feel magnanimous and strong.

Still, from what I've read in Margot's research notes, she sensed an undercurrent. To her, Harry was a real wheeler-dealer, someone untrustworthy. She couldn't help feeling he was up to something and guessed he was involved in illegitimate, and legitimate enterprises. Margot suspected the illegitimate ones were used to make lots of quick money. That's how he could afford the fancy car and home he shared with Georgia.

Later on, she found out her instincts were right. Harry was a gambler who rubbed shoulders with local mobsters. He packed a derringer, liked to play craps, and bet on the horses. He was good at it too. Real estate was a legitimate side of his business; the dry goods store his cover. He also prided himself on being a successful player in the stock market. Margot was certain that despite all the other get-rich-quick schemes Harry ran, playing the stock market was his greatest downfall, and in the end, this was what ruined him. But that came later.

After Harry drove away, Margot said she strolled down the block. Feeling she'd seen enough, she slipped around the corner of *The Marqueen Hotel* and reentered 2012. Once back at Georgia's trailer, she made a few notes about the encounter and spent the evening thinking about Harry. He had been different as a young, aspiring—if somewhat crooked—entrepreneur. She softened her opinion of him then and this made her ponder the meaning of life, what it brings forth, what it unfolds, and how, through unforeseen circumstances, it changes people.

The next morning when she woke, something gnawed at Margot. She said she wanted more input about Harry, needed to see firsthand the fulcrum where things turned for him. So, Margot went back to 1929 again to take another look. This time, she walked into a different set of circumstances. When she landed near the dry goods store six months later on the timeline, she thought she had miscalculated and missed the right time portal. To her surprise—and she only realized this later—Margot had arrived at the right moment and walked into a complicated, telling situation.

Before she went into the dry goods store, Margot spotted Harry through the storefront's large plate glass window. He waved his arms, jabbed the air with his hands. It appeared he was in a heated argument with a man she presumed was the proprietor. When she entered the store, Margot went over to the counter where the men were standing. They immediately stopped quarreling. Harry, red-faced, swung around and stalked out without looking at Margot. There was dead silence in the store after he slammed the door. Clearing his throat, the store owner said, "Can I help you, Madam?"

It was obvious to Margot the man was trying to contain himself, so she waited a minute for his anger to dissipate. "Well, I wanted to talk with that gentleman who just left. He said he had a real estate business. I'm, uh, interested in a bungalow he has listed."

Twisting his lips into a scowl, the proprietor said, "Hmm, that would be Harry Swan, my *former* employee."

"Oh, he said he worked here."

"He *used* to work here, but not anymore. I just fired him. He doesn't seem to want to come to work on time, or at all lately."

"I see. Well, I'll try to locate him another way." Margot pulled out a business card from her pocket. "He gave me his card. I guess I didn't realize there was a conflict here."

"You might say that. Excuse me." The proprietor turned away from Margot, picked up a large package and began unpacking the box of goods. "If you need anything, just let me know," he said. "We have some lovely new fabrics down the left aisle."

Margot said she politely smiled at the man and peeked down the aisle. Still standing at the counter, she glanced around the store, stalling for a few minutes, wondering what to do next. That's when her eyes landed on the calendar behind the counter. Margot said she was dumbfounded when she realized what day it was. "Well," she said, fumbling, "uh, well, uh, there *is* one thing—" Trying to form her next question into the attitude of the day, Margot clasped her hands together and used a demure voice. "What is the date today, sir?"

Peering over his glasses, the proprietor said, "Why it's Wednesday, October 23rd." Smiling at her, he quipped, "Do you need the year too?"

"No. No, I know it's 1929. Thank you." The man was so curt that Margot couldn't wait to leave. But then, she changed her mind and looked back at him. "Listen, sir, can…can I give you some advice?"

The man raised his eyebrows and glared over his gold half rim glasses. "What is it?"

The store owner's brusque manner didn't deter Margot. She knew she had to warn him, so she said, "Do you own any stocks in the market, sir?"

"Yes, some." The man frowned. "Why?"

"Well, if you do, I mean, if you've got anything at all in the stock market, sir, I'd sell it today, and fast." With that, Margot walked out the door.

That was the last time Margot ventured to 1929 and the last time she saw Harry in the flesh. Her other encounters with him—fieldwork, she called it—were in dreamtime states or visions, or through conversations with Georgia.

Margot told me Georgia's pregnancy was a real turning point. As far as Harry was concerned, Georgia deceived him. He was angry. His negative reaction was the beginning of a downward spiral for him…and for Georgia too. Margot said it was a classic case of projection, for it was Harry who deceived Georgia. Investing heavily in the stock market several months before the ill-fated 1929 crash was a fatal mistake. After losing everything, Harry couldn't cope. He turned abusive, often staying out late. There was little money or work, so he drove a truck, hauling dry goods long distance. He didn't stick around long after Sandra was born, but bolted when he couldn't take the humiliation or make ends meet.

But you know all this, don't you?

I have to remind myself that I'm writing a chronological order of events you *don't* know, things that only Margot and Georgia knew…and now me, but what I'm writing about seems unbelievable to me even now.

Allow me to continue.

After Margot returned from her last visit to 1929, she went through the time portal again to the Contemplation Bench in the hope she'd find Georgia waiting there. Margot said she wanted to tell Georgia she'd been right, that her judgment had been too harsh. Now, after two trips back to 1929, Harry had redeemed himself in her eyes. Margot wanted to admit that Harry wasn't as bad as she thought. He'd simply handled his life situation poorly, made bad choices. He wasn't a bad person, just mixed up.

To Margot's dismay, Georgia did not return to the Contemplation Bench, nor did she appear at the trailer or orchard. When Margot realized Georgia wasn't coming back, she sank deeper into depression, took a real nosedive, and stalled out. She quit the rewrite. Neom was the one that came forth and prompted her out of her shell, urging her to continue the project.

Now, it's a stretch for me to think Neom exists, but according to Margot, he does. She told me he lives in the higher realms, and as a result she wasn't able to see him like she saw Georgia. I didn't understand then what she meant, but after reviewing her notes, I sort of get the picture.

In her journal, Margot refers to having a *sense* of Neom and The Group and writes that she *heard* him inside her head and *pictured* him in her mind's eye. That's how they communicated—through telepathy, visions, and dream states.

Since Neom and The Group became her new contacts for the manuscript, Margot assumed Georgia had gone to join The Group, and that was why she didn't come back. But Margot was never sure where Georgia went. Neom wouldn't say.

According to Margot, her first conversation with Neom went something like this:

"We're here now."

"What? Who's we? Is that you, Georgia?" Margot twisted in her chair, hoping to find Georgia across the room smoking. But she wasn't there. Certain she'd heard something, Margot called out again. *"Georgia, is that you? Where are you?"* When there was no answer, Margot shoved her computer back and went outside. *"Georgia?"*

Confused, Margot said she glanced down the field. A thin layer of morning fog coated the land. A few chickadees hopped along the cluttered deck, but that was all. There was no sign of Georgia. When Margot ducked back into the trailer, she heard a distinct voice inside her head.

"It is I, Neom," the voice said. *"We've come to help you."*

"Neom. Oh, Neom, it's you! I was wondering—" Margot searched around the trailer but saw nothing out of the ordinary. *"Where are you? Where's Georgia?"*

"We are here on a higher level. You cannot see us from your dimension, but we are here. We will communicate with you through telepathy. It will be easier for you."

"I see. I…I mean, I think I see. "

Margot said at this point she was not sure how to take the new twist in communication. It was the first time she'd heard Neom's voice inside her head.

"Well…well, I want to know where Georgia is," Margot said. *"Why doesn't she come to the Contemplation Bench anymore?"*

"It is not desired."

Margot told me she still did not get the relevance and scanned the room for any sign, any shimmer, outline, or shape, but the room was empty. She felt bewildered and vexed.

"What do you mean? By who, uh, er, whom?"

"The self, the one you call Georgia, no longer desires the lower realms. There has been a release, an advancement."

"Huh? What are you saying? Are you saying I won't…I won't see her again?"

"That is correct. You will not see her as you once knew her."

"Well, that's just great. What am I supposed to do now? What about her story?"

"We are here to further your efforts and to help complete the manuscript. Do you wish to begin now?"

Margot said she sat down at her computer—collapsed, actually. Tears ran down her face as she tried to imagine Georgia somewhere else—as something else. She didn't know what to say or how to go on. She realized how much she missed Georgia's presence and their interaction.

At that moment, she struggled to reply to Neom—if it was Neom. She wasn't sure about that either. Completing the project would be difficult if she couldn't see or talk with Georgia. How could she finish Georgia's book without Georgia? It seemed too complicated, too convoluted.

For a long time, she sat in silence and deliberated. What *did* she want? Then a sudden spark came into her thinking, and she whispered:

"An ending...I want an ending. I need to know how the story ends."

Well, I have to tell you when Margot asked for an ending, in the end, that's what she got. There were a few sidesteps along the way, and parts of her story remain baffling to me to this day, but here's what happened next.

Once she felt confident about the new arrangement with Neom, Margot brightened up a bit and worked again. With his gentle reassurance, she found her voice and became less depressed, more animated, more talkative. Margot told me she was sure she was doing the right thing, on the right track, but she still missed her chats with Georgia.

I was relieved to see how Margot had grown in confidence now that Neom and The Group were helping her finish the book. She told me a spiritual venue opened between them and constantly spouted about her evolutionary progress and new spiritual understanding.

One day, I found her standing near the door of her trailer. She quickly waved me in. "Lisel, guess what? Neom was here again today," she whispered. Her voice sounded staccato— almost giddy with a slight nervous edge. "Shh, quiet." Margot glanced over her shoulder as if someone stood behind her.

Not again, I thought, and hung up my jacket. I knew she wanted to talk about her session with Neom, but I didn't. I was beyond tired of it. "Oh? What did he say?" I pulled off my rubber boots and gave her a hard look. "Did he give you any clues about how to fix that silly fence?" I pointed out the window to the path, which had just disappeared in the brush. "You know, the one that keeps vining and winding shut without notice."

"Oh, shush, Lisel. You're making fun."

"Certainly not. I want to know how to make it stop. It's creepy."

"Oh, never mind about that. We talked about something *far* more important." Margot stubbed out her cigarette and went to the stove. She snatched the teakettle. "Want some tea?"

"Yeah, sure." I eased into the kitchen nook. With relief, I noticed the table looked uncluttered. The previous squalor and scattered debris were gone, the inevitable ashtray was half-full but tolerable. Stacked in a neat pile near her computer was the manuscript, surrounded by another stack of research material. The shelves above were dusted, the books lined up. At last, visual progress—Margot was coming out of her depression. She appeared happier too.

"Okay, now..." Margot said, not missing a beat, "What Neom *did* talk about was multiple lifetimes and how they all connect energetically and can be accessed through a series of connected portals or worm holes."

Margot headed over to the table. I knew she was about to begin another in-depth lecture. She clasped her hands in front of her as if guarding something precious. "Neom told me that each lifetime carries within it certain purposes, reasons for being in a physical body, and that one can draw upon the experience of another lifetime if needed to help with this lifetime. It's kind of like a past life regression, simultaneous time continuum you can tap into when needed. Am I making sense?"

"Sort of." I sighed, and stirred honey in my tea. "Well, not really, but go on." Honestly, I tried to take in this new concept Margot espoused. She seemed excited, happy even, and for her sake, I stayed open. That's when Margot launched in at great length about Neom's hub and spoke concept. She went into detail about how it worked and how important it was for spiritual evolution. Her platitude sounded like esoteric mishmash to me, but I remained quiet and let her go on. When she finished, I asked, "Am I part of your hub-spoke relationship too?"

"Well, no, not exactly. You and I have *mutual* hubs." Sheepishly, Margot looked at me as if sorry I had been excluded from an elite class of souls. "But," she said, smiling, "they're similar in vibration. That's why we get along so well."

"What? You mean we're related here on earth but distant relatives *up there*." I pointed to the ceiling. Just between you and me, I *did* try to keep the sarcasm out of my voice and stifle my laughter.

"Well, yeah, sort of." Margot glared. "We're not connected to the *same* hub, but out in infinity," she spread her arms wide, "we are connected—the same. Everyone is. We really *are* all one."

Reaching across the table, I touched her arm, alarmed at her facial expression. She had a dazed look, like she was in a trance. "Margot? Are you all right? You look a little odd." She appeared exhausted. I wondered how long this work would go on. It didn't seem like she could take much more.

"Yes. Yes, I'm okay." She shook her head and came out of the stupor. "I just had an immense epiphany. Wow! This whole thing makes so much sense now." Margot lowered her eyes and whispered, "But I can't put it into words just yet. Well, what I mean is that I have no words for it now. Later. I'll tell you later when I can think it through." She pushed herself away from the table and went over to the door. "Let's go for a walk. I need to move around."

A few days later, Margot and I had another daunting conversation. This time we talked over the phone. I suspected Margot had not been in town because of the work. The last time I was at the trailer, her cupboards looked almost empty, so I called Margot in the morning to see if she had enough food to eat. I knew her nerves were ragged, and I wanted to be sure she was eating, not just drinking coffee and smoking cigarettes. She had to come up for air to eat once in a while. As her concerned sister, I could help with that.

She didn't pick up at first, so I spoke into her message machine, "Margot, how's it going? I'm going to do some food shopping. Do you need anything? Give me a—"

"Hello? Lisel?" Margot said. "Hi, I was working. I'm busy and haven't had time to go into town. Can you pick up a few things for me?"

"Yes, sure. That's why I'm calling. What do you need?"

"Uh, let's see, a six-pack of beer. Get the Modelo Negro if they have it. Two packs of Marlboro Lights and—" Margot paused.

"Margot? Are you still there?"

"Yeah, I was thinking—and, oh yes, a quart of milk and some granola. You know the kind that I like, don't you?"

"Sure, is that all? Don't you want some veggies, meat, tuna, eggs? Something else besides beer, cigs, and granola?"

"Oh, don't be smart, Lisel. I've got stuff here. Plus, the garden is producing now. I'm fine. Really."

"Okay." I made a mental note to pick up a few more things that weren't on her list.

"Guess what, Lisel!" There was a slight tremor in Margot's voice. She sounded almost feverish.

"Margot? Are you feeling okay?"

"Yes. Yes, Lisel. For heaven's sake, I'm fine," Margot snapped. "Listen, Lisel, I know why Harry is so important. I didn't grasp the significance until today, but now…now I understand why Georgia wanted me to meet him."

Good Lord, I thought, rolling my eyes. "Why?"

"It's so simple. I don't know why I didn't pick up on it sooner." Margot's voice escalated. "He's part of our hub, Lisel!"

"What? What are you talking about, Margot?"

"Harry. Harry is part of our hub! He was…or is…the missing link. I have to find Harry and help him, help us."

My blood pressure soared. "Margot. Calm down. You're sounding a little over the top. I mean, you're not making sense. You told me Harry died over thirty years ago. Remember? He's not here anymore. You won't be able to find him. He's dead."

Things crystallized for me then. Margot needed help, not Harry. Harry was dead. How was she going to find him? I panicked. "I'll be out there in about an hour, Margot, after I pick up the groceries. We can talk about it then. I'll get some takeout and we can have lunch. Okay?"

"Sure. Sure." Margot's voice sounded distant and a little dreamy. "Oh, I know Harry's dead, Lisel. Don't be silly. But don't you think that's great? I mean, Harry's one of us. That's why Georgia wanted me to find him *before* the crash." Margot's voice went up a few more notches, sounding shrill and unnatural. "That's why she forgave him. She had to. He was part of her. It was like her forgiving herself. I have to find him, Lisel, and tell him he's forgiven. He needs to join us."

"How are you going to do that, Margot? He's not here!" Trying not to sound alarmed or patronizing, I took a deep breath. "Listen, Margot, why don't you stop working for a little while? Take a break. Go outside. Walk around down by the orchard. It's so nice this morning. Some fresh air will do you good. I'll be there in a little while."

"Okay, okay, Lisel, but this is so exciting. We're so close, so very, very close."

That was the last conversation I had with my sister. When I arrived at the trailer, Margot was gone, literally gone. Frightened, I called out for her and scoured the property, but there was no trace. She had simply disappeared into thin air. After a few hours of searching, I didn't know what else to do, so I called the police. I had to. But even then, I knew we'd never find her.

Several days later, after the police roped off the area and left, I sneaked back to the trailer to take a better look around. I knew Margot wouldn't leave without some sign of what happened, especially after our phone conversation. She and I were all the family we had left. I didn't think she'd desert me without telling me why.

When I stepped into the trailer, it was almost dark. Afraid to flip on the lights, I used my flashlight to peruse the area. It had to be inside, I thought. I knew in my heart my sister had left a clue, something for me. The police found no note or any evidence of violence. I searched her work area and stacks of paperwork. That's when I noticed the manuscript was gone.

In my furor the day Margot disappeared, I hadn't searched for it. A thunderbolt struck me. "Of course!" I said aloud, and went over to the closet where she kept the old suitcase of

Georgia's. It was the most likely spot, the place only she and I knew. Holding my breath, I peeked into the closet.

In her haste to clean up last week, Margot had stuffed the closet full of odds and ends, linens, extra pillows—you name it. I pulled out the top layer of goods and there, underneath a pile of blankets, was Georgia's suitcase. The police had overlooked it. "Thank God," I murmured.

When I opened the suitcase, the same hodgepodge of flimsy scarves camouflaged the secret compartment. Lifting the old, stained fabric lid, I found what I was hoping for—the typed manuscript. "There you are," I said, and let out a long, grateful sigh. The printed pages were bundled with large rubber bands. Tucked inside was a CD in a white paper jacket labeled Georgia Swan manuscript. Underneath the manuscript was Georgia's notebook and on top of her notebook was an envelope addressed to me, written in Margot's hand. "Thank you, Margot," I said, and kissed the envelope. Trembling, I opened it.

"Lisel, I hope you will understand why I left so suddenly. I had to—"

I couldn't stop sobbing. I felt abandoned and alone. Holding the letter away, I wiped my tears.

Once I calmed down, I reread the letter. Margot wrote that after we talked, she took my advice and went down to the orchard. Kitty followed her. At the instant she entered the orchard, Margot said she experienced another phenomenal epiphany. This time she understood there was no place for her here anymore.

She said that despite what she thought at first, she knew she didn't have to search for Harry. By finishing the manuscript, she had completed her journey, her mission, her earthly cycle, and was free to leave, go to other realms where she could be more comfortably aligned. This knowing, this guidance from an exalted voice, as she called it, made perfect sense to her, and a deep peace enveloped her. "Besides," she wrote, "I live mostly in the other realms now anyway."

Convinced of the rightness of her revelation, Margot said she hurried back to the trailer, dashed off the letter to me, and hid the work. Intending to leave permanently, she went back to the orchard and disappeared with Kitty into the vortex, just as Georgia had done.

After putting the letter down, I didn't know what to think. I still don't, and it's been months since Margot left. When I brought the note to the police station, Cliff, the sheriff, just snickered. He didn't believe anyone could disappear into the ethers. "Where is the body?" he asked.

"Well, I don't know," I told him, "but I know Margot won't be back."

A few weeks after Margot left, I paged through Georgia's notebook and read *Notes on Neom* several times. The information was so fascinating I practiced Neom's meditation techniques. Surprised how easy and useful meditation was, I decided to meditate daily on the hope I'd connect with my sister. Sometimes I think I have. But I'm never sure, not like Margot was.

Two days ago, in a lengthy meditation, I asked Margot for a sign and pleaded with her to send me something—anything that would show she was around and happy. I had to know she was okay.

Then the unexpected happened. I dragged myself home late after a long day of work. Tired and grumpy, I flopped down on the couch and took a brief nap. I woke thinking I'd heard a noise in the house. For a few minutes, I strained to hear any unfamiliar sound, but the house was quiet. Just the wind, I thought, and hobbled my aching body into the bathroom to take a hot shower.

After starting the water, I glanced over at the hand mirror Margot had given me years ago. Handcrafted from koa wood, the round beveled mirror with a sleek, long handle is a favorite of mine. Margot purchased it from a local Hawaiian artisan while living there. I picked up the mirror and turned it over. I gasped. Stuck to the top of the mirror was a note written in Margot's distinctive handwriting:

With every ending, there is a beginning. Love

Island News

2014

In a conversation at the editorial office of the Islands' Sounder *months later:*

"Wow. Look at this!"

"What's up?"

"Here's a typed press release about the Swan property. Looks like they've donated some land to a spiritual organization. Double wow."

"What? Lemme see. Jesus. What next?"

"Should we run it?"

"Well, why not? It's local news. We need some filler this week, anyway."

"Yeah, I guess you're right. Well, you can't blame them for wanting to get rid of that place, especially after two people disappeared from the property. Remember? That old lady who vanished over fifty years ago—wasn't she a famous author or somethin'?"

"Yeah, she had a bunch of money. The other person was a woman too. A writer, I think. She rented the place last year. Isn't that right?"

"I'll look it up. I think she…she dematerialized too."

(The sound of nervous laughter.)

"Well, better get back to it. It's four o'clock and we've only got 'til eight. Put the bit on page seven in the local business column."

"Okay, sure. Geez, I hope it doesn't dissolve on the page."

(More laughter.)

PRESS RELEASE
July 2014

Institute of Oneness funded in part by Swan Family. Construction planned on Orcas estate

Orcas Island will now be home base for a recently established, nonprofit organization called the Institute of Oneness. The Institute will reside on land donated by the Swan estate located on the IN Road, just off Dolphin Bay Road. According to Billy Swan, part owner and executor of the Swan estate, the Institute of Oneness, a secular, New Thought foundation, will be on ten acres of estate property given to the Institute by the family in honor of Georgia Lee Swan, a renowned author and artist. At the behest of Sandra Swan, daughter of Georgia Swan, the family will also contribute initial funding of one hundred fifty thousand dollars to the organization for construction. Funds will build a library along with a series of six small, individual art studio/loft spaces to be used by local and/or visiting writers and artists; a sculpture park is also planned.

Institute of Oneness Executive Director, Lisel Bridges, longtime resident of Orcas, will oversee all aspects of construction and day-to-day management. "We are very excited about this project and expect construction to start within the next sixty days," Bridges said. "Georgia Lee Swan came from humble beginnings to become a talented, award-winning artist and author. The family wishes to carry on her tradition of creativity." Bridges also said initial plans are in the offing for a five-acre sculpture park. "We've sectioned off a beautiful area for the sculpture park, which was at one time an apple orchard. We have also commissioned a local sculptor to create a large, wooden, hand-carved bench as the centerpiece for the park," Bridges added.

Bridges also indicated that starting mid-September there would be a grant and application process for aspiring writers and artists of all mediums who want to apply for studio occupancy. Projected completion of the studio construction is July 31, 2015. Applicants can petition for six-month, ninety-day, and thirty-day studio spaces that will rent for a nominal fee. Availability will be on a first-come basis. Along with that, there is a *Call for Artists* for those interested in displaying their work in the sculpture park. Contact Lisel Bridges for more information, lbridges@instituteoness.com

Afterword

At the age of fifty-three, I enrolled in the Academy of Art University as a freshman, carrying with me a few leftover credits from my college days in 1967. The thought of going to art school in my fifties seemed scary but I was determined to fulfill a lifelong dream and met with the acceptance board holding a portfolio of past work I hoped would suffice. It did.

AAU is known for its demanding art curricula and excellence in all types of design, animation, and fine arts fields. At the time, the school was revered by animation companies such as George Lucas's Industrial Light & Magic, Pixar, DreamWorks, and on. A rumor ran through the school that the big animation companies hired direct from AAU. *Perfect*, I thought, and gravitated to the city campus feeling like Mary Tyler Moore who, at the beginning of each TV show, tossed her hat and twirled between the Minneapolis skyscrapers.

Finding myself living near the Bay Area and still young enough to start another career, I set my sights on animation and Industrial Light & Magic. I fantasized about working for George Lucas, but when I researched the job requirements, I qualified for only secretarial duties. My twenty-plus years in front of a computer as a graphic designer didn't count.

Since I lived in Sonoma, California, a hop, skip, and short ferry ride from San Francisco and AAU, I accepted the challenge, applied for a government loan, and enrolled.

Little did I know what was ahead or how long it would take to graduate. To quote Bob Seger: "I wish I didn't know now what I didn't know then."

A year into the school's rigid curriculum, I realized animation wasn't for me. My middle-aged body wouldn't be able to withstand nine to twelve tedious hours working on a background or character animation every day. Plus, no matter how qualified or highly trained I became, the odds of me being hired were slim, if next to nothing. The fact is/was: I was too old for a new hire in the animation industry. In a sea of talented, young artists at AAU, all eager and qualified for the chance to work at a big animation company, *who was I kidding?* Still, I pursued an art degree, thinking I'd fit *somewhere*.

AAU educates its students on how to tell a story. They teach the classics in drawing, painting, figure modeling, and illustration. For an animation degree you must take acting classes, learn digital photography, digital animation or 2D animation, plus calligraphy, typesetting, story boarding, and creative writing. I took them all.

In my second year at AAU, *Narrative Storytelling* was a required course. I enjoyed the creative, free-flowing writing assignments and received high marks in class and an A on my final four-thousand-word story. Thrilled with my grade at the end of the semester, I tucked away my final paper, and subsequently forgot about it. Five years later at a local holiday gathering, a friend of mine and journalist graduate reminded me of the story, which she'd previously read. "You should do something with that," she said. "The story still haunts me."

"Huh. Okay," I said, and dug out the paper. *Not bad*, I thought after reading it, and asked my sister to give it a read too. She gave me a nod.

So, I dreamed the story into a novella-sized, magical realism story with the intention of making the finished product a short ebook. But my muse wanted more, and the words kept coming. In the end, the story grew into a full-fledged novel with more twists and cosmic flavor than I ever imagined.

Suffice it to say, I truly hope you enjoy going out the IN road.

Acknowledgements

I extend a great deal of appreciation and gratitude to all who encouraged me throughout the years in order to keep this story going: the college professors, friends, writing groups, beta readers, family members. There have been stops, starts, turns, and dips with multiple nonproductive years in between. I wrote and rewrote, and rewrote again, as this story continued to expand and nudge me to fruition.

I'd like to thank all the beta readers: Mosa Baczewska, Libby Cook, Leslie Harrison, Raeleen Hunter, Lisa Murphy, Kat Rose, plus my former Whale Tale Writers group (you know who you are) for listerning to bits and pieces and aiding me with helpful critiques. A special thank you to everyone at the Friday Harbor Open Mic, especially to those on that first fateful night when I sat trembling and nearly lost my voice while reading the first few pages.

To my editor and judicious proofreader, Billie Hobbs, a special *thank you!*

Another big thank you goes to Janet Thomas, who continued to encourage me through the tough, formative years, and for my good friend, Elizabeth Forlenza, who at ninety-nine, passed on before the publication date. "Thank you for sending down a good word now and then, Elizabeth!"

Above all, I'd like to thank my muse, who never let me down when I needed it the most.

Author Bio

As author, illustrator, and book designer, RA Cook published her first book, a children's picture book entitled *Calvin Splinter & His Splendid Splinter Ideas* on her seventieth birthday in 2018. Inspired by a five-day visit to Iceland, *GIGANTA, An Epic Tale*, a middle grade book about a troll in Iceland, was written and released in 2021; *Lola's Muse, A Story of Whimsy and Wonder* came down the pike in 2022.

Cook lives with her dog, Stuart, and works out of her home studio in the San Juan Islands of Washington State. To keep posted and for more information on RA Cook and her latest work, go to: www.hmapublishing.com, RA Cook/Becca's Books on Facebook, beccasbooks.calvin on Instagram.